ALSO BY ELWIN COTMAN

Dance on Saturday
Hard Times Blues
The Jack Daniels Sessions EP

WEIRD BLACK GIRLS

STORIES

ELWIN COTMAN

SCRIBNER
NEW YORK LONDON TORONTO SYDNEY NEW DELHI

Scribner
An Imprint of Simon & Schuster, LLC
1230 Avenue of the Americas
New York, NY 10020

This book is a work of fiction. Any references to historical events, real people, or real places are used fictitiously. Other names, characters, places, and events are products of the author's imagination, and any resemblance to actual events or places or persons, living or dead, is entirely coincidental.

First Scribner trade paperback edition April 2024

Interior design by Davina Mock Maniscalco

Manufactured in the United States of America

10 9 8 7 6 5 4 3 2 1

Library of Congress Cataloging-in-Publication Data is available.

ISBN 978-1-6680-1885-9
ISBN 978-1-6680-1886-6 (ebook)

For my father

CONTENTS

THE SWITCHIN' TREE

I

These days ghosts visit me in the way a lock of hair will kink, or the way someone stirs their tea, or the competitive crack when someone slams a domino down on the table. Mine is now the eye that would miss a girl stealing my diamonds. I search the mirror for my mother before realizing I never saw her this old, and even days I lived through become a void behind me, like the unknowable hour before that hour I first opened my eyes to the sun.

When it comes to speaking fact, memory is insufficient, and fact is as changeable as the morals that beast once carved into my skin, but I believe, I know, the whole damned deal started in 1958, during a summer unkind. Late in the day with mullet, cornbread, and string beans warm inside me, I watched Jesse emerge from the palmetto, his dinner cold on the table. "You disrespected your mama," Pa snarled from the stoop where he cradled his flask. "Get a switch."

Unsteady in the boot-sucking mud, I accompanied Jesse under the trees. No matter how tall he grew, or how much bass maneuvered from his pointy Adam's apple, Jesse needed me whenever Pa'd see fit to whup him, my ear a piggy bank for him to drop rusted quarters of fear.

We walked until Pa couldn't see us, the effort being very much the point, else he'd grow angrier to think we hadn't done the proper questing for this cudgel. On the riverbank it took time to find a switch among the palms twisted at the waist like so many church ladies eavesdropping on the conversation of gulls. Bulrushes curled about our legs like inquisitive cats. Hyacinths gleaming whitely on the bashful blushing water blended salutations to the waking stars. I asked Jesse, "Where you go?"

"See the turnpike," he mumbled.

I'd seen it once, and once sufficed for me, after a mile-long trek to perch my mud-splattered butt on a log fence and stare in disappointment at what they called the pinnacle of modernity, a wonder on the level of Sputnik and microwave ovens. Cars zoomed past with the recklessness of unhindered things. Once or twice, an androgynous blur in sunglasses would yell "fucking nigger" out a window. The wind snatched that curse from their mouths right before the highway swallowed them up in gray nothing.

Secretly I thought it unfair Pa'd punish Jesse for his hobby, but kept my tongue cleaved to the rafters of my mouth. Like our supernaturally gifted parents could put food on the table for us all, they seemingly possessed a thousand ears to hear the slightest word spoken against them, a superstition eight-year-old me feared to test. Even so, I knew I had it easier than my brother; Ma's slipper was nothing next to getting whupped by a man.

To distract Jesse, I asked what cars he'd seen. He puffed his chest toward the sunset and described two Ford Edsels, one red, one whitish; the navy Chevrolet Nomad, silver Cadillac Coupe DeVille, lime Coupe DeVille, rosy Studebaker, and a Tucker Torpedo. He said he'd met a colored man selling paintings out of his trunk, something he considered the coolest thing ever.

Beneath a violet sky with pink welts, we found a cherry tree. Pulling the lowest branch, he grunted, "Come on and help me, Man," that being my nickname. Save my white church dress, all I had to wear were Jesse's hand-me-downs. They called me Mannish Girl, Man for short.

We cut the sprouts with pocketknives to make a proper switch, the kind that whistled before it struck your backside. On our way back I could hear the breath tremble between his lips. Nothing shamed the soul worse than knowing you'd messed up so bad your own parent had to forget they loved you, expose your bare ass, and beat atonement into you.

At home we found Pa on the porch, the back of his bald head gleaming like a brass brazier in the kerosene light. Jesse, eyes downcast, held out the switch for his appraisal.

"Find a better one," Pa slurred.

Again, we sojourned to the woods. Could barely see a thing in the dark. To Pa, *better* meant *longer* so we returned with a lean, mean chinaberry branch.

"You fuckin' with me, boy?" he shouted, launching to his feet. He cut a terrifying figure, John Henry gone to seed. When he stepped he stumbled over the seventh and eighth floorboards, the rotted ones. "I'ma whup you twice as bad for wasting my time," he promised, grabbing the lantern off the hook. "Come on, Man. You watch your brother get licked."

Most dads would've postponed the whuppin' till the next day; make a real terror of it, something to dread all through school and the walk back home. But Pa was sailing a moonshine sea. We trailed him to a road. We followed the road to a path. In the gnatty dark, his lantern jostled like a one-winged robin struggling to fly as, drunkenly confident, he led us deep in the direction of nowhere. Jesse followed like a soldier marching to defend his hometown, while I struggled to breathe, afraid to fall in one of the pits hidden around the swamp. Finally the earth hardened under my boot—the bridge over the St. Lucie—and I gripped his long sleeve, faithful that inch of fraying hemp would save me from the monsters wrinkling the water below.

Across the river, the tree. A thing so mesmerizing in its hideousness I had to wonder if we'd been following it since we left the cabin, drawn through some dark mirror of the seductive magic known to beautiful things. In its frail and piecemeal canopy, moldering oranges hung like a baby mobile constructed from doom-blighted moons. Decay made patchwork up a trunk that curved scythe-like, and that of a second, slimmer, equally deformed trunk grown like a parasite from the fungal roots where they met in a lopsided *V*, same as the *V*s I thickly penciled in class, sometimes within the lines. Pines hemmed the grove where the tree reigned alone under turgid night, sounds of wildlife and windblown fauna muffled in the awesome and terrible aura it shed. Unable to look away, I wept from its ugliness. It seemed my world, along with any small comforts I held dear, ceased to exist in the anti-material shade of the decaying monarch. I clutched Pa's brittle denim pant leg. "Can we find another tree? There be pines right there."

Suddenly he cried out, threw both hands to his ears as if in terrible pain. Jesse shouted, "Is you okay?"

Surely the tree was to blame. I yelled at the thing, "Stop hurting my pa!"

"Mama?" Pa cried through tears and snot, his tobacco-stained teeth a rictus. "Is you . . . No . . . Boy wandered off . . . Yes . . . Yes, ma'am! . . . No! Not that!" he pleaded. "All's I want's a switch! Why?" asked my father, almost childlike. "Ma'am! Please listen! Was a boy in Mississippi. Crackers said he whistled at a white woman. They beat him. Shot him. Cut his penis off. Tied a fan 'round his neck and drowned him. All's I wanna do is protect the boy."

With a snap, a sharp branch came pirouetting from the

canopy to land like an eyelash at my feet. Reluctant at first to pick it up, Pa fell as if pushed, and, keening on all fours like a lonesome dog, fumbled the thing into his sweaty fingers. I switched my gaze between him and Jesse, who waited with palms on hips, overalls unbuttoned to expose his backside.

Having barely the strength to raise the cruel branch, Pa struck Jesse a glancing blow he endured with barely a moan, stoic, until that second lash made him holler for mercy. With every strike, his screams grew less dignified. Pa's blows grew stronger even as he struggled to stand, as if the branch thirsted for blood, Pa a podium from which it delivered its sermon. Flushed and breathless, Pa hollered: "Don't . . . you . . . ever . . . run . . . off . . . like . . . that . . . again! You . . . tryin'a . . . get . . . killed?"

I watched him chase Jesse around the dell, a Punch and Judy act that might have amused had it not been men I loved trapped in that infernal puppet show. Jesse sprinted my way, to dig his blunt fingernails in my arms and cringe behind me. "I'm sorry! Take her instead!"

Nothing to do but screw my eyes shut and think of Jesus. Then I heard Pa's arm fall. His knees smacked the mud where he statued in wretchedness.

Rather than let the tree revel in our humiliation, I helped him to his feet. I buttoned Jesse's overalls and, seeing he could barely walk, let him lean on me as we staggered to the bridge. In the psychotic shadows, I dared like Lot's wife to look over my shoulder. There the creature remained, infinitely vile and pitiless.

II

I remember Pap Pap as a surly, small man who'd beat Jesse, call me ugly, force kisses on Ma, and call Pa a disappointment until one day he vanished and reappeared in a pinewood box. Dying being the most useful thing he ever did, second place went to building our house: a living room, two bedrooms, and kitchen under a shingle roof. Out back a well, henhouse, smokehouse, and pigpen Pa led us to the moment we got home, that night the tree found us.

No one spoke as he fed Big Ma and her babies slop, sweat thick like Vaseline on his mustached face. I kept looking to Jesse, who stood a ways from us with his back to the outhouse. Whatever tears remained on his cheeks were drying rapidly. In their stead, hardened vigilance kept his eyes and ears trained on the swamp.

Sounding frail and sober, Pa swore us to secrecy. As if we had a choice. Once obliged to our parents' thousand eyes, we answered to a new authority.

Tight lips made for vivid nightmares we yearned to whisper to our classmates and transfer the dread from our skin to theirs. But we chose sleepless nights if they meant keeping the tree in its glen, harmless, a memory to fade.

Harvest season became hurricane season. Watching Pa pickle yellowtail in the smokehouse, I knew this storm would be vicious. Winds made the pine trees loll side to side and grunt like frustrated men, and so did the pinewood moan in our porch, as if the living and the dead were speaking to one another.

For three days we stayed inside, subsisting on fish and other reserves, while all the swamp supplicated outside the rattling window. I prayed for the demon to perish in the torrent, dared to hope our humiliation over when the clouds departed like a fleet of burnt pirogues above the weeping cypress.

Then came planting season. On our walk to school we passed felled palmettos. We went to class. At recess I hung around the boys in hopes they'd pick me for their ball games.

One day word spread that a terrible thing happened to Amos Barnes. We gathered in a small group at the edge of the yard, around the log where Amos sat, spindly and gape-mouthed, hair cropped and curly. Afraid to talk at first, he gave in after we all screamed at him, perhaps none louder than myself.

What happened was, on the way back from school, Amos, feeling grown, called out "Howdy, Edna" to Miss Edna on her porch. Addressing any grown-up like that, let alone a woman of Miss Edna's stature, was an execution-worthy offense. Naturally she set for the Barnes cabin to tell Amos's mom, her words a bullet in the chamber soon as Mr. Barnes came home. First Amos's daddy "punched the freckles" off him (Amos's words). Then he sent the boy for a switch. But whenever Amos tried pulling the branch off a cherry tree or chinaberry, a breeze whisked the limb out of reach. So he returned home and, according to Amos, who lacked the imagination for guile, the pecan in their yard gave his daddy instructions, in a voice Mr. Barnes at first took for his beloved grandmother. It forced him to the ground, like what happened to Pa.

"I can still feel the switch," Amos murmured. "It was like getting hit with pure hate."

"From the pecan?" asked Jesse quietly. For a second, his eyes met mine.

"Nah." Subsequently he described following his daddy over the bridge, where the tree waited for them, and every word out his mouth put strain on my bladder. Of all things the hurricane felled, that devil survived. Indeed, I wondered if it could die, or if we'd stumbled upon a creature as immortal as demons who torment sinners eternally.

After Amos's story, his words lingered like acrid smoke. Jesse sat in the grass with his knees to his chest. He knew better than to share what we knew, but he was thinking about the whuppin'. Pure hate. Then, from the crowd, someone chuckled.

"It's weird you're all scared of a tree," declared Carrie Mae Sawyer.

She'd been sitting to my left: a chubby, blond, sunburnt mulatto who excelled at granting wishes. For example, our teacher Miss Sandra took joy from Carrie Mae's hand shooting up like a dandelion all day. The church ladies celebrated their successful efforts to imbue the youth with Pentecostal values when Carrie Mae offered to do charity. That I knew her blue polka-dot dress and penny loafers hid a mendacious nature made me feel like the keeper of a maddening secret.

"You calling him a fibber?" I challenged, trying to look mean and at the same time hold my piss.

Pink like bubblegum, her lips veered sideways when she smiled, a saucy expression borrowed from her mother. "You mean a *liar?*"

"Ooh, I'm telling! She said *lie*. I'm tell—"

"Shut up!" Jesse cut me off harshly. "You ain't telling nobody."

We weren't supposed to say *shut up* either, but I got the point. It was hard to keep secretive with Carrie Mae spouting bad words. In any case, she went on, "Amos would never fib. He says it's real, it's real."

"Then I hope the tree get you!" I said.

Artificial innocence quivered her gray eyes. "But doesn't your daddy work at a sawmill? He cuts trees all day. If he's not afraid, I shan't be afraid."

If only I was Jackie Robinson. Then I could take a Louisville Slugger and knock that round white head right off her shoulders. Unable to stop the pressure any longer, I dashed into the brush, looking for all the world like I was fleeing Carrie Mae, to unbutton my overalls, squat, and wet the mud for what felt like forever.

Before long, five, ten, twelve kids along the river met that tree. Our parents learned our misdeeds from the murmuring jasmine outside Miss Edna's cottage; from the feral roses on the riverbank; from Ma's tomatoes that at twilight, when the sun angled just right, looked like a fire in our backyard.

Not even the eldest among us had seen or heard of the tree before. One would think, at some point, someone would have discovered that glen on the St. Lucie, yet the beast seemed to have materialized straight from Hell into our time and place.

I watched Ma and Daddy become anxious, morose people. If either even looked at me askance I'd apologize because, contrary to what everyone said, I wasn't made of hickory, or gristle, or snakes and snails. My being tougher than most girls meant nothing to the tree. Imagining its splinters in my flesh filled me with mindless panic, mine an obedience for which my parents took no comfort, helpless themselves to the beast's demands.

Commonly Pa worked double shifts at the mill, meaning he might be away for two days at a time, during which Ma tended her garden and listened to radio preachers, or at least she did until the tree decided, since she was at home all day, she should spend half her time whuppin' neighbor kids while their parents worked. Seeing her on the porch at night, crumpled in the rocking chair and cradling her arm, I blamed myself. I remembered the warning she said her ma told her: if you spoke something often enough, those words became a spell that manifested, and I had no doubt that actions held similar power. That some combination of Pa's drunkenness, Jesse's disobedience, and my femaleness had summoned the demon, sure as anything.

Ma had whupped six of my schoolmates before the afternoon when I came home tracking mud. Naturally I dashed to the well for water and scrubbed that living room floor celestial.

When Ma returned, she found me grinding a bar of Ivory into the floorboards.

Such was my terror, I retreated to the wall, to put distance between us.

"You done got it in the wood." She dragged her fingertip over the film with a piteous expression. For which of us, I couldn't tell. "You doing the floor, use Spic and Span."

"I . . ." Words and tears choked me. "S-sorry . . . Please . . ."

She snatched me up in her arms. Cheek to her bosom, I breathed deep the smell off her sweaty neck, like pine. She said, "I know you meant well. Go outside. I'll get it."

"You ain't mad at me?" I sniffed.

"I'm upset at what you done, but I could never be mad at you."

To distract myself I changed the straw in the pigpen. Then I grabbed Jesse's BB gun from under his bed to go shoot birds. Around an hour later, I'd killed a woodpecker and was gearing to snipe a warbler when I heard Ma scream. Fast as I could, I ran back from the trees, over the ripe tomatoes and sickly cucumbers to find her genuflected in the fresh-watered soil.

"No, Meemaw!" she cried to the collard sprouts. "I'ma do it! Just please stop!"

Before I could say a word, she grabbed my hand and rushed me to the glen. I pleaded for mercy the whole way. When we came to the bridge, I ran for the water, certain neither mom nor tree could snatch me from its green arms. I was halfway submerged when she lifted me out and, likewise soaked, dragged my dead weight over wood and mud. From upside down I saw the beast descend like a dredge net. Since last time it had grown in bleak grandeur: the trunks now bore holes larger than my head, sapwood exposed where the bark had rotted, and both fruited abundantly with oranges spotted in hairy gray cankers. Such was the perverse cheer in the citrus smell over the glen that my tongue stilled in awe. For Ma, there was something alluring to that great, decayed, two-horned protrusion because she stepped to it, placed her palms on the sapwood, and begged softly for a switch. I wondered if she, having often done its bidding, had learned to sweet-talk the thing, right when the tree delivered my mother a fable, and she threw me across her knees for the moral. Fifteen lashes on my backside.

That night in bed, my smarting body was forgotten in feeling the tree had smeared its vileness on me. Our parents whupped us so we'd respect them. Respect for them meant respect for their house. Respect for their house made that house a sanctuary. Their authority usurped, the demon made its home in every creak from the rafters, every jesting shadow its shed skin.

Grown folks named it the Switchin' Tree. Kids called it the Old Gray Aunty.

Nightly I'd beg God for the power to take it down. If He saw the righteousness in me, I promised, He'd grant me the horns from Jericho to blow that monster back to Hell.

On the other hand, our parents never spoke against it. In fact, whatever it said to them through rustling leaves rendered them fearful almost to the point of worship. One time Pa declared, "We must listen to our elders. And ain't none elder'n that tree, children."

On Sundays we filled our souls at a one-room chapel off the road. I remember scraping the dirt off my penny loafers before I stepped inside, and right away noticed something off about Pastor Dinkins. From the pulpit he spread his arms wide as an ocean, his perm plastered to his sweaty forehead, his handsome heart-shaped face consumed in a smile that failed to reach his eyes. And when he stumbled his words like a skipping record, I knew he was drunk.

"A tree! You think it's a *treee*?" he emphasized, disgusted at us. "The demon told me to scourge my own dear son. And I let the devil sway me. I am here to beg forgiveness for my weakness. Forgive me, Lord," he shrieked, raising his clasped hands to the steeple.

Behind him, the choir hummed. Parishioners absorbed his rant like they would any sermon, arms up, amen, hallelujah, yes. Ma's grits turned to mud in my guts.

"Leviticus!" he roared, a wobble in his righteous tenor. His long fingers gripped the edge of the scarred old pulpit for dear life. "Leviticus . . . Revelation! Revelation said this day would come." Tears descended his sharp cheeks. "The Beast will strike through the children. But we love our children. I love *my* children because they remind me of me. Let children come."

I clenched Pa's hand. "Can I *please* stay here?"

Last night he'd left the house right after dinner, since it took awhile for Jim Freeman's mule to haul five men into Fort Pierce, where they drank for hours at the neighborhood hooch, plus a stop at Miss Edna's backyard hooch along the way. Since breakfast Pa'd looked like he was going to cry, and I felt beastly for heaping stress on his aching head. But I refused to move, so, placing his pointer finger on my shoulder, he forced me into the aisle, alongside everyone else who could be called a child. On the dais, Pastor Dinkins embraced the nearest boy and girl with a grin so tight a hydrogen bomb couldn't have knocked it off his jaw. Curiosity dragged my gaze to the pews where Carrie Mae remained next to her mom, who like every adult was on her feet, chanting. Carrie Mae looked gleeful.

"The Lord strikes down sinners," howled the minister before he stumbled backwards into the altar. The collective gasped watching him fall. Helped to his feet by Jesse, he brushed off his black robe. After reciting a verse from Job which was actually quotes from Matthew, Song of Solomon, Ruth, and Exodus jumbled together, he reached behind the altar. Too late, I saw the slapjack, no time to warn Jesse before his shoulder was struck a glancing blow. Then the reverend laid out a girl in my grade. "Corrupted! Back to Hell, you corrupted things!"

I tackled him around his legs. Together we tumbled down the dais. And like that, his spell over the people shattered in a wail. The choir avalanched, thirty parishioners in turquoise robes, the indecisive ones buried under those desperate to attack Pastor Dinkins. Parents ran on top of the pews, and some glorious person dragged me by the collar to a wall where I watched, heart rampaging, the pastor get stomped into the floorboards.

The tree found no fault in my attacking a man of the cloth. And since nobody stepped up to lead the flock, we stopped going to church.

In eighth grade, boys learned roots and soil in preparation for farm life. Once, at the general store, Jesse told me his theories regarding the Old Gray Aunty.

"There be a world under the world," he explained, a pickle jar under his arm. "What we see ain't the plant but the genitals of the plant—pardon my French," he apologized to Joe Landon behind the nickel-plated register, a scowler with a lazy right eye and large hands. "Underground the roots is connected. That's where the Switchin' Tree tell them other trees, 'This my territory.'"

He practically had to shout over Joe Landon's phonograph, *The Exciting Lloyd Price*. That toe-tapping boogie-woogie kept Pa on the porch; acolyte of the old school, he considered "doody wop," as he called it, too fast.

I grabbed saltines off the shelf. "I hate that tree 'cause the tree hate coloreds. There plants in Fort Pierce, you don't hear 'bout no crackers getting whupped. I bet that's why Carrie Mae don't get whupped!" I gripped Jesse's sleeve when he seemed to ignore me. "She mulatto."

"Hush your foolish talk!" Joe Landon ordered in a voice sharp and remorseless, like the crack of ball on bat when Mantle hit a line drive. I shut up.

One of the loungers in the store, Jacob Ruffin, roused from his string-bottom chair. The mouse-voiced man told the others, "That girl got a point. I heard that tree was telling Ben Peterson his boy messed up. And it spoke just like a Confederate." To amuse his friends, he put on a redneck voice. "'See here, I ain't bury my body for Ol' Dixie just to see jigaboos *not* get whupped.' I bet it be a cracker ghost—"

"The tree talk like a woman!" I broke in before I could stop myself. "You ain't got no kids, Mr. Ruffin, so why is you talking like you know something?"

That got me switched for sassing at a grown-up.

As the months wore on, the Freeman twins got whupped for digging a well two feet wide, instead of three. The undertaker Mr. Dickerson whupped his daughter Loni for giving their cow a name. It had been my personal tradition, once a week on shopping day, that the first thing I'd ask Joe Landon upon stepping inside the store was if any mail had come for my family. Whether or not he handed me a parcel, seeing to our affairs made me feel grown. Unfortunately, the tree took offense. It had me whupped for henpecking the man.

Franklin Smith stepped on a crack in the cabin floor, something the demon interpreted for a plot to cripple his mother. We thought Mr. Dickerson had just the six kids with Mrs. Dickerson, but, according to the loungers, the tree had him going downriver all week to beat six unofficial kids from four other women.

Surely the tree got a laugh out of this.

Fifteen years old in the sixth grade, slow-thinking, thunder-sounding Buford Wooderson looked like a dad in the back of Miss Ethel's class. As a game, the boys would taunt him until he went after them, and whoever he caught got Buford's palm like a skillet upside the head; Jesse claimed fleeing Buford was what turned him into a good base runner. It came as a surprise, considering Buford was at the age when dads used fists on their sons, if discipline was called for, when one day he, too, unbuttoned his shirt to show ten angry lashes on his batter-fat back.

"Jesus Christ!" Jesse blasphemed. As soon as he said it we froze, breath clutched, his words like stalactites in the air.

"We was doing roadwork," Buford said at last, though we stayed listening to the grass, and Jesse had brambles in his breath. "Sammy took a piss. Boss man come back and say, 'Y'all break while I was gone?' I say, 'Sammy took a break.' Tree said I was tattling. I cried when Pa lashed me," he admitted.

"You *cried*?" I laughed. "You supposed to be grow—"

Jesse cuffed me on the back of the head. Softer than a real punch, harder than a play punch—a tomboy punch. No further comment from my brother, whose gaze stayed fixed on Buford, as if an archangel spoke to him from the ruined flesh. None of the boys gave my aching head the least bit attention, and, figuring I deserved it for acting uppity, I held my tears.

The tree didn't care he hit me. That was the funny thing—for all its violence, the demon found Jesse more agreeable than Pa ever had. I had to wonder if my brother wasn't glad to some degree that he could walk to school, most days, without stinging pain.

However, rather than pacify our home, this period saw Ma and Pa at each other's throat. Usually it came after dinner when she'd call him a degenerate not worth the three bucks her daddy spent on marriage papers. Then he'd pop her in the mouth. That got them brawling. It scared me how far she'd push him, never one to let him cool down with a smoke when she could snatch up a pan and threaten to bash his brains, her desire for pain clear in the bloody noses she wore like a badge. Were I allowed to talk back, I would've yelled, "Stop hurting my pa!"

Because the tree followed its own schedule, Ma'd rouse me from bed sometimes, throw on her robe and shoes, and march me to the grove. After a whuppin' she'd stumble to the river, roll up her sleeves, and wash her arms to the elbows while I watched in hiccuping shame.

If she whupped me in the evening when Pa was up, he'd take me off her hands the minute we returned, to buy me a ginger ale at Joe Landon's.

Five thousand, eight hundred breakfasts Ma cooked over the years, and each was the hour of the day I cherished. Her sweetly singing voice as she braided my hair. The way she'd anoint my knees and elbows with Vaseline before sending me to school, shiny like a cat's nose.

Periodically I'd wake early to catch Pa before he left. Run out the front door and around back, the dew like fairy kisses on my toes, to peek in the kitchen where, two fingers to his temple, a man who started each day worried he'd destroyed his life the night before, he'd fill his lunch pail with care, every piece of sandwich in its place.

A time he sat at the table to stretch his legs, I climbed in his lap like I'd seen Carrie Mae do with men. It startled me how unsteady he felt as I scaled the fat on his creaking bones. His fingernails were brown like a tree without madness. Sunk deep in their sockets, some might call his morning-grimed eyes tired. To me, they looked like puddles in puddles.

"Come on, Man." Gently he lifted me off him. "You too heavy for that."

III

White pinstripes on watermelon pink. White polka dots on lemon yellow. Red-and-green plaid. Cream skin. Fog eyes. Carrie Mae Sawyer never got whupped.

I can recall a summer, years before the Switchin' Tree, when a scream interrupted our dinner and Carrie Mae, barefoot, in a blue puffed-sleeve dress and white pinafore, came crashing through the palmetto, over the lawn, up the back porch, and into our kitchen where she threw her arms around Pa's leg with a ceaseless wail.

"She trying to kill me!" cried Carrie Mae. Persecution unspooled from her pink lips until my parents offered a plate of fried mullet, corn bread, ham hock, string beans, and potato pudding the heathen consumed bare-handed. Her patronizing smile upon receiving Ma's gift, a stuffed doll with button eyes and a red yarn smile, rooted in my memory like a fossil in peat.

Soon her mama, Miss Carolyn, arrived wreathed in scowls, a woman whose large bosom was matched in size by her behind. Her hooded eyes, maybe beautiful, once, resembled rusted nails hammered in a plank, gummed in fluid and lusterless. Watching Ma set a steaming coffee before her, I saw a trace of sorority tense between them like a golden thread. I remembered Ma saying they were friends, long ago, during their concurrent pregnancies.

"She killed the chicks!" Miss Carolyn hollered. "Murdered them right in the nest."

"We got wolves 'round these parts," Ma reminded her.

"A *wolf*? Them chicks weren't eaten, Barbara. She *crushed* their heads. All ten of 'em! I was gon' sell 'em when they was grown. That little girl got the Devil in her."

Carrie Mae, acting terrified at the sight of her mother, took Jesse to the pigpen for some silly game. I eavesdropped on our parents through the window. Pa leaned in the kitchen doorway with his arms crossed, a patriarchal vision before drink turned his gut and arms to suet.

"Carrie Mae a sweet girl. She ain't the kind go killing chickens. And even if she did," he qualified, "it ain't like she know better. Kids is curious."

Over time Carrie Mae would seek harbor in every house on the river. These melodramas embarrassed Miss Carolyn to the point she gave up disciplining her child. I knew from the salted, larded dialogue Ma conducted with herself in the kitchen that Miss Carolyn used to be a juke-joint harlot. A shame that white man made her carry his child, my mother would tsk, eager to recast this fearsome woman into a figure of pity.

While Miss Carolyn permed hair in town, Carrie Mae barricaded herself in their bungalow with coloring books and Archie comics, Bazooka Joe and chocolates. As far as I knew, she spent hours in front of her mom's RCA Victor Eyewitness TV. She could describe in detail Howdy Doody, Marshall Dillon, Lucy Ricardo, and Scrooge McDuck's adventures. That way she drew in other kids who, bored from chores and picking berries, endured her maltreatment so long as she taught them about imaginary Caucasians and birds. For her they'd act out Shakespeare; they became Merry Men waiting on Maid Marian; declaring herself General Jinjur, she'd recruit girls into her army to attack whichever unfortunate boy agreed to play the Scarecrow. On the playground she'd call her "friends" insulting names and mock their sun-dried accents.

An ambivalent student, except for phys. ed., my favorite subject, I came to love the gray building as a neutral zone where the tree ignored us. Perhaps the routine of the place prevented us from doing anything displeasing, even by accident. I did my best on Miss Sandra's assignments. Because she never whupped us, I loved her. I doubt she even believed in the Switchin' Tree. The one time a kid told her about it, after she had complimented our politeness, her pleasure switched to anger in an instant.

"Only the Lord could speak through the plants," she shouted, and made us write THOU SHALT NOT TAKE HIS NAME IN VAIN a hundred times while she stared out the window.

Typically, Carrie Mae would find some blurry-eyed girl to escort her home from school. But one May afternoon, I saw her head down the road with Amos Barnes, an eighth grader. The way she looked at him! Plain scandalous! The next morning she came skipping into class, arrogant like a luscious jungle queen in a pulp novel.

"She grown!" I whispered to the next kid over. "She should be ashamed of herself."

A lady would never admit to going out with a boy, so, naturally, Carrie Mae gathered us girls during recess to brag about her exploits.

"Amos took me to the cinema!" she declared. "He thinks he's my boyfriend, but I just don't know if I'm ready. You gotta let a boy court you. We saw a *sp-oo-oo-ky* movie. Vincent Price"—spoken like we should know who that was—"invited these white people to a haunted house and he said, 'I'll give you ten thousand dollars if you can last the night.' And they all needed the money. Me? I woulda been outta there. I'm afraid of spirits. Anyway, there was this big vat of *acid*!" she screamed in my face, trying to scare me. I scowled back at her. "And somebody got knocked on the head. Then this lady saw a ghost. Then—"

Curious as to the other half of the story, I crossed the field to where the boys played ball, and found Amos, usually shortstop, with Jesse at the edge of the woods. My brother had an arm around him. I asked Amos, "What she do?"

"That little girl crazy," he muttered.

"I know that."

"She kept saying she gon' see the movie no matter what. I wasn't gon' let her go alone. What if the crackers got her?" he cried, looking to us for understanding. I supposed his heart was in the right place, but when it came to boys I had trouble telling the difference between chivalry, stupidity, and plain horniness.

"We was in the balcony with the colored folk," he went on. "And there was this part a skeleton fell from the ceiling to try and scare us." A disbelieving boy. "Carrie Mae took out scissors and cut the string and it hit the white folks below on the head. Then the crackers came up, dragged a colored man down the stairs, and beat him." A guilty boy.

"You shoulda known better'n go with her," I lectured. "She mischievous, and she too grown. But"—I put on a confidential whisper—"the tree ain't get you?"

A weird, saccharine smile tugged the spokes of his lips. "Daddy said, 'That tree don't raise my kid. I'll discipline my son how I see fit.' He beat me with the belt."

It got my heart racing to know Mr. Barnes resisted the tree. Maybe if our parents stood up to it, like that time they beat the pastor, they could deny the thing its pleasure.

We walked Amos home. What he'd been through seemed beyond my understanding, and, in truth, I had trouble sympathizing for such a dumb mistake. It mattered to me because it mattered to Jesse; my role, it seemed, was to be a bridge for him to walk when the waters grew treacherous. I tried inserting myself in the boys' baseball talk, same as I'd ask Pa to take me fishing in spring, but it seemed men viewed me as an incomplete male, neither fully ignored nor welcomed in their fraternity.

Halfway to his cabin, Amos clutched his eyes and emitted a noise like the cry of some animal, maybe bird, maybe mammal but certainly the last of its species, gray, blind, an invalid crying in vain for his dead mate and nonexistent children. He cried, "No! I don't want to see!"

Before we could stop him, he dashed into the palmetto. The trail of trampled plants led us to the creek, where we found him naked and splashing water on himself. Chilled at the sight, I hitched my overalls to my knees, waded in, and slapped his cheek, twice. "Snap out of it!"

Amos spoke to the air above my shoulder. "It be endless, Man. Deeper and deeper and deeper . . . *Don't wake the dreamer!* I see it . . . Hear it . . ."

It took all we had to get flailing, biting Amos into his clothes and escort him to the general store. There Joe Landon suggested we take Amos to *our* cottage, and the laziness of him—the outright *immaturity*—woke in me a display of shameless, girlish, teary-eyed begging till he had to either help or risk his manly pride. A spoonful of medicine knocked Amos out on his feet.

Then Mr. Landon carried the boy to the Barnes house. For reasons I didn't understand, he told us to accompany him. When we reached that quiet cabin, and I followed the men down the flagstones, I passed the pecan tree, under whose witch-green flowers I felt naked. To stay calm, I gazed over the lawn, at the red mule impassively watching us from his stable, until I paused next to Jesse at the foot of the porch. Three knocks and Joe Landon presented Amos to his startled mother, a homemaker in a flour-spotted apron. She asked Mr. Landon to carry him inside before shutting the door.

The next morning, I woke with a troubled feeling different from my usual anxiety. Like my belly had been hollowed to a rind. Not hungry, because hunger pains were still a sensation, but truly empty, my guts as muted as my heartbeat. It was Pa who got us dressed and off to school earlier than the normal hour. Certainly the Barneses would get Amos right, I told myself. The doctor would come from town to treat him with that know-how he learned up north.

While we were in class, the women, the homemakers, went searching for Amos, who had vanished in the night along with his daddy. Galoshes on, they tramped for hours through sawgrass, combed the river until, the sun at its zenith, Miss Edna discovered a body in the shallows. Amos had been mutilated beyond recognition.

It fell on Miss Sandra to deliver the news. Only later would I learn the specifics, and for the life of me I can't recall how; over the years I've convinced myself that Ma's tomatoes, violating their orders that only adults should hear them, came alive to mock me with grisly details. True, untrue, that's what I see.

Tearful Miss Sandra said she'd lost a brother in the war, her way of letting us know she understood. Not like this helped me, in fact I barely heard her, I wept into my hands for long minutes, and when Carrie Mae cried her own fat tears, fake as they seemed, and her grief had teachers fawning over her worse than ever, I felt like she was spitting on Amos's grave.

At home I cried more, out on the porch, in front of the swamp where, if the tree had any shame, it would notice and know itself for a devil. Eventually Ma, frustrated with my weeping, furious at the burnt pork in the skillet, ordered me into the kitchen, where, pinching my nose, she forced me to drink rancid medicine. She sent me to bed early. I prayed for Amos, but even as I spoke the words, I realized I saw no point, no reason to believe God would reward my piety, surely nothing to be grateful for.

In the dark, I lay awake and bedeviled when Pa came in. "Get dressed."

Minutes later I hustled after him, through the kitchen where Ma squatted over a tub, washing dishes. When our eyes met, she snatched up a plate and dashed it to pieces on the floor. "She in mourning, Bill! You think she need to be tough? She ain't a boy!"

"Barbara . . ." He paused. Then he said, "Wasn't no one's fault the others didn't make it. This what we got. One kid near grown"—he tossed me a denim coat several sizes too big—"t'other a little girl. Them's our babies. They need love and a firm hand. Let's go," he told me.

Jesse had been feeding the chickens, but Pa told him that could wait. We followed him to the store, where a half dozen men gathered on the porch, under three lamps burning bright, as if the weatherbeaten dais were a lighthouse. There we learned the sheriff had driven past.

"I don't want to believe it," one of the loungers muttered, "but it had to be his daddy. They say Matt led him in the swamp—"

"*They* say a lot of things," Pa sneered, lighting a cigarette.

"I think it was a mercy killing," another man proposed. "That boy lost his mind."

Joe Landon shook his head. "It still ain't right to kill him."

"I heard he snuck off to town," Pa gossiped. "With Carolyn's girl. I think the crackers did him for that. Just their style."

"Maybe he killed himself," I offered. All at once the men stared down on me, and though part of me liked the attention, I hid behind Pa's leg.

Shortly Carrie Mae came up the road, pigtailed, red-coated like an evil Englishman in a history book, hand in hand with her mama. I suppressed revulsion watching Miss Carolyn embrace every man in turn. Carrie Mae stared at the road from the top step, still, like a featherless buzzard watching her prey gasp its last from her perch on a parched yucca branch.

A mechanical growl drew our gaze down the road. Toward us shambled the green snub-nosed police cruiser. Through crimson lasers I made out Sheriff Norvell at the wheel, a rumpled man held in place by the twin poles of his belly and hat. It struck me as strange how ordinary he and the deputy looked. Not at all menacing. I asked Pa, "Is he Carrie Mae's daddy?"

"Hush," he whispered. Peering past his leg, I glimpsed Mr. Barnes in the backseat, hunched under the low ceiling, his soul gone.

Carrie Mae bounced down the porch steps. Her mother yelled, "Stupid! Get back here!"

But she caught up to the slow-moving car and banged on the door, right on the five-pointed star. The deputy rolled down the window and stared at her through cigarette smoke, curd-colored jowls slack from confusion. Carrie Mae clasped her hands behind her back and addressed the sheriff. "Mister, is you my daddy?"

Her mother wailed.

IV

No one investigated the deaths of black folks. Mr. Barnes went to the farm. Amos got buried. Cherries blossomed in June.

Then one bedtime, I put on Jesse's woolen socks over my own. Just to see how they felt. Not five minutes later Ma barged in, dragged me off the mattress, and hurried me to the grove, where she demanded a switch. "I agree! The girl gon' get worms!" Tugging at her robe to keep it closed over her nightgown, she sat in the mud and demanded I bring myself. As hard as Pa hit her, she whupped my ass and thighs. "Un . . . grateful . . . piece . . . a . . . shit. . . . Always . . . crying. . . . Acting . . . like . . . a . . . boy. . . . Why . . . is . . . you . . . so . . . weird?"

Three days later and the welts, thick as fingers, made sitting impossible. Up to that point, Ma'd rub salve on my wounds every night, her touch obligatory, her eyes annoyed. Her remorselessness felt worse than the injury I'd done her when I summoned the tree, any contrition I may have felt turned to vengeful thoughts, and, though the salve stung, I never cried.

Around noon I was hiding from the heat on the porch, switching my hips to relieve the itch, while inside Ma and Pa danced to chirpy Mexican music out of Pa's radio, a rocking kind of dance that had me surprised one of them didn't accidentally fling the other through the wall. That was when Carrie Mae came skipping over on her own invitation, in a white polka-dot sleeveless dress with a Peter Pan collar. Watching her kick off her saddle shoes and plump down on a rope swing hung from a pine, a *Saturday Evening Post* in motion, I imagined my welts bursting.

It shocked me how quickly she reached Superman height just by pumping her chubby legs. "Mama wants me to sing at the retirement home today," she woe-is-Mae'd. "I love it so, but it gets lonesome sometimes."

Ma came outside with a pan in the crook of her arm and rhythm in her slippered feet, scraping corn bread batter with a spatula. "Go with Carrie M— Oh!" she exclaimed, surprised at a kiss from Pa.

Thus shanghaied, I found myself in the back of Miss Carolyn's Buick, on our way into town. Near feverish with pain, I cast my evil eye on lawns adorned in armless goddesses under effeminate palms. Storefronts displayed the rebel flag, that inbred *X* of death. Gazing on the sidewalks, I noticed the small ways negroes snatched happiness from under the white man's nose, and this felt like betrayal.

Miss Carolyn left us at the two-story retirement home before driving to the bar, as Carrie Mae informed me the moment her mother left earshot. A smiling, round, bespectacled matron ushered us through a dusty hallway hung with dour portraiture into a parlor where two dozen elders waited in hickory chairs, some of them already asleep. Among their ranks I spotted a plump woman in tan capris, blue-and-white-striped shirt, gold earrings shaped like maple leaves, and a blue headband over her obstinately black curls. Arms folded under her heavy bosom, she looked annoyed to be there, yet we had her attention, like she saw in us a potential story. Of everyone in the audience, I feared her judgment.

The matron played "This Little Light of Mine" on the upright piano. From the first note, it became clear Carrie Mae had the sweeter voice. Not content to merely outclass me, she started singing in cursive. "Thee-hee-ee-ees! Lee-hee-hit-tool-hoo-hoo-hool li-eye-ee-eye-hight! Of my-ee-eye-ee-eye-ee-hiiiine!"

Her vanity flashed red to the snorting bull in me, so, tossing aside sweetness, I sang *harder* for the Lord. "Je-*ZUS*! Jee! Waaaaah! Zus! LOOOOORD! WAAAAAAH!"

Neither of us could sing a lick after caterwauling the first verse. Some elders looked confused as they shuffled to the veranda, others clenched their eyes in pain. "Them little girls got the spirit," I heard a man say.

"That was very impressive," the annoyed woman told us, far kinder than I'd expected. Her accent had me picturing humans packed in streets like pickled tadpoles. She escorted us to the veranda for tea and cakes, and, though my parents put food on the table, and I wasn't hungry, I snatched sweets off the antique china and stuffed my face. To hell with the elders glaring at me.

"There goes the anthropologist." One of the wizened

men mocked her from the domino table. While they laughed *kee-kee-kee* like squeaky wheels, I noticed sinister thoughts play behind her eyes. Internally I laughed at her, too, righteous in my belief that, though I'd been taught to respect classy women, this yankee clearly considered herself better than us, her humiliation good old-fashioned street justice. While this went on Carrie Mae, standing at the window, stared through the bug screen at a blue iguana staring back from the porch swing.

The woman allowed us scant time to eat before she led us inside a small sunflower-yellow room. Overfull bookshelf. Cosmetics on a pinewood vanity. Fumed finishing on a nightstand, straw basket, a plastic bunch of grapes gone silver with dust. Baby-powder-smelling bed next to the open window. Complicated undergarments chimed as she rummaged her drawers for the jewelry box she smilingly presented to us. New York City photos. Chiaroscuro negroes posed in fur coats on concrete stoops, or barelegged on the beach, or flaunted meat dishes that looked like flower arrangements at tables where they languished on colossal tufted couches.

Carrie Mae had questions. "Did you go to the Cotton Club? Did you know Cab Calloway? Did you see the follies at the House Beautiful? Did you sing at the Apollo?"

The woman ignored her, as I suppose in her mind only she deserved to show off, her back to us while she returned the box to its spot. Far older than Carrie Mae, she seemed her mirror—two stupid girls who would rather drug themselves on Befores and Nevers than pick the swamp grass from their shoes and carry on. I was imagining pissing on her photos when Carrie Mae slipped a pair of diamond earrings in the pocket of my overalls.

"Do you have any more artifacts?" she asked when the woman turned back around, her grinning teeth sugar-glazed.

"She was very interesting," Carrie Mae said to her mother on the drive home, precociously excited. "She was a writer and she—"

"Shut up," Miss Carolyn groaned.

A drama took place on Carrie Mae's face in which disappointment overcame her need to impress before both surrendered to pouting fury. Turn off the praise and she wilted. Silent and still, I feared to breathe too loudly, should I jangle the contraband hot against my sternum.

Two minutes from my house, Carrie Mae snarled, "Let us out the car."

Miss Carolyn called her smart-mouthed but brought the Buick to a halt, glad to be rid of her. Helpless against my curiosity, I followed my nemesis into the undergrowth.

"I gotta show you something," she panted, moving swift as a balloon through the thicket.

The cypress closed around us. Stamp AMERICA on a map all you want, but the quatrosyllabic trill from birds as colorful as their trees were dark made it clear the world we swam through, because the humidity and shy sunlight had us moving like mermaids in the deep, belonged to the same tropical climes where Indians still fished with spears and dove for oysters, as far as we knew. Deeper in the manchineel green I grew repulsed at Carrie Mae. Why did the Lord abide her? I wished she'd fall in a hole and break her legs and take mud in her lungs and die.

Under Spanish moss teardrops, the river laughed to accomplish such a bold cerulean hue. Here the air smelled sweet—what summer was this that burned the leaves to sugar? Carrie Mae flashed me a wink before she counted ten steps to a pile of bricks nearly hidden in the grass. Frightened of her careless touch, zebra longwings fled so high they hurdled her yellow gables. "Help me," she ordered, giggling at their wingtips on her ears.

"No." I recalled every rotten thing she'd done. "Why you make me steal from that lady?"

"I didn't *make* you," she responded, easy as anything. "You could've turned me in. You didn't 'cause you don't care."

Now disgusted at both of us, I snatched the earrings from my pocket and chucked them in the grass. Carrie Mae, calling me words I'd only ever heard from Pa in his angriest moods, searched until she found them. "Stupid fucking tomboy!" she said.

"Yellow slut! I hate what you did to Amos. You's a lie—" I nearly stopped myself but the profanity had left my mouth, a poisoned syllable for the swamp to relay.

"His daddy killed him." Carrie Mae sighed. Even *lie*—the worst thing you could say outside of insulting someone's mama—failed to shame her. "Or not. What did I lie about?"

Honestly, I struggled to recall her lying more than the average person. That adults loved her seemed tied to our collective desire to please them—she was simply best at it.

"Shirley." I flinched to hear my name, which no one but Ma and our teacher called me, though Carrie Mae's tone suggested indifference to whether or not I took offense. She said, "You're my enemy, kind of. I don't think you're mad at me. You're mad at somebody else, and you take it out on me."

To this I had no answer. Nor could I pull myself away from the scene before me. First, she lifted the bricks individually and tossed them aside. Next, she lifted three rotted wooden planks gummed on the undersides with dirt and earthworms. The effort left her breathless, her hair snarled, her fingernails worn to the quick. From the hole she lifted a cigar box illustrated with pictures of a tropical port town, proud as Aladdin to present me her rattling treasure.

Among crumpled dollar bills glittered rings, watches, and necklaces. She let me explore the trove, but I did so with a swelling bladder, aware of the eyes on us, servants of the tree who whipped me like a dog yet made allowance for the thief.

Such rage swelled in me, I could barely speak. "That's what you do when you go out singing?" I said through deep breaths. "Steal from people ain't got nothing?"

Her laughter sounded coarse and animal, as if she'd never learned the process, her attempt based on instructions from a book she'd read. "I'm saving to buy a ticket to New York. I'm going to be a Broadway star. And you better not tell," she warned, then, falsetto, "*I swear I didn't do it, officer. It was the little darky girl.* You can stay here if you want. Marry a drunk like your daddy. I'm leaving—"

"Shut up. I'll join you."

She blinked in confusion. "What do you mean?"

"You can only steal so much yourself. I'll be your partner."

On the jocular riverbank, I suggested we steal the silver candlesticks from the Dickerson home. Then we could snatch those heirloom rings Miss Edna wore. It stood to reason Miss Clara Barnes, with her son dead and her husband locked up, would be too depressed to notice us sneak inside her cabin for loot. If I was to be beaten like a rogue, I would act the part. More important, my fear was gone. Knowing Ma held no power over me except to batter my toughened flesh made her seem pathetic, and I so strong I found myself anticipating the whuppin' as reward for my magical, beautiful wickedness.

Carrie Mae, if not overly enthusiastic at my change of heart, embraced it with the full of her craft, as any chess player would a situation where a pawn suddenly became a rook. Malice made her eyes an amen, an invitation to embrace her, however weakly she returned my affection. I nearly wept to stand on the winning side for once.

We meandered in what I guessed for the direction of my

cottage. Dreams filled the hollow between my ribs. I wanted dresses and honey and rock'n'roll and movies and pianos and cars. Carrie Mae would marry Johnny Mathis and wear Schiaparelli. She would buy a four-bedroom house for her mother. She would stab her white father to death with her own hands. Bold as Broadway, I sang "Shuffle Along" and she joined me, in harmony.

Halfway through the song a gasp from Carrie Mae shivered the back of my neck. There it stood several paces ahead: the big-dick bastard who spoke like your mother. Summer oranges blossomed in its twiggy branches like a Dantean Hesperides. I was struck with phantom pain everywhere it had touched me. As urine polluted my leg, the space between the trunks fixed me like a serpent's eye and from its blackened corruption pulsed such judgment I'd pictured only in the descriptions of damnation served with poetic fervor by the minister at the A.M.E. Church before our parents beat him half to death. I tried to yell "Run," but my throat closed.

Then a crunch sounded from the grass. I turned and gaped upon a hole where Carrie Mae once stood, a drop into darkness.

Then every leaf, flower, and blade of grass screamed at me in a wordless, idiot cacophony that scarred my brain meat with endless fields under endless stars. I grasped for the white hem of Jesus but each time his name stumbled from my spit-clotted lips, the plants mocked me. *This is not Hell. You will never see Hell.*

Around me materialized beings whose bodies made no sense, shaped like a mad god had gifted three dimensions to the whorls dancing feet imprinted upon mud after the rain, then animated those forms and coated them in millions of fine white hairs writhing along their headless, limbless bodies. Over the fields and cities fluted a melody from no earthly pipe, and its chords split my head open, aided in their assault by a barrage of raw-meat-smelling fragrance. I knew at last what Amos saw when his family defied the tree, and I wished for the mercy he'd received. Stars fell from black sky that folded upon itself like velvet. Buildings made from chaotic mineral compounds grew out of the earth for hundreds of stories to intersect in the air with other buildings that branched like veins, an aerial labyrinth. All through streets wide as meadows, the earth spongy beneath my feet, reptilian skeletons stood waiting the day they would again terrorize the earth. In the homes, fungal citizens sensed my presence, and as one they warned in a voice that rumbled through my chest, "Let the dreamer dream." From the suicidal stars, "Let the dreamer dream." From the bones, "Let the dreamer dream." I pleaded for mercy from the dread unity of the place as, borne under no power of mine, I approached the featureless cylinder I knew for the dreamer's dwelling. Through the door and into a bedchamber I drowned in the reek of unimaginable decay, such that I craved to wash the stink from my skin, even as I observed several dozen shadowy figures attendant to an earthen mound, what a person might call a cairn or pyre, in this place a bed where the dreamer lay rooted by fine hairs that ran the length of its body. I stared on the thing, and the dreamer stared back.

Eloquent and vicious, it promised that as seed and sower, father and mother, king and queen it would eat my pain. It told me I, an accident of nature hardwired to narcissism, misread biological life for an eight-decade tragicomedy of acquisition and loss. However, the dreamer, born wise, without sanity, knew what we called Time for a set of rings radiating from a central point. It felt the vibrations in every ring between parallel walls of mist marking the hour before it took seed and the hour its existence would cease in days when the land I called home was a watery tomb beneath an overheated, lifeless ocean. It recalled falling into a semblance of what we called sleep, and in that state grew attuned to man moving fleet like doe upon the soil. Simultaneously it felt a sonar of stomping feet, as of men who thought themselves gods, accompanied by footfalls slower than anything had ever moved. Of the vibrations pouring endlessly through its consciousness, the dreamer came to love that cadence. It delighted in the agony its kinfolk felt when their branches cracked under the weight of mine. What we called plantations it called a feast, a grinder of black flesh from which blood poured into the soil to slake its decadent thirst. It spoke of pain like Pa spoke of whiskey, an addict delighted to be conquered, and with imbecilic cruelty told me my vibrations sounded no different from those of my ancestors. It promised me aeons of pain before it was satiated of me.

"Not my daughter, motherfucker!"

Pa swung an ax into the nearest trunk and the tree exploded with centipedes. Jesse rushed in, howling, his blade lightning in the dusk, and one half of the Switchin' Tree toppled in a cloud of black rot. Wolf-eyed Jesse fell upon the log like a butcher. Roaring profanities, Pa chopped the other half, an act I beheld with love and awe.

All at once, the dreamer's visions blurred in my fevered brain, like a last attack in revenge for its castration. Distantly I heard a cry. I heard Pa's ax hit the dirt. Through the fog of other worlds, I saw him, on his knees, rip at the bark until a piece of pale skin gleamed. "No," he whispered, reaching inside to lift Carrie Mae from the carcass, unconscious, blood in her yellow hair, covered in webs and insect husk.

The world lurched beneath me. Carried on someone's back, I recognized Jesse's strong arms under my legs. Holding Carrie Mae—holding *you*—Pa ran ahead of us. Though I wanted to thank Jesse, or warn him, the dreamer had robbed me of thought. Like I remained underground.

Carrie Mae—my pa saved you that night. But it tore him up to believe he was the one who'd hurt you. Caused the injury that broke your mind, except you and I know it was the dreamer's realm, and whatever you saw there. I suppose it's a mercy Pa died soon after. We found him floating in the St. Lucie. Gambling debts, they said.

You would've known he had nothing to do with the asylum if you got my letters. My heart broke to learn what those monsters did. It wasn't enough to cut pieces from your beautiful brain. They used your body, too. I can only hope you died there, freed from suffering.

The white man needed a letter, a plane ride, and a Vietnamese person to kill Jesse. But even when he lived, I was never his sister. Not really. That afternoon on the St. Lucie I got to be *your* sister, which I will always cherish. You were right, Carrie Mae. About so many things.

The state tore down our houses to build a freeway extension. Motels, gas stations, roadside attractions, and diners like the one where I worked awhile. Our neighbors came to think of that tree as our guardian angel. Pathetic, right? One of the Dickerson boys told me to my face it was Pa's fault we lost our homes. I poured a pot of Folger's in his lap. Funny, right?

For years I suppressed the thought of you. Yes, I used your treasure to buy that bus ticket. I waited for you! But how long could I wait for a girl I knew would never return? If I caused you any pain in our brief, strange friendship I am so, so sorry.

The truth is, I'm afraid. I'm approaching the day they will put me in a box and plant me in the ground. What do you know of that place? What secrets were revealed to you in the dreamer's realm? Oh, Carrie Mae. I am ecstatic to know we are speaking again. I will tell you all the joy I've seen. Until then, I remain your friend,

Shirley

REUNION

Halfway through breakfast at the Mexican restaurant, Kalonji was delighted to find the restroom could talk. A husky female voice coming from somewhere around the air vents said, "*Lava tus manos*. Wash your hands. *La cuenta, por favor*. Check, please." A robot Spanish teacher. Especially impressive considering Kim had taken them to a normal restaurant, nothing gentrified, a fifteen-minute walk from her Bushwick apartment. A normal restroom made of grimy surfaces and soggy toilet paper rolls. In the stall he listened carefully to the words, testing his dormant Spanish, at the same time peeling the Band-Aid on the back of his right calf. Last night he'd injured himself hauling his suitcase around Penn Station. The wound was cherry red and ringed in black scabbing.

He washed his hands. *"Me ama Nueva York,"* said the bathroom. "I love New York." He'd left Kim in the middle of a conversation about a TV show filmed in the city. She often saw one of the cast members, a British artist, walking her children around Bushwick. "People say the show's too white," she'd said. "I guess I can see that. But I like *Broad City*," she added quickly. Another show about Brooklyn hipsters. "The black guy on it? Hannibal? He's hilarious."

Anything about race Kim said with a mix of apology and

defensiveness, wanting to balance being a "good" white person with her veneer of Noo Yawk tough. It was November 2014, a time in which whiteness was attacking Kalonji from all sides. Over the year:

1. Police murdered a chubby black teenager for crossing the street, then left him dead for hours on the cement, as if he were a vampire they intended to stake should he rise. When black people fought against this, whites sent in the National Guard. They made his murderer a millionaire. They ejaculated the darkness of their souls online, rejoicing in Mike Brown's death like they did Trayvon's. The internet became a Nuremberg Rally.

2. They failed to cover up a rape scandal in the New York literary establishment. Kalonji had never heard of Alt Lit, but felt a familiar, blunted anger to read how the main rapist admitted his crimes via self-pitying tweets. None of these men went to prison. None were shot dead in their own neighborhood.

3. A white woman informed him she was pregnant with his child, a fact he took with philosophical calm and secret excitement. Thirty years old and unemployed, he welcomed the sense of purpose this could bring. Then, to be cruel, she stopped returning his calls, torturing him for ten days with her silence. A piece of him was floating unchaperoned in the great, wide universe. The baby consumed his thoughts and he got little sleep.

4. Another white woman (younger, saner, one he'd never slept with) agreed to do a reading with him in Bushwick. All five readers were poet friends of his who'd found their way to the city. It would be a reunion. Before leaving Oakland, he built anticipation by googling beer-filled photos from hipster literary salons, or listening ad infinitum to a Rick James song about New York that was short and groovy and always left him wanting more. Every visit he got to play the artist—that strange breed of half child, half adult. Then Julie sent him a Facebook message saying she couldn't do the reading. A friend from her MFA committed suicide and the depression had her in bed all day. Don't worry, she told him, the other readers agreed to reschedule. Kalonji was livid. Her myopia felt comparable to killing a child because of his melanin, sense of perspective be damned. He wrote her back to tell her in clear—but restrained—terms how flying across the country to *not* do a reading would inconvenience him. She apologized, uncanceled, and asked a friend to take her place.

Kalonji paused in the restroom to think over his next conversation starter. He'd spent most of last night complaining to Kim about point #3: his regret over an angry message he'd left on his ex's machine, his fear of having a child with a crazy person, concerns she'd listened to with a coolness he found troubling. Boring her didn't bother him. It was the risk of reducing her to a vessel into which he poured his thoughts. Twelve years of friendship deserved more, he told himself. He considered combining points 2 and 4. In a way, the Alt Lit scandal was karmic. Every novel that came out of NYC was about some fresh-faced girl's love life. Or the drugs she did, followed by narrations of the miserable sex she had while on those drugs. The reasons were obvious: white men ran publishing. White men took a personal interest in when white girls would start breeding. As student loans and the job market pushed back their immaculate baby boom, the leaders of the master race grew impatient and took what they wanted.

He returned to point 4. "Julie's young," he told his mirror reflection, "pretty, award-winning poet. Then this guy kills himself so it's like, that's what she has to look forward to? Or getting raped by some motherfucker who wears pink shorts? She's having an existential crisis and I don't blame her."

Yes, that's what he'd tell Kim. He didn't blame Julie at all. Part of him felt silly for talking to himself but, as a writer, verbalizing his mental tangents helped wring a little sense from it all. He was headed to the door when the smoky voice said, "*Hay mierda en el inodoro.* You left shit in the toilet."

He looked to the ceiling for security cameras. None. Must be its programming. "So what?" he said to the recording.

He gave the handle a tug. The door wouldn't open. This time the voice came from the walls. "You think it's okay to shit inside someone and leave it there?" Algae-green water poured from the grout between the tiles. Kalonji shuddered. The bathroom was *salivating.*

"You have terrible breeding." She kept that same lungless, android delivery. Hint of a Brooklyn accent. "You're tacky and weak."

The light tubes in the ceiling flickered. Pipes groaned. This was a bathroom that had seen too many horror flicks. Panicking, Kalonji remembered Jonah in the whale. He remembered he had no god to pray to. The Xlerator hand dryer whooshed to life with a spear of hot air directly on his Converse sneaker and the foot inside. He yelped. Purple pain swelled his toes and, like a pigeon who'd lost digits to hot asphalt, he hopped to the toilet and pressed the lever. The shit vanished. He tugged the door handle once, twice. At the third try it swung back and he was running like a cartoon character down the tiny hall decorated in paintings of tanned Marilyn Monroe wearing bandoliers and a sombrero.

His shame was pumping harder than his heartbeat. Should have stood up to it, he thought. Asshole bathroom . . . let it bully me. On the other hand—and this made him giddy—he had a new story for Kim.

She was picking at her rice and beans, drawing stick figures in the sauce with her fork as she considered what to talk about next. That time in college they threw a Weezer dance party in her friend's bedroom? The day they'd spent in Montreal last summer? Kalonji slipped into the plastic seat on his side of their booth, boyishly exuberant, as if rejuvenated by the burrito shit he'd just taken. He was massaging his left toes. "Kim," he said, "the craziest thing ha—"

"So you know," she interrupted, "I believe in Black Lives Matter. You know I do. But the next time you want to talk about that kind of stuff, don't post it on my Facebook wall."

It took him a moment to remember. "You mean that article about the Staten Island teachers wearing the NYPD shir—"

"Exactly. I hardly ever post on Facebook because I like my privacy. And you put that on there for everybody to see. Next time send me a private message."

"I just wanted to know what you thought about it."

"Again, send me a private message."

"I'm sorry." He didn't see what she was complaining about, but his apology seemed to satisfy her. He recognized her condescension as Kim acting out the small cruelties she didn't often get to indulge. It felt sweet, how instead of hiding her insecurities, she used him as an excuse to wallow in them. He watched her brush chemically auburn hair off her cheek. Within seconds the strands magnetized once more across her nose. She was pretty but not beautiful, with florid cheeks and tired eyes. He thought she looked better than she had in college, slimmed down from her former alcoholic puffiness. Her teeth crowded together like tall and short members of an overpopulated family all trying to get in the photo. The hairs on her upper lip were soft and white like a butterfly's belly. Elbows on the table, she slouched forward, parenthetical fingers cupped under the coffee mug she'd occasionally lift to her lips. He said, "Well, what did you think about it?"

Industrial stoves hissed in the kitchen. She sipped coffee, held it in her mouth until it grew painful, and swallowed. "I think it's horrible those kids have to go to school with those racist teachers. And that's one reason why education is broken. For what it's worth, every teacher I'm friends with marched for Ferguson."

"Including your boyfriend?" he asked.

"We went to the march together."

"That's cool."

"Isn't it? He's not a real political guy. He's kind of a bro. But he wanted to go with me. That was one of the first things we did together. A year, two years ago."

"It couldn't have been a year ago if it was Ferguson," Kalonji reminded her. He pictured a slideshow of black faces, the carousel clicking as they flashed by. Mike Brown. Trayvon Martin. Oscar Grant. A travesty how he only saw "thug" photos the media used to make them America's nightmare.

Kim bowed her head and rubbed her brow in circles, a séance for her thoughts, until she slapped her palm on her cheek. "Trayvon Martin. It was a Trayvon protest." That day they'd gone for Chinese food after the march, then a stroll through Washington Square. "I really don't get them mixed up. That's bad. That's so bad. That's really bad, isn't it?"

"You're so racist."

"Okay, fuck you."

"It's all right."

"No. Don't let me off the hook for that. I *really* don't get them mixed up." Kalonji noticed her jaw muscles clench. "I'm sorry. I interrupted you. What were you going to say?"

"About what?"

"The crazy thing that happened."

"I forgot." Something strange in the restroom, but the memory was gone. Besides, that sounded gross, talking about the shitter. "How long have you been together? You and Jake?"

"A year," she said.

His brows rose, contracting the space between his deer-colored eyes and inch of mossy 'fro. He looked good, she thought, a soft-featured man with a flirty smile and a nose like *Off the Wall* Michael Jackson. Maple skin. Ears that stuck out. Slender fingers.

"I can't imagine that," he said. "A year."

"I'll bet you can't," she spoke into her coffee, a mistake. The steam stung her eyes.

"What's that supposed to mean?" Kalonji asked.

"You break up with a lot of girls," said Kim. "You date a lot of girls."

"Well, what the hell else am I supposed to do with them?"

She'd taken a wrong turn, she knew, turning the subject to his love life. No topic pleased him more. Ever since women started liking him as much as he liked them, he'd grown an effeminate, showy confidence, along with the annoying vulnerability pretty boys had. His emotional softness stuck out like a deformity, like a gunshot wound in the middle of his face. In college he'd been endearingly unaware of his beauty, interested only in protests and parties.

Except when it came to her—he was in love with her. The

night of Bush's reelection he showed up at her apartment, where they drank whiskey sours and said *Fuck America* until three in the morning. One time he called her a slut when she arrived late to a party. *I don't care who you're fucking,* he slurred, beer-breathed. *Showing up on time is simple fucking manners.* Thinking about it made her smile behind the ceramic muzzle.

"I don't date that many girls," he continued with a self-assured smile.

"Yeah, you do." Breaking from her nostalgia took unexpected effort. "Last time you came here, you were engaged. Which, by the way, I knew wasn't gonna work out."

"You didn't like Caitlyn," he stated.

"I liked her! She was nice. But she just kind of seemed eager to please. Like, 'Oh, I'm just along for the ride.' A little flaky, y'know?"

It amused and intrigued him to learn she'd had such thoughts during her pleasant conversation with his ex, last year when he'd read at Molasses Books. That underneath her chirpy anecdotes about the subway system and the horrors of "teaching to the test," she was brimming with contempt, thinking, *This woman is a fucking child.*

She watched him scoop a rubbery forkful of burrito off the plate, then leave the fork lying in the sauce. A slow eater. Kim wondered if she'd gone too far. The hurt might still be fresh. At last he said, "When we broke up, there wasn't anything I could do about it. We'd been building to it awhile. A bathroom fan here, a lock there—"

"What the hell are you talking about? Bathroom fans? Locks? What?"

"She would yell at me for not . . ." He paused, then backtracked. "For forgetting to lock the top lock. 'Cause somebody tried to break in her apartment once. That's not a deal breaker."

"It kind of is. That's a matter of security."

"You're being white right now."

She threw her hands in the air. "Oh, what . . ."

"You are!" he said. "Black people can't walk down the street without wondering if a cop's gonna kill us. No, that they *want* to kill us and will get away with it. If somebody's like, 'Woe is me, you didn't lock a lock,' I don't speak that language."

She chose her next words carefully, resisting the urge to argue. He could say vulnerable and honest things in ways that made her want to dismiss them, either being hyperbolic to the point of silliness, or simply arrogant.

"I guess I see that," she said. "But it's not a race thing. It's about being a woman and feeling, you know, safe. 'Cause life is unsafe for us. You should be sensitive. Like what you were saying about your friend. The one who can't do the reading . . ."

"It sucks that guy killed himself. But she screwed me over. This sounds bad, but at the end of the day, ain't no flags at half-mast over her friend."

She had no reply. The hole of silence quickly deepened into a trough. Like a moon-eyed girl, he squeezed a knee against his chest with both arms and stared at his food. His inability to finish his plate seemed emblematic of his ineptitude, which over the years had yielded dead-end administrative jobs and toxic love affairs. She was aware her exhaustion with him had gratitude at its bedrock—his foolishness was a reliable thing, after all. Or perhaps she was overthinking it, and she was simply a pig who ate too fast. His expression told her he was thinking about the baby. She regretted bringing up his ex, any of them, and sought to bury her mistake under words.

"How's your cut?" she asked.

"Good." He stuck out his leg to show her. He peeled at the Band-Aid in hopes of getting a girly reaction. He was successful.

"Ew!" She cringed with her palms out. "Man, don't show it to me!"

"Sorry."

"I really don't like blood!"

He liked giving her a fraction of his pain from last night. Maybe it was a sex fetish he wasn't aware of. The metal hand truck on which he dragged his suitcase with the missing wheel broke apart five minutes after he'd touched down in LaGuardia. If only the buses took cash, as buses did in logical cities, he wouldn't have to haul fifteen pounds of clothes and chapbooks to the next terminal, buy a ticket from Hudson News, then back to the first terminal to wait in the cold. As he watched the lights from the Q70 weave through the snowfall, a shriek from above pummeled his ears. A great winged shadow fell over the sidewalk. Kalonji hid with two other commuters behind a trash can as, preluding its descent with a deluge of snow, a pterodactyl sailed earthward from the parking garage to grip its claws in the bus. One beat of its leathery wings hit Kalonji with a windy battering ram that sent him tumbling into the nearest wall. Lying prone, he watched the dinosaur carry the vehicle to its lair like a thirteen-ton trout. Dazed, he forgot the incident in the bone-chilling wait for the next bus—in his mind the first one never showed—then the ordeal of carrying his suitcase and reconfigured cart down subway steps. The cart lashed out and sliced through his jeans to the calf. Around one in the morning, he finally saw MONTROSE AVE. in white mosaic outside the subway car, and arrived sodden, shivering, wounded, possibly tetanus-infected at Kim's apartment, where she greeted him with Chinese leftovers in a foam carton. She insisted he put cream and a Band-Aid on his cut.

He looked at the wound again. Growing from it was a red rose in bloom. Grateful for the unexpected gift, he pinched it under the thorns and uprooted it from his skin. Only hurt a little.

Kim thanked him for the flower, embarrassed and charmed at his affection. She put it in water after a long, pleasurable sniff.

Kalonji heard the Mexican family in the next booth having a lively conversation. A cowlick-headed boy asked the mom why she'd bought two gallons of milk. "Because our household goes through milk like"—Kalonji waited for the simile—"like it was nothing." Disappointing.

"Didn't you cheat on Caitlyn?" Kim asked him.

"We were poly," he said pithily.

"Oh god." What California nonsense.

"She said it was fine sleeping with somebody else as long as I told her after. Which, by the way, she had other men." He knew she found him tedious. All he could do was double down. If she saw narcissism, make it a joke. "You think about it, I'm not responsible for anything."

Kim blew a derisive syllable of air from her nose. "You just tripped and fell on top of that lady." The waitress came with a pitcher, and Kim thanked her for the refill before noticing a rose in her water. Strange. The bemused waitress left to get her a new glass. Kim chewed the tip of her straw, an old habit. "So Cait kicked you out and now you're back in Oakland."

"Not a bad place to land," he said.

"That's why I could never do poly. I admit it, I get jealous. And I'm not perfect. The first time I got with Jake, it was cheating."

"I don't remember," he lied.

"I was dating somebody else. Another coworker. From my previous school."

He laughed. "I was about to say—"

"I know what you were about to say. I'd never date two guys at the same place. I told myself not to get involved with guys at work at all. It was a drunk hookup. The next day I cried about it. I felt really bad."

"How are things with Jake?"

"He's . . . I don't know."

"Wow. That's how you describe your boyfriend?"

"You know. He's a photographer. And before me he slept with a lot of girls. His whole thing was sort of like . . . you know . . . how artsy guys are. Sort of a Peter Pan complex. Like, 'I'm just flying through the world without a care.'"

"What—"

"And one time he was like, 'Kim, sometimes I just want to murder you!' Isn't that crazy? Why would you say something like that?"

"What changed? You've been together a year."

"He's very even keel and that works for me. 'Cause I'm more intense. Especially with my manic episodes."

"He—"

"He keeps me grounde— What?"

"He said he was going to murder you. How's that even keel?"

"He said he *wanted* to murder me. That's different. Right?" It shocked her how easily she could tell him that. Like a therapy session, the productive kind, and when he said nothing she kept going. "That sounds bad. I was being mean to him at the time. I got drunk and thought he was trying to leave me and I got really paranoid. He's put up with a lot of shit from me."

"You told me you didn't date white men."

"I didn't." He was getting smirky, trying to rile her. She could play along. He finally put the piece of burrito in his mouth. "I mean, I didn't date them, not I didn't *say* that."

"You said they were cocky. They think they own the world."

"Jake's the first white guy I've dated in years."

"I can't relate. I don't know why anybody dates white men. They're not even attractive."

"How many white guys have *you* dated, Kalonji?"

"None that I recall."

"So there y—"

"But unlike you, I never swore them off."

"Black guys got a little . . . there's a thing with black guys."

His eyes widened. "Yes?"

The waitress returned with her new glass. Having gnawed the straw to plastic paste, Kim tossed it aside. "Do all black guys feel the need to act . . . how do I put it . . . act theatrical . . . during sex? Like, they get pumped up and . . . say things."

"What in the hell are you talking about?"

"I don't know. It's just, every black guy I was with, they liked to get real into it. Like, say they're my daddy and . . . I don't know."

"As the representative of all black men . . ."

"Porn language! They talk like porn people!"

". . . it's because we invented fucking."

There were kids in the other booths. She checked to make sure they didn't hear. She lowered her voice. "Forget I brought it up."

He didn't lower his voice. "It's the Mandingo fantasy. We're all about that dumb stereotype. And I'll bet you any black guy who did that thought he was giving you what you wanted. If you didn't like it, maybe that's something you didn't communica—"

"I know, man! I know there's stereotypes. Black men. White women. I don't care about that. We're talking real life, not some fucking, fucking, old-ass Amiri Baraka play. Shit!"

"My people are naturally empathetic," he said after a pause, careful to not wind her any further. "That's why—I'm told—sex with white men is weird and gross. Self-entitled pukes just want to get themselves off."

"Look," said Kim, "I'm pretty vanilla. And don't think I forgot that time you called me a slut in college. That was really hurtful."

Kalonji almost said he'd never called her that. She'd gotten wasted and thought he did. Seeing no purpose in correcting her, he let it go.

"And I'm not saying you were like that all the time," she continued, to not sound judgmental. "Just when you were drunk. Most of the time you were quiet and gentle."

He searched for words. He wanted to turn back time to when she'd admired him, resented her for not telling him then, when a kind word, even if spoken in friendship, not an ounce of romantic feeling, would have eased the self-doubt he moved through like quicksand. For her part, Kim was looking at the table as if thinking of the younger him.

"You know," he finally said, "I like to sing opera when I'm doing it. Theatricality."

"Stop!" She moaned. "C'mon, I'm a schoolteacher. Okay, there was one time . . ." She let it trail off, to be dramatic.

He could feel his dick press against the back of his zipper. "And?"

"Me and Jake had sex in the same room with some cousin of mine when we were at a wedding. But I'm glad we did. He was this Republican asshole. It felt good, like I was disrespecting him. The whole time he was just being racist and sexist and it's like, well, here's something carnal in your face. He was probably asleep the whole time. I don't know. And there was one time I hooked up with a Turkish guy I met on the subway."

"Right after you met him?"

"It wasn't my safest moment. He was a construction guy. He came over the next day and fixed my door." She felt nostalgic for meaningless hookups, the temporality of sleeping with a near-stranger. How it made her feel unanchored. Then the mischievous, whorish walk from his apartment, feeling his eyes linger on her back, same as the morning sun on her face.

Kalonji pictured her having conventional, competent sex.

Pictured her back muscles pinching in and out like wings as she rode her faceless boyfriend. For some perverse reason, his mind fixed on imperfections. The lines around her mouth would deepen as she screamed. Her naked breasts would sag between her sticklike arms.

He was disappointed in himself.

"Are Turkish guys theatrical?" he thought to ask.

"Stop."

"You were never wholesome! You were the party girl in college."

"That's still there. I'm a teacher now. Or I was. I'm gonna teach again. Sometimes I want to party like Rihanna. Just rent out a floor in a club and pick random people on my way there. If I could do that once a year, I'd be good."

They both laughed, laughter that seemed to float in the air between them after it was done. She wanted to ask him: Why me? In college she'd been a drunk, depressive mess. Suddenly ashamed, she felt like she existed in a small room, apart from Kalonji or anyone who cared, alone with the memory of wandering the highway shoulder in her underwear, pursued by terrors they told her were imaginary. Back then she'd found little to love about herself.

"You want to be Rihanna?" he was saying. "That's good. I'm like Kanye in every way."

"Oh my god."

"Why does everybody like *Yeezus* so much?"

"It's a good album!"

"*You* too? The only songs I heard off that album was the one from that video where he's on the motorcycle—"

"That was terrible."

"And that 'I Am a God' shit. 'Hurry up with my damn croissants!'" Laughing, he brought his right hand down, accidentally flipping the dish spoon to upend the cup of creamer. When his wrist hit the table's edge, his hand came off. It dropped to the linoleum and bounced three times on the fingertips like a little man running away. Kalonji held his wrist more out of embarrassment than pain, because there was little blood, and it didn't hurt. A dairyfall was pouring off the Formica. His hand lay like a brown starfish. He reached for it and, in his haste, nudged it with his toe so it went spinning halfway across the room and under another table. The family of six screamed and lifted their feet like it was a five-pound subway rat.

Feeling the waitress's stare on the back of her neck, Kim flashed the woman her most schoolmarmly smile. Kalonji started wadding napkins. "Forget about the milk," said Kim, harsher than she meant to. "We have to get your hand."

While the waitress cleaned their mess, Kalonji and Kim got on all fours next to the other table. The family twisted so they could get through. Propped on his elbow, he kept losing his balance trying to reach with one hand. They butted shoulders like two lovestruck, tragic cows trying to walk side by side into the slaughterhouse when the end was nigh. She reached for his hand in the cobwebs. "Oh no," she said. "It's getting dirty." Kalonji's stomach twisted to see the blood crumb trail he'd left across the floor, everyone glaring at him for ruining their meals.

Kim stretched her fingers, clamped his thumb between her middle and ring, dragged it out, wiped it on her jeans, and, still crouching, jammed it back on his wrist. Turned it three times until it stuck like a new lightbulb.

"Flex it," she said. "See if it works." It did. The family resumed their amiable crunching, a pack of short-necked giraffes.

Back at their booth, his hand was a ball and chain of humiliation. He would have preferred anger to the friendly detachment she was showing. He'd rather she called him an asshole like the week before graduation when she'd wept in the passenger seat of his Toyota because he'd said taking psych meds was a sign of weakness, and he could only sit like a block of wood and watch her, and hurting her sent him into such a shame spiral that he drove around town for hours singing along to angsty alt-rock songs.

She noticed his mortification. "I'm sure it happens to everybody!" she said. To test this, she turned her right wrist counterclockwise until the hand popped off. It wobbled like a rubber chicken in her fist. She stared in fascination at the stump, the two bumps of bone lodged in red muscle that reminded her of cherry pie. She reattached it. "See?"

The look he gave her was shy and appreciative. "Got that Kanye in me," he said.

If she was ever going to kiss him, she thought, it would have been Montreal. He'd been on a book tour that coincided with her Canadian vacation. Something about him driving through North America in a rental car, doing readings in bookstores and living rooms, seemed youthful and adventurous. They spent twenty-four hours in each other's company and kissing him would have been right, but never *felt* right.

"You're not white, by the way," said Kalonji. "You're more red. Like, Irish red."

"Well," she said, "you look brown." Under his jokes she could see the injury. She wasn't helping him by skirting the real issue. It occurred to her that a good friend was a surgeon who prodded the painful spot in order to heal it.

"You said you apologized to your ex?" she asked. And added, "The pregnant one."

"Yeah. First thing this morning."

"What was it you called her on the voice mail?"

"I believe it was 'trailer park psycho cunt.'"

She sniggered. "I like that one. Okay. Show me the text."

He handed her the flip phone. He shouldn't have enjoyed her reading it aloud. Regardless of being rude and supercilious, it still felt like someone reciting his work, which made the tiny artist inside him dance at his typewriter.

"*I'm sorry about last night,*" she read. "*It was immature. The thing is, trust between us is low.* What is it, a gas tank?"

"I didn't want to just say, 'I don't trust you.'"

"You should have. It's honest. *You fell out of contact for ten days.* You really said the number. *I shouldn't have to have this stress.*"

She said it with a whiny tone. "It sounds emo," he said, trying to laugh it off.

"It's a little self-centered. Okay. Gotta finish this. *Call me back. I'm in this. I'm a part of this. Be in touch.* That's a dramatic way to end it. I can tell you're a writer." She handed the phone back. "It's good."

"You really think so?" He stared at the message, then her. "You think I'm self-centered?"

"She's pregnant!" said Kim. "There have to be all kinds of things going on in her head. It sucks for you but, y'know, she's pregnant!"

"She's toxic! Everybody hates her!"

And you fucked her anyway, she thought. Men always wanted sympathy for that.

"She had her sister call me to yell at me," he continued. "What kind of redneck shit is that? I can do that. I have an ignorant-ass sister, too!"

"I'm not defending her," Kim said, which she knew for a lie, as well as a stupid thing. His bitch ex deserved scorn. "Just, you carry someone in your womb, you get attached."

She hadn't thought her words would offend him, but Kalonji

turned livid. He snarled, "She's not attached. She's terrible. She's the worst person and she's not gonna keep it, anyway."

His viciousness hit her like bullets to the chest, made it hard to breathe. She bit a thumbnail. "Hmm," she managed to say.

"Which, y'know, it's her choice. Ain't shit I can do about it." He manufactured a chuckle. "I mean, once I start makin' that paper, I'll get everybody an abortion. I'll pay to get you one, if you want."

She needed to escape this conversation. "I don't mean to be rude, but I have to go. It's almost noon."

"How much do I owe?" he asked.

"I got it."

He watched her lift a tote bag of groceries from off her seat. He asked, "Can we stay an extra minute?"

"Of course."

"You ever had times when you weren't sure of the world? Like, maybe your reality wasn't actual reality?"

"Um, all the time."

"I don't feel like that now. I feel real centered."

Outside, snow filled the air like sawdust. Flakes coldly prickled their cheeks. He kept his tote bag of chapbooks under his coat and wedged in his armpit. Like a vinyl record, Brooklyn rotated around them. He picked a rectangular piece of black bean from his teeth and flicked it away. It bounced off the ski-capped peak of a homeless man's head. The man transformed. Like a video game glitch, the world in front of them seemed to crash, but instead of a keyboard blitz of numbers and symbols, he saw the radio waves of sex and agitation that made up their universe. Before them appeared a ferret in a tiny crown standing on hind legs.

The little furry thing addressed Kalonji. "Many thanks, O lord of givings! For years I have been imprisoned in the body of a man, when truly I am Skalalala, the prince of ferrets!"

Kim clasped her hands and squeaked, he was so cute.

The prince twitched his tail that looked like an old bath brush. "My Moorish benefactor! I have waited millennia for someone to break the spell of manhood by tossing a bean on my head. Now that you have freed me, I will bless you with good luck."

Kalonji almost thanked him, then said, "It wasn't me. She did it."

Skalalala opened his mouth and screamed a burst of orange magic at Kim's stomach. It hit her like a ferret-sized punch, so she doubled over. "Fuck your mother!" she grunted. Kalonji was asking if she was okay. The prince of ferrets ran into the sky and toward the white sun. Annoyed, she nonetheless watched him depart with gratitude, and grateful for Kalonji being with her in this moment, one she knew would not happen again.

They walked. Smells braided together: roasting lamb from the Arab butcher shop, ice on concrete, car exhaust, until those scents muted by a fresh-paved road and the tar played its solo. A low, black blues. "Where are you going after New York?" she asked.

"I have a reading in Philly."

"Are you going to see Caitlyn?" She remembered the ex-fiancée lived there.

"Doubt it. I think I made her mad last time I was there."

"What did you do this time?"

"I texted her and she said she'd like to hang. I told her I was staying with a partner. She said she was busy. Isn't that funny?"

"A partner? Say you're with a *friend*, Kalonji. That it's a friend you're sleeping with isn't important."

"I hope we'll be friends again," he mused. "I have to think the passage of time can give us things. Like, there's people who I wasn't close with in college, but now we're great friends. Cait hates me now but all that antipathy fades."

"It fades to indifference." They'd reached the subway stop. Black icicles dangled a foot long from the grating above. "This is me. I'm crashing at Jake's tonight, so you have the place to yourself. You have the keys. You have my number. Have a good reading."

She was wearing a winter coat. Hugging her felt like holding a bag of packing peanuts. "I love you, Kim."

"I love you, Kalonji."

It was cold. The clouds were a herd of steel beasts migrating across the sky. Printed directions in hand, he tromped through the snow to another friend's apartment. He loved the sensation of walking, of being a flaneur. He wanted to strut Broadway like an eighteenth-century freedman, sash around his butterfly waist, top hat looming like a steeple, twirling a cane on his way to the follies. Or lose himself in Williamsburg until he stopped at the coziest overpriced café to unleash pages of built-up prose onto lined paper. In a court, Puerto Rican boys were shooting ball at a netless hoop, striking reverb off the rubber halo. The brownstones made him feel like the star of a Spike Lee movie, bricks singing "People Make the World Go Round" like the opening to *Crooklyn,* a movie he'd watched with his dad, the man who took him to libraries and Waldenbooks. It would be a gift to give that to someone else. To be a father.

And Kim really defended that bitch. Sided with the person who looked like her. Something cruel clawed at his insides as he remembered her smug comments he'd been too infatuated to call her on. To calm the rage he focused on the trees in their leafless trance, the desolate and timeless warehouses. Finally he arrived at his friend's steel-and-aluminum home. They'd met in Baltimore a decade ago, when both were spoken word artists. Now this friend studied poetry at NYU. Before he entered, the friend instructed he take off his shoes. Then they hugged. For the next three hours, Kalonji workshopped with the MFAs, drinking wine and eating Salvadoran food. He felt tenderness from these strangers. New York shrank to fit him.

Kim arrived at her boyfriend's basement apartment. He was naked, his freckled chest and boyishly soft pubic hairs waiting for her. They kissed. He took the groceries from her bag to start cooking. "That's impressive," he said, "your friend's so young and already published. Why don't you want to go to the reading? Sounds fun."

She said she'd seen him read before.

"I wanted to be a writer once," said Jake. He tied on an apron, the strings in a bow above his ass. "I got published in, what was it, *ZYZZYVA*, I think."

"He's a sad guy," she said. "Got some lady pregnant and wants her to keep it. Thinks a baby will complete him."

Frowning sympathetically, Jake cut carrots into strips.

In the bathroom, she opened the medicine cabinet. Her row was the one with a half dozen orange vials. Her school had been understanding to give her as much leave as she needed following her episode. And she felt no shame with Jake. Like some girls kept a toothbrush at their boyfriend's, she kept Rx pills. And a pink toothbrush.

She heard him through the half-closed door. "The students were asking about you today."

"Aww. Who?"

"Valentina, for one."

"Oh. She's such a sweetheart."

"And José was asking when you'd come back. You should visit."

"I want to," she said with Kalonji in her thoughts. He had to be cold right now. Driven through the snow by dedication to his art. She remembered what he'd said about the police and hoped they passed him by. Hoped today was a day he not only reached where he was going, he felt safe once he got there.

A sad guy, she repeated in her mind. Years ago he'd started telling her he loved her. And sometimes added, "as a friend," which meant, "as a man loves a woman." Her belly clenched involuntarily as she reached in her bag for Ativan and came out with a handful of words. She gasped and dropped them in the sink.

"Are you okay, babe?" Jake asked.

"Yeah. It's nothing." Chilled into paralysis, she watched the letters ant-march across the porcelain. They'd brought periods and ellipses with them. . . . *ever since I was a kid. You were so fun . . . kind . . . beautiful . . .* The fucker left words unsaid in her bag. How did Jake miss them? Her heart racing, she was stunned at her good luck. Her nerves twisted to see many *S*s. Versatile, unpredictable letter, beautiful and deadly as the serpent who shared its coils. Progenitor of uncomfortable words. Submit, she thought. Supplicate. Submerge. Unwilling to kill them, but unable to look at them any longer, she gathered the words on an MTA ticket and slipped them inside an empty Rx bottle she then hid behind the hamper.

She would throw them out in the morning.

OWEN

She called me up and said the boy pushed his sister. You don't hit girls. Certainly not my little girl. So I get in my station wagon and drive from Edgewood to Garfield to spank my son.

Because I do the spankings. Pam has no stomach for it, and we agree that discipline is a father's job. When it comes to teaching a lesson, you need a man's physicality to make it stick, and Teddy stands near eye-to-eye with his mother these days.

Filthy rain pours almost horizontally under spiteful winds. I ascend deep-treed hills through Highland Park and then Garfield, former enclaves for mill hunkies with the stink of Ellis Island still on them; I remember the foreign bastards had no tolerance for darker complexions. Now black folks live in the postwar bungalows, the sleepy town houses. In the oaks I can see dilapidated Victorians rise like leviathans from weeds grown tall like elephant grass, their boarded windows like so many blinded eyes.

Parking in front of Pam's town house, I see in the rearview three punks noticing me from the dead end of the street. Clowns in ski caps like dunce caps, they have the nerve to stare me down like those guineas and Polacks used to.

I think of real outlaws. As a boy I'd see them drive Lincolns past my cottage to the hooch—card sharks, number runners, knife hands—and knew it was they who inspired the murder ballads bluesmen sore-throat-croaked out the brass flower of Daddy's 1907 RCA phonograph. They wore Stetson hats and high-ankle boots to hide their razors. Real deadly cats.

As a grown man who should probably know better, I style myself like them in dress shirts, slacks, suit coat, flat cap, and polished wingtips. Say what you will about their profession, they were men. Not little shits thrown in the street by moms too lazy to raise them, pants round their asses like prison bitches.

On the doorstep I shiver at the weirdness of coming over Pam's on a weekday. I ring the security buzzer and my daughter answers. "Daggy?"

I smile into the machine. "Hello, mouse!"

It takes composure not to push down my wire-rim glasses and stare hot fuck-you at these teen shits eyeballing me. I am tall, heavyset, and light enough people tend to give me a second glance in hope I am what they are. I get Italian, mulatto, Filipino, Mexican. Even Thai one time. And as much as I want to call out these boys, it stands to reason the cowards might shoot me. So, trying my best to not look like a target, I mutter for Kimmy to hurry up.

It made the national news: wrestler plummets seventy feet in a stunt gone wrong and dies in the ring. Shocking, because I knew wrestling was theater. The sudden injection of realness shook me up, though I'd never call myself a fan.

Maybe it got to me because the kids loved wrestling. Theodore Jr. and Kimberly, eleven and nine. The year before Owen Hart died, I took them to the Civic Arena for a pay-per-view because that was the only activity they could agree on, and I'd never seen either so happy.

I'll always remember that view from the nosebleeds when

the Undertaker threw Mankind off the top of the steel cage. Till that point the show had been pure vaudeville: some buffoonery, some impressive athleticism, even some big-titted women, then out of nowhere I had my heart in my throat, scared for a man's life. Meanwhile, the Undertaker stood on top the cage like a black-garbed demon gloating over his infernal handiwork.

As they wheeled out Mankind on a stretcher, the chants started. "No-more-Man-kind!" "We-want-re-fund!" Disgraceful. What if he was really hurt? Or worse?

Mankind didn't die. In fact, he ran back and kept fighting. One of the damnedest things I ever seen in my life. My heart kept racing the rest of the night till I found myself in the parking lot with a kid on either side, both crestfallen because Stone Cold lost the WWF Championship to Kane in the main event. The black foam middle fingers on their hands were pointed sorrowfully at the pavement.

Hearing the news of his death, I struggled to recall whether Owen had wrestled on that show.

"Can we give money to his charity?" Teddy asked me on the phone, Monday night after the accident.

"Charity?" I asked.

"Owen's favorite charity. It's in Canada."

He was watching *Raw Is Owen*, a night of remembrances and matches in his honor. Owen had a wife and two children, and that seemed to hit Teddy the worst, knowing the wrestler had a family. The boy said he'd worn an Owen bracelet to school that day.

"I don't know about charity," I told him. "But ask your mother if you can help around the house. Charity starts at home."

Monday through Friday I'm the associate at Jacob Maiselman, DDS & Associates in Monroeville. Mine is the face most patients see. Dr. Maiselman comes in three days a week: an old elf with a grievous air, he mostly stays in his lemon-smelling office, among plaques from innumerable local organizations and masculine brotherhoods he belongs to. He hired me nine years ago, after his son left to start a rival practice, and while some would call his employing a black dentist progressive, I doubt Dr. Maiselman had ever heard of affirmative action, let alone made it priority; it had been my military service that got me in the door. He calls it a national tragedy, how this country treated men like me when we came home. I see the patients he no longer bothers with as, nearing retirement, his clientele has narrowed to friends and their families, whose teeth are so familiar to him he can predict each new rugrat's dental records while they're nursing. A straightforward man. A boss. I work too much and my commission could be better, but starting my own practice had never seemed worth the trouble, and I'd long ago lost the right to be choosy.

On Tuesday, I found time after my morning patient to speak with the receptionist, Tilly. I'd grown curious about this person my boy was mourning, and she was the closest I had to an expert. A rotund woman from Nor'side with an eager smile and a taste for flower-print dresses, carroty hair moussed high in honor of her groupie days, she liked to reminisce about painting her face Italian flag colors to cheer Bruno Sammartino in Madison Square Garden. Billy Graham, Ric Flair, "The American Dream" Dusty Rhodes—she loved them all.

I told her the only one I knew was Dusty. After the war I went to Howard College of Dentistry, two hours from Richmond by Greyhound. Every Saturday, I came home to find my youngest brother on the shag rug watching Dusty cut promos. That white boy must have spent some time on the black side of town; close your eyes and you'd think a Shaft flick was on.

"My brothers love Dusty!" Tilly gushed. "They were always arguing with Dad because he was a WWF guy and they liked southern wrasslin'. Dad was like, 'We're Italian! We like Bruno!'"

I asked her, "You wouldn't happen to have information about Owen Hart?"

"I'll see what I can do," she said, like an ace reporter.

The next day she came to work with a printed history of the Hart family she'd found on Yahoo. Born into Canadian wrestling royalty, the baby of a multitudinous brood, Owen trained under his father, Stu, in a school called "The Dungeon," got his start in the family promotion Stampede Wrestling. After signing with the WWF he gained a reputation as a high-flying technical wrestler awarded many accolades in their fake sport. He often worked with his brother, Bret, which I imagine must have been fun for them. Eventually Bret left the company after getting screwed out the title ("One hundred percent shoot," said Tilly seriously) but Owen stuck around. At the time of his death he was doing a superhero gimmick. He was thirty-four.

Just a tragedy. Over the day, I performed oral surgery, filled out insurance reports, stewed over the latest doughy white man to address me as "buddy" with my Doctor of Dental Medicine degree framed on the wall and my drill in his yellow mouth, unable to stop thinking of my siblings in Virginia. Counting all the halves and sibs, I have about a dozen like the Harts. It would kill me to lose any of them.

And I thought: What kind of carny company would let such an accident happen? Did they catch his death on camera? Should I let my son watch such things?

Wednesday night, Pam called. "He's lost his mind, Theo. He's mourning a white man."

"Part of growing up," I said to put her at ease. I grew thoughtful. "It's his first taste of mortality. I don't remember the first time I learned about death."

She acted like I hadn't spoken. "He wants to have a funeral for the wrestler."

I tried not to say something smart at the fact she'd ignored me. Leave it to Teddy to find the creative side of things, the sensitive side. One time he threw a birthday party for a kid he'd never met—just a name on a calendar. Threw a Happy Birthday Gaia party for Earth Day. Dressed up as his original comic character for Halloween. I loved that about him.

"We need to put him in therapy," said Pam.

Then on Thursday I got the call saying he pushed his sister down after she laughed at the memorial he made. And I wanted to tell Pam I'd seen them fist-pumping in unanimous exultation at the wrestling show just a year before. Now look at them fighting. All the Dr. Spock in the world and this woman wouldn't know parenting if it chomped on her narrow ass.

But you don't hit my little girl.

I hear three locks turn and Kimmy opens the door, embraces my waist. "Daggy!"

My baby girl is beautiful and charming, chubby, gingerbread brown, dressed in pink pajamas, large front teeth, her hair in that inexplicably popular style called afro puffs. I follow her up a short stairwell. In the living room, orisha idols stare me down from pupilless eyes. Lions snarl from quilted tapestries and other African art pieces. It all feels disturbingly like voodoo. Pam likes African men, too. All kinds of Kunta Kintes coming around my kids.

She'd wanted to give them crazy names, too, Ujima and Nia. My foot came down on that one, before every job app they ever filled got thrown in the trash because that woman was having an identity crisis. My kids have perfectly fine Anglo names and if, when they grow up, they want to ditch their slave names for a Kunta or an X then so be it.

At the coffee table Kimmy shows me the A on her math test, Daddy's little girl, a flirt. I check her face for bruises but she looks fine. She asks me to buy her lip gloss from Claire's.

"You're a bit too young," I tell her.

"Then buy me the *getter* eye shadow." She means glitter. She likes malapropisms.

"Too young for any makeup."

"I want the getter!"

It's then I notice the remains of Teddy's memorial in a corner by the TV cabinet, a dinner tray flipped over, its adornments spilled on the beige carpet. Charmingly, he'd been attempting a Gothic thing: a linen doily, gargoyle bust, the name OWEN on an index card, four pink scented candles, and the plastic ivy Pam uses for fall decoration. His mother must have been pissed—she hates anyone touching her things.

"Did you knock it over?" I ask Kimmy.

"It's stupid," she says.

"Don't say *stupid*. It's a stupid word."

She shrugs. "Teddy's weird."

"That's your brother, mouse. That's the only brother you got."

"Whatever," she sasses, working her charm.

Secretly I hate when she badmouths him. From the back of the house I smell sautéed chicken and collard greens with maybe a side of corn bread. A recipe Pam got from her mama, who I miss having for a mother-in-law, a godly woman who worked fifty years cleaning white homes, who performed as wife and mother with equal duty.

Pam appears from the kitchen in a purple terry-cloth robe and curlers. A good-looking woman, short and dark, she glowers at me with domestic weariness and bald disinterest.

"Can we talk?" she says.

I want to say, Jesus, woman, give me some time with my

girl. But I cross through the dining room to do recon. A sense of wrongness crawls through my skin seeing the dining table, silverware, and walnut armoire we used to jointly own.

The rolltop desk, another fossil of our marriage, she's made a shrine to herself full of plaques and certificates from her HR job at Pitt, interspersed with the kids' report cards and Black History memorabilia. Woman always had a stagey love for milestones. When Denzel won Best Supporting Actor, she had me wash dishes so she could call everyone she knew to gloat like she'd catwalked onstage right with him to accept the little gold naked man from Geena Davis.

We join in a kitchen so small I can see the pores on her face. Greens sizzle in the skillet. There is a bean-shaped stain from cooking grease on her robe, above the heart. Her petiteness has me remembering her second pregnancy, how low her belly hung on her frame, the gauntlet of anxieties, meals I cooked, massages I gave, baths I drew in fear that childbirth might break her.

To think I loved her once. Now it is like a story I read about people I could never picture as us. I ask, "Are those little pussies always out there?"

"All day." She grunts with distaste. "And the girls are even worse. They go out dressed like sluts. No wonder they all get pregnant."

Another thing we agree on: keep the kids away from ghetto negroes.

"So tell me what happened," I say.

"I already told you." She speaks like I'm a child. "Kimmy started picking on him and he pushed her. What happened to the wrestler again?" she asks abruptly. "How'd he die?"

"He fell doing some kind of stunt."

"I thought it was fake."

"Why were they unsupervised?" I say, to get on topic.

"They're old enough to be unsupervised. I was cooking dinner. I'm the only parent here. A single moth—"

I cut her off. "You know how I feel about that single mother thing. Ain't no mother single unless the man is a deadbeat or she's a widow. You got me, you got your daddy, you got whatshisname . . . Thaddeus? A black man named Thaddeus. You still with him?"

She rolls her eyes. "Jealousy. Very original, *Theodore*. Work through that on your own time. We're talking about the boy."

"It's 'cause you keep him in the house all day. The child gained twenty pounds sitting around. I told you to get him on a football team."

"Those boys would eat him alive. Will *you* pay for his medical bills?"

"I could if I had to." A lie. I want to hurry it along, knowing the boy waits upstairs, dreading me. But her sass has me raw. "He can't be inside all day. Especially with Kimmy picking at him like she does."

"Blame it all on me," she says with a martyred air. "You're the one supposed to provide an example."

"There you go again talking like Doll."

"Do *not* bring Doll into this."

"She never liked me."

"That's my sister, Theo. You gon' say something about my father next?"

"I have nothing but respect for your daddy. That man was building airstrips on Okinawa with kamikazes shooting at him all day long. Hell yes, I respect him. I don't even care that he never learned my name—"

"This again."

"You want somebody to stick around, try learning his name. The man called me 'Bruh' for nine years."

She makes a sarcastic face. I remember her telling a white man in a black dress, *He said he'd never love me,* whining over hurt feelings in a court of law. Like love means anything next to responsibility. Charged with giving those kids a family, the woman failed.

I collect myself before she gets me worked up. "Where's the boy?"

"In his room."

For some reason, I hesitate. "Fuck," I say at last. "Let's get it over with."

She switches from condescension to unearned tenderness. "If you don't feel up to it—"

"Jesus Christ! The things I've seen would *blow* your mind!"

"I don't know why you feel the need to say that as if I don't know." She follows me upstairs. "It's not my fault you got drafted. Maybe you should talk with a psychiatrist."

Her mouth never stops. The older I get, the more I understand why Daddy smacked Ma every once in a while. Bless their hearts.

We find the boy upright in bed, gingham bedsheets rumpled around his waist. He has a well-kept room decorated in video game posters, comic books, and classic literature stored neatly in cubbies. He wears black sweatpants and a white T-shirt with a cartoon tiger saying "Earn Your Stripes!" in the word bubble. Stocky, eyes the color of bourbon, pretty long lashes that curl back on themselves, he sees us and begins to hyperventilate, his tomato face dewy with tears.

I remind myself that fear is the point. Else he'll never learn. When I used to mess up, Daddy would promise a spanking in the morning, a guillotine over my head on the mile walk to school in heel-blistering shoes, eight hours in the schoolhouse, the walk back home, and even then Daddy'd see fit to extend the terror. Make me go in the woods and find a switch and strip the branches, and if he disliked it I had to get another. Then, and only then, did he beat my ass.

Black boys have to learn some act right. Any lesson he doesn't get from me, the honkies will teach him with more permanent consequence.

"Stop hyperventilating," I order. "You'll make yourself sick."

"I didn't mean to," he pleads between hiccupy breaths.

"Shut up when your father is talking," says Pam.

I can take it from here, I think.

"That bitch started it!" he blurts.

"Watch your language!" we say at the same time. I add, "Call my daughter that again and see what happens. Come on. Pull down your pants."

Meek as dust, he complies. His mother watches from the doorway. I remove my leather belt, fold it in half, and sit on the bed. He lies across my knees. The weight of him hurts.

I dread when he'll get too big. The one time I thought myself grown enough to sass my dad, I was in fatigues, on leave from boot camp. One sock to the jaw put me through that hideous accordion closet door and broke it off the wheels. The next day he made me repair it.

Hopefully it would never come to that.

Teddy's high, wide behind looks puffier than usual. I pull down his Fruit of the Looms to find him wearing five pairs, one on top of the other.

His mother bursts out laughing. "He wore extra undies?" She staggers off down the hall, doubled over in laughter. "Oh Lord, that's funny. I need to call Tina."

I want to throttle her. Again Teddy cries, hands clasped

protectively over his butt. I gaze through the blinds at a sodden hillside. "Go take it off," I say.

Mercifully he doesn't take long in the bathroom. Still, he forces me to hold down one of his arms as he thrashes and begs. Like he's trying to make my work harder, so, pissed off, I hit him harder. Thirteen lashes like the Bible. Worn out, I tell him to go wash up.

After he finishes, I wash my own face in Pam's bougie upstairs bathroom. Brass faucet. Do-not-touch hand towels. African trash can made of bronze. Supposedly fragrant yellow hand soap in what looks like a Victoria's Secret perfume bottle. Her sacrilegious laughter booms in my mind and my legs tremble, like she has upset me on a cellular level. I stare in the mirror at a middle-aged man.

"Nigger," I scold, "get it together."

For a while in Kimmy's room, she fills me in on the newest drama with the Baby-Sitters Club. Terrible books below her grade level, but they make her happy. Downstairs I find Pam on the phone, still laughing to some girlfriend. That alone would enrage me, but on top of it she's ignoring me, as if I serve no purpose anymore. My gaze drifts to a tapestry of an African village done in collage style, three huts and a river snaking through them.

"Is that mine?" I ask.

"Huh?" She looks up from the phone. "Is what yours?"

"This collage. It was a gift from my roommate in dental school."

She glares. "That was from my friend David."

"The Ghanaian you dated two years ago? No, I believe this was hanging on the wall in *our* house for nine years."

She exhales audibly. "What is wrong with you? Are you just a crazy person? Huh?" She addresses the phone. "I was talking to Theo. He's in a mood."

"I'm taking Teddy for a ride," I declare, expecting an argument. But she says sure without looking at me.

At his door I knock and he says come in. He sits at his desk doing a social studies worksheet; it shames me to notice the pillow under his butt. He regards me with the stoicism of a movie Indian, like Tonto.

"You want to go for a ride, Bub?" I ask.

"I don't like when you call me Bub," he says softly. "Yeah. I'll go for a ride."

Soon we're driving past Highland Park Cemetery, a sprawling golf course for the dead. The rain has let up. Teddy sits in the cracked leather seat, wearing a hangdog expression. It would be easier, I think, if he had a real affliction other than trouble keeping his hands to himself, something we could cure with a pill, like Pam wished. Curtis thumps on the tape deck: *"The doo doo wop is strong in here . . ."*

"Somebody get the deodorant," I joke, "the doo doo wop is strong in here! Where's your sense of humor?" I ask because he refuses to laugh. What happened to my bright, giggling boy? His mop-water mood is pissing me off. "You don't hit girls," I remind him.

"Yes, Dad," he acquiesces in adolescent misery. Then he adds, "She started it."

"It doesn't matter."

"I hate her."

"That's the closest—" For a moment, my voice snags on the thorns of his anger. "She's your closest relative, son. You're getting too old for that. You're gonna have to protect her soon."

"I told her to shut up," he insists, desperate for understanding. "She wouldn't stop."

"Women never shut up. All they do is talk 'cause they don't do nothing else. Men are too busy getting things done to talk."

I picture his mother in the windshield. "Women get to be little girls their whole lives. *You* have to grow up."

Around Wilkinsburg, close to the apartment, I try to show off my newfound expertise. "Owen Hart. Bret Hart's baby brother."

"Bret's in WCW now," Teddy states. "He's probably gonna lose to Hogan. That's why WCW sucks—Hogan wins too much."

"All I know about Hulk Hogan is"—I do the voice—*"Let me tell you something, brother! Say your prayers, eat your vitamins!"*

"He's Hollywood Hogan now. He sucks." Out of nowhere, he becomes a loquacious bard of wrestling legend. "Bret got screwed by Vince McMahon. Then Stone Cold beat Shawn Michaels and got the belt and Mike Tyson was the referee and he punched Shawn Michaels. Shawn Michaels is gone but Triple H and Chyna are still there. Then Vince McMahon tried to screw Stone Cold and he fired Stone Cold but Stone Cold kidnapped him and held him at gunpoint but it was a fake gun."

"A gun?" I exclaim in alarm.

"That wasn't the first time they had a gun!" he says with chilling enthusiasm. "Brian Pillman was gonna shoot Stone Cold when he invaded his house. Brian Pillman's dead now."

I can't tell if he means in storyline or real life. Either way, I'm left speechless from the irresponsibility of these wrestling people.

After the divorce forced me from our yellow house in Penn Hills, I moved to Swissvale, a neighborhood grown on the Monongahela to feed the riverside mills. Together with Braddock, Rankin, and Edgewood it forms a desolate Neverland where unsupervised kids roam the alleys between dilapidated vacants. Seeing them amble in packs under the streetlights reminds me of when the mills started closing. Guys would drive to Texas and return with trunks full of newspapers they'd sell to steelworkers interested in the want ads, desperate for employment anywhere. And, one by one, those workers left. Or died and bequeathed the Victorians to their children, who left.

Which is better? Racist mill hunkies or black Lost Boys? I don't know. Whether you're staring at Franklin Roosevelt, or an olive branch and oak branch about to catch fire, a dime is worth only ten cents.

To cheer up the boy, I buy dinner from his favorite Caribbean place, run by a friendly Haitian chef and his son. Collard greens, black-eyed peas, jerk chicken, mac and cheese. Then back to my place, a building made from orange, lichened brick. I live on the ground floor in a former storefront with a long window I keep curtained. For that reason, the apartment stays dark.

A floor above me lives a girl with a baby and a boyfriend who stomps up- and downstairs in the middle of the night. My third-floor neighbor is a widow, abandoned by her worthless kids to climb those steps. I check on her now and then, buy her groceries with her SSI. It's the least an able-bodied man can do.

At the tin kitchen table, watching Teddy tear through the meal, all I can think is how long his nails have grown. On top of looking like a girl, it's plain slovenly, though I admit I don't provide the best example. I clean when I can, but bachelorhood encroaches from all sides. I see Ninja Turtles, Lego, Care Bears, and Masters of the Universe gathered round like they're waiting to come alive behind my back. At my elbows, a snowbank of bills. VHS tapes lie on most surfaces; every night before bed I put one on, to drown out street noise.

When Teddy's finished I make him brush his teeth to get the seasoning off his breath. Then I have him stand still while I clip his nails. I send him to the living room with a nod, uncomfortable at the vindictive undercurrent he leaves behind, and I'm wondering whether this disrespect will become a problem when

I notice he's left his plate on the table, a pile of bones in grease. I wash it, open a Schlitz.

Later I find him on an Indian kantha quilt whose origins and how I came to own it are a mystery to me. Teddy sprawls in front of the TV, plump and content in his kingdom of amusements, playing Zelda on the SNES, an X-Men comic to either side of him. I leave him be. At the table I examine a stuffed toy of the Rock: he has a plastic head with oversized features, giving me the People's Eyebrow; dangling Popeye arms; a big heart-shaped torso that squawks catchphrases when I thumb his fluffy solar plexus.

Perhaps, I think, I made Teddy soft with all the toys. Not to the extent his mother made him soft, yet I worry how he'll survive on his own. Then again, I'm happy to know he'll never dread the lottery. Never see Armageddon in my eyes, like I saw in Daddy's when the letter came. My dad worked his whole life in a paper mill. Granddad sharecropped and my great-granddad was born a slave. My son goes to school with white kids, has white friends, gets good grades. He can be anything he damn well pleases.

Including, I note with beery affection, the kind of boy who mourns a stranger.

I wonder what the guys in my platoon might say about him. Of those I keep in touch with, some would say raise him military-style like they do their sons, but the way they brag about making their boys run laps and do push-ups sounds like they brought the war home. It seems a strategy born out of fear, like the world itself is the jungle, and whether or not that's true, I cannot allow that fear in my house.

An infantryman with an M16, I did two tours. Most of the time I could barely breathe, my nose stuffed and eyes itchy from newborn allergies. When a gunfight broke out, I snapped into action, pure adrenaline, my desire to survive. For seven hundred thirty days, death controlled my world like the weather, and, like weather, I hid from it behind heroin, booze, and hookers. How else do you forget?

My eyes burn. A miracle that I ever convinced a woman to offer me her still-hopeful heart, the shelter of her cunt. My love for her was like a honeybee: born beautiful and propelled by urgency until it died from exhaustion.

Three beers later, an idea emerges from the rusted septic pipe I call a brain. I'm mulling it over when the phone rings in the living room.

"Let it go to the machine—" But Teddy has already picked up.

"Hello?" he says. "Theodore? Yes. Hold on—"

I bash my palm down on the switch button. With the dial tone Oming mournfully in his ear, Teddy gives me a terrified look that knocks me back to my senses. Suddenly faint, I stumble back until I'm sitting on the stool for an electric organ I used to be able to play.

"Whenever someone calls, just let the machine get it. I'm not angry," I assure him. "Just let it ring. Okay?"

In the span of two heartbeats, I see his fear of me replaced with fear *for* me, intrigue on his pinched face. Old enough to know what a debt is. Wise enough not to ask.

Regardless of this iceberg I've landed on, I focus on pressing matters. I propose we hold a funeral for Owen.

First, we choose a white JCPenney shoebox for the memorial casket. In goes Owen's 1995 Topps trading card, an action figure, and, why not, throw a Bret figure in there too. "Nugget" being one of Owen's nicknames, we throw in a nugget of fool's gold that happens to be lying around. An afro pick to represent the Nation of Domination, a black separatist wrestling stable Owen was inexplicably a part of. The boy draws and markers a crown, cuts it out, paper-clips it into a makeshift Burger King crown representing Owen's King of the Ring win.

Teddy, who insists on wearing a suit, has grown too fat for the dress pants I keep for him. He enters the kitchen from my bedroom, shamefaced because of the button he can no longer do up. "Sure you can't wear jeans?" I ask.

"Nobody wears jeans to a funeral," he moans. "Can you buy me new pants?"

"It's nine thirty," I remind him. I add with aplomb, "Let's be creative!"

So I cuff a pair of my own black slacks using Ma's Singer from the '30s. Takes me half an hour but I make him a presentable pair of pants, if baggy, belted tightly round his waist, falling in folds down his legs. Next he tries on the first of three dress shirts, miserable at his reflection in the hand mirror. "This shirt's too shiny," he mopes.

"We doing this in the woods, son," I remind him.

"I look like a traffic cone."

More dressing and undressing follows. There comes a point I remember he hasn't finished his homework, at which I can only smile to myself. Of all the roles I play as his dad, being the academic police seems like one I can put on hold for a night. I finally get him suited in pants, shirt, a snug black jacket, brown slip-on loafers, and a skinny tie I haven't worn in years.

At the last minute he wants to include a Canadian flag in the box, the emblem of that magical northern kingdom where Owen was born. What I have is a red T-shirt and a white T-shirt. I make Teddy trace the two bars and maple leaf on the red cloth, then I cut them out. I run the leaf under the mechanical needle and, thinking him ready, give him a shot at the last few stitches. Not five seconds pass before he stabs himself in the thumb, red on red, blood for country. No sound escapes him. I run to the bathroom and grab the first-aid kit, assuring him this is a part of learning, dreading what his mother will say, while he stares in fascination at his stuck flesh.

Memories crawl through that blood of my dad, a square-jawed, mustached figure who always seemed taller than he was, quiet and masculine. Before we had luxuries like a TV or indoor plumbing, I was reading a Donald Duck comic in the yard when he called me to the porch. Rapt, I watched him repair a tear in his overalls with needle and thread.

At half past ten we park on the Braddock Avenue side of Frick Park. Teddy, the box tucked snugly under his arm, looks like a future mortician in his black suit. Past the playground, we reach the entrance to a trail, the flashlight I carry illuminating Pennsylvania oaks hunched like old men. Nocturnal radiance throbs from their beryl leaves. Invisible squirrels and maybe coyotes skitter in the mud. A sign reads: DO NOT WALK TRAILS AT NIGHT.

Momentarily we hesitate before throwing ourselves into the dark like a pair of trapped moths butting against the glass jar. I feel him fumble his damp, nervous hand into mine. I squeeze his palm tight. A strange compulsion tells me we'll find our path in and out of the wilderness like anointed apostles. Except we bring neither fatted calves nor bread loaves—we bring ourselves, backs straight, breath clutched.

"Not much farther," I tell him.

I think of my mother, bless her heart. Zipped in my pea-green whipcord jacket, ax over my shoulder, I followed her broad, checker-shawled back out the cottage door, past the well and chicken coop into the pines. Amplified by the frosted earth, the air smelled muddy, like a landslide. The shoes Ma bought me in

June, two sizes too big, now fit my feet. Out of curiosity, I gazed north to where our closest neighbors lived: a father, mother, and three curly-haired daughters I'd sometimes glimpse through the pine needles, at the edge of their property with buckets in hand and cardigans tied round their long, defiant throats. Protective of Ma, I walked ahead of her. Before long we arrived at the stunted firs grown up round a wooden fence, where springtime sparrows would rest and shit seeds. Every day I chopped a tree for her. She'd weave the leaves into wreaths she'd sell at the roadside. If she made enough money, she'd buy us Christmas presents.

I lead Teddy off the trail, my footsteps made eerie from crackling leaves; I have him hold the light while I kneel and take a garden trowel to the black mud. Tough topsoil makes it harder than I anticipated. When the hole is large enough, I'm panting watching him lower the box, and I pass him nitrile gloves. He covers up the hole. We each take turns saying eulogies while the other holds the light.

"A seed is planted in the earth," I say. "It grows to be a beautiful flower. In time, the flower starts to wilt. It returns to the earth from which it grew. On May 7, 1965, the flower of Owen Hart came into our lives. He enriched us with entertainment. His athleticism showed us the possibilities a man can accomplish. He was a son, a brother, a father, and he was loved. There is nothing quite so sad as the passing of a young person," I add, speaking for my friends, long-dead and faceless. "Lord Jesus, we ask you take his soul to your kingdom where we will all be reunited on the Judgment Day. In your name we pray. Amen."

"He was born in Calgary, Alberta, Canada," says Teddy. "First, he wrestled as the Blue Blazer. Then he wrestled with his legendary brother Bret, who was tragically screwed out of the WWF Championship." His voice catches at the remembered betrayal. "But Owen grew jealous of Bret. He thought Bret was selfish and so he kicked him in the leg. Then they wrestled as enemies." As he speaks, I cross my arms over my chest, freezing. "Owen beat Bret in the opening match of Wrestlemania X but nobody cared. They just wanted to celebrate Bret beating Yokozuna. Owen was the King of the Ring. Then he joined the Nation of Domination. They're black and he was white, but he didn't care. They were his brothers. Shawn Michaels called him a 'nugget' but he wasn't a nugget—he was a great man."

Hurriedly I say, "Ashes to ashes, dust to dust. The circle of life continues."

On our way back to the car, I let Teddy hold the light. The woods teem around us. Every snap has me jerking my neck to stare into the dark. Breathless, I take back the light, twining my fingers in Teddy's. As I start to fear I've gotten us lost, we emerge into the empty playground.

Sickened at the mud on his loafers, I remove a napkin from my pocket, spit on it, kneel at his feet, and clean them carefully. The whole time, he watches me with his mother's eyes. At the station wagon I unlock the door for him, and he gets in, and we drive home.

TRIGGERED

1

Two or three years ago, in Davis, Spike met Tiffany. Back then, bosomy blond Tif worked as a librarian, wife in all but name to a sociology grad. Her partner, a chubby white guy in love with his own voice, naturally appointed himself media liaison when hundreds of students, Spike included, occupied a lecture hall to protest tuition hikes. Spike could recall cozy parties at a white clapboard lake house owned by the Sociology chair (a molester with a coke habit, fuck that guy) where punks mixed with academics; idling on the wraparound porch overlooking the goat pen, Spike would listen, mildly amused, to self-important babble from outdated Trotskyists who nevertheless made her blush when they called her *comrade*. Shyly she'd nurse a Four Loko and wait for the drugs to kick in, or for someone cute to make out with her.

Tif attended those parties. A woman in her thirties, a laugh in a sea of laughter, pretty and unremarkable like the Cézanne reproductions on the walls.

Now, sitting cross-legged at the edge of the driveway, her pulse racing from the previous bout, Spike beheld the librarian from Davis ready to get it on. And Tif looked *pissed*.

Handsome and curvaceous, nearly fat, Tif had a masculine jaw and striking eyebrows that started blond and bushy above her nose, vaulted over her lids, and tapered to white tufts at the borders of her skull. Her high ponytail displayed her face in all its aggression. Black spandex shorts clung tight to her hips. Her gigantic breasts strained the lycra in her sports bra. Staring across the driveway at her opponent, she huffed with hateful breaths that made her long upper lip billow like a parachute around her black mouthguard.

The punk boxing event was affiliated with the Bay Area Anarchist Book Fair scheduled for the next day, April 1. Proceeds from the anti-capitalist pugilism would benefit the Occupy Bail Fund, a mutual aid group for comrades arrested at protests. Whichever idiot organized this had equipped the fighters with gloves but no head protection; Spike would cringe every time someone took a fist above the neck. Nevertheless, the beauty of red leather bruising tattooed flesh mesmerized. Plus, she took comfort in familiar faces. To her right sat a street medic she'd seen give head stitches amid flash grenades. Behind her, at the backyard firepit, a Filipina with a serious expression was chatting up a willowy grad student, the latter of whom had famously gotten her hand crushed by UC Santa Cruz police at a sit-in. Spike had a hazy memory of smashing a cop car with either or both of them. This bungalow on this night took on a we-made-it grandeur she felt no shame in comparing to the saga-ending Ewok party in *Return of the Jedi.*

(And D stopped by to watch a fight. Strange, Spike later thought, for her to attend such a white event. But the eulogies said she liked to build bridges, so there was that.)

The other combatant looked about Spike's age, a pretty girl with long lashes and short brown bangs breathing nervously as she danced in place. She looked unprepared, and, judging by the betting in the crowd, everyone could tell.

A cowbell rang and it shocked Spike how quickly Tif crossed the cement to deck the girl with a sound like a tire puncture. Spike felt a shudder travel from her shoulders to her crotch. Some guy behind her shouted with a lewd thrill: "Don't fuck her up too bad. She's cute."

"And you're not fucking cute," Spike shouted back at him.

The beating that followed felt disturbingly personal. With every blow, Tif shrieked through her mouthguard, her weight advantage augmented with rage, then she would return to her stool and soak up the crowd while laughing like a woodpecker. A flanneled ref with Dewar's in hand circled the combatants, pointlessly gesticulating.

Three rounds later—two more than necessary—Tif's opponent threw in the towel. Spike cringed at the sight of her blood goatee. Before the loser could stumble to her stool, she was seized in the quivering pink arms of her opponent.

Spike could hear Tif rasp, again and again, "Thank you."

Elated disgust constricted Spike's chest. After the scheduled fights came impromptu bouts for anyone who wished to step in the "ring." Spike volunteered. Her thought when she stared across the cement to a skinny girl asking for help lacing her gloves: *This is gonna be fun.*

Forty minutes later Spike was puking in the kitchen sink. Holding an ice pack to her cheek, she watched the bruise turn from red to black to purple. She drank coppery water out the faucet, then whiskey to numb her shame upon seeing the girl she'd drunkenly pulverized.

Around the whispering fire, she made acquaintance with the only person she could see clearly, every other face liquefied under smoke. Changed into a light blue tank top and jean shorts, Tif's tremulous cheer seemed one broken plate away from a meltdown. Her bob haircut and elastic headbands from Davis, a pretty look, paled in comparison to her present-day golden zigzags Spike wished to braid. Or maybe chew. At the ends of Tif's plump wrists were long, dainty, elegant hands. When she smiled, her stringy lips stretched taut over teeth that shone like lights on the last subway car of the evening.

Up close, Spike noticed that her eyebrows imprinted on her face either concentration or panic depending on the angle, her eyes a relentless blue. Anxious under that gaze, Spike found herself rambling. In answer to her question of whether Tif knew her opponent: "Sadie? We're great friends! That's what's so fucking rad about punk boxing! We've been having drama but we totally hashed it out tonight. I feel closer to her than ever. I *love* her. And you! Fucking Kite—"

"Spike."

"You sure your name isn't *Kite*? Oh, I'm sorry! Embarrassing! It's those pesky long vowels." Tif gave her shoulder a slap. "You kicked ass out there, Spiky Loo!"

"Yeah, well," Spike replied, trying not to think about it.

"Our friend circle is badass," the other woman declared with obnoxious pride.

From there Tif recounted her tragic year. Apparently her milquetoast partner had abused her, and after much debate—"I was in love," Tif demurred—she'd kicked him out their apartment last summer. He stalked her at her job. He entered the apartment while she was gone and rearranged her things like a childish bully. All this led to Tif becoming a homeless wanderer.

Intellectually Spike knew better than to develop deep empathy for someone she barely knew, nonetheless, she felt powerless to stop herself from caring, even as Tif's tale of fleeing the patriarchy devolved into an insufferable vacation story about the trails she'd hiked on her cross-country road trip. Fragrant smoke off the redwood logs roiled the air so majestically that, in her relaxation, Spike half expected a unicorn to emerge from behind the cacti and join them. Before she knew it, she was offering to let Tif crash with her in her tent near the highway. To hoard resources when she had the opportunity to share, Spike reasoned, would be stinginess worthy of a yuppie, not a punk.

"Let's get some snacks," Tif proposed, driving her red Toyota Camry down MLK Way. Through the tempered glass, Spike gazed on humans shuffling block-long tent cities. "I just got my food stamps today," Tif continued. "Only took me three hours 'cause I have a parasite."

"Huh?" said Spike. "Like a tapeworm?"

Tif's lips parted to reveal both rows of teeth. "You can't tell?" One hand on the wheel, she lifted her shirt to display the tops of her breasts, veiny, comically swollen. "I'm preggers. Twins."

"Oh, your poor vagina," was Spike's reaction.

Tif laughed from her gut—"Ooh-hoo-ha-ha!"—so forcefully her chin collapsed into her neck. "San Francisco social services! They're all about the children! Gotta save the children!"

Spike recognized that tug in her clit for excitement over something so nihilistic as a pregnant boxer. Tif said she'd shacked up last winter with the father, a high school friend in Michigan who now wanted nothing to do with her. The sole man she'd met who could match her sexual stamina. "He was a freak! We'd fuck ten hours a day!" She sarcastically called him her *baby daddy*. "He's a jerk! Well, not really a jerk. He's just scared." Her talk of parasites was a rubber mask over heartache and Spike adored how broken she was. Like a vain and needy cat who refused to move from her lap, the weight of it warming her crotch until she wanted to shove it off, or rub its scruff to hear that melodious purr. Right after Spike suggested a parking spot, one close to the highway and well-lit, Tif accelerated four more blocks to park on a side street, a sizable distance away. "My car's been broken into," she said in a serious tone, even though her words explained nothing. With that they stuffed their valuables in their backpacks, locked up, and made for 580.

Peel back the chain-link fence like a scab. Run through the stygian murk as the concrete sky thunders. Climb the hill between West and East, wading through weeds that bite at the knees, Maglite at war with the greasy dark.

Behind her Tif was boasting how she grew up in the woods; indeed, her navigation of the undergrowth belied the woeful image of her in that oversized backpack, like a suburban camel. Tif singsonged: "Freddy Fungus and Mary Moss took a lichen to each other. It lasted until their marriage hit the rocks." Cringing at her corniness, Spike stooped to knuckle her way up the incline. Through rifts of cool blue shade, fungal alcoves indifferent to stone and silence and time, Spike followed graffiti beckoning through the thicket—THIS IS OHLONE LAND—to a clearing ten feet below the highway, her tent camouflaged under branches. Above, cars roared in either direction. Here the grass grew tall and ebullient. Tif joined her in howling at the stars.

Once she'd zipped the flap, Tif unpacked a rice cooker, three pots, a pound of rice, a battery charger, a stack of paperback science fiction novels, nine tinctures, a thermos the size of a fire extinguisher, sleeping bag, MacBook, blanket, and afghan until she took up two thirds of the polyester bubble. Considering the koi swimming inside her friend, Spike gave her as much space as possible. The passing cars sounded like the tide along Half Moon Bay.

"You should know I have PTSD," Tif said, straightforward

and selfless, pulling the sleeping bag to her waist. "So I might have night terrors." She put an episode of *The Office* on her laptop. The ambient glow washed over them. "You wanna snuggle?"

Spike had met this particular Occupy type before: the middle-class liberal making stupid mistakes in a quest to regain her lost youth. Though she'd never admit it out loud, Spike appreciated any comrade who shared her origins in that fiefdom of mediocre whiteness called the 'burbs. Four years ago, her software developer dad left her mom in Palo Alto for a twenty-year-old mistress. Her older brother, once her confidant and friend, went full Zionist and moved to Israel to flip real estate stolen from Palestinians. But it was her mom's quivering voice that periodically attacked from her subconscious with *Nobody will like you if you dress like that, Zoe. Why do you look like a lesbian? People will think you're in the lifestyle!*

Constant handwringing over her clothes as if her crime hadn't been engorging her veins with heroin, but looking tacky while doing so. Clean for almost a year, Spike considered it best she keep Mom at a distance, until the exhilaration over her rehab faded and with it any embarrassing behavior the anxious, uptight, selectively liberal woman might exhibit at this vicarious accomplishment. Spike sneered to picture Mom reducing her to a redemption story, a chance to score points with the other ex-wives opiated on mimosas. *Zoe's doing much better! And she's in computers just like David!*

Spike knew that Tif, like herself, would sooner self-destruct than become such a woman.

She woke to sunlight on her forehead. Tif lay sleeping a foot away from her. Rest revealed the lines of her skull and her modest throat wattle squished like a stack of pineapple rings. Every few seconds her exhalations would flutter on Spike's chin in such a way the girl ached with intimacy, like the bones inside her were blushing.

2

After five intermittent years of college—the life of a student had always felt like wearing a suit made from cardboard—Spike was set to graduate in a month with a computer science degree. It seemed the right time to leave Davis; her roommates at Poopie Haus were starting to catch on that she was the one stealing electronics. Time to pocket the two grand she'd made off their shit and set up tent in Oakland.

She did Web design under the table, not a dime to the government. For the revolution she encrypted comrades' phones against surveillance and this made her feel noble—a bizarro world version of the Silicon Valley yuppies driving up rent prices. That way she met most of the communists, anarchists, nihilists, squatters, addicts, oogles, and adjuncts in the scene. So it came as a surprise the next morning, at the book fair in Golden Gate Park, when she desired no company but Tif's. Her friend wore different athletic gear than the day before, light blue spandex pants and a neon-yellow tank top. Embraced in those strong, fat arms, Spike felt cared for.

They attended a panel called "Where Does Occupy Go from Here?" Of the four panelists Spike recognized D, a petite black woman with an attractive smile and high, serious forehead. D expressed optimism about the movement, her caveat being that black and brown organizers deserved credit for making the occupation *real*, whatever that meant.

Spike knew D from protests. Always, the woman had a megaphone in hand to shout insurrectionary slogans that kept the march stomping. Typically she wore a Raiders jacket and sweatpants, her hair a hasty ponytail that resembled a radish stem. It came as a surprise when, during the panel, D made an offhand comment about her *twenty-three years on this planet,* meaning she and Spike shared an age. But D was a *woman,* whereas Spike wouldn't have been too upset if she woke up tomorrow to find herself back in seventh grade sleepaway camp.

Throughout the discussion of goals and tactics, Spike and Tif played a comedy duo, rolling their eyes whenever the white dude panelist rambled on. Then the Q&A where Tif would raise her hand with observations for the panel, really aimed at D. Such as, "Um, could you speak more about the people interviewed on TV being middle-class and white?" Or, "We can't let the movement die! Police just evicted the biggest homeless camp in San Jose. I put out the call and nobody came."

D leaned into the microphone. "That's fucked nobody showed up."

"I showed up!" Tif cried, insecure as hell. Embarrassed for her, Spike squeezed her hand, grateful to know such an earnest person, annoyed at herself for that gratitude.

Her whole life people had been drawn in by Spike's long face and large, dark, antipathetic eyes. In her sloped shoulders and wiry arms, her knife-edged hips and nonexistent bosom they saw frailty or danger, depending on their kink. White men told her to smile. Middle-aged barflies rubbed her back as they asked her to move one stool over.

Eventually those strangers found her a condescending killjoy. They found her silence sly and aggressive, her jokes inappropriate, her clothes unflattering and sexless. The subtle cruelty in her features created expectations—like they wanted her for a dominatrix or something—that always left prospective friends disappointed to discover she was just a sneak.

Spike hated to think she liked Tif purely because the woman reciprocated her feelings.

Around noon she helped Tif run the Occupy Bail Fund table. Like a retail manager, Tif insisted on arranging the zines on topics such as prison abolition and Black Power a certain way, and, blowing her puckered lips in frustration, would move them as soon as Spike laid them down. An exhausting, admirable perfectionist. For hours Spike watched her engage disheveled leftists on the need to support jailed comrades. She'd hype the Bail Fund with companionable, cartoonish energy impressive for a middle-aged organizer. In conversation she kept unwavering eye contact and enunciated the last syllable on every sentence. Versed in history, able to switch from anarchists in the Spanish Civil War to Paris '68 without missing a beat, also opinionated, critical of what she called the "self-congratulatory Californy bullshit" of modern protest.

Between bouts of shilling for the cause, Tif waxed nostalgic. "I saw Green Day at Gilman! This was right before the one album came out. The big one. What was that called?"

"*Dookie*," Spike said.

"Yeah! *Dookie*! They played 'Welcome to Paradise.' That song was about my *life*. I moved to the big city and wasn't sure I could make it. But I survived. And I rocked the *fuck* out. My friend circle held it *down* in that mosh pit," she said in a rapid string of words.

"What song spoke to me?" Spike mused. "I guess 'Happy Birthday.' I remember being so impressed that so many people could memorize the same lyrics."

Tif laughed at her dry humor, thank God. Like everything about her, the Green Day story was unapologetically cheesy and fed Spike's nostalgia for days she'd never known; the adventures you found dodging 24th and Mission on your way to warehouse shows in untamed San Francisco, the queer-punk-artist Mecca she'd read of in Michelle Tea novels and old issues of *Ker-bloom!* Tif spoke about her polyamorous foursome in the Sunset in '98. How she paid her way through college selling X at raves. How she saw Nine Inch Nails in somebody's mildewed basement and Nirvana at the Cow Palace and Butthole Surfers at Lollapalooza One. There were many protests and—if she was to be believed—Tif knew every radical in America.

"I was in a reading group with Elaine Brown," she proclaimed. "The Black Panther. I was starstruck! I was such a dork around her!"

"Is it true Elaine Brown was a government agent?" Spike asked.

"Huh? I don't know anything about that." She darted her eyes as if trenchcoated G-men had binoculars on them. Spike felt guilty for bringing it up even as she adored Tif's absurdity. How in that moment the white slash of her lips combined with her eyebrows in a severe expression that made her look ancient. The look of a beleaguered mother, and Spike wouldn't have minded playing her daughter.

At five p.m. they packed up and hauled boxes past baseball diamonds and greenhouses lush with floral imports to their parking spot half a mile away. Wheezing like a pig in a slaughterhouse cage from carrying one box, Spike reminded herself to quit smoking. Tif, damn her, carried two. Spike would look to her belly; however preposterous the thought, she was going to be a mom. Three hearts beat inside her, a marvelous and alien reality.

"I love being pregnant!" Tif said as if she'd read her mind. "All those mommy endorphins! It's like being high all the time!"

"I thought pregnant women glowed," Spike countered. "Like sugary piss."

Fortunately her mockery flew past Tif. "We don't glow! We grunt and puke and fart!"

When they reached the car, Tif dumped the boxes in the trunk, plumped down on the grass, and wept into her palms. "I can't believe he did it!"

Spike's stomach heaved at the tonal shift. "Did what?"

"I can't believe he came inside me," she elaborated in an awe-struck whisper. "He knows I'm fertile. Every time a man's come inside me, I've gotten pregnant. This is my third."

At that moment she *did* look pregnant, at least how Spike viewed the mutation: her skin oily and porous, shoulders hunched beneath the weight of female servitude. Tif blew her nose in a Kleenex and moaned, "Homeless, jobless, and knocked up."

"What happened with your other pregnancies?" Spike was curious.

"I didn't carry."

"You have support," Spike replied desultorily as a jolt rocked her crotch like an erotic sneeze. Two abortions! That meant at least *four* unborn children! This woman was an impossibility; a powerful, feminist, evil abortion machine.

Tif sounded accusatory. "Do I, Spike? *Do I?*"

"You have so many friends in the scene. Right?"

"Who I can depend on?" She exploded with laughter, and when it seemed she might stop she laughed more. "April Fools! Ha ha ha ha!" She resumed her misery. "You're sweet, but I didn't just fall off the turnip truck. Child-rearing is very gendered. The women always end up alone," she sneered.

"I can't stand kids." Nasty, immoral little creatures.

"I expected better of you," Tif snapped. "I *really* expected better. Ooh, you hate children? You're so edgy. Well, I hate black people. Hear how that sounds? You kids think fucking ageism is cool? I shut that shit down immediately. *Sooo* maybe try to have some fucking tact and not say offensive shit," she concluded with a hostile grin.

Spike wanted to punch herself in the face for triggering Tif. In the dispiriting silence, she observed the world beyond their bubble of shame. An older couple, a black woman and white woman, drifted hand-in-hand down the sidewalk. An ice cream vendor bicycled her cart across the intersection and onto the grass. The air smelled of salt and eucalyptus. Finally Spike said, "I once asked my mom why she had me and my brother. Not like I wish I wasn't born. Just: why? And she said, 'I felt like I had all this love to give. And I just wanted to give it to somebody.'"

Tif's grin came so suddenly it could only have followed despair. "That's beautiful." She took on a fierce, maternal gaze. "I'm having my babies. I told Tom: you can be daddy. You can be uncle. Whatever works for you."

It was then Spike knew she'd have another abortion. She had to wonder when she'd turned schmaltzy as she imagined Tif in a thin-walled apartment, a single mother bathing her golden lambs in the kitchen sink. This odious sentimentality externalized in her mind as Tif's kids begging her to save them.

Nobody gets what they want, she informed the doomed twins, who couldn't hear her, meaning, she grimly realized, she was reminding herself.

A month later she escorted Tif to Planned Parenthood for her third abortion. Shielded her from protesters and had the satisfaction of slapping one large-nostriled Republican in the teeth. In the waiting room they chatted about the sexist articles in women's magazines.

Tif fell into a depression after the procedure. They spent a week in an airport hotel courtesy of her father, a physicist she'd never mentioned up to that point. They cuddled together and played board games. That summer of 2012, when Tif was thirty-six and Spike twenty-three, they started a house with three other Occupy comrades. A West Oakland duplex off Market Street, where Spike discovered she loved nothing more than porch-step cigarettes in the twilight.

3

OAKLAND—January 4, 2014—Police have identified a woman found shot to death in a West Oakland street as the mother of a small child.

D—— S——, 25, was unresponsive when police arrived at the intersection of 29th Street and Telegraph at 5:31 a.m. Saturday; a passing motorist had seen her body and called police. She was declared dead at the scene.

S—— was a graduate of Skyline High School in 2006 and had studied at Laney College in Oakland. She was active in the Occupy movement.

A Facebook page set up by friends to commemorate her life shows a photo of her smiling broadly while holding an infant boy.

4

For the remainder of 2012 there were demos every month. Some became riots; others remained tame affairs. A soldier in a movement, Spike looted businesses rather than steal from friends. She smashed yuppie restaurants rather than shoot dope. On protest nights she'd drink a fifth of whiskey, mask up, and hop in her housemate Rachel's car with their squad of Davis oogles turned O-Town hellraisers, the unfutured hordes left for dead by capital, zealous to paint their vengeance in the ash from burnt dumpsters.

Bandana over her mouth. Sirens in her ears. Breath clutched. Downtown Broadway a nightmare of looming skyscrapers and riot pigs goose-stepping a block behind. "Keep it peaceful," the liberals would plead in lukewarm voices. They made her laugh. The revolution would be spontaneous, not choreographed by gatekeepers.

Sometimes Tif tagged along. On the sidelines—claiming that even if she masked up, a single loose hair would identify her—she dubbed herself a *riot cheerleader.* Her plaudits—"You can do it! Fuck the system!"—made Spike grateful for a bandana to hide her mortification.

After one demo Tif said to her, "You're *hard*! You kicked drugs *and* you fuck shit up in the streets. You're a badass bitch."

5

Spike made their house a home by building things, like a bike shelter in the backyard, like the coop for Rachel's chickens. When Tif proposed they build bookshelves for the living room, Spike purchased the lumber that same day. Embracing order and cleanliness, she grew to love the pleasant tingle in her scalp when she stared upon a rack of clean dishes, or a toilet that flushed, or the smell of a bathroom floor freshly Lysoled.

And she had a room! A cozily dingy cube on the ground floor with vine cornice moulding, milk crate bookshelves, and a duct-taped air mattress. Not a busted couch or windowless loft where she'd wake in the afternoon with her spine petrified and her mood bitter like the cold coffee in the French press in a punk kitchen smelling of bread and lethargy. In her room—her room!—she decorated the walls in screen prints of proletarian warriors such as Assata Shakur and Lucy Parsons; Annie Golden, Poly Styrene, and other femme punks; magnificently putrescent genderfuckers like Wayne County and Wendy O. Williams. She'd dance to post-punk with Tif, or alone, her hair dyed black with poodle bangs like Lydia Lunch circa '85.

Rachel, the second-oldest housemate, started coming over to smoke and discuss protests. Rachel was a Latina from Davis with a radio-friendly voice, possessed of a calm maturity Spike appreciated after an infinitude of hot-mess roommates.

During one such marijuana session, a cathartic bitchfest about a local Marxist group, Tif entered uninvited. She had to tell them about this book *The Ethical Slut.*

"It should be required reading for any female-assigned person," she insisted, pacing back and forth. "You have to start fights with your male-assigned partners. If you start a fight and he hits you, you know for sure he's an abuser!"

When Spike glanced at Rachel to see if she, too, found this delightfully kooky, Rachel smiled flaccidly, as if to say, "No judgment! It's just not my thing."

"She's funny," Rachel told her later, chuckling off-beat. "It's just, yeah, she's so funny."

6

Though Spike liked both sexes, she had little luck with either. Moreover, she found penises boring. It seemed every time, without fail, whenever she met a cute boy they would flirt, kiss, and play kinky games until the fun abruptly ended, and everything became about ingurgitating his spindly pink udder, while above her he mooed and slapped at her hair like a giant baby.

Spike was starting to see the appeal in asexuality. She pictured herself a middle-aged, loveless, and perfect creature in a voluminous paisley nightgown, living in an RV.

But she wasn't asexual. When Tif went on errands, leaving Spike in the house alone, she'd pleasure herself to the thought of Tif losing her virginity at thirteen, in the woods with a high school senior she claimed to have loved too deeply. Facedown on her pillow, Spike would picture Tif as Lolita, ripe with sex at an age when Spike herself sought annihilation.

Not once in her life had Tif been unwanted, and, freed from monogamous constraints, she reveled in the *de facto* promiscuity of American leftism. Usually Spike would be smoking on the porch when Tif opened the gate for some blandly handsome college boy who'd limply wave at Spike before Tif hurried him upstairs. Then Spike would run to her room, dive on her mattress, and plunge her hand down her jeans like a moviegoer grabbing popcorn during an action scene. She could hear through the ceiling: "You, you, you! Oh youuuuu!" Always the interchangeable second person. Sex with her sounded gluttonous, stupid, and strenuous, the boys' eagerness colliding with the practicalities of her womanly body. Envisioning Tif insatiable and voluptuous, Spike would come so violently she hated herself, reduced to animal lust by this ridiculous woman.

For a couple of months, Tif dated a socialist boy around Spike's age. Brunette, medium height, one of those O-shaped-earlobe punks hiding his goofy looks under a Stalin beard. He and Tif met in Anti-Capitalist Judo around the time hand-to-hand-combat became the rage among anarchists. Many nights Spike would sit in the stairwell listening to them grunt and grapple behind the bedroom door. It excited and embarrassed her to think Rachel, in the room next to Tif's, content to wear headphones and argue on Twitter as sex noise pounded her wall, might step out for a snack and catch Spike rubbing the denim over her crotch.

One night she listened with similar pleasure to Tif berate him. "If you can't bone me then you need to give me head! I mean, how lame are you?"

The next morning, smoking with her on the porch, Spike asked if she was okay.

"I'm sorry, sweetie! Was I too loud?" Tif said bashfully. "He's just a spoiled little rich boy. And he's totally absorbed some toxic ideas about how male-assigned persons and female-assigned persons should interact. He's cute, though," she added fondly.

The night before, Tif had sounded downright abusive. Spike resisted the urge to sympathize with the boy. Fuck a romantic rival.

7

Tif volunteered at a black radical center on some trashy West Oakland block, a place Spike visited once to install antivirus software on their computer. From the bookstore section of the rambling black-walled warehouse she watched the woman D organize clothing in the free store. She heard Tif read picture books to their brats while the dashiki-wearing male "volunteers" smoked weed outside. When Spike asked them about the Wi-Fi connection, a lanky man with more beard than face informed her she, as a colonizer, had no right to ask black men for anything. Also, he thought she looked like a person who called herself a Jew, meaning she should know Africans were the true Twelve Tribes of Israel, and her people nothing but pretenders.

Spike swallowed her retort. Sometimes, in Oakland, white girls had to take one on the chin. But what shitty misogynists, those men. What irrelevant clowns.

8

Nights grew colder. In Tif's room they'd cuddle under blankets and watch Netflix, slatted blinds closed, the laptop a rectangle of hyperactive light at their feet. Those dreadful boys got nothing so intimate as Tif's head on her chest, eyes closed, her lashes like white fringe hanging from a swaybacked branch.

Never truly relaxed, Spike would anticipate an intimate gesture, or for Tif to reveal a piece of her life. Every revelation created pictures in her mind: eleven-year-old Tif getting hollered at by her mother, a weepy and casually mean fat woman—"You think you're so smart? I'm the mother! I'm the smart one!"; she saw Tif as a Sisters of Mercy–loving goth bored in class after finishing her work early; she saw Tif on a dorm phone, the cord twisted in her fingers as a relative told her the state had custody of her brothers, that Mom was truly gone this time; she saw Tif as a three-hundred-pound blob at a telemarketing job, her desk covered in Pop-Tart crumbs, black gel thick around her narcotized eyes.

Spike admired her resilience and her lack of awareness, how easily she mythologized herself as a hard-luck queen of sorrows. Spike wished she, too, could turn off regret.

One November night, half watching some dull show about cyborgs, Tif told her she used to work three jobs in Davis to support her ex. Spike asked, "How did he abuse you?"

She'd always wondered. In the dark she could see Tif blink rapidly like some secret part of her was trying to escape through her face. Then her expression turned inscrutable. "He would get drunk and depressed and have breakdowns. I would have to give him care. It was hard."

An evasion. Unsurprising, it left Spike disappointed nonetheless. "I can't imagine being with somebody ten years," she mused, neither happy nor sad at the fact.

Tif shifted so the back of her knee rested atop Spike's knee. "Believe me, ten years is a long time to put up with somebody else's shit." She paused. "That's why I have night terrors. That's why I needed this room."

"It still would've been nice if we had a conversation about it," Spike said, chuckling to show no hard feelings. But Tif replied with an irritating, confused look. "Seriously?" snapped Spike.

"When we moved in, we said we'd have a meeting about who got this room. You just put your stuff up here and when I asked you about it you said 'Fuck that' and—"

"I never said that!" Her breathing grew labored. "I need the lights on."

She rolled out of bed and flipped the switch. Brightness stung Spike's eyes. Through the pain, she watched Tif clench the doorknob. Her collarbones stood out, and her nostrils shuddered with panicky breaths—a look of such extravagant terror it was impossible to take her seriously.

Spike fought to keep exasperation from her voice. "That's kinda fucked up you agreed to do something and then—"

"I never said that." Tif was looking at her askance, hoarse like she'd been screaming for hours. "I don't know what game you're trying to play, but I'm not gonna let you."

Spike tried to dial her down. "I'm sorry! I'm not trying to trigger y—"

A laugh, half dolphin squeal, half hyena howl, erupted from Tif with such suddenness Spike cringed an inch under the blanket.

"Are you serious? *This* isn't triggering. I know what it's like to *really* be triggered. Audiovisual hallucinations, sweetie!"

This bug-eyed woman wielded the power of Zeus. She held a lightning bolt of drama in each hand, poised to cast them on Spike, and the girl felt outnumbered by Tif and her paranoia. "You need to leave," Tif said.

"Fine." And gladly.

Tif came to her room an hour later with a sheet of gluten-free cookies as penance.

Spike tried vindictiveness—"That rectangular piece of wood

is there for a reason"—but welcomed Tif, who apologized for her outburst. Then she blurted, "You know what? I'm not sorry!" Paralyzed with fear, Spike listened for an hour to Tif call her a drunk who took advantage of her friendship. Told Spike her constant negativity was bullshit neo-leftist behavior and she, Tif, was a true revolutionary.

9

Tif could be a marvelous friend—driving Spike on errands, listening to her complain about her family, a companion at awkward parties. One night they prowled Half Price Books in their most innocent college girl sweaters, casually, discerningly shoplifting anything that might inspire the black and brown kids at Tif's story times. Unlike the days when Spike would dash-grab through an electronics aisle and out the door with a manager at her heels and dope on the brain. By the time they strolled out the exit, each with two hundred dollars of merchandise in her backpack—for the kids—Spike knew that life felt *better* with Tif around.

So when Tif filled the house with her furniture while everyone else was at work, when she obstructed the dining room with four dozen boxes of books while she and Spike built shelves, when she reneged on those shelves being communal and filled them with her books alone—her selfishness wounded Spike.

Tif, first to the living room for house meetings, greeted stragglers with an aggressive, "Hi, Cupcakes!" She'd accuse their pothead housemate of stealing utensils. She'd accuse the other timid male of not paying rent, even though he did. Quick to point out the sacrifices she made being on the lease, she said Spike "stole" the blanket off the couch one night when she was cold—"You made it stink! Sometimes you smell so bad I have to leave the room!"

Spike excused herself to cry in the backyard. Concerned, Rachel sought her out. They sat at the firepit, where Spike snuggled one of Rachel's Bielefelder hens, for comfort.

"Tif's got trauma," she told the woman. "She hurts others to avoid getting hurt. We shouldn't trigger her."

Their male housemates agreed. Don't trigger Tif. Let it go when she gets in a mood. Sometimes Spike convinced herself the accusations and childish insults were part of a sadomasochist game they'd wordlessly agreed to. Nightly she'd masturbate to her own dread. This didn't feel like desperation, but she knew it was.

From January till August, Spike deferred to Tif. In doing so, she got the friend more often than the monster. That made her happy.

10

OAKLAND—June 11, 2014—A six-time felon has been arrested and charged with murder in the fatal shooting January 4 in West Oakland of a 25-year-old woman he did not know before the confrontation, authorities said Wednesday.

V—— M——, 57, a self-employed electrician from Oakland, is accused of killing D—— S—— about 5:11 a.m. January 4 in the 2900 block of Telegraph Avenue.

Sgt. Robert Rivera said Wednesday that M—— admitted shooting S—— after getting into an argument with her. What the argument was about was unclear and Rivera said there was nothing to indicate the two knew each other before S—— was killed.

11

In autumn 2013, five months before D was found dead from three shots of a .38 special, a suspected drug deal gone wrong, Spike found herself worried about rent. She'd spent the summer doing

Web design for a local DIY porn queen, all on IOUs that were never paid.

"How'd you even take that job without a contract?" Tif said over porch-step cigarettes. Her lips flattened and she gazed across the street, as if willing her brain far away from Spike.

"I guess I'm stupid," Spike said. "Just a fucking idiot."

"Now you're gonna feel sorry for yourself?" Tif blew smoke contemptuously. "I really don't like emo narratives."

"You listen to Nirvana."

A pause. "My interest in Nirvana is primarily nostalgic. Look"—she stamped out her cig in a pewter ashtray that needed cleaning—"why don't you come trim?"

These past five months, her search for library work a dead end, Tif had been trimming weed for a rich kid. Spike reminded her, "Jeff sold crack out the Occupy supply tent."

"That wasn't his finest moment," Tif conceded. "But I think he has a number of good qualities."

"I agree. Zero is a number."

"Sweetie," Tif cooed. "You have a thing about drugs. That makes sense given your past."

Spike absorbed her words with a sense of privilege, appreciating the compassion for her old—yet never truly beaten—addiction. Tif opened her arms and Spike relaxed in her embrace.

"You're adorable," said Tif. "C'mon, it'll be fun! It'll be like *Breaking Bad*!"

"That's about meth," Spike replied with automatic dolorousness. "And isn't there a show about pot dealers?"

In the street, two indigenous children were pushing their sister on a pink bike, a rusty heirloom with a banana seat and tasseled handlebars. Everyone shrieking in Spanish, they launched the girl, who slipped on the pedals a few times before she gained control enough to bike toward Market. Tif shot the children a gaping smile over the iron gate.

"My life isn't fucking *Weeds*!" she said with joyous indignation. "I'm *Breaking Bad*!"

12

That Saturday they drove to the Lower Bottoms. Tif parked behind warehouses in the shadow of twisting highways. Walking three potholed blocks, Spike, arms folded, struggled to look like a streetwise punk and not some frightened hipster. From the outside, Jeff's home looked narrow and prissy, an average Oakland domicile if one discounted the trash bags on the windows. She bit her lip as his tall black lackey patted her down; once inside, her skin crawled from his violating touch.

Jeff occupied a leather sofa in the living room, the coffee table at his knees haphazardly arranged with incense, sage, and glass pipes shaped like mythological beasts. Tense and watchful, Spike shivered to glimpse beside him a haunted-looking teenaged punk girl sucking smoke from a dragon's tail. Jeff was thin, average height, uneven ears, one pointed like an elf, his jaw shaved smooth as a soft-boiled egg, his auburn shitlocks like hairs pulled from a shower drain and Scotch-taped to his scalp. This silver-spoon-sucking desecrator of the Oakland Commune probably thought he came off like a laconic hippie in black Ray-Bans, his dirt-colored corduroy pants slung inches below the hem of a faded Oakland A's shirt. As he rose, the sofa farted. Tif introduced them with a pressurized grin.

"This here's my road-dog Spike!" she said, arm around her shoulder.

"Everybody knows Sketchy Spike." She winced at her

nickname from Davis—*Watch your shit around Sketchy Spike!* Jeff's voice sounded robotic, his words meaningless. "Welcome to the beautiful family, you fucking pirate."

Gazing into the kitchen, her guts twisted at D giving her infant son a sink bath. D wore black sneakers, gray sweatpants, and a gray shirt to her knees. Her being there made sense because everyone needed cash, yet Spike grew nauseated watching Tif embrace her and sing the baby's name like good news: "Omari!" The baby bleated and made scary choking faces.

"Dealing with anybody under eight is like being with somebody who's perpetually stoned," Tif said, yodeling with laughter. "Huh? What's this? What's this?"

Spike watched D's face. Within her smile, condemnation and false gratitude. Any dubious anticipation Spike had of enjoying the drug trade evaporated like moisture off a July sidewalk. In the kitchen she grew dizzy from the flowering buds' earthy odor, a smell she'd never liked, despite the expectation that she, as a Californian, should cream her panties at the mere mention of a drug she considered purely utilitarian. Faking patient beneficence, Jeff sat them at the table with scissors and a pound each of lilac indica that had clearly been planted in cramped confines, requiring Spike to shear through mold to uncover the dollar-bill-green beneath. She recognized the seven punks and hippies at the table from Occupy. How funny—wearing bandanas in the chemical air, they looked ready to smash Starbucks.

Intermittently addicts would stagger through the back door, through the kitchen to the living room, where Jeff handed out cash on a loans-and-credit system. Their slack faces taunted her with the pleasures of one more toke. It was Tif's tactile face and palpable laugh that reminded her she'd seen, accomplished, and fought more than that junkie preserved in regrettable Polaroids and mistrustful glances around Palo Alto. As she loosened up, she noticed D kept to herself, a black bandana over her nose, the baby in her lap screaming unmet needs.

13

In the downstairs bathroom, under headlamps blazing and humming, Jeff grew his own Purple Kush. Stunted buds on the cracked floor tiles, in the tub, the sink, the toilet bowl. Daily he dispensed the wet crop from a trash bag and onto their trays. The job was tiring. Bits of stalk and stem clung to Spike's fingers. The sugary mold smell got in the black sweatpants and long-sleeved shirts she wore to work. Following an eight-hour shift she got cash in hand, plus complimentary scissor hash to light up with Rachel once she came home.

Much as she struggled, Spike liked making $500 a week, sometimes more. Relief at her newfound solvency led to a revived interest in sensual excess. At the Indian buffet, hers and Tif's favorite spot, she'd eat until her stomach ached. She'd guzzle loads of coffee purely for the satisfaction of pissing it out later, then drink herself to sleep with potent whiskeys.

Before every shift, workers would pop the batteries from their phones and drop the devices in a bucket. Barred from the upstairs bathroom, they did their business in the fly-infested rear hall, where, squatting over another bucket, Spike enjoyed the rare solitude. A set of age-blackened net curtains, textured like gouda cheese, turned the window to an oily triangle through which a hint of street could be seen. She'd glimpse Jeff's two thugs on the other side of the fence talking pussy and violence. They looked brutish with long bodies and slouching postures, oversized hands made for breaking, guttural voices for snarling broken English.

One afternoon she was shitting while listening to the thug

with face tats describe an especially savage beating. "Hit that nigga hella hard. Smashed his cheek. I ain't never seen that shit done with a fist, my nigga. I seen it done with a bat, not a fist."

The other shook his head in contempt. "Till them Mexican niggas can do that shit, I don't wanna hear how hard East Oakland niggas is. 'Cause all they can do—"

He stopped when he noticed Spike with her ear to the glass. Her heart pounding, she did up her jeans and rushed to work.

14

Around the table, comrades talked upcoming actions. They talked Marxist theory. Anything to break the leaf-crackle monotony, on the condition it didn't offend the lord in the living room, who smoked away the hours to obscure soul vinyls, his incremental movements causing the sofa to creak like a haunted house. In their sillier moments the table discussed pitching their story to Hollywood—a sitcom about trimmers. Call it *BUDdies*. The potential hijinks of anarchists running a weed business stimulated Spike's creativity. One day she proposed, "What if we do an episode where we challenge a Grass Valley company to a trim-off?" And Tif said, "Then we accidentally set the weed on fire! And the other trimmers fall in a river!" And Spike said, "Then the Park Service thinks it's a wildfire and evacuate the area! And they get mad and I try to smoke them out but it's funny 'cause I'm, like, serious." Naturally she saw herself as the straitlaced Ross of the group. Tif pictured herself the lovable manager, like Steve Carrell on *The Office*.

Secretly, Spike enjoyed D's annoyed expressions during their tomfoolery. The woman held tight to her misery, silent, except when she'd tell certain people to pick up the pace.

Generally, if Tif finished her pound early, she would watch

the baby (a strangely light-skinned baby—Jeff's?) while D went into the living room to grouse at him about ridiculous drama. After one boring demo: "These niggas come from L.A. and do that wack-ass, safe-ass march? That shit was embarrassing. Got me hella fucked up! Is we trying to end black genocide or what? We should make a rule: you wanna march, you ask Oakland's permission."

By *Oakland* she meant herself and the wannabe Huey Newtons in her clique. The rev reduced to bullshit hierarchy. It seemed an extension of that dynamic to watch Tif clutch the baby to her bosom, such a bleeding-heart liberal that Spike imagined her breastfeeding the boy white guilt instead of milk from her melon tits.

Even after D brought a bassinet to keep Omari in the living room, his crying continued. Spike hated having a baby there. Hated D's pissy little mood swings. Hated her I'm-from-Oakland arrogance. Hated her sleepy ponytail. Hated that Jeff let her argue with him over money. Hated that he probably put her at the table in the first place to spy on the other workers.

15

"Do you wanna smoke?"

What Tif meant: *Do you wanna be a body for me to talk at?* Come December, as reward for their diligent work, Jeff let them smoke on the former second-floor patio. All that remained was a periwinkle door overlooking a backyard Jeff's hirelings kept mowed, raked, and decorated in astrological knickknacks, deferential to blight laws, unremarkable. Perched on the ledge, Spike exhaled arsenic paper airplanes into the rain-scented wind. Somewhere a BART train slowed with a noise like whale song.

"Your generation is really impressive in bed," said Tif in an aquamarine hoodie, black tights, and ass-hugging black shorts. She kept her knees together to look adorably plump rather than merely fat. Spike thought she succeeded. "These guys really practice consent. Look!"

She showed her phone. Onscreen was a brown dick.

"Caption says 'Happy Kwanzaa!'" Laughter. "I think dick pics are the new Hallmark cards! It's always some caption like 'Thinking of you!' 'Happy birthday!'"

Spike averted her gaze. "Nobody sends me those," she said gratefully.

Laughter. "It must be something about how I carry myself sexually that makes guys want to do that." Her eyes lingered in satisfaction on the photo. "I don't know what it is with black guys, but for some reason they like sleeping with me."

Five hours of snipping leaves had Spike's brain unqualified to contemplate Oakland black men and their white girl obsession. She said, "Sex with most guys lasts as long as the average punk song. If I have three minutes to spare, I'm listening to Fugazi."

"I never thought I'd be sleeping with so many male-assigned persons," Tif continued as if she hadn't heard. "I was a forty-year-old lesbian. Well, I still am a forty-year-old lesbian. Just with a lot of male-assigned partners. *Young* ones," she mentioned again, then lightened her voice to sound like a naughty preteen. "I'm banging guys I could have read *The Cat in the Hat!*"

Spike chose self-deprecation to deflect her creepy boasting. "I call myself pansexual."

"Heck ya! Fuck sexual binaries!"

"As in my lovers turn out to be like Satan." She wondered why her best witticisms were at her own expense.

"Aww. That's so sad," Tif stated, hugging Spike until her ribs hurt. "I have to remind myself you're a woman and not a puppy. It's the big, sad brown eyes." Laughter.

Spike hated this conversation. The pattern of boorish dialogue followed by passive-aggressive quips felt so husband-wifey to her. So banal.

Before long, the door behind them opened, and D entered the empty room. "Y'all need to finish your break," she demanded, standing there with the dignity of a wet umbrella.

"It's only been," Spike checked her watch, "six minutes," and dismissed her with a wave.

"I know you did not just wave me away." She sounded gravely defiant. "My shift's almost over. I worked ten hours. My baby is hungry." Was this guilt trip necessary? "I need my break. What you gotta say to that?"

"Almost done!" Tif exclaimed, and Spike swallowed her pride once more. No point in arguing with either of them. She waited for D to leave.

"Raging fucking bitch," she growled. "Like it's my fault you ruined your fucking life."

Tif looked shocked.

16

Jeff extended their hours to *beat the holiday rush*, which in his mendacious language meant something had gone tits up and they needed to get these drugs on the street pronto. More than ever, Spike mused, he was a rich boy playing kingpin. One rainy Monday he placed a hand mirror in front of her. She looked down at her face chopped into thirds by two white lines.

"Holiday rush!" he beamed. "Everybody does a hit. You should feel honored you're getting Colombian for free."

When Spike hesitated, he leveled her a cold gaze she shot back at him. For several moments his mouth opened until his jaw gaped like that of a sock puppet, his teeth saffron, possibly a startled expression, hard to tell from his lifeless eyes as he edged closer. Gold necklace dangling above her forehead, he continued to hover, his silence a boot on her throat, and Spike fought her gag reflex, the heavy odor from his scorched breath driven into her tonsils. She wondered what to do. Beg him to care whether she relapsed? Run away? Ashamed to pussy out, especially for a pussy like him, she accepted the rolled hundred from his fisted hand. It had been years since she'd last done blow. The rush hit hard.

"Pass it!" Jeff roared. Eyes screwed shut from the dopamine, she fumbled the mirror to Tif. "This feels like grad school!" she heard Tif chortle, then a snort, then she opened her eyes to the blonde entertaining the table with a cheesy half-grin, powder on her upper lip, palms raised and shrugging like *Whaddaya gunna do?* Then they worked ten hours.

December 16, 2013. Less than a month before police cordoned off the block in West Oakland where D had lain dead for twenty minutes. At first residents assumed the cops shot her and let their rage be known. Told them they would die for this.

Nine hours into a coked-up shift, Tif was regaling the table with tales from the student movement. She was dressed like a winsome grunge kid in jean jacket, gray hoodie, short red cotton skirt, black tights, red wool socks, and half-laced black work boots. "We held it *down* in that lecture hall," she bragged. "And the thing is, the security guard understood what we were doing. He was totally *down*. Working-class solidarity."

Spike struggled to recall Tif having been in the occupation, then she remembered: *riot cheerleader*. D stared up from the pound she'd been erratically scissoring. "What do you know about working-class solidarity?"

Tif looked over her shoulder, then back at D. "Who? Me?"

"Who else would I be talking to?"

"What do you mean?" Her smile trembled like a driftwood log being bent in half before it broke into a frown, her bottom teeth upthrust like splinters. She looked hideous.

"You was saying you let security in the building 'cause he got you. Did *he* ever say that? Did you ask him? That was hella stupid 'cause he was probably snitching to the admin."

Tif protested, "I'm a woman. I understand oppression."

"A middle-class white librarian," D chided her. "What do you know about it?"

Tif laid a conciliatory hand on her wrist, a move Spike queasily recognized. "Oh sweetie, you know I—" Before she could finish, D flung up her arm to break the hold. Tif raised both palms in a sign of grungy denim pacifism. "Why are you being so aggressive?"

As other punks pretended to count leaves on the schwag, Spike grew outraged. All Tif did was lie. Just another stupid lie and what was the point of this?

D spoke like there were multitudes behind Tif. She spoke like a hero. "If you really a ally, the first thing you can do is shut up and listen. Being a black woman is hard. Living in a world where your only expectation is to give white men babies ain't hard."

The thought of Tif giving anyone a baby caused Spike to snigger. D must have taken this for laughter at her expense, because the glare she shot Spike promised she had vitriol in her lungs for both of them. Spike averted her gaze.

"I was homeless," Tif insisted. "I'm there for everybody. I've helped thousands of—"

D cut her off. "What do you have in common with the average never-had-a-job, never-graduated-high-school nigga on the street? You got all the power."

Tif jumped to her feet. "I don't have any power! I don't have any power!"

"What's going on?" Jeff groaned from the other room. Hearing him extricate himself from the sofa, Spike brought her fist down on the pinewood hard enough to make the legs twitch in their moorings. Startled trimmers covered their cannabis like soldiers diving on a live grenade.

"No!" shouted Spike. "We are not doing this anymore!"

"Spike," Tif pleaded, "stop . . ."

D was screaming and crying. "Don't get all up in my face, little girl."

"Can't you see she's upset?" said Spike.

"Of *course* you defend each other!"

"I have to listen to your baby crying all day!" Spike accused, noticing for the first time that Omari had been quiet.

D bristled. "I know you did not just say some shit about my baby—"

"We're fucking drug dealers! Just shut up and trim weed!"

Spike readied for her to attack. If this mentally ill bitch expected to bully the little Jew girl, she would learn her lesson with a capital-A anarchist beatdown. The next moment, Jeff came stumbling in and Tif made her eyes round and terrified, fingers laced over her lap. Jeff's face made Spike want to kill the whole world.

Moaning, D clenched her head in both hands. "Oh my god, I *hate* white people! Why won't you leave me alone?"

Jeff grabbed D by the elbow and, no hesitation, she slapped him across the cheek. Rapt with mingled shock and respect, Spike tensed when Jeff's thugs came in from the yard. One of them made for her. Backed against the table, she pictured his hands around her throat but he froze, then he retreated, almost apologetic in his posture. He and his partner sized up the situation before they lifted D off the floor, one with an arm, another a leg, to haul her outside. Manhandled, D ceased in that moment to be anything resembling a woman as Spike knew it and became a five-foot mass of bulging eyes, unclean teeth, unlaced sneakers, neck veins, braless tits, clutching fingers, threats, and profanity; a person altogether pathetic, unimportant, and victimized to the point Spike grew aroused.

Her pleasure was interrupted when someone grabbed her arm, and she was spun to face the male of the species. Her heart battered her ribs like a crowbar to a windshield when Jeff pinned his dry white tongue between his crooked teeth, ready to spout more noise.

Tif was shaking her. "Stop! You're getting blood on the weed."

Dazed, Spike looked to her right hand, a bloody pair of scissors in her trembling fist, then to the half dozen stab wounds in her left arm. She saw Jeff pale from the sight of his plant drenched in her cells. Tif rushed her to the sink.

17

A scared voice. A declaration of victimhood. After hearing Tif's side of the story, Jeff spoke gently to Spike. "I forgive you about the weed. Tell me the truth: Did D threaten you, too?"

What was she supposed to say with a drug lord demanding answers? That she'd started the commotion that made his weed unsellable? It took all she had, in her semiconscious state, to keep pressure on the bloody towel, barely able to think over Tif brainstorming, out loud, what lie they'd tell the emergency room. Why defend D? Who was that woman to her?

But she didn't do it like Tif. Never like Tif! Spike remained a punk, a hard motherfucker, not some melodramatic Becky who for the rest of the week, at cafés and parties, told every white man in earshot she felt threatened at work. These aging punks would grind their bearded jaws and say, "He fired her, right?" and Tif would say, "I hope so. I don't know her intentions. I don't know if she's going to threaten me, or yell at me, or argue with me. I just feel like I don't have support!" she'd squeal. A tacky, gendered performance.

Spike wanted to yell: "You dumb, horny male! She's just gonna use you!" But that would anger the monster, and in the end Spike didn't love them. She loved herself. Spike. It was empowering to admit she cared nothing for these people.

18

Ten stitches in her arm. At least she left the trimming game with some rad scars.

Tif proposed they open her "magical" walnut jewelry box and celebrate the holidays with a Nicaraguan shroom party, and Spike, terrified what demons might emerge from Tif in an altered state, chose to vacation in Palo Alto.

In a town she once despised, she found herself relaxed biking University, a street with too many Stanford students, but more palm trees than she recalled. She smiled to find, among the corporate chains, resilient mom-and-pops whose hippie owners, longer yet in the teeth, still whiled their hours behind the register. Old haunts like the Fro-Yo shop filled her with such nostalgia, she could ignore the wealth behind the quaint mood, no different from the other villages clustered like polyps along rail lines cast from San Francisco to harvest the milk-and-honey, deer-and-antelope fields, yet the light never left these towns, which, as time rushed toward catastrophe over the terra-cotta roofs, kept right on slumbering.

Her greatest pleasure, however, came in her welcome reception from old friends. It seemed, over the years, enough worse people had passed through the scene that her kleptomania had been forgiven. The mechanic at Peppy's Bike Shop praised her for kicking ass in the streets. On the Southern Pacific track she got blackout drunk on forties with Joe Crust, recovered from his overdose and flummoxed at how good she looked.

"You look healthy," he said with a gap-toothed grin. She! Spike! Healthy!

High on their forgiveness, she danced every night with punks on the beach, any beach, so long as the sand was smooth and clean.

19

She returned home to a grieving activist scene. On January 4, 2014, a passerby discovered D's body in a vacant lot on the corner of Telegraph and 29th. Shot twice under her left breast, once in her throat.

Spike spent hours reading remembrances on social media, a neutral observer, like an alien studying human grief. Fascinating how D chose to spend one of her last days of existence arguing with them about nothing. Why had it been so important to her? Spike regretted her role in the fracas, a minor shame easily strung behind the greater ones she'd learned to live with.

That night she joined Tif on the porch. Streetlights dusted the sky above the duplexes shale gray. Tears streamed Tif's cheeks. She kept her hands clasped to stop their shaking.

"I feel sorry for her son," Spike felt compelled to say.

"Don't," said Tif between sniffs. "Because our friend circle holds it *down* for that kid."

Spike put out her cigarette. This small act caused a throb in her disfigured forearm. Damn lucky she'd missed the artery.

"Omari is taken care of," Tif continued, "by Jeff. He won't become *ward of the state*." She said it like a disease. "She was an amazing organizer, a strong feminist, and a great mommy. I told her, 'I want to be like you when I have kids.'"

Her smug faith in her drug friends came off like cynical theater. To coddle the monster, Spike attempted profundity. "It's disturbing—the sexualization of how she died." She made her finger into a gun. "Shooting. Climax. As a woman . . ." Trying to verbalize it had her stuttering with fear. "I-I th-think we shouldn't mess with these people anymore."

"Who?"

She shrugged. "You know. The Black Power types."

"You mean people like D."

"It's not a racist thing. Just, what do we have in common?" Spike rushed to clarify. "And I'm no angel. I was that fucking junkie stealing from my parents and friends. Palo Alto. Fucking bourgeois paradise. I had friends OD. I had a friend get shot in a drug deal—"

"What is your intention right now?" Tif's composure shattered like D's rib cage into the tiny stakes that pierced her heart. "What you're saying is really disturbing."

"Tif, don't—"

"Are you saying we can only organize with people who share our values? Look, I've been organizing for twenty years. Just because we don't agree on everything doesn't mean we have to throw each other under the bus." She yanked a lock of hair with both hands, staring down Spike with a sickened expression. "That's a cliquey, childish, middle school way of looking at revolution. I mean, what kind of person *are* you?"

20

In January Tif was hired as children's librarian at the Santa Clara Library. She started leaving home before Spike woke and returning around six p.m. She dressed like a wizard in flowing, multipatterned shawls. She talked about cashing in her 401K to start a land project in Oregon. She gushed over her patrons, whom she called *llla-tee-nohs!* and *ob-wo-lee-tahs!*

"Library science is deteriorating," she would say, her hands thrown up like Atlas bearing the globe. "These librarians are a bunch of white college kids who don't understand the populations we work with."

"Yeah," Spike would say, obedient and spiteful.

21

It stood to reason somebody who'd had a public row with a black activist—let alone a murdered one—would tread carefully when it came to brown people. But Tif claimed certain black male comrades made her feel unsafe because they dealt drugs. *You're a good person. You understand,* she told comrades whom Spike would have envied, once, for being treated as confidants. Now she saw cowardice and hypocrisy. —*What she said triggers me.* —*I feel like she's exploiting my emotional labor.* —*I need a break.* Words spoken only when Tif was gone. Women from the Bail Fund complained about her while smoking Kush with Rachel, who suggested they kick her out of the collective before she caused any more chaos.

Spike—so scared of Tif she would never speak against her—felt neglected. All this sanctimony over the ways Tif hurt people, not a word of sympathy for the person most abused.

22

Their male housemates were Davis punks whom Spike had grown to dislike the last two years; one an "Occupy poet" more concerned with broadsides than rioting, and after that time Spike told him "art is dead" he stopped talking to her; the other a redhead who'd grown addicted to opioids. For Spike, forced these last few months to cover his rent, often late, with her own money, the hope was he'd finish repaying her before his inevitable overdose.

But she liked Rachel, and, more than that, respected her. Sometime in early March, Spike arrived home from her anarchist reading group, rain-soaked and craving a blanket, when she was confronted in the dining room by Rachel in jeans and a plaid shirt. "I know she's your friend," Rachel prefaced, "and I've tried—"

"She's not my friend," Spike said. "I hate her."

This seemed to take the pressure off Rachel somewhat. She got to the point. "I heard she's the one who had Jeff fire D. I heard she was saying she was scared of D. Is that true?"

Breathing came hard. Though Spike wished to lie, she cowered before Rachel's seriousness. Told her about the people to whom Tif named D a menace.

"People?" Rachel said disgustedly. "You mean white men." She proceeded to speak of lynchings. She spoke of black women as targets. "I'm not saying you specifically, but to a lot of you it's just a game. You come to the hood and want to be bad. But when shit hits the fan, it's black and brown people who suffer."

"It's about race?" Spike snapped. "Not the bookshelves? Or that time Tif came out of the bathroom naked and your boyfriend 'accidentally' saw her?"

That gave Rachel pause. She sat at the glass-topped table to collect her thoughts before she spoke again.

"If she had a black woman fired and that woman ended up dead for whatever reason, I can't live with her. I tried talking with her about the other stuff and . . ." She made a hand motion at the futility. "I can't do it. I'd rather just close up this house and move than put up with her lying anymore. I've spent years watching everybody just try not to deal with her. It hasn't helped us and it hasn't helped her, that's for sure. All this tiptoeing around is not radical. It's not feminist. It's just really fucking tiring."

Spike sank into a recliner and wept. How many times had she fantasized the downfall of capitalism? She couldn't even stand up to one woman. "Tif . . ." She choked on the name. "D . . . I . . . We were on coke . . . Tif started it! Oh god! What if they think it's my fault?"

"I know none of this is your fault," Rachel assured her.

"What if *they* think I had something to do with it? I could get jumped or—"

"Nothing's going to happen to you," said Rachel, deadpan.

Why did everyone think being white made you immune to violence? "I'm sorry I brought her here. I can't do it anymore. I'm such a coward."

"You are so brave, Spike. You are handy and tough and smart. Let's call a house meeting," Rachel proposed, embracing her around the shoulders. "Only if you're comfortable with it. We should *all* talk to her."

23

"Why should there be a house meeting?" Tif asked archly. They were in her room. Changed from her work poncho to a jogging outfit, Tif still had on her story time hat, shaped like a bunch of grapes. Deliberately calm, Spike explained Rachel's concerns. Tif began to pace.

"She's saying I got D fired? Oh my god. I feel vertiginous. I need air." She struggled to open the window, mouth agape as if in feverish orgasm. "The worst thing anybody can do is gaslight me. I knew she wasn't a safe person."

"She never said you did that. She's just wondering."

"So we need to have a house meeting just for her? 'Cause apparently we have nothing better to do, O Rachel, O center of the universe! I'm a target person. Maybe it's because I'm a woman. Maybe it's because I give so much of myself"—her ranting became white noise until Spike heard her shout through tears—"*you* want to have a house meeting where I get accused like some witch trial?"

"No!" Spike capitulated. "It wasn't my idea."

"And why are you her messenger? Are you leeching off her like you leech off me?" Laughter. "A dope fiend who became a drunk. The only direction you know is sideways."

Her mockery hit Spike in the gut like shrapnel. Doubled over at the waist, she groaned, "I tried to tell her to stop! But the race thing bothers her."

"Are you saying I'm a racist?"

"Of course not!"

"I loved D. *Loved* her." Tif reached out to cuff both her wrists. "Thank you," she rasped with intense gaze. "Thank you for telling me what she's trying to do. This is truly horrifying. I could get kicked out of spaces! I could get beat up!"

24

Spike, anticipating Rachel would issue an ultimatum, dreaded a housemate war. It kept her up at night imagining the horrors to arise if the monster felt cornered.

A week after Spike passed along Rachel's concerns, Tif sent the housemates a mass email saying she'd move out by the end of March. To live closer to work. Rachel ran into Spike's room, seized her by her ams, and bounced around. Spike fought to keep composure. A plan came to mind that would need Rachel's cooperation.

"She still thinks I'm her friend," Spike told her. "I'll be nice to her so she leaves quicker."

Rachel looked concerned. "You mean hang out with her? Just don't do anything that hurts you. Okay?"

"This is how we get rid of her. I got this."

Dance parties. Wine parties. Bonfires. Bike rides down MacArthur. For once, Spike considered herself admirable—a sneaking, lying, flattering fraud.

At home Tif would close her door and crank up industrial rock "to avoid Rachel's aggression," she would say. Spike would venture upstairs through misanthropic classics like "Irresponsible Hate Anthem" to sit at the foot of her bed, an emotional sponge.

"I think her behavior is typical of a certain type of woman," Tif yelled over the music one time. "Tom always told me his ex-wife was like that. Tom. My baby daddy."

Because of course she still mourned the life she'd missed out on, a dream collapsed when it became clear she could have the babies, not the man and his six-figure house in Detroit. Spike, picturing Tif's four skull-faced bastards, almost admired her for a nihilist hero sparing so many the horror of existence.

Color bled from the world. Food tasted like ash. Spike missed deadlines and lost coding gigs. She accompanied Rachel to protests that, no longer empowering, felt like aimless walking. She'd cry herself to sleep after drinking all day to quiet the monster's insults, now one with her internal voice. Her face in the bathroom mirror looked pale and swollen. Her alcoholic belly bulged like a tumor under whatever foul-smelling band shirt she'd thrown on. She'd grin at her reflection and say, "I hate you, coward. You suck."

25

"I'm sorry," Tif told her one night, like every night the culmination of hours spent mistreating her companion. Aside from the torture, ennui made Spike curl up in bed, like a piece of tissue paper in mud, heavy, yet at the same time prisoner to the breeze, unclear what day it was let alone which specific insult had prefaced Tif's fraudulent remorse. The beast said, "I didn't mean to say those things. I'm just stressed. Remember those French hipsters we met at the party? They came over to plan a camping trip! Come join us. If you like," she offered sweetly.

To stay in bed would make the beast feel unloved. Summoning her willpower, Spike pushed herself up on her hands, then her elbows, to rise and follow.

Entering her room, Spike smiled to see the floor mostly empty, everything in boxes except for her desk and damnable bed. Next moment she noticed three French boys in tight band shirts and skinny jeans, one wearing a laughably choppy mullet. She didn't recognize them. A boy put techno on a Bluetooth speaker, and Spike, her back to the wall, observed the four others dance as if each had on headphones and was listening to a different song from the rest. Someone passed her a joint. She hit it, then, arms around her nervous stomach, watched Tif stomp through the room in tank top and jean shorts, throwing herself from boy to boy. "Vous avez l'air mignon se soir," said Tif. "Avez-vous des bonbons, bébé?"

The blonde smoked deep from their joint before busting out her glowstick moves. Spike wondered: What did her mother do to her that caused this madness?

Time slowed. Dancing bodies left rainbow trails. In a panic, Spike tried to move off the wall but found herself rooted there by literal roots. Tif undressed and the boys followed suit. Paralyzed, Spike watched one of them wrap a hand around Tif's back, hold her other hand like a waltz, and lower her to the hardwood. Then they rutted. The other Frenchmen, seemingly less interested in Tif than in watching their friend, beat their dicks to his ass puckering in and out. Poorly assembled mannequins, long limbs attached to boxy torsos stickered in pointless tattoos bold as bruises against their impractically pale flesh, they said, "Slut. Petite pute." Two more pumps and, with a growl-sigh, the one fucking her flopped to the floor, leaving a cum trail from her labia to the smooth ass-fat protruding from between her legs.

"Hey!" Spike fumbled to unlatch the pepper spray from her carbuncle and destroy all three rapists; her dousing had no effect because the can didn't exist. She locked eyes with Tif across the puddle of hungry flesh that was her. Lightning-shaped blood crept toward the gas flames of her irises, and Spike, filled with sewage to witness her pleasure, wanted to squat over her fake dyke face and shit down her shameless throat, even as she masturbated, hemorrhaging love. Tif rolled bonelessly in a circle until she came to face Spike with her breasts smashed flat, her pelvis raised for the next boy.

"Are you just gonna fucking stand there?" Her moan sounded all the more chilling for its lacking urgency. "It's now or never."

Once disrobed, Spike felt ashamed of her hardened brown nipples, hairy arms, fat gut, and wet little vagina. When a boy grabbed the back of her neck and forced her to her knees, she thought, *Can't leave her alone*. Anything could happen to Tif without a friend there. Dreamy acquiescence fell over her until he thrust inside. She screamed.

26

"They raped us," Spike told her the next day.

"I wouldn't go that far," Tif scoffed. There followed a pause as she stared into space, seeming to deliberate the pros and cons of comforting Spike. Whimsically, she said, "It was always my fantasy to try a group scenario. Thank you for sharing that moment with me."

27

Less than two weeks to Emancipation Day, Spike house-sat in Palo Alto over a rainy weekend she spent inside, mostly. Since writing her mom a Happy Hanukkah email in December, they'd been messaging and, periodically, speaking on the phone, their reconciliation unceremonious, like Spike had hoped. In a role reversal, it had been her mom, Ava, who kept canceling coffee plans, focused, so she said, on training for her hypnotherapy certificate. Spike was thinking she might have to crash Passover at Uncle Avi's to see this flaky woman, when she was asked to watch the two-story Mediterranean while Ava studied *goddess energy* in Mexico.

"For my practice. Not a vacation. I'll ask Ixchel to bless you," she told Spike in a brief, upbeat message.

Spike availed herself of the wine closet, Trader Joe's, Netflix, a cuddly white tabby named Bryce, the bathtubs their housekeeper sparklingly maintained. A pleasant home, no longer burdened by a father hidden away in his deadlines, his PC games, his chatrooms, a man unseen yet present everywhere, like a fog made from despondency.

Over three nights, sauvignon and crap TV rendered her near unconscious by the time she hit the Anasazi comforter on the guest bed, her old room having been renovated into a home hypnosis studio. Around midnight the evil idiot faces that orbited her waking consciousness grew hands to tear her open again. Alone in a house large enough that four people could hide for years from one another, she could scream her throat to shreds and never have to explain herself.

Before picking up Ava she slathered her face in makeup, confident she looked less deathlike. A hoodie hid her fucked-up arm. Later, idling in the family Prius, she made out her mom through the rain, the most attractive woman at the terminal. Short and wide-hipped, elevated in heeled sandals, she wore a jean jacket over her azure knee-length sundress. Silver curls framed her tanned chubby cheeks, simian upper lip, buckteeth, and dimples. Noticeably vigorous, Ava sauntered to the car while a Mexican handled her luggage.

Hellos. Kisses. A girlish tee-hee-hee ferried Spike to childhood and the stuffed animal plays Ava would perform for her. Such a charming laugh, which had felt inappropriate for her high-strung parent, sounded just right coming from Melanie Elephant. Presently Spike watched in quiet appreciation Ava remove a bag of grass from the glove box, sniff the leaves, stick her tongue out, then roll a fat joint, anyway.

"Hope they don't drug test hypnotherapists," said Spike, headed for the highway.

"I hope they do." Otherwise occupied, she patted Spike's knee. "I love testing drugs."

"You're cute." She'd been staring at her mom's calves long enough to wonder if she had the hots for her. She told Ava, "You lost weight."

"What do you call this, then?" Ava gave the roll around her waist a good-natured squeeze. "What's this? Enchiladas. That's what this is."

"I mean you lost two hundred pounds of deadweight."

"Zoe, stop talking like a Woody Allen movie." She'd no desire to discuss Spike's father. Nevertheless, equal parts ironic and enlightened, she said, "Not being bitter has done wonders for my skin."

That was her mom, post-divorce: pragmatic and dispassionate. On 101 they shared a joint for the first time. Spike remembered picking flowers for Ava, who, compared to most adults in her childhood, was the kindest person she knew. In high school she'd wanted to murder her for being a self-deluded Palo Alto capitalist. Interesting, to think of love and hate as artificialities, born from environment and emotional clutter.

Over the ensuing minutes she got a sense of their rapport; she'd meet Ava's wan comments about the world with sardonic reply, less witty repartee than a verbal badminton game that felt comfortably weightless, like neither were truly there. She had to laugh at the assumption their neighbors, possessed with a distinctly Aryan undercurrent to their snobbery, would have ever accepted their family, as strongly as Ava once desired this. Time and struggle had unmasked the droll yentas they always were. They cruised University past Pizza My Heart, Cheesecake Factory, L'Amour Frozen Yogurt, Il Fornaio, and Joya to Starbucks.

Over lattes Ava asked: "Whatever happened to your friend you told me about? The one who was being dramatic in the meetings?"

Are you some kind of leech? Burying her scream under an arch expression, Spike rubbed the smooth denim over her inner thighs. "It's the Bay. Everybody's dramatic."

"Your housemate," Ava elaborated. "The shiksa who took out her issues on everyone."

"We kicked her out months ago. I haven't spoke to her. I think she went—"

"Wherever losers go. Didn't you say she was almost forty?" Ava guzzled her drink. "Oy vey! She sounded like a nightmare."

28

Three days later Spike missed her period. She called her dad for the first time in years for abortion money. He agreed without hesitation. Finding him generous, she asked for a thousand bucks to buy a 1990 Chevy RV and he gave that, too. She planned to take a long vacation before deciding her next move.

Emancipation Day arrived. It was nearly four p.m. when the monster returned late from a dentist appointment. Loading the remaining boxes took another hour, time enough for Tif to ramble about John Waters movies, standup comedy, the impending destruction of California via earthquake, '80s music videos, and the Yip Yip Martians from *Sesame Street*. Nothing to see here, neighbors. Only gentrifiers screaming White People Shit into the evening.

Finally finished stacking boxes in the RV, Spike got in the driver seat and slammed the door shut. She took 880 South through parched yellow countryside to Santa Clara. Any asshole drivers, she slammed on her horn and cursed at them.

"I can't believe Rachel said I'm a racist," Tif said from nowhere. "She's afraid of intimacy. It's sad." She looked like a farm girl in a well-used plaid shirt, jean shorts, and boots, her hair a tightly woven braid. Laughter. "Did I tell you she told me I reminded her of her mom?"

Spike remembered damp between her legs. Bruises. Fingerprints like acid on her taint. A damning prayer unuttered.

Late afternoon they arrived at a stucco apartment complex where Mexican families gathered in open garages, their lives on display. Tif greeted her neighbors by first name. Dodging children underfoot, Spike carried boxes up the steps to her second-floor apartment and deposited them in a spacious living room. They set up furniture and soon the place looked homey, modern accoutrements mixed with heirlooms—somewhere a woman could settle.

Tif poured two glasses of lemonade. On the fleece carpet, doused in twilight through the blinds, under swirling dust motes, Tif said she planned to spend a year in Santa Clara before joining "the flow of nature" in Oregon. Increasingly Spike felt like she had food poisoning.

"You're wonderful," Spike told the inhuman cunt. "You spread your love like lice." A line so corny Tif could have thought it up herself.

"Aww, sweetie," she replied through a pungent grin. "You say so many cute and sweet things. I don't know how to respond. Hmm . . . Thank you!" To Spike, her voice sounded like a hemorrhoidal dog barking out of its ass. "And thank you for warning me Rachel's been trying to manipulate and get me kicked out of spaces."

Spike suppressed a shiver. "I never said she was doing that. I just said—"

"Sweetie, you're the eighth person to warn me about her." Laughter. "Telling everybody I'm a racist. She only pretends to be Guatemalan. She's really a rich white lady!"

An exuberantly nonsensical lie. "You shouldn't take that," Spike managed to say.

"I'm not. I texted her. I'm gonna confront her."

"What did you say?"

"That we need to meet up. I'm gonna tell her to back the fuck off."

Spike saw her reflection in the monster's eyes and thought, *A librarian.* Twenty years of working with black and brown children. A career spent pursuing the vulnerable. Feeling trapped in a great violence, Spike said, "I have to go."

Tif looked taken aback. "So soon? That's weird. Are you sure you're okay?"

Spike hugged her goodbye. "I'm okay. I love you. Be in touch. I love you."

When she tried to break the hug, Tif held on. She leaned away to regard Spike with deep, purposeful breaths, the hysteria gone from her demeanor.

"What's going on here?" she said in a low voice.

Spike slipped from her grasp and made it to the door. "I have to go."

She'd been driving for five minutes at ten over the speed limit when Tif called. Against her better judgment, she answered. "Hey, sweetie," came the cautious voice on the other end. "I'm not comfortable with how abruptly you left and I'm crying now. If something's going on—"

"Leave me the fuck alone! Everybody hates you. Do you understand? You crazy, toxic bitch. You fat, old bitch. You're the most terrible person I've ever known. You . . ." Words strangled her. "You got me raped." Weeping, she pulled onto the shoulder. She turned off the ignition and screwed her eyes shut as the quiet pulsed. She sobbed, "Don't bother me, you fucking vampire. Don't bother my friends. Go suck somebody else dry."

Tif called back immediately after she hung up. Spike hurled the vibrating phone under the seat before expurgating herself from the RV and onto the shoulder along a barbed-wire fence. In the distance grazing cattle looked like burnt marshmallows against hills like burial mounds. Here the earth smelled of mud, mulch, and the death of things. From her subconscious emerged a vision of D rotting in the sun. In a strange way, the woman had helped her by dying.

"Thank you!" Hands cupped over her mouth, she called to D in the racing clouds. "Thank you! Thank you!" Memory of heaving chests, pot, and sex brought her knees to the gravel. She fought with deep breaths to keep her coffee-and-pancake breakfast from ascending her gullet. At last she gasped, "I'm okay. Thank you, D. I can breathe."

THINGS I NEVER LEARNED IN CAITLIN CLARKE'S INTRO TO ACTING CLASS

Today I wear eyeliner, cheetah-print pajama pants, hype sneakers, and a pink crop hoodie under which my long, narrow torso greets the world. I look fabulous.

Come to Bloomfield, where bags of uncollected garbage sun-ripen and rupture in alleys and where weeds break the cobblestones like zombie fingers. On my way to the Hollow, where I intend to smoke indica on one of the secret stairs built into the hillside, a place to think, I detour through the back door into Crazy Mocha. Longer than it is wide, the café has a video rental section in the back, inscrutable sketches from some local artist on the walls, a creepy old man in a long dung-colored T-shirt who sits by the supply closet all day with a managerial glower yet works neither there nor anywhere, and, at the front of the store, a crescent-shaped counter bulwarked in tall bottles of artificial sweetener.

Like a basic bitch, I order a latte. Through the three-paneled window I notice three old men in red chairs around their little table, sipping cappuccino, and recognition brings animosity. These wannabe Sopranos think themselves hard holding down the Little Italy franchise of a corporate coffee chain with a dozen identical stores around the city. Once, in college, they called me a moolie—one of two obvious insults they could have thrown my way, so maybe they opted for the more traditional one—so I returned with a group of queers to let them know, in no uncertain terms, they could become better acquainted with that sidewalk they liked to occupy if they kept fucking with us. And because they're softer than the ice cream that spirals out the spigot at Old Country Buffet, they shut up and took it.

Part of me wants to read them for old time's sake, but, annoyingly, age has made me cautious about scaring white people. So I take my latte to the wall, and a table and chair that are Spirit Airlines levels of uncomfortable. From my red Gucci purse I fish a sketchbook, then, on the first available page, write RACIST in blue gel pen with an arrow pointing down, about to ask the barista for tape when I lock eyes with a man across the aisle.

He hesitates before standing. His reluctance confuses me because we're both clearly gay, myself particularly. Only thing straight about me are my edges. I invite him with a rueful smile.

Chubby, dark, and genially handsome with a clean-shaven face, he approaches, remains standing at a respectful distance. His eyes are charcoal gray. He says he performed with Sonia Sanchez at the Kelly Strayhorn Theater, and after a moment I realize he is referencing the book sticking out of my purse, *Autumn Blues*. Named Leroy, he pronounces it "Le Roy," like a French word. How pretentious, I think. How delightful! I ask him to sit. I wonder what detergent keeps his brown pleated sweater so fluffy.

After he sits, we pass some minutes in desultory conversation. We discover we graduated the same class at Pitt. Sophomore year, we both took Intro to Acting. My professor was Doug Pona, a character actor/Al Sharpton lookalike who maintained a lighthearted class. Lots of improv exercises. Lots of talk about Cuervo and weed.

"Pona's a sweetheart," Leroy says, starry-eyed. "I did Shakespeare in the Park with him two years ago." I notice his hands are soft. His striated nails shine like piano lids. "I had Caitlin Clarke for Intro. She was a pretty big name."

"What was she in?"

"You remember that show *Moonlighting*?" asks Leroy.

"With Bruce Willis! You have to call it *Moonlighting with Bruce Willis* like that's the whole title."

"I like to think of it as *Moonlighting with Cybill Shepherd*."

This is going great.

"She did Broadway," he continues. "She was in a movie called *Dragonslayer*, I think."

Saying the name, he smirks, because what a cheesy title, right? I slam both palms on the waxed tabletop, startling him against the back of his seat. I demand to know, "Did she play Valerian or Princess Elspeth?"

He sounds warily intrigued. "The princess, I believe."

"My nigga, you don't even know! That was my shit when I was little."

My pulse clangs like an alarm because, somehow, I know she portrayed Valerian. Leaning close to Leroy, I declare *Dragonslayer* classic '80s fantasy. The premise: killing a dragon is very, very hard. Charged with this task is the wizard's apprentice, Galen, played by Peter MacNicol. No feather-haired beauty like Mark Hamill in *Star Wars* but an average, insecure, slightly effeminate kid whose safety I, a child in front of my wood-sided Panasonic babysitter, would fret for during commercial breaks. Watching plots and counterplots unfold as peasants, warriors, and royalty each pursued their solution to mankind's secondary status on the food chain, the moral ambiguity on display stretched my black-and-white mind to gray putty.

"The dragon's name was Vermithrax Pejorative," I tell Leroy. "How cool is that?"

"What a name!" he exclaims. All through my monologue he's had the knuckles of two fingers on his throat. At first I assume my attentions have him checking his pulse, and these narcissistic thoughts embarrass me. Then I realize that's exactly what he's doing.

I tell him about Galen's friend Valerian, a husky-voiced boy with cautious eyes. In a shining example of '80s PG rating, a skinny-dipping trip with Valerian leads Galen to discover his friend's buoyant breasts. Her whole life she dressed as a boy to avoid the lottery through which, on the king's orders, virgin daughters were sacrificed.

"I thought it was so cool the love interest was androgynous," I say. "As a femme, I know it was formative. And Galen *loves* his girl. He chooses her over the princess. It's kind of dorky, but I'd write fanfic about them going on adventures." It's the first time I've told that to anyone, other than my mom.

"That is *chaaaar*-ming," Leroy compliments. "Speaking of femme, you must tell me what nail polish you use."

"Maybelline." I present my cherry nails for his inspection. "Boy, this shade be giving me life. It looks so much more expensive than it really is."

Unexpectedly, Leroy replies with a grunt that shivers me in its carnality.

"You know she was from Pittsburgh?" he says.

"Who?" I ask from the depths of distraction, the whorls in my brain a violet cloud.

"Professor Clarke."

"That don't surprise me," I reply. "She didn't have the *awk scent.*"

In Medieval Fantasyland, actors in Ren Faire costumes employed a variety of awful British accents that ranged from laughable-but-noble attempts at posh (Chris Sarandon in *The Princess Bride*) to none at all (Tom Cruise in *Legend*) to Matthew Broderick in *Ladyhawke* playing a Frenchman with a Cockney accent while sounding like a kid from the Valley, to Christopher Lambert playing a Scotsman with a French accent in *Highlander*. Caitlin Clarke made up for her awkward inflection with her earnest recital of lines like *You're going to die, you know.* Or *I can see why you love the princess. She's very beautiful.*

She performed the character as someone grown angry and fragile from a life of hiding. I doubt any role she played, before or after, equaled that of a dragonslaying Yinzer trans man.

"Sorry for rambling," I rush to say. "I wish I took her class."

He frowns with his whole face. "She would have loved to hear that. Rest in peace."

My heart contracts. "How'd she die?"

"Ovarian cancer."

"Shit."

"I know, right? She died in oh-four." The year I took Intro to Acting. He continues in a choked voice. "She really helped cement my love of acting. I was just reading lines for an audition. Always on that grind," he adds, his amusement forced.

Lately I've been fashioning my life into a rebellion against America's obsession with hustling, grinding, whatever they call it these days. When people ask what I do, I refer to myself as a bum who smokes too many cigarettes and recreationally reads essays on Ralph Ellison at the CMU Library before finding a restroom in which to recreationally masturbate.

At twenty-six, I am young enough to fall in love from a

gesture, and the dewy sadness in his eye does it. Rimmed in long lashes, his irises, of which the right contains more bronze than the left, halo my smitten visage. I reach over the table for his shea-soft hand . . .

. . . and I'm struck by a force that numbs my jaw and vibrates down through my chest. I am flicked like a pesky mosquito out of my skin.

I fall through blackness until I come to a stop that jars the soles of my feet and rattles my teeth. Leroy has vanished. In his place, a dozen young adults sit in a circle of folding chairs, in a basement with windows set high in white, featureless walls. At one end of the room stands a black Steinway surrounded by music stands like a cluster of skinny groupies; the other end has three-tiered wooden seating, decorated with tasseled pillows.

My hands are now four shades darker. Longer, fingers thicker, the nails manicured.

At the head of the circle sits a slender woman in a black turtleneck, dark blue jeans, and leather boots. Curly black hair rests across the broad plane of her shoulders; her nose is long and bold; her cheekbones like slashes pulse artificially with blush; her rouged lips resemble twin mountains on the shore of a bay. Large and tired, her eyes shimmer darkly, deceptively blue.

A cry for help crackles down my brain stem to disintegrate on the back of my studious tongue. Realizing where and who I am, my spine jolts. *His* spine. I scream without sound. Even panic has been robbed from me—the heart in his chest beats calmly, like the dumb organ it is.

"Two pieces of advice," says Caitlin Clarke in a low, hoarse voice. "One: no matter how small the role, that part helps create the fabric of the story. In the movies—of course I'm first and foremost a stage actress—in the movies I was always the girlfriend, the prostitute, the girl who gets killed. But those roles were just as important as a lead role. Two: look for yourself in your characters. In *Dragonslayer* I played a girl pretending to be a boy—"

"Was that hard?" As both thought and words, his voice blasts between my ears. I grit my nonexistent teeth, thinking, Idiot! *That's* your *Dragonslayer* question?

The professor purses her lips at our interruption. Before she can speak, she bends at the waist and coughs into her fist. I shudder. His salivary buildup starts to choke me, and, when he swallows, it makes the sound of snow falling off the roof, a catastrophe in miniature.

"Well, I've never been a boy," she rasps after drinking from a thermos. "But I wasn't a girl at the time, either. I was close to thirty when I made that film. We all hide things. And that's how I found the character. Now, think about the character you're portraying for your monologue. What would they wear? What is their background? In a conflict, how would they react?"

His hand moves a stubby library pencil across the notepad balanced on his corduroyed knee. I watch his fingers write TROY—FENCES at the top of the page, then proceed with lines of tight cursive. Trapped, I surrender to terror, screaming like an animal . . .

I come to as if pulled from the water where I drown. Gravity tackles me facedown on the pinewood floor, taking a table and two scoop-backed chairs with me.

On his feet, Leroy throws his hands over his mouth. "Oh my god! Are you okay?"

"How the fuck did you do that?" I scream.

"Do what?"

"I was . . ." People are staring at me like I'm crazy. *Am* I crazy? Breathing, trying to recenter, I snatch my wrist back from the stranger taking my pulse. Bitch, you don't know me. For a time

I expectorate the taste of dish soap from my mouth. I tell Leroy, "It's the heat."

He collects his satchel. "It looks like you had a stroke. I'll take you to West Penn."

"I'm fine, sweetie." I reach to touch his cheek but catch myself. After a torturous pause, he searches his satchel for a ballpoint pen and writes his number on the back of a receipt. He tries to appear calm, but the upper right corner of his lip quivers.

"I'm going to go," he announces, holding my gaze until the blood fizzes in my ears. "But call me and let me know you're okay."

Watching him leave, my mind's eye follows him to the sidewalk, where he berates himself, though he did nothing wrong. I sit back down. The barista asks how I'm doing. I lie and say I'm fine, and she commences mopping tea and spit from the floor.

Over three years at Pitt, I probably crossed Caitlin Clarke's path unknowingly. What was her class like? Would I have annoyed her with questions about some movie from her Betamax years? Would I have been wowed by her stage actor's acumen? Or would I have been petulant watching her phone it in, unaware the woman before me was her own ghost?

I snatch up my purse and run after Leroy.

He lives a short walk from the café, on Penn Avenue in an apartment over a hardware store. On his walls hang framed playbills. A hundred halide eyes belonging to aunties and uncles smile from photos of picnics and church functions.

While he boils water for tea, I wander between living room, kitchen, and bedroom to discover he likes nice things. Big-screen TV, sound system, cooking doodads. It pleases me to find black authors populate his bookshelf, a literary barbecue. Multicolored linens neatly decorate a queen-size bed that brings to mind a slice of king cake. Condoms in the fishbowl, ha.

On the leather couch, an oaken table shaped like a chestnut at our knees, I twist my body to give him the strongest possible signals. He seems unaware his shirt has ridden up to expose the bottom of his chocolate gut. Lust inches in, a desire to lift that shirt the rest of the way and play with his fat. While I fantasize, he grinds weed noisily. He rambles about indie movies.

"Never seen it," I respond, again and again, suspicious of his stalling.

This might be new to him, I think. Wouldn't be the first time a closet fag roped me into his shame parade. A depressing thought.

Rather than get strung along, I rise onto the toes of my left foot, twirl, and death drop to the carpet. Starfished on my back, I shoot him a deadpan look.

"So," I say, "are we gonna fuck or what?"

Leroy glances away with a Mona Lisa smile. "Isn't it a little soon?"

"I'm easy." I shrug.

Nearly a minute passes as he slips to the floor in an irritating show of reluctance. Like any black boy, his body is a city where angels dwell with warriors, his gestures an equation he yearns for me to solve, even if I must cheat. I tell myself I am ready, could never not be ready, but when he moves in, the distance between his mouth and mine the wingspan of a ladybug, I recoil. His face crags, and I hate myself for instigating such a disfigurement. "I'm confused," he says after a sigh.

I choose truth. "I'm afraid to touch you 'cause I got trapped in your memories last time."

After giving him a just-the-facts report on my experience in the café, I wait for him to break his stunned silence. At last he cries, "That's amazing! I just knew we were meant to meet each other. You know," he adds, "my horoscope told me something like this would happen this week. Are you Virgo? It said a Virgo would be involved."

I am, but that is beside the point. Gratitude and contempt well up inside me. He should call bullshit on my story, even if it happened. Gullible niggas get hurt.

"You have no reason to lie," he says. "You just described a class she taught in detail. I believe in spirits. It feels like she's an ancestor reaching out to us."

"But she's not our ancestor," I retort.

"Biologically, she isn't. I meant spiritually."

"I've been trying hard to de-mayo my life," I inform my potential hookup, letting bitterness show. "White people are the worst. And not just 'cause they racist, 'cause everybody racist. Mexicans gon' be racist. Arabs gon' be racist. Chinese gon' be racist. Whoever's convenience store you walk in, you'll get shit for being a nigga. White people are just pussies," I opine. "Never had to struggle. Never had to fight for they lives. White man gets challenged, he throws a tantrum and shoots up the place. White woman gets challenged, she cries. These people are babies. I'm a grown-ass man and I ain't wanna deal with them any more than I have to."

"It's not like I can argue with that," he replies.

"Damn right, you can't. So no," I conclude, "I'm not enthusiastic about having a white woman show up when we touch."

He waits a beat to make sure I'm finished before saying, "I don't want you to be scared to touch me. Professor Clarke wasn't like a *white* white woman," he asserts, publicist for the dead. "She was blue-collar Pittsburgh. I think it's dope this happened." His dreamy smile makes me desperate to kiss him. "It's like diva worship. Do you know that theory? Because gay men can't have kids, we make ancestry through mother figures. Like, uh, Marilyn Monroe."

"Marilyn Mon-*no*," I counter.

"Marlene Dietrich."

"A German? Fuck off."

"Madonna."

"Let me dress you up in fuck off."

He undoes my jeans and grabs me in his manicured fingers. "Grace Jones."

"There we go."

"Aretha. Patti. Whitney. Janet. Beyoncé. Rihanna."

"Go on."

"Janelle Monáe. Josephine Baker. Lorraine Hansberry. Tina. Betty Davis."

"Fu-u-uck!" I crunch my molars into his neck. His laughter sounds drunk, like my worshipful teeth have detached some part of him from the rest. "I don't usually do this," he cackles, to convince himself.

This time, leaving to his memories soothes me, like I'm consuming a handful of chocolate, and returning from class injects in me such euphoria that the moment I open my eyes to the popcorn ceiling I come all over his hand. After that he sweeps into the kitchen to get Crisco and I breathe a small "Thank you" to Caitlin Clarke.

Seemingly the magic has exhausted itself for the moment. I tell him his past in the breath between kisses. Considerate of each other's body, we check for cues, ask permission. It has been a week since my last fuck, a long time since I made love.

Eleven fifteen. In bed, the linens we've disturbed lumped and twisted, my chest to his spine, I wrap my arms around his belly. "Stop," he begs. "I'm self-conscious."

"I like it."

He demurs, “Feel this love handle. It’s so big.” I take up his invitation. “No! You’re not supposed to touch it.”

“You said touch it.”

“Just let go.”

“A’ight.”

Under a blanket of street noise, I wait for dreams. But he says, “You should go.”

“Did I do something wrong?” I ask, quickly.

“No,” he answers as quickly, upright and naked. Cold and slow as snowflakes, words drift from his lips. “It’s not your fault. You’re really interesting and . . . self-possessed,” he says, and I hear the pause. “But I have work tomorrow. If you stay here, I won’t get any sleep.”

“It’s late,” I groan, burrowing my nose in the pillow like a truffle pig.

“It’s not you. I just know I won’t get any sleep,” he repeats.

“What you’re doing,” I explain, “is using a bullshit excuse to get rid of me instead of telling the truth. Whatever you’re dealing with, we can talk about it in the morning. Or never. Right now, the human nigga in your bed is tired, and it’s fucked up to kick him out.”

He refuses to take no for an answer. So, bitchily, I get dressed. Before long we’re in his red Toyota struggle box, outside the Wilkinsburg duplex where I sublet a $200 attic from an illegal tenant who ran to France on that James Baldwin tip and might never return to this barbaric nation. We agree to dinner tomorrow. His parting kiss frustrates in its ambiguity.

In my garret, I lie awake on the frameless mattress and wonder: am I an asshole for asking to see him again? All signs point to him being an insecure, indecisive dweeb and I’ll tire of him quickly. On top of that, I prefer solitude, and the space to follow my own interests, no apologies to anyone. Yet I want this man to adore me.

Thinking, thinking, thinking. At two in the morning, I fall asleep.

Whether I reach REM at three, four, or six a.m., I'll usually rise at noon for my abbreviated day. Today I wake at half past seven. My housemate Sharonda watches me stagger into the kitchen in my gym shorts and she raises her plucked, fashionable eyebrows.

"I guess Hell froze over," she quips. A stout woman with round cheeks, pointed chin, and ropelike purple extensions in a bun, she texts someone while coffee brews.

"You is annoying," I chide. "Now finish making the pot so a nigga can *carpe diem*."

She wears a teal pencil skirt, cream-colored blouse, and Miss Thang heels for her job at the Department of Health. Eight hours a day she sits in a cubicle explaining to poor people the meager financial aid available to keep them alive. Lately she's been talking about changing careers to event planning. We converse. It delights her to learn I knocked boots with Leroy.

"Give me life, my nigga!" she screams so loudly I'm certain techies can hear her in the gentrified Victorians a block over. "I know him! He used to come to Black Queer Art Night."

I snort. "Girl, every black queer in this small-ass town done slept together."

"You get laid and you still salty?" she counters. "That ain't right. When will you see him again?" she inquires with gossipy interest.

My gaze drifts out the window to our serviceable backyard that ends at a cinder-block garage the color of microwave popcorn batter. No one uses it, not even Sharonda, paranoid the motor oil smell might seep into her upholstery. The grass needs mowing.

I pour black coffee in a Snoopy mug and drink a harsh, bitter mouthful. "Tonight," I answer.

Then, because I need to vent, I complain to her about Leroy's little mood. "He's sensitive," she tells me afterward, her eyebrows arabesque with sympathy.

"Every gay nigga sensitive. *This* gay nigga sensitive."

"You should be considerate of his boundaries."

"That nigga need to be considerate of niggas tryin'a sleep."

"You sound like you're repressing something."

"Thanks for the therapy," I snarl. "Leave it to a dyke to say a gay nigga repressing. Y'all the ones constructed the closet in the first place. While y'all Cleopatra-ass bitches was marrying men and writing sapphic poetry, us niggas was in Africa and Greece, ass-fucking."

We bicker, gently, same as we did in college. An astounding number of my cohort at Pitt stuck around after graduation. With a degree to prove they could commit at least four years to something, they fell into sanitation, service, medical, library, drug dealing, and bartending jobs as easily as we'd fall into bed at the Towers after a night of malt liquor and O fries.

"I'm happy you're going out with Leroy," Sharonda coos, snapping me from my reverie. She makes a ham sandwich, trimming crust from the bread. "You know he lived in New York, too? I'm surprised you never met him."

"New York is literally the biggest city on Earth."

Beneath my sarcasm hides appreciation to hear her stand up for Leroy. We need to have each other's back, even when it comes to each other.

A year ago I would have donned a crop top, spangle earrings, and falsies for a date. Western Pennsylvania has me turning butch. I throw on tight jeans, shit-kicker boots, and a tank top. The five o'clock shadow in the mirror strikes me as too manly. Eyeliner, then.

As the sun reclines in purple cadmium I wait on the porch. Across the street, five vacants kneel like penitents upon their crumbling foundations; on my side stand three duplexes and a single Victorian whose brick porch juts over the lush grass like an overstuffed belly, upon which the widowed owner sits most days to watch the world go insane with an elder's irate acquiescence; the brick street ends against a sand-hued wall supporting the East Busway.

Leroy pulls up to the curb. Today he wears jeans and a caramel sweater that's as crisp as a hundred-dollar bill. My excitement turns to caution at his expression.

"Yo' attitude be sharp today," I commentate, paused in the open passenger door. "You look like 'I don't wanna talk with nobody, I don't wanna look at nobody.' I love it, though," I add, attempting positivity.

"I work at an after-school program." He groans. "These kids and they drama got me staying late. You know they don't be acting like that at they mama house."

"You know for a fact them badass kids be acting like that at they mama house."

Weekdays I can hear the buses from a block away. Inside, kids brawl while the driver screams, and their classmates cheer from on top of the black vinyl seats. When it comes to gladiators, Russell Crowe wouldn't have lasted a day in the Woodland Hills school system.

"I came straight from work," Leroy goes on. "Ain't had time to shower—"

"Hold up, my nigga." I refuse to go out with him in a mood. "Come smoke my shit."

Sharonda and our housemate Kathleen, a design student at CMU, have decorated the living room in African and Black Power art. On the enclosed veranda where I like to read, Kathleen studies, and Sharonda does yoga, I sit on the rug and Leroy the calico armchair. To Orpheus my man from mental Hades, I roll a fat joint. I notice he passes it in a way as to keep our fingers from touching, a game I start to like. Meanwhile, Caitlin's words pinball around my brain: *Nothing is more important than play. It carries us from birth to death.*

Three puffs make Leroy verbose. His dad was a Baptist minister, his mom a nurse. He has two older sisters. In Garfield he got bullied for being a sissy, so, to rescue him from other black kids, his parents sent him to CAPA for high school. The summer before he started at Pitt, his dad, realizing Leroy would never be the son he wanted, cut him off financially. In secret, his mother continued to support him until his sophomore year, when she divorced his dad, after which Leroy found himself working to pay expenses. He nearly flunked out.

In New York he acted in Off-Off-Broadway plays and had a recurring role on some Web series. He made friends in the slam scene. Because he loved acting, however racist the casting directors, however poorly the black theaters paid, he continued to hustle. To escape despair, he took pills, then to escape pills he dated an abusive narcissist for six crushing months. He had to leave New York before it killed him. Now he auditions for local theater.

"My ex was femme," he sighs. "My weakness."

"Fuck New York queens," I malign, sincerely. "Them bitches really think they women."

I heat up leftover pasta and vegetable stir fry, sprinkle on garlic powder, and we eat at the living room table. Though I enjoy learning his past, at the point he seems ready to complain about teaching again, I change the subject to myself. In the '90s, when simply reading books would get a boy branded gay, I, a bratty ultra fag hurling grenades of drama, refused masculinity. Generally speaking, breaking the rules is a black kid's power, school our window to get away with deviltry before adulthood, when a sneeze can land us in jail. So, like a nigga, I cussed out teachers. I gossiped girls' reputations into the mud. I smoked dope and vomited champagne. I played hooky. I laughed at ugly people.

Starting in ninth grade, I'd sneak out to East Liberty, to the bars and the embrace of older men, in whose cocoa butter hands I came to know my beauty. On the sidewalk, the taste of them in my mouth, I might run into classmates trailing their dope-dealing sugar daddies, dressed like vamps, and, upon seeing me, would catch me up in their arms, girl to girl, sister to sister.

"Bitch, I'm lucky my ass wasn't sent to reform school. The girls would be like, 'He a fag, but he a cool fag.' And the boys be like, 'I don't fuck with no gay shit, but he a'ight.'"

"Black kids respect bad," Leroy answers evenly. "That's 'cause it's socially rewarded."

"We was fucking *bad,* my nigga. We was some drugged-up little nymphos."

'That's why I appreciated the good kids. I'm like, 'Okay, I see you. You do you.'"

"I liked them, too! I made life hell for 'em. But I liked 'em."

We wash our plates. I propose we visit the Bloomfield baseball diamond. "Yeah," I smirk for him, "it's one of my spots."

In the passenger seat, I tuck my legs under me to get comfortable. Leroy plugs in his iPod and we sing "I Want to Dance with Somebody." There follows, after much debate, "The Way You Make Me Feel," and "Breathe Again" to satisfy our mutual need for Toni Braxton.

At midnight we park on Liberty and walk two blocks to a stone stairwell nearly obscured behind overgrown bushes. "It's really pretty," he says on our descent to the hollow beneath Bloomfield Bridge, the air humid, the diamond doused in halogen like *Field of Dreams*, and above us five hundred tons of steel thunder from the passing cars, an industrial ode to winter summer nights. How his hand tenses in mine says he likes the thrill as much as I do. I lead him beneath small oaks. Shadows whisper affection from their fragrant throats, while make-believe light fouls the leaves with the threat of homophobic murder.

His back to a tree, one hand down his jeans, Leroy strokes his cock. I crawl through the nettles to unzip his jeans with my teeth and kiss the cotton over his crotch, the fabric warm with rushing blood. His trembling knees butt against my shoulders. His cheeks bright with sweat and tenderness, he screws his eyes shut, gasping, "You a bad bitch, huh? You gon' be bad to me?"

"I'm a nasty slut. Thank you for your patience," I say, when I remember the acting class. "This whole magic thing is new."

He sounds impatient. "Do it a few times and it'll be old."

"It's kind of kinky having a woman involved." My attempt to make things sexy again. "Maybe we should invite a living woman."

"Why would you say that?" he grunts.

No sooner does he shame me than I put that shame in my pocket, drive to the Forgettery, and toss it in the furnace. Since he needs to hear "I'm sorry," I say it, not with words, but my tongue. I take him in my mouth like I'm a spoiled child and he a piece of birthday cake.

"Open your books to page thirty," says Caitlin Clarke.

On our third date, Leroy wants to catch a scary movie at the arthouse theater on Melwood, and I reluctantly agree even though the movie he proposes is Scandinavian, plus I tend to find horror flicks corny. More fool me—minute by minute, the story of the little boy who falls in love with an androgynous vampire turns my guts like a well winch until my intestines are tangled inside me. Later, at the bar, we chug whiskey and hurl questions at each other. Was the vampire a girl? A castrated boy? Did the vampire love the boy back? Does it even matter if they're queer when they're also a murderous, immortal cannibal? What is this movie even trying to say? Is it homophobic? Or just Swedish?

His sweet whiskey tongue takes me to class. I enjoy being in his head, where imagination and insecurity battle at a frenetic pace I find relaxing, an all-too-human chaos. Younger Leroy has an affected, smarter-than-thou tone he dons when lecturing his classmates about theater.

Leroy, my dear Leroy. Even your classmates roll their eyes at you, you hand-raising teacher's pet. Slow down, my nigga. You doing too much.

Meanwhile, Clarke, sitting with one black-skirted knee over the other, writes in a notepad. She keeps a thermos nearby. She smiles but rarely laughs. She wants us to work on character. Put your character in a setting. "Now put them in a new setting," she repeats, using her pointer and middle fingers to flip the egg timer. Every so often, she critiques body language. "Unless you have a receiver built into your pinkie," she says sternly, "you have to form your hand like you're actually holding a phone."

After exercises, she summarizes her experience with casting agents, ranging from demoralizing to gross, her lesson being we must push through adversity.

On our fourth date, we get tested together at the clinic. Then we get ice cream.

As the group improves on pair work, Caitlin Clarke refuses to coddle us, her feedback blunt. Jostled from the force of Leroy's nodding, I scream at her to take a vacation. Don't spend your last days babysitting college kids.

Five days later we get our results. Both clean.

The program where Leroy works segues into a day camp over the summer. He helped write a grant proposal to some foundation and was awarded the funding. Now he works longer hours to spend that money, on the phone with places like Phipps Conservatory to get his kids out of their beleaguered neighborhoods into somewhere green. This he tells me over the phone, his job talk cathartic for him, the insincere colleagues and prickly children a tapestry of problems he finds nobility in solving, or at least attempting to solve.

On a Tuesday he invites me to a rally he's helped organize outside City Hall. Some funding bill on the council docket. An hour late, I arrive at brown, dingy downtown in a tropical print scarf, dressed up for him. I easily find his group in bright purple shirts that read GIVE OUR KIDS A CHANCE. One after the other, people get on the megaphone to make earnest pleas for equal access, end the school-to-prison pipeline, etc. While Leroy and his colleagues take smiling pictures around a banner, I think on the bleakness of blackness, our time and energy wasted begging for money, as I scan the sidewalks in hopes that nobody I know passes by and sees me.

The Pittsburgh City Council chambers, where plebeians fidget in leather chairs and politicians go over motions at a long oaken table, looking like the world's most bored college study group, has the effect of making me feel one with the yellow wallpaper. Out loud I wonder if this is the same room where Alex did her audition in *Flashdance*. People stand at the podium. A woman around forty who apparently comes to every session, seeing as the council people address her by first name, shames the councilman from the Hill for a corporate crony who should know better, and I snap my fingers and say, "Yes!" Five guys in black-and-gold face paint come up, I think to argue for some motion involving Heinz Field, I don't know, because when they start singing a hymn to the Steelers, and rhyme Pittsburgher with Roethlisberger, I can't hear them above my own laughter.

Then people argue for the school bill. Heartfelt, heartbreaking speeches one after the other from parents aggrieved at the conditions their children must learn in. The politicians receive these platitudes without emotion. I whisper to Leroy, "Someone could straight knock the fuck out these council people right now. You ever seen *Dead Presidents*?"

He whispers back, "You don't have to stay."

"Why would I come if I didn't want to? Do I do *anything* I don't want to?"

That one doesn't count. Our actual fifth date is Chinese takeout at my place, and he chats for a long time with Kathleen about the famous actors who graduated the CMU theater program, which he almost attended before Pitt gave him a scholarship.

Upon my return he wants to hear about Clarke's class. Cradled in his arms with my ear against the dark, curly hairs on his inner thigh, I say, for a bunch of college kids, I find our classmates surprisingly unannoying, even likable. The standout is a small, black-haired, ethnically ambiguous girl who always compliments his performances. "I hate you," she'll tell him, "because I wish I knew how to do what you do," to which an embarrassed Leroy will twine his fingers like a cobra and mongoose locked in combat.

"I can't stand that bitch," I say, kissing his thigh. "She keep making you hurt me."

He smiles into the air. "She was sweet. I remember she had a real shitty boyfriend, that one time we hung out. Boy, I wish I remembered her name. What was it?"

"I forgot." I'd need her standing in front of me to match the face with a name. Even in Leroy's head, I can get distracted.

On our sixth date, Sharonda invites us to a get-together at her friends' Garfield apartment. This night we wear our finest threads, as we intend to go dancing in the Strip later on. Under Leroy's approving gaze, I preen in slim-cut black pinstripe slacks, a chest-exposing vest with coattails, and heels. He wears slacks, a sweater, and wingtips. "You got the finest mess in Pittsburgh," I brag, lest he take me for granted.

Before heading out, he proposes we do some two-year-old coke he keeps at the bottom of his underwear drawer. Maybe it's expired, he jokes, and I say that's impossible, and he has the nerve to pretend like he's struggling to open the bag, like he's afraid I'll see the look on his face.

We're already in the car when he gets paranoid about driving under the influence. I call a jitney and twenty minutes later a fat-assed Cadillac shows up. Chauncey, the driver, smokes a cigar and monologues on the way about the changes to Wilkinsburg. He'll glance in the rearview at my outfit. Three times he does this until I pinch my nipple at him, and he stops.

Something about him reminds me of my father. Last time I saw Dad he was on the corner of Forbes and Penn haggling over bootleg watches as I pedaled from 7-Eleven on a stolen bike with a backpack of stolen food, and there passed between us a nod, neither malice nor resentment. I don't know him well enough to hate him. One day I may take care of him. When I told Mom I saw him on the corner, she snatched the afro pick out of my hand and threw it in the sink, and Chauncey cannot look like Dad because Dad never knew me well enough to judge me, and when I think of him what I picture is that comb, and my hairs curling into spirals on steel.

At some point Leroy says, "When is this blow going to kick in?"

"Y'all must be on some o' that cut snow," Chauncey belly-laughs. "Back in my day we called that yellow snow. That's the snow you do when you gotta go to work in an hour."

"Nobody ever called it that," I retort. Then I say to Leroy, "You done been high. That's why I called a jitney."

"That's not being cranked. That's being cautious." His spine stiffens. "Ah. There it is."

In a buppie home resplendent with expensive pottery, I have a great time shooting the shit, and Sharonda, ever the romantic, aunties over me and Leroy, taking our photo like we're on the red carpet. She wants to hold a support group for black femmes, and he readily offers his apartment for the venue.

Finally I get some time away from Leroy after an hour standing next to him, and he seems to appreciate the chance to breathe because he slides into conversation with some other nigga who is gay in such a bored, disingenuous way I'm fighting the urge to like him for his commitment to mundanity. Watching them from the kitchen table, I'm not jealous. Or maybe I am—I'm mentally reading this nigga. He really paid someone to give him that fade? Spent legal tender to have his edges looking like a leaf on an aloe vera plant?

From nowhere, Sharonda comes up behind me and plants both elbows in my shoulders. Her black blouse has sheer sleeves. "Y'all are cute together," she says.

"Girl, get out my face with that JCPenney two-for-one sale."

"Bitch, I was not even sassing you. What is wrong with y—

Oh," she whispers when she sees Leroy with him. "Jealousy is normal."

"Black woman—"

"When is you gon' try the casserole? It'll take your mind off it. Cleanse your thoughts."

"Black woman—"

"I slaved over that casserole."

"They should write a book about your suffering. *Twenty Minutes a Slave*. Black woman, I love you, but I'ma slap you."

"Try."

Accepting her challenge, I can barely twitch my forearms with her elbows on me. I try again and yell, full force, "Yo! Let me move my fucking arms."

"I learned this in self-defense class. I'm Jason Bourne in this bitch."

"Get off me!"

She does. Instantly I'm on my feet, and we circle with our dukes up, play slaps our love language.

"Oh my gosh," I hear Leroy chuckle. "Y'all are like my kids."

How embarrassing that I'm embarrassed. Even as I resent his condescending words, his indulgent wholesomeness leads me to take his hand and hurry him to the bathroom, slam the door, push his back to the wall, and, before I kiss him, grab hold of him, one hand to his gasping throat, the other the carafe of his cheek.

I like my midterm partner Juan, a plainspoken kid who seems intimidated by Leroy's passion. Together they have to devise and act a scene based on a random dialogue Professor Clarke has given them. Juan suggests two kids arguing over whether to shoplift candy. No, says Leroy, their characters should be in the middle of a Vietnam battlefield arguing whether to retreat as shells rain around them, and oh, we should get soldier uniforms, and I'm free this afternoon and can pick you up from Posvar and let's go shopping.

Clearly Leroy has a crush on Juan. And poor Juan, well, he abides.

Coming to in the bathtub, I'm confused as to where I am, afraid I've found myself at a party where people get violated. My vision solidifies upon Leroy sitting hunched on the pink-sweatered toilet seat with his knees on his elbows, my return to lucidity met with patience. Through the door I can hear the others sing "Nasty Boys."

Chuckling as he lifts me from the tub, I recount his conversation with Juan. He throws both hands over his face. "Oh no," he cries. "I was *awful* to him."

On our seventh date I help him practice. Next week he's auditioning for Shylock in *The Merchant of Venice*. I read Antonio's and Bassanio's parts. After an hour I conclude he's got it on lock, call him a dope-ass actor, but he wants to keep rehearsing.

"And can you tone it down?" he asks. "You're acting the part. It distracts me."

"An actor's supposed to act," I point out.

"Please just read the lines."

All the girls want to partner with Leroy for pair exercises, and the one he chooses, the ethnically ambiguous girl, smiles the whole time, charmed by his seriousness. They have to describe a time someone made them angry. Thrilled to spill the tea, she tells him about the time her roommate redecorated their apartment and inadvertently misplaced her history essay.

Come his turn, Leroy recalls the weekend he spent on the streets in tenth grade after his dad kicked him out. "Couple years later he cut me off," he concludes. "I'll never talk to him again."

His partner retreats into silence, while I taste Leroy's dad's evil like venom on my tongue. Mercifully, Caitlin Clarke rasps, "Everybody come together," then coughs.

When Leroy asks what I saw, I say, "Just some boring pair share." In bed we kiss fervently. The moment I enter him from the front feels like triumph, his belly in the air like a mound, his presence in my hands a tonic.

For his depression he sees a therapist once a week. The other six days, he smokes weed.

One Friday I come over to find a bong buffet on the table and five people partaking of cannabis served with fried chicken. They're slam poets and seem to believe I'm one, as well. An hour later they love me because of course they do.

I'm not even properly drunk before everyone sits on the couch to watch YouTube videos. They love that True Crime stuff. This comes as no surprise; though I avoid social media, I'm aware Leroy frequents several sites because he's always updating them in front of me, with quips about TV shows. At present, feeling like I might devolve into my basic biological components out of boredom, I steer them into debating when was the last time we saw Beyoncé's real hair. Destiny's Child? *Star Search*? (A trick question because the answer is never.)

But here's the thing about domesticated negroes. 1. They call Pittsburgh a backwards, redneck city. 1b. No one is forcing them to live here. 2. They hate the honkies at their bougie jobs and colleges. 2b. Don't enter a space where no one wants you and then try to act like Robert Williams or Assata when you get put in your place. Get over yourself.

On our eighth date I come over to find ribs, collard greens, and sweet potatoes on the kitchen table. A real-ass dinner. Watching him set the plates, something in his body language puts me on alert, a caution in him where there should be none after four weeks. Perhaps this is why I drink too much wine.

Leroy, to my surprise, shows up stoned to class, an unprofessional move that leaves me disappointed in the younger, squarer version of him. The haze in his brain weighs on me like shackles, more than ever a prisoner of his consciousness. I wonder if this is around when his parents divorced. Throughout discussion, Caitlin calls on him with sarcastic meanness, shaming him in front of his peers, who snicker like squirrels in mating season at his five-second delay.

"Acting is fifty percent preparation," she says sagely, "fifty percent instinct. And sometimes one will take precedence over the other, but there's always that balance, right? Leroy, you've acted professionally in commercials and such. What have you found?"

From north, south, east, and west a hum blares as he struggles to think. "I don't know."

"Thank you, Leroy." Cunt.

She makes him stay after class. "You were being very disrespectful today," she scolds.

"I'm sorry," he says, like a pussy. I'm fighting to lift his gaze from the melamine floor.

"If this was an acting job, you would be fired." Shut the hell up. "And it would go all around the community—which is very small—how unprofessional you are." Bitch, get out my face. "Just because you have passion and experience doesn't make you better than anyone."

"Actually, it *does* make me better."

Moments pass before I realize I spoke the words. Caitlin Clarke stands speechless. Keen to my newfound power, I read her. "What are you jealous of? My youth? My potential? Woman, your greatest accomplishment was running from Cybill Shepherd in a bowling alley. Scoop your coins. Back the fuck down."

Speech is physical action: contract my lungs for air, move my jaw to exhale; adjust my lips for volume; clash my teeth in thunderous *t*'s and hissing *s*'s. A single word puts my whole head to work. Leaving her humbled, I spin on my heel and attempt a swaggering exeunt. Fall, right heel, bend knee, lock knee, switch hips, fall, left heel, bend knee, lock knee. My stumble becomes a strut through the Cathedral of Learning and then smells strike me. So many smells . . .

My back hits the floor and the air rushes from my lungs. Voices skitter over my brain in senseless, painful gibberish. Above me, Leroy sits in bed, naked, hugging one knee to his chest. In the lamplight his eyes gleam cold with contempt.

"She almost kicked me out the class," he says. "I remember all of it. I had to beg her to let me stay. How *dare* you?"

"Beg?" I spit back. "Stepping and fetching. She publicly shamed you! That bitch can eat a dick. Or is *you* a bitch?"

"She was dying," he reminds me in a deep, dark voice. "She moved back here to teach because that's what she wanted to do with the time she had left. Of course she took it seriously, you asshole. Now tell me you'll never do that again. Please."

One day I wake in my attic at noon and spend an hour on the beer-stained mattress, gazing on islands of unwashed clothing, my every neurological impulse occupied by endlessly branching musings on death, environmental collapse, and method acting before I roll out of bed and amble naked to my dresser like some ghost fresh off the misty moors of a Brontë novel. Dressed in boots, jeans, and a crop top under a purple windbreaker, I walk to, then down Penn Avenue in a state of perfect indifference. The sun-kilned streets smell of mud. Before long the sandy old Wilkinsburg two-stories become Point Breeze manors separated from the common folk by tall black fences. Then East Liberty, which they are trying to rename East End. In Garfield families gather on town house porches with fans blasting from the windows. Boutiques, takeout restaurants, decapitated parking meters, graffiti over boarded storefronts. Here and there, an art gallery displays overpriced junk, yuppie condos on the way. I catch up with friends at the cafés, bars, and tattoo parlors. In the park behind West Penn Hospital, my body putters like a vintage roadster pushed past its mileage and I relax on a bench. More charming than a kennel of puppies, a black boy shows skateboard tricks to his girlfriend, who wobbles on the board with nerve-racking ineptitude, but my heart beats triply fast to watch the girl embrace him, a goth with red hair to her waist and a black hoodie to her knees. I tell myself to stop staring at children, but nearby two brats beg their dad for candy in voices like sped-up records, spellbindingly atrocious.

Famished, I sit down at a storefront diner and order a hamburger with fries. Small talk with a waitress in a red-and-white-striped shirt reveals she went to Allderdice. We had a mutual friend at CAPA, a punk who lived in Squirrel Hill and at whose manor house I'd smoke weed on hooky days. How is Dori? Three kids? Wild. Good to see you, girl. Here's a twenty-dollar tip.

Waiting for the 61B at the corner of Forbes and Murray, I check out a boy who possesses an exhilarating, guarded air. Tall and whip-thin, dark, maybe eighteen, a rounded jaw and scowl on his careful lips. His red-dyed mohawk forms a strip like dead leaves. Haphazard phrases and drawings comprise the tattoos across his tank-topped torso. That he looks like he'll threaten anyone who steps too close makes me want to get closer.

A text from Leroy. Apparently we were supposed to meet for lunch half an hour ago.

I text him back apologizing, promise to call him later. But that night I smoke and forget about it. He calls me and I say, "Bruh, I am so high right now."

"I can't just do for you," he says, like I ruined his life. "You need to do for me, too. I need *attention*," he pleads, practically shouting the word.

"Is you keeping a scorecard of who do what when?" I sneer, feeling a headache come along. "Today just wasn't my day."

Eleven hours later I'm at the dentist in Edgewood, to get five cavities filled. Afterward some white lady tries cutting in front of me when I'm trying to pay, demanding the receptionist answer why this or that can't go on her insurance. The devil's maiden wears a leather jacket and stretchy black cotton skirt to hide all manner of disaster on her lower body, a short woman with a broad forehead above close-set dark eyes pinching an aquiline nose, her hair a tawny rug over her left shoulder, all of which I insult her for over the course of a minute, unconcerned that the anesthesia has me reading her out of one side of my mouth. Then I plunk down a thousand dollars cash and read her again for needing insurance.

Outside, Leroy waits in the car. Academically suave in his beige sweater and new leather loafers with tassels, he looks upset. Me, I'm riding high.

"Drive fast!" I shout as he peels from the parking lot into midday traffic. "Oh my god, fam! I'm a bad bitch. You shoulda seen me roast that bit—"

"You're such a Virgo," he says in a tight voice.

"What? Yo," I level with him. "You got something to say, say it."

"Sometimes I wonder if you're just using me for my car."

"If you said I was using you for the metaphysical acting classes, it would at least sound like you respect me. But obviously you don't, so maybe you should do some soul searching about these issues of yours."

He drives back roads that bend like twigs on the way to Wilkinsburg. At one point the woods clear and there stretches the football field where I refused to play, where I once met a boy named Avon. Hard and unquestioning like a teakettle, his midriff gleamed in the moonlight, this boy raising his Wu-Tang shirt with one hand and unbuttoning his jeans with the other, and my breath stilled at the gorgeous dick he unsmuggled from his Calvins, this track star who liked me to watch, and proceeded to twist his manhood with the efficient delicacy of a concert trumpeter dismantling his instrument so he can place each part in the sateen-lined case. Presently that field, mine and Avon's, is overgrown with wildflowers.

Leroy says, "Don't do that."

"Do what, babe?"

He stares hard at the road. "The passive-aggressive comeback under your breath to get the last word in. You sound like some bitchy middle-aged queen from the Castro."

"Never heard *that* before. I know exactly what this is. Some femme nigga was bad to you and now you projecting it on me."

"There you go again!"

Talking so much, drool flees my slack mouth like bats from a mine shaft. A bolus splashes my jeans near the crotch. "I ain't taking the blame for the other nigga shit. I got dirt of my own."

"You're right." He looks guilty, regretful, his eyes fixed on the past. Moment by moment, his grief draws closer, opening cracks in him from which his soul gusts like farts. "I'm overreacting," he tells me. "I know you're making up for yesterday and Lord knows I need—"

"I don't need your car," I interrupt. "I don't need your anything. I sold coke."

"For real?" His disbelief sounds genuine.

"Yeah, nigga. I got fifty grand in the back," I claim, less than the real number, my business being my own. "Oh! Now you quiet? 'Cause when you thought I was a do-nothing nigga, you was one loquacious motherfucker. Bitch, fuck you." Disgusted at the saliva on my thigh, I wipe it into the denim. "Got me drooling on myself. I was in a good mood, too."

What story do you want to hear, Leroy? The one about the weird, artsy kid who chose his friends unwisely? The talented mind fallen in with a bad crowd?

Fine. Here's a story. Since everyone heralded NYC as the place for artists, I moved after graduation to a Brooklyn loft with six queer and trans punks. I worked three jobs. Parties, sex, and poppers made us glamorous, for a time. Between jobs and hedonism, I worked on a sci-fi abolitionist opera about the Tulsa Massacre. Sometimes I'd take the subway to Columbia to spend hours writing in my Moleskine.

What will give you satisfaction? To hear my years of hard work yielded sleepless nights and drawers overstuffed with paper? Maybe a tired tragic-queer narrative about the friends I watched waste from HIV? Do you want to hear my criminal activities so your Urkelly ass can feel superior? An outlaw ballad for your straight-laced, straitjacketed ass to jack off to? I'm Terri Nunn up in this bitch: Tell me why you need to hear those stories from my lips when you obviously hear them every time you look at me?

You want me to say I was beaten, shot at? You want to hear I threatened people with violence? How about how I sold them the coke that killed them? What if that never happened? What if I moved through the drug world as easy as Dave Hampton did the downtown glitterati? Can't we chill and watch shitty movies? Why can't you accept the fact that I won?

No, I will not whine like you. Sobbing school of negritude, get off at this stop. I'll be chilling with Zora at the front of the bus.

After our ninth date, Leroy, having exhausted his questions about selling coke in Brooklyn, searches the Japanese bathrobes in his closet for a rose yukata illustrated in white lilies that he puts on in time for me to disrobe, a blank page for him to write upon, a New York gangster in his bed, if that's his pleasure. The pause when he looks at me confirms, from his caring demeanor, that he pities me. Fine. I'll take it. He sits on the edge of the bed.

"You're the good kind of lazy," he muses. I ask him what that means. He explains, "When most people say lazy, they mean burnt out from capitalism. Real laziness is when you just have time to be. Real laziness is going on a hike, or reading a book. That's the lazy that heals."

"I'm not finishing my opera."

"You done some crazy shit to survive," he smiles, "and lost your creative energy. But the good part is you can start again."

"It ain't that serious."

Isaac Hayes's "Walk On By" radiates from the stereo, sonic perfection, a song I associate with the final scene from *Dead Presidents*. I hear Larenz Tate yell, "Life? Fuck you mean, *life*?" before he hurls the chair at the judge. Then the bus ride to prison. If I tell my lover his song shuffle has me ready to cry over a movie it would sound ridiculous, so, treating this for the slow jam Isaac intended, I lean in to touch him, but he says, "Not tonight."

"Fuck you mean, not tonight?"

There's too many questions about the magic, he claims, after weeks of begging me to summarize his past to him. Even after that time I changed history, he never suggested we stop. Gripped by fear and anger, I remind him I'm neither his dad nor his ex nor his pill dealer. But his hyperventilating makes me drop the matter, for his sake.

On opposite ends of the bed, he falls asleep and I lie awake, thinking about Caitlin's last class. She spent ten minutes assigning our final projects: a dramatic dialogue we must select from the Stanislavski book and perform with a partner. When Leroy heard this? His spine stiffened. His toes curled. Spotlit in my mental theater, Caitlin dresses casually in red tennis shoes, black cotton skirt, and a Pitt sweater. My classmates blink to life one by one, and I imagine her lecturing us on vocals. As I make my dick hard I think of her voice and Leroy's bodily tics alchemized, a perfect fit yet tragic to an almost comic level, like the Steadfast Tin Soldier and his ballerina burning in the stove.

For decades Mom saved her money working the register at Giant Eagle in order to buy a house in Highland Park, far enough from Negley that urban agitation fades among deep-treed hills and apartment complexes built from porous brick. Last year she converted the front room into an appointment-only hair salon, six barber chairs, three dryers. Sometimes we drink rosé in the garden, her own purple-flowered oasis with a patio table in the center of spiraled paving stones, peaceful as any mansion hidden at the end of a driveway. She never asks my plans.

Biking Negley, on my way to her shop, I see a hooker working the day shift. Immediately I recognize her because her energy, once inquisitive and creative, if a little too ingratiating, is still present in her body, only manifested in the addict's eternal thirst. I examine her leather bustier and shorted legs that look atrophied, as if barely used; her golden arms bear dark blotches over premature wrinkles. Out of instinct, I smile and shout hello to her as I pass. She bugs out her eyes and shrugs at me, annoyed and confused. I will never tell Leroy I saw her.

What I feel, when at last I sit with a flourish in Mom's chair, is gratitude: that whatever Leroy and I have gone through, we've come out the other side. How wonderful! Today she braids my hair in zigzag cornrows. Mom, a small and thin woman, young in appearance, wears jeans and a short-sleeved black T-shirt. Her hair plunges to the small of her back in a single nylon braid woven with the complexity of cybernetics.

"The braids need to be thin," I remind her. "I gotta be able to fit the wig on."

"Remind me who you're trying to look like."

"Jennifer Beals from *Flashdance*. And it better work, 'cause that wig be expensive."

"I told you he was serious," she tells the tall white man in the opposite chair, name of Dirk. Dirk wears khakis, a black windbreaker, and loafers without socks, one bony ankle crossed on his knobby knee.

"You know what that means?" he says. "That means you raised him right."

"He loved the pretty stuff when he was little," she reminisces. "*My Little Pony. Rainbow Brite*. He would dress up like Punky Brewster. They said, 'He's going to turn out soft if you let him do that.' I told them, 'My baby's going to be himself. You worry about your own baby.'"

"You're embarrassing him." Dirk laughs.

"Nothing embarrasses me." I make sure to correct this displaced polar bear. "I looked cute in my Punky pigtails."

"You can't reach judgments about people when you haven't lived their struggle," Mom continues. "I won't lie—raising a boy was terrifying. There's so many people out to hurt boys. But I don't hate anybody."

"Well, I would hope you don't hate me!" Dirk chortles.

"My religion is love," says Mom. "I was raised Baptist, but I don't belong to any church. They ask me, my religion is love. Speaking of love"—she wrestles a comb through my hair—"I bought a ham for that dinner with your boyfriend."

"You didn't have to."

"Baby, I want to. Any news about that spirit?"

Dirk cuts in. "Spirit?"

Admirably succinct, my mother tells him I experience time-travel astral projection whenever I'm with my partner. His smile is made of plastic. "I've had some spooky boyfriends," he laughs, "but never any ghosts involved. I'll tell you what—I can't say for sure if I believe, but I believe you believe. I don't mean to stereotype," he prefaces, "but sometimes there's a grain of truth. And in my experience, black people I meet don't like spirits."

"Being black is scary enough!" she exclaims. "When that man I met at Shadow Lounge wanted to take me on a picnic at the cemetery, I said no. Not with all those spirits. But I believe most spirits are good," she adds sincerely. "And one or two evil ones."

"Caitlin Clarke's an okay spirit," I groan. "But she's more like a memory."

"Memory or not, if you treat your man right, his spirits will be right, too."

"Are you saying I don't treat him right?"

She keeps combing, unconcerned. "If I had something to say about you, sweetie, I would say it *to* you. And let's not talk about the gray hairs you gave me back in the day."

"Let's *not* talk about it. I done told you I'm sorry."

"You've always been aloof, even as a baby. Off in your own world. I think you're perfect the way you are. Just know it won't work for everybody, and that's fair, too."

Hours pass. Mom and Dirk remember the salad bar at Rax

Roast Beef, Wednesday morning Bible study at Peabody, the adventures that found you while you were shopping with George Romero's wife.

What to wear the night your man meets your mom? Something special, for sure. After searching town for the right ensemble, I bike home with overstuffed plastic bags tugging at my handlebars, carry them upstairs, and put the Go-Go's *Talk Show* on the record player. I crank that shit, too. This weekend Kathleen is in Youngstown visiting her parents, and Sharonda cashed in her vacation time, rounded up her girls, flew to Atlanta, and at this very moment she's invading the clubs like a slasher villain armed with a cocktail. Part of me wishes I went with her, but I'm here, more than happy to air guitar like Jane Wiedlin.

For Leroy I put on pantyhose, a leather miniskirt, and black ankle boots with charms on the zippers, and, though Jennifer Beals doesn't wear them in the scene I've rewound endlessly for reference—the one where she kicks it in her loft with the supposed-to-be-a-nice-guy-but-actually-kind-of-creepy-and-girl-now-that-I-think-about-it-ain't-he-twice-her age love interest—black leg warmers are a must.

For Leroy I wear a baggy aquamarine sweater with wide sleeves, one shoulder down. On my face go cleanser, moisturizers, concealer, foundation, bronzing powder, blush, eye shadow, mascara, ChapStick, and Revlon 5 to evoke Alex from *Flashdance*, a steel-town girl, a nymph terrified the dance school will reject her, slutty enough to feel you up under the table at a fancy restaurant, tough enough to punch a strip club sleaze, any ethnicity, mass market appeal, curly wig to my shoulders, hair-so-big-because-my-brain-holds-so-many-dreams '80s It Girl with a heart as pure as the cocaine grown by Reagan's contras. I kiss the mirror. Mwah!

At a quarter to five, Mom arrives in a black chiffon sleeveless drape dress with a diamond brooch on her chest. "Beautiful," she calls me. "He's lucky to have you."

Another woman says, *Breathe like the character.*

We cook honey-glazed ham served with a side of bruschetta with tomato and basil, and a caprese salad. I splurge on a $120 bottle of pinot. When he arrives with a box of chocolates for Mom, they cheek-kiss and hug in the best kind of way.

"You look lovely," he tells me, dressed in black jeans, brown sweater, and black dress shoes. Above his tired smile, his eyes crinkle thoughtfully. "Jami Gertz in *Lost Boys*?"

Always remember, Caitlin Clarke says, *what would the character do in this situation? Let go of yourself.*

"Oh, you." I peck him on the cheek. "Jennifer Beals."

"What happened to the 'no white divas' rule?"

"Jennifer Beals is black," Mom and I correct him at the same time. And she says on our way up the steps, "I just love this whole diva worship memory thing. Good spirits have blessed your relationship."

At first he gasps to learn she knows about that, followed by a sardonic grunt.

"What?" I ask, hanging up his coat.

"Nothing," he says, his expression bereft. "Just, you don't always act very worshipful."

Wrapping him in my arms, I say, "Maybe *she's* not the diva I'm worshipping." I show him the table, already set. "Who says you can't turn a ho into a housewife?"

Over dinner, Mom asks him how work is going. "Yesterday, I took the eighth graders to the Warhol," he answers, after chewing and swallowing with his mouth closed. "They acted so nervous around the erotica. And I'm like, 'Y'all see worse than this on the internet!'"

For a time he prattles like an old man about his distaste for these modern teen dramas where the characters are always having sex. Says it verges on kiddy porn. I wish to mock him and say, *Kiddy porn with thirty-year-old actors?* Instead I say, “You’re so dedicated. You know what we should do at the end of summer? We should go to Paris!”

“Ooh la la!” Mom agrees.

“End of summer?” Leroy chuckles. “Isn’t that in a week? Kind of last minute.”

“He’s always been like that,” Mom assures him. “Impulsive.”

I touch her arm. “It’s like you used to say: ‘Don’t go through life with the brakes on.’”

“A wise elder,” Leroy says into his glass.

“Stop it!” she cries. “Calling me an elder. Shame on you. But I stand by those words,” she concludes and sips her wine, pinkie up.

Find the conflict and play with that.

“I would pay every expense,” I propose, and Mom gives me a look, curious how I would do this. I go on. “Wouldn’t you like to see La Comédie-Française? You *are* a thespian.”

“I’m also a teacher,” he responds. “I might get my masters in secondary ed.”

Mom uncorks a second wine bottle. “I will drink to that. We need more black male teachers in these schools.”

“How did your audition go?” I ask.

His smile veers to the right. “We already discussed this last week.”

“And what was the answer? You know me. Forgetful.” I shrug.

“I didn’t get the part. But it’s fine.” And he clinks glasses with Mom.

You’re doing wonderfully. Finish the scene.

At his car I toss my hair over my shoulder, flick my eyes to the sidewalk, then his eyes, then the sidewalk like a yo-yo. "I'm glad you came. I'm serious about Paris."

"I have to plan for the fall," he reminds me.

"Then let's go in late fall. Think about it."

"Yeah."

"I love you."

He smiles. He gets in his car. He drives away. As if psychically attuned to my withering, Mom meets me at the top of the stairs and leads me to the couch. I weep in her lap.

A full week later Leroy finds time in his schedule to meet me at People's Indian Buffet. My fear of losing him becomes a mission to numb myself, furious pedaling down Penn, the Dollar General, a dumpster where D'Anthony meets me on his break. A beefy guy I know from Pitt, two chromosomes shy of handsome, he sells me oxy and a Fanta to wash them down.

Adrift on a painless sea, my eyes follow the Newport smoke spiraling around his blocky skull. Ashy from his croissant-shaped lips float thrilling words: baby mama, Harmerville, connect, fentanyl, fifty-fifty. To think of partnering with him has me feeling like I felt the first time I shoplifted, powerful and alive. But I decline.

Luck carries me the next three blocks without getting run over. On my way into the restaurant I'm adjusting my scarf, but I've no chance to fix this knot before Leroy, already at a corner table, gestures for me to sit. He doesn't hug me. His goatee has grown in, two gray hairs in the middle the prelude to an erudite stripe, a compliment to his August Wilson cap.

Here it comes. "I think you're great. But it seems like you're getting stronger feelings, and I don't feel that way. But I really want to be friends."

I wasn't catching feelings! I scream in my head. *I just wanted you to think I was.*

Folded up in the chair like a napkin in a cup holder, I try to reach him. "Do you think friendship is what I want? I have money. I can support you while you audition."

"I got a full-time job," he drones.

"Teaching? That's what artists do when they give up," I say at the same time I spread my arms over the table and lay my cheek to the plastic laminate, it feels so good.

For a long moment he sits with his hands over his face. "You high."

"Fuck you! You never invited me to meet your fucking mom! I never met your sisters—"

He speaks low. "Slow your fucking role. This a grown man you talking to."

"Motherfucker, you never told me the reason you wanted to be a fucking actor is 'cause you and your mom watched *To Sir, with Love* a hundred times and you idolized Sidney Poitier. I had to hear that shit from Sharonda when she read it on your Facebook. You think I'm shit."

He almost touches my hand, stops himself. "Listen to me. Just listen. I do *not* think you're shit. You're brilliant, and special, and sweet—"

"I ain't *sweet*! You just saying words. Look at me!" I shout, now he's glancing around. "Look at me, not these honkies. Am I too loud for y—"

"Are you trying to get us kill—"

"You been kept me at arm's length—"

"Letting you in my memories ain't no arm's length," he says through tears.

"Nigga, I went to a city council meeting for yo' ass. Then I miss one date and you *shame* me. Now you gon' throw me away?"

The wait staff come running from around the fish tank with their fingers wheeling toward the door. Before I can read them, my attention is hijacked by a woman at the next table over, who has the audacity to make a sniffing noise. I wheel on her. "Meth-looking-ass bitch. Mind your business."

Her boyfriend rises from the table. All I can think is how dumb he looks with that bulky torso and tiny bowlegs. He roars, "You nasty fucking faggot! I'll kill you!"

The chair is in my hands and I'm ready to swing when I see Leroy almost out the door. I fly to him. My arms around his waist, I humiliate him. "You can't leave me! I'm inside of you!"

He narrows his eyes, draws back his arm, and blesses me with the lifelines on his palm. My soul rises from my feet and out of my skull. Gratefully I let go.

Standing, I breathe deep and open my eyes to face my partner, the ethnically ambiguous girl whose name, I have learned, is Kaitlyn with a K. Our classmates surround us in quiet interest, come to expect something good from me. The heartbeat in my throat comes close to choking me like a necktie. Otherwise, I stand calm, while Caitlin Clarke watches at the head of the circle.

Leroy, your voice emerges from my chest as a tinny vibration between our ears. Call it bottled intensity. Happy to ride you, I am rattled with the stiff, precise movements of your leather-shoed feet over the lacquered floor. Our eyes follow your dance partner, improved over the semester to the point I wish to keep watching her even as our eyes pivot south and east to convey aversion, contemplation, and rage. We are a couple going through a divorce. She threatens to take our son away and our lungs burn from your furious bellowing. Like Denzel in his most intense moments, you sharply enunciate and rock the syllables with a bebop cadence that leaves me feeling like I'm in a hall of mirrors. How could I not love you?

Ten minutes later, we bow to the class. "Wow," says our professor. "That's acting."

Our partner beams at her. "When we were practicing, one of the janitors stepped in. He thought Leroy was going to hit me!"

Our cheeks burn with embarrassment. But we are proud. I expect at any moment to be ejected from your body like tobacco spat in a cup.

In her jeans and Pitt sweater, the professor speaks to the class, a slight tension drawn across her face. "It has been my honor to teach you all. Thank you. And have a good summer."

They applaud her. At my command, your hands rise to do the same. Yes! Struck with a plan wondrous and terrible, I dash for the door.

"Leroy," says Caitlin Clarke. A glance at her blue eyes shows us admiration, but more than that hope for the future of her profession. "Leroy, I just want you to know—"

"No time." I'm sorry, love. That's the last she'll ever see you. I'm sorry. Other than bringing us together, Valerian doesn't matter. My love for you carries me out the door.

Nothing looks different except the fashions students wear. Controlling your body has me relearning how to walk, and, in too much of a hurry to take my time, I move like a giraffe trying to duck a hunter's bullets. Through the gridlock on Bigelow, assholes honk at me. Muscle memory carries me past the William Pitt Union, up the stairs framed by faux-Grecian columns, up more flights of steps to a landing crowded with idiot college students, perhaps none dumber than the one I find smoking menthols outside Tower A. He wears ripped jeans, Jordans, and a Nirvana shirt festooned in safety pins. Something on my face unsettles him.

"Do I know you?" he questions after spewing a gray rainbow. "I don't like niggas getting close to me. Why don't you step back?"

His friends look wary, except for Sharonda, who happily

asks our name. And I say to him, "Do you remember *Dragonslayer?*"

His grin flashes white. "A strange pickup line. But effective. Maybe I should take you upstairs and dress you in some boy clothes."

Did I really talk like that? Sounding like a damn serial killer. Regret swims like the movement of tiny fish in our guts. I lead him around the tower to the terrace overlooking Forbes, where none can see us. He leans back with his shoulders against a rectangular flower pot. "Girl," he purrs, "if you tryin'a cruise, this is not the place—"

"Shut the fuck up." My voice sounds feeble. Remembering our lessons, I breathe to calm myself. I treat the boy kindly, as you would. "You don't know me, but I'm the one. All these hookups you're doing are fun. But you're going to need more. Because next year you're going to New York. And you're going to tell yourself you're okay, but it's a lie. You're going to be stressed, and depressed, and do stupid shit, and convince yourself you're making it while you lose your passion. That's because you need me. And I need you. You're a playwright, I'm an actor. This world can't break us if we hold on to each other and, and, and I'm a good man—"

"What the fuck is this, fam?"

"Look in my eyes and tell me I'm wrong." I stare the kid down. "Tell me you don't see my kindness. Tell me you don't see my strength. My wisdom. My patience. You don't know me but you *will* love me." Now sounds from another time and place encroach. "You remember the end of *Dragonslayer*. Galen's magic is gone, but he wishes for a horse and a stallion appears over the hill. Galen and Valerian ride off together into the mists of time. You wanted to ride with them. It's not just a fantasy. I'm Galen and you're Valerian. This is where our story begins."

The cup of tea is warm in my hands. I am me, at a table in Crazy Mocha. Across the table sits Sharonda in a fuchsia shirt that reads SHAR'S EVENT PLANNING. "What was that?" she asks. "You having a seizure or something?"

Hurriedly I check my phone. The digital numbers claim it is the year and day I left. Reading, chatting, texting, and coding, the people around me feel like they exist on the other side of glass. I grab her wrist and ask, "Is Obama still president?"

"Ow! Why wouldn't he be?"

I let go. "Thank fuck."

"What?" A socialist, she never liked him much. "Are you all right?"

That is when I hear the barista say, "What's up, Leroy?"

Over my shoulder, I see her serving him. He is clean-shaven and looks, if not happy, content. There is a man beside him. Their easy rapport speaks to the long term.

"I know that brother," says Sharonda, who closes her eyes to think. Four heartbeats later, she snaps her fingers. "Isn't that the guy who proposed to you outside the Towers? Oh my god! That was the weirdest, most beautiful thing. You just thought it was weird, but, I don't know." She sighs. "You never see people being vulnerable like that anymore."

The events of the last four years return to me. I am a twenty-six-year-old former playwright, well off financially, living in an attic in my hometown, comfortable, left so sleep-deprived from my time selling coke I may never recover the deficit. And something deeper has vanished from me, something that makes the world opaque.

Leroy, you step past me. As your boyfriend pulls out chairs, you steal a glance. There has to be a way we can jump over our chaotic selves to the part where we work it out. To melt the small grievances in the heat of greater truth, and, having accomplished that, be as one.

If luck prevails, you know the secret. Because it's something I never learned.

TOURNAMENT ARC

For nearly two decades every crumb of energy I possessed went to teaching high school history, while Sean worked a cushy supervisor job at a drug-testing facility, if one considered watching men urinate for half your life a cushy thing. I'm talking endless penises, and not the happy kind Sean enjoyed watching, but the persecuted kind he was forced to study all day like the contents of the Zapruder film, recalcitrant phalluses unsure whether to stretch or shrink, every desperate twitch a struggle to meet that court-mandated line.

During COVID the government deemed drug testing an essential business. On top of watching urethras open and shut like the mouths of eyeless, hairless choir singers, Sean now had to brave airborne pathogens in a fundamentally fluidic, close-quartered job. He got sick. He spent a week in bed, his lungs barely responsive, death a certainty in his feverish mind.

His reward for survival was being sent back to work. There, smug drunks and junkies called him a liberal liar. They threatened to kill him because he dared wear gloves to handle their piss. His second infection put him on a ventilator, tethered to this world by oxygen delivered to him in syringe-thin drips.

Daily I teetered between rage and despair at the possibility the pandemic might claim him, as it had my dad. But Sean stayed knotted like a dreadlock to life. Upon leaving the hospital he cashed out his 401K and retired. Months later he'd yet to fully recover his sense of smell.

"I done seen it all, anyway," he reasoned to me over beers, his lips a tight smile. "Remember I told you about the dude who was peeing out a fake dick? Dark nigga with a redbone dick. My nigga, that was the first month I worked there!" Regarding his loss: "There ain't much in Columbus I wanna smell anyway. But it still sucks."

Sometime in the fall the usual suspects passed a bill banning "divisive" topics from Ohio public schools, which brought me to an impasse I wasn't ready for, even though I'd seen it coming. All through my career it had been my honor to teach black children their history, from maroons to Panthers, Shaka Zulu to Zulu Nation, Yaa Asantewaa to Mandela. Republicans figured, in erasing our triumphs, they could write their own narrative of the inhuman horde besieging their civilization, justification for their sins against us. While I hesitated to leave a job I loved, you couldn't fight Capitol Square. All I could do was refuse complicity, so I put in my two weeks, told the kids to challenge authority, and cashed out my 401K.

That very afternoon I joined Sean at his bungalow in Maize-Morse. In a tartan-wallpapered kitchen he fixed me a K-cup while searching a cupboard filled top to bottom with jarred cannabis, like some stoner doomsday prep. From across the table I watched him pack a bowl. Back in college he'd been pretty, delicate in face and form. These days his belly protruded under a dilapidated Robotech shirt, Bengals sweatpants and brown Crocs completing his indifferent appearance. His beard looked like a black horsetail on his chin. Fed-up eyes, bronze, like a pair of weathered gongs under a low forehead crowned in curls like melted licorice, their bags shaped like hammocks, as if some part of him would forever stay catching up on sleep.

I tell you this to set the scene, not as a judgment. Everyone gets older. I had a full head of hair once, then a widow's peak that over the years became a widow's peninsula, until at last I saw no choice but to shave my head bald, leaving the poor widow with no landmass whatsoever to call her own. In any event, I'd still say Sean had matured from a pretty youth to a man who was handsome, in his own grubby way.

"Honkies," I sneered. One toke of Humboldt County rustled like redwood leaves in my belly. "Can't let their precious babies *not* grow up racist."

"Fuck them," Sean surmised in his bone-weary tone. "*And* their fucking kids. You should start your own school. The Panthers were right: we need our own learning centers for *our* kids, teaching *our* history. You can do it."

"Stop trying to make me feel better," I ordered him, "and let me fucking vent."

Starting my own school sounded like an idea . . . for later. For now, I considered being an overweight nerd who smoked reefer and watched VHS anime the noblest pursuit. Indica, sativa, edibles, resin. Blunts, joints, bongs. Harem comedies, superhero teams, intergalactic war dramas. Pirate ninjas, giant mechs, cyborg cops, yakuza. *Alien* and *Blade Runner* and *Mad Max* ripoffs. Gory horror steeped in Shinto lore. Uncomfortably prescient cyberpunk. Magical girl transformations, atom bomb imagery, speed lines, nosebleeds, and hot springs. Classics like *Akira* and *Ghost in the Shell* still held up. Even the bad stuff remained gloriously trashy.

Over time Sean's disenchantment, which I'd thought unchangeable given his decades in the trenches of America's war on common sense, morphed before my eyes to cool determination. From the attic he retrieved armfuls of half-assembled, cobwebbed

Gundam model kits he proceeded to finish over seven hours at the kitchen table; he catalogued his two-thousand-plus comic book collection; twice a day, he set out tuna for the neighborhood cats. It heartened me when he shaved his beard and clipped his fingernails, even if all he did that day was sell old figurines online while I smoked on the sofa. Still, his chronic cough worried me.

He spoke of moving to Belize or Costa Rica, inexpensive countries home to a growing black expat community. This talk of a Palestine where our people could sip from coconuts without fear of a white bullet sounded like marketing to me, but I left my cynicism unvoiced. Instead I pictured him flying south of the equator, or joining an Arctic expedition, or fleeing this planet on a hot-air balloon.

Finally, after months in his house, he was ready to find new purpose in life, whatever that may look like. He abhorred geeks who—rather than strive for something on the absurd battlefield called adulthood—asked nothing more than to keep playing with their toys.

"Being a grown-ass man ain't no matter of opinion," he told me. "You grown whether you like it or not. Is you a grown-ass man worth a damn, is the question. You remember how cute I was back in the day. You don't hear me crying 'bout, 'I ain't cute no more.' 'Cause what kinda grown-ass man be crying 'bout that?"

Our local anime con would be our last hurrah for nostalgia. I brainstormed an "old-school" panel. Two guys reminiscing on the artery-spraying, boob-jiggling trash we grew up on.

"Know what we should do instead?" Sean proposed, aloft in smoke like Juliet on her balcony. "What if we ran a LARP? Watch white folks beat on each other."

Contrary to his assumption, I knew several black LARPers. Like my friend who hit up tristate Ren Faires dressed as a Barbary corsair, his wife a Dahomey Amazon; amid the fried turkey fumes and body odor, they struck a fearsomely handsome vision. Another friend traveled on weekends with his all-black unit to Amish Country, where they donned crested helmets to thunder across the field as Hannibal's legions.

Anyway, I thought this was a fabulous idea. Since I had experience in drafting friendly emails—as opposed to the kind Sean used to write, dour lab reports for probation officers—I wrote to the programming committee. They accepted.

Wednesday before the con we drove a U-Haul into the countryside, the hills rounded with six inches of snow that had been falling and melting on a 24-hour cycle all through this nominal winter. Two hours later we pulled into the cedar-fenced parking lot of a campground owned by a polyamorous threesome, two gnomic men in tunics and a stout woman in a bell-sleeved dress. The men wheelbarrowed foam weapons from the barn as Sean rocked back and forth on his heels, a cigarette in his lips. His brush with death, it seemed, had made him more loyal than ever to his vices, something I observed uneasily. Soon we had halberds, warhammers, spears, glaives, staves, broadswords, greatswords, bastard swords, shields, battle-axes, poleaxes, dirks, daggers, poniards, flails, maces, morning stars, claymores, and lances stacked on racks in the truck. His eyes bright, like two windows to the surface of the sun, Sean paid cash for a weekend rental.

Friday at sunrise he picked me up in the truck from my Franklinton home. Along the way we hit up Kroger for snacks. I wore a Blind Guardian shirt. Sean wore a *Battle Angel* shirt with a picture of the titular heroine gazing at the sky from a desert dune.

At the convention center we carried the weapons upstairs on the freight elevator. Breathless from four trips, irritated to start my day on a calisthenic note, it nonetheless gave me pleasure to help Sean roll the racks against the window overlooking High Street. Downtown Columbus, seen from above, looked primordial in its emptiness. Sean did inventory. I made five duct-tape squares on the floor for children, youth, introductory, intermediate, and advanced fighters. I wrote on the whiteboard:

1. There are five skill levels. Children are 7–10. Youth are 11–13. Anybody under 18 needs parental permission.
2. No headshots.
3. No hitting below the belt.
4. If you get hit in a vital organ, you lost the round. If you get hit in a limb, you lose that limb. Lose two limbs and you've lost the round. It's NOT just a flesh wound.
5. Have fun.

By ten a.m. fans were trickling in. A safe thing to do during the latest variant? Hell no. We knowingly risked our lives in search for normalcy. You couldn't convince us these few days of controlled amusement wouldn't eventually fall prey to the next disaster, so we gathered in fanatical opposition to chance, even Sean, who had faced eternity, his concession to caution a mask slack beneath his nose like my widowed mother's clothesline.

Within the shopping-mall noise of the crowd I heard chipmunk outbursts from adolescents gushing over fanfic and memes. A girl called to me: "Mister! Is that you, Mister?"

I smiled watching my former student Aaliyah zigzag through the crowd. Dark and petite, she wore a schoolgirl skirt, white dress blouse, tan combat boots, and shaggy tangerine wig. Above her collar was the serial number 63194 in black eyeliner. Over her amiable nose a black mask read in white letters: MORE YAOI.

Small surprise, then, to see on her phone a gay romance comic which, though I didn't recognize the series, woke memories of comic book shops and the beat-up boxes where they stashed foreign, indie, and gonzo titles. I remembered paper rustling, cheap, thin, and brittle like communion wafers, as Sean tossed aside grotesques spewing bodily fluids and debatable anatomies inked with the blackest brushstrokes in sexed-up Batman ripoffs, on the hunt for Captain Harlock. Translated, untranslated, whatever, he needed to know if Harlock defeated the Mazone Queen.

"You're Emma from *Promised Neverland*," I told Aaliyah, meaning her costume.

Her moonstone eyes widened. "You watch *The Promised Neverland*?"

"I'm fire!" I bellowed. "How's schoo— Hold up! Shouldn't you be there?"

She didn't even try looking guilty. "I'm sorry, Mister."

Teachers got addressed as *Miss* and *Mister*. There'd been a time I'd wield the disciplinary power at my disposal to make kids say my name, but with every successive year they wore me down. Now, hearing the impersonal title moved me almost to tears.

Before I could insist she return to second period, Sean reminded us of my words, *challenge authority*, which she cheerfully confirmed: "You said that, Mister." As if a grown man wasn't entitled to hypocrisy. Didn't matter if I told that girl to put the lime in the coconut, we shouldn't be encouraging truancy. So I told Sean, "I'm trying to teach her the right thing."

"Oh, I agree!" he said, then to her, "You're a weird black kid. All you need to know: you ain't better than any other nigga, white people ain't your friends, respect your mama, them Hot Topic contact lenses gon' give you glaucoma. Shit! *I* shoulda been the teacher."

Then he asked if she'd like to organize our weapons, and her willingness to do so, kind as it was, seemed overeager in a way I disliked, as if she still considered me an authority figure needing placation. Watching her struggle to lift a spear off the racks, I called out, "It's fine. Really. Go have fun." To Sean, "Don't be using my student for labor."

"Least she doing something today." Then he noticed the look I was giving him. "Bruh—"

"You got time!" I snapped. "Go 'head. We got time. Say something else stupid."

All morning we remained at our table stacked with snacks and many, many waivers. Rarely was there reason we should leave, even to give instructions, seeing as combatants took it upon themselves to uphold the rules, veteran duelists keen to show newbies proper weapons use, maybe too keen. You never heard so much mansplaining in your life.

Around eleven, during an advanced bout, one of the fighters swung an ax at his opponent's head. Thank God he missed. This clown wore a kilt and leather jerkin over a fur pelt, his mohawk dyed black, his wispy goatee like raven feathers glued to his chin.

Sean reached down for a megaphone, spilled a bag of chips on the floor, cursed, coughed, and shot up from his folding chair like water from Shamu's blowhole. "All y'all hold up! William Wallace! Raggedy man! Yeah, I'm talking to you. No headshots."

The guy said, "It's a fight!"

"Is this motherfucker arguing?" Sean whispered before saying to him, "You think this is medieval times? You got most of your teeth. You don't have any plagues that I know of. And I believe in ye olden days they weren't wearing S and M leather. That pelt ain't even real fur."

"Sean!" I pleaded. "This is a family-friendly event."

"That's your one warning," Sean told the man, who looked

upset at this, his goatee twisted in a hyperbolic paraboloid from the scowl on his trout lips. "Oh, you mad? Go storm the Capitol, then. I shall have my skalds sing ballads about your inability to follow rules. No headshots! Any y'all got a problem, it's *my* LARP. You know what else? Batman ain't no hero. He's a billionaire who could solve global warming and instead he beats up poor people."

I laughed. "Now you clownin', dog."

"*Star Wars* is a hate crime. You got a whole galaxy and one black person per movie? Miss me with that ethnic cleansing."

Unanimous silence from the crowd. He took a bow and collapsed into his chair. At his high, fragmented breathing I asked if he was okay.

"Headshots in *my* LARP," he growled. "Fucking punk. The corn in my stool is harder'n that motherfucker."

On the other side of the table a person waited, hands over their lap, for Sean to finish. Tall, broad-chested, long-limbed, they wore armor from precolonial Benin: a black-and-gold skirt sewn with traditional patterns, and a red quilted, short-sleeved surcoat that smelled strongly of years and miles. Less authentic was the crimson silk scarf over their collar, anachronistic and a bit flouncy, but admittedly stylish. Long black gloves, black stockings under leather boots, and a black lycra mask under a dome-shaped, red-beaded helm concealed their identity. Perhaps, I thought, they wished to portray a "dark" character. Or, well, germs.

"Benin!" I yelled, hurling out my fist for some dap. "That's what I'm talking about!"

The stranger gazed cluelessly on my fist. Must be a white guy, I thought. At least he had the decency to hide his face while pillaging my culture. The stranger said, "I ask the honor to participate in war games," their accent and cadence like that of a Nigerian scholar I'd known, if you elevated his pleasant baritone to something light and androgynous, and recorded him speaking onto lo-fi tape that distorted the breath and spit from his speech, the resulting sound smooth and windless like desert rain.

If they turned out to be white, I was going to act a fool over the accent. Sean, fully on board with this person, gave them the Wakanda salute. I watched in interest as the newcomer tried out weapons before choosing a spear and shield. Sean smiled like a pelican the whole time.

Starting from beginner, the mystery fighter quickly advanced in levels. They fought with grace and fairness. I looked forward to their matches, as did the cell-phoned spectators recording their powerful strikes, their footwork a dance transporting me to those days when black kingdoms flourished like Heaven's reflection between Egypt, Zululand, Ethiopia, and Yoruba.

When they faced William Wallace, the wannabe Celt/Viking/whatever charged, roaring, swinging his ax for the stranger's head. Quicker than a housefly, the Benin cosplayer stabbed at his sternum, allowing William Wallace a gasp before he flew from the square to lie prone on the linty carpet like a G.I. Joe disfigured with acetone and chucked in the grass for a yard sale.

Sean got on the megaphone. "I would like to call attention to the fact you got knocked the hell out. You got whupped in a most embarrassing fashion. Praise the Lord. Amen."

Afterward, I got up to congratulate the mystery fighter, my ass cheeks atingle from hours in the chair. "That was dope! You gotta tell me your name, bruh."

"I have no name," they said.

Annoyed at their preciousness, I said, "At least let me see your face."

"I need to show you in private," came their reluctant answer.

It seemed a good time to take lunch, anyway. We'd need energy for running the tournament later. Our weapons secured with chains and padlocks, we followed our new acquaintance in the direction of the men's room. Along the way, I saw Aaliyah on a silver vinyl couch with other spindly urchins, violently thumbing their phones in contentment, sharing memes, communally dialed in. Being an old-head, people expected me to mourn my students' tech dependency, but, really, they looked no different than me and Sean when we used to trade Yu-Gi-Oh cards. Nothing had changed now that the toys were online. I was reflecting on this in the restroom, when Wę opened a stall door and motioned we should enter.

I rolled my eyes. "Come on, man."

Sean yelled, "Ask their pronouns!"

"Who you yelling at? Ain't no reason to get turnt up. Do you go by he, she, or they?" I asked the mystery fighter.

"My lord called me Wę." *You* in Edo. No gender. Just Wę. "My appearance might shock people, so I would much prefer privacy."

Two guys with hemispherical bellies and a warrior walk into a bathroom stall. Sickened at the piss in the toilet—apparently nerds these days lacked potty training—I was stomping the handle when Wę unstrapped their helmet and lowered their mask. Nothing underneath. I stared down their neck hole at emptiness, the smell of cobwebs.

Over a year and change I'd seen pandemics, wildfires, and white supremacist coups. A sentient suit of armor—the breaking of the fifth or sixth seal, I'm losing track—made no less sense to me than going from the first black president to a man-baby with cotton candy hair. We took Wę to lunch at the Mexican joint down the street.

"I knew there was something different about you," Sean smiled, noshing a quesadilla. "How'd you hear about us?"

"I was asleep," Wę recounted. "Then a voice in the dark told me, 'Go to the tournament.' I woke to find myself in a glass box. On the other side was a shrouded figure holding a great book, and from that book it read my name. Then it vanished. Discovering a spear in my hand, I smashed the box. I was in a room full of armor in boxes. That is no way to treat us," they huffed.

I grew excited at the potential divinity involved. "That figure you saw. Would you call it . . . the voice of God?"

"Sounds like Destiny from *Sandman*," Sean mumbled through beans and cheese.

"Can't be," I retorted, "'cause Destiny's fiction and God's real."

"My nigga! You gon' ask 'em how they speak English next? Let the magic happen."

First of all, Sean would defend his position to the point we'd spend our entire lunch arguing, and second, I wanted Wę to think well of me. So I changed the subject to Africa, to show off my knowledge. "You're sixteenth century," I told the armor. "Tell us about it."

During the fabled reign of Oba Esigie, Wę protected a member of the Village Regiment. Wę remembered their owner as a man of the earth, a yam farmer fallowing along the Niger, a gourmand who loved kola nuts, a storyteller ready with a proverb when his children went astray. Bliss colored Wę's days in a corner of their lord's house, observer to man's quiet desires.

But peace never lasted. Wę witnessed fields aflame; thundering hooves and horses pinioned with arrows; shattered spears and blood-mouthed hyenas; savannah heaped with dead in the shadows of circling vultures; acts of monstrosity and heroism. Between battles, when soldiers gathered at the fire to pass what each man knew could be his final night, their armor held council. Stained with blood, crusted in mire, disfigured from the blade, it fell on them to soothe one another with proverbs, and mourn those lost, in their impassive way.

First in the Igala War, then the campaigns against the Enogie of Udo, Wę's humble man proved exceptional at survival. Fight after fight, Wę observed him—*felt* him—outmaneuver men who yearned to live as surely as himself. And in the mud and screams, Wę protected him.

There were battles and sieges and sorties, including, Wę said with an even tone that shivered me, the raiding of smaller nations for slaves to sell to the Portuguese.

Like any child of Africa, I wanted to believe the motherland a utopia, damn the truth. It didn't help hearing the armor speak lovingly of a thug who'd consigned my people to Hell. "Did you ever think it was wrong?" I asked in a low voice, aware I sounded accusatory. "Slavery."

They answered, "All I thought to do was protect my lord. It was not my place to question men who never questioned the practice."

My anger would have me blaming a pile of hide, beads, and wool for the Middle Passage. May as well blame murder on a bullet. I choked my opinions back down.

Wę lowered their scarf to show the hole through the front and back of their beaded collar. It happened during a raid on Igboland; they recalled screaming, though they had no mouth, as the arrow spun closer. Despite years witnessing death, including women and children desecrated, the charred and blackened bones, the swollen throats and tumors, Wę had been a stranger to grief, unprepared to find themself in that black country where huts fell to ruin and crops blighted beneath a ceaseless wind called pain. Immobile, trampled, buried under bodies, filled with decay where love once stood. At length they found themself on a caravel to Lisbon, among African spoils tossed about like junk. Alone without purpose, they fell asleep.

"When I was fighting," they explained in a voice bright with wonder, "I was *moving* like my lord. It felt like he was there again."

"I lost my dad recently," I told them and, finding I had no appetite, pushed my half-eaten burrito to the center of the table.

Węʼs mask indented slightly where the mouth should have been. A kind gesture of condolence, I decided.

"I am sorry for your loss," said Wę. "And I am grateful to fight in your war games."

"The land where you used to live is called Nigeria now," Sean informed them. "You should visit. *After* the tournament. 'Cause you gon' win, my nigga."

I wondered: How on earth was a sentient suit of armor going to board a plane? Instead of elaborating on his novel idea, Sean told Wę about the weekend he and I first met at Otakon.

I was an undergrad at Ohio State when I drove from Columbus to Baltimore with my homeys, all of us obsessed with bushido. Raised on *Ninja Turtles, Street Fighter, Ronin Warriors, Mortal Kombat, DBZ,* and *Ninja Scroll,* we believed in the honor to be found in the simple, sacred practice of punching and kicking people who also like to punch and kick. Never mind I only made yellow belt at the Buckeye Dojo next to the Auntie Anne's in the mall.

At the time we loved *Naruto,* an anime we'd watch in the dorm, the experience made all the sweeter from the hours we'd spend waiting for the file to download. With its massive cast of ninjas seeking honor and destiny, we all had characters in the show we could relate to and, come the con, dress as. That weekend I was wearing the orange tracksuit of Naruto Uzumaki, a cheerful underdog whose journey to overcome his lowly status I connected with on a spiritual level. On the convention floor we chanced to meet the University of Cincinnati Anime Club and—destiny!—combined into a black nerd mega-clique.

Captivating was the gossipy, snobbish, dramatic, black-belt-in-shit-talk club treasurer Sean, or Shinji, he liked to be called. At no point did he formally introduce himself, mainly interested in pointing out "bandwagoners" in their "heinous" *Naruto* cosplays. I struggled to remember where I knew him from until it hit me:

Fan's View. At that time one of the few websites for anime fandom, the site was maintained by an older black man named Kevin who uploaded convention photos from across the country; the tiny boy in front of me, wearing his homemade cosplay with swagger, attended every Rust Belt con.

What a bitch. A beautiful bitch temperamentally at odds with the blue sandals, baggy black shorts, beige hoodie, black wig, and lavender contacts he wore as Hinata, the shy Hyuga clan heiress who secretly pined for Naruto. He was an Asian studies major who answered "Moshi moshi" when his mom called to check in. When he removed his wig to primp it, the hair underneath was permed into a dry, lumpy cone struggling to maintain straightness against a thousand defiant curls. I'd have dismissed him for a sorry Japanophile, were he not gorgeous. Though I'd my own list of merchandise to purchase in the dealer room, Sean said he was broke, so I bought him $150 worth of visual kei magazines and porn.

Like myself, Sean "shipped" Naruto and Hinata, which meant he believed in true love. I held his hand through the crowd. I shielded him from horny girls trying to hug him every five steps. When we went to lunch, I didn't think twice about lifting him on my back to protect his prissy, stupid, precious, baby-carrot-looking toes from the pavement.

Night rose from the irrepressible streets. Neither of us knew our way around Baltimore, and unlike some of our friends, for whom gang turf existed only in rap songs, we knew better than to explore. Children of Oshun, we kept to the harbor. An algae aroma hung thick upon the glittering waves. It was the kind of walk I'd dreamed of taking with someone, though not without altercation—"Fuck you and everybody who look like you," Sean said to some rando overheard besmirching his beloved cognac.

His fandom went *old* old school, *Star Blazers* and Captain Harlock, and, though I dismissed that stuff as '70s cheese full of square-jawed beefcakes making speeches about manhood, the passion with which he argued the mythic humanism in those samurai–spaghetti western–Horatio Hornblower space operas made me want to both rewatch them and slap him for saying I should stick to populist crap like *Cowboy Bebop*.

"You told me," I digressed, amused at the memory, "the episode, uh, one with the boy in the coma—"

"Episode twenty-three," he interrupted. "'Brain Scratch.' Boy sends his consciousness to the internet as a cult leader. Heaven's Gate–type douchebag."

"And you were mad at me—"

"I wasn't mad. Ol' acorn-headed dramatic-ass—"

"You said their critique about technology was superficial. And I said, 'I never thought about that.' And you said, 'That's 'cause you're not supposed to think about *Bebop*. You're just supposed to consume.' Talking about consumerism after I spent a hundred fifty—"

"Man, I was a little bitch! And youse a bitch, too, if you still crying 'bout that buck fitty when I done did pay you back. 'Sides, I like *Bebop*," he whispered after a rattling cough. "I had to grow up first. See, when we was kids, all the niggas wanted to be Spike Spiegel—"

"Then we get older and realize we're Jet Black." I grinned. "You right. The show didn't change. *We*—" Puckering then widening my lips on that particular pronoun was like a record scratch over my consciousness. Concerned we were leaving Wę out, I asked the armor their thoughts on the matter, to which they tilted their chin to the left, then to the right, then regarded us for several heartbeats.

"My lord used to discuss philosophy around the fire," they replied, not really answering the question but sounding, to me, satisfied.

The day Sean and I met concluded with us on the wharf,

staring at yachts, their prows outthrust like collagen lips on rich bitches displeased with the pinot. While Sean talked at length about *Battle Angel*, I grew embarrassed at the erection I sought to hide with my hips aimed away from his peripheral vision. Finally, grown impatient at my hesitation, he kissed me deferentially, his tongue tenacious, his breath like an ashtray. To kiss another man in downtown Baltimore had me terrified I'd be killed, true, but it didn't feel right, either.

"It's not you," I tried telling Sean before shame consumed us. But he wanted to save face. Called me closet case, down-low fag, pussy.

Why do I bring this up? Because Sean brought it up. There in the restaurant he told Wę 110 percent of our business. *Battle Angel*, water, kiss, everything.

"It's hard," he said, fighting the tremble in his voice, "when you think you connect with somebody. Then it's like, he just a straight boy trying to experiment. It ain't no big deal." Eyes glistening like honey, he looked over Wę's shoulder at the exit. "We grown-ass men now."

Wę nodded with sympathy. Sean shook his head, as if to throw off the last bit of hurt. "Now y'all sentimental niggas got me going," he said. "Let's get outta here. I need to watch some niggas get they ass whupped."

On our way back to the convention, while Sean and Wę chatted about fighting stances, I wondered if I should tell my friend the truth: that I'd never taken that night personally. Almost immediately I decided against it. In the end, a man had better things to do than stretch out the past like an old shirt too small for his gut.

An overwhelming smell of leather hung over the fighters waiting in line for us. Bystanders gathered to take photos. At the front of the line, a graybeard with a hawklike face and bald pate stood erect, callused palms on his hips. Cybernetic gadgets booped on his naked chest. His legs bulged with impressively taut muscle in red leather boots and matching pants. Also, he wore a spiked codpiece. Can't forget that.

"Cormac the Man-borg," he introduced himself in a martial voice. "Summoned at the Shroud's behest from my castle on Europa Seven, I have been called foremost to battle."

Who was I to argue, with him or his codpiece? But Sean said, "Slow your roll, OG. You can be first but the contest'll show if you foremost. Put your name down."

The old man unsheathed his broadsword with a sanctimonious ring. Up and down the blue steel, rainbows flashed. Rubies winked on the golden hilt from pommel to crosspiece.

Sean said, "What's that shit? A surrogate for that wrinkly, raccoon-tailed dick of yours? Mine's bigger. Now put your name on the board or step." Abashed, Cormac the Man-borg wrote his name. "And put on a mask!" Sean hollered at him. "We still in a pandemic, bruh."

Before I could flag a staffer and tell them one of the cosplayers was massively violating the rule saying no live steel, I found myself staring at a squat, sea-green, bowlegged goblin in a velvet doublet, smiling from both heads. As one, they called themselves Baron Twice di Twice.

I whispered to Sean, "That ain't no cosplayer."

"Grand prize is a fifty-dollar Red Lobster gift card," Sean informed the conjoined twins. "If you win, y'all gots ta split it. Write your name." As they did, Sean told me to relax. "We done been had a walking suit of armor, bruh."

Honestly, I'd been relaxed the whole time. Feeling obliged to show discomfort at our escalating situation, though uncertain for whom I performed this theater, I murmured in my throat, curious why I didn't fear the double-headed goblin already blending into the crowd. For the next several minutes, I watched Sean interact with sign-ups: Xentax the Great, a nine-foot-tall, eight-armed vermillion mech with extensive battle damage on its steel carapace; Dalra the bounty hunter, an elf, dusk-colored and silver-haired, her dented plate armor pinned with scalps; Ludwig von Bloodfang, a seven-foot-tall, nude, copper reptilian; robots, mutants, and djinni. All shared the same story of being summoned to the tourney by a shrouded entity. Enveloped in cacophonous odors, I reminded myself some of these folks had literally been woken from their tombs, a situation worthy of compassion, though I secretly envied Sean's olfactory limitations.

However fearsome their appearance, whatever distant soil they traveled from, Sean owned the ground he stood on. The phrase *real recognize real* came to mind.

The fifteenth sign-up wore a tattered black cloak over a suit of clanking mail. A cowl concealed their face but for the pair of fanged mouths where their eyes should have been. They stank like a marsh, and the hem of their bedraggled robe made a dismal wail over the carpet. They wore an armored band above their mouth-eyes, and, gripping a green marker in their gauntleted hand, wrote *Le Marquis d'Oblivion* in the most exquisite cursive I'd ever seen.

I was curious. "Is you that shrouded dude?"

"'Twas another," said the Marquis in a whisper like the sound of water thrown on a grease fire. "'Tis not they you should fear, but I. I am the architect of the Malnerean Genocide."

"And we grown men," Sean broke in. "When was this genocide?"

"Aeons before the birth of your galactic star."

Sean looked annoyed to hear his voice echoed back at him from under the Marquis's hood. Impatiently he said, "What have you done lately? Nothing. So quit wildin'."

It was like that moment in a concert film where they cut from the singer to some dude in the audience who's trying to sing along but doesn't know the words so he's just kind of slurring syllables to the beat and then he notices he's on camera right before they cut back to the singer. That level of embarrassment somehow emanated from the Marquis's unface. Nevertheless, the five banshees who made up his cheer section continued to sing in harsh, asymmetrical voices of the Malnerean Genocide, the Desecration of Arcturus, and other grave misdeeds.

Nobody had time for that. I left the table to speak to them. Their smell carried visions of temple ruins like broken teeth on a tundra, where the cold preserved rime-pearled lotus grown over magic mirror and shattered rune. Their jade tie-neck dresses had me craving madness and delight in their bosoms; ashamed to sexualize women for doing their jobs, I took a moment to collect myself. Then I told them, "I know y'all wanna hype your boy, but you doing too much."

The colorless women quieted their howling to a murmur. Wę took the sixteenth slot.

After that, you never heard so much bragging in your life. "I slew the Neryon Cyclops! Here is his eye!" "I outwitted the Saturnian Sphinx!" "I stole the Wand of the Witch-queen!" However boastful, the competitors seemed, to me, cordial sorts, happy to reminisce on old battles, no hard feelings to discover some of them had fought for opposing sides. It dawned on me that our visitors were centuries past their prime. Call it a senior tour of badasses. Just as this last chance for glory put them in a celebratory mood, Sean and I, our anticipated leisurely day changed into a genuine tournament arc, sang *Naruto* theme no. 2, "Haruka Kanata."

Wę searched the racks for a spear they liked best.

Close to the three o'clock start time, Ludwig von Bloodfang, the self-proclaimed *dread champion* of twenty intergalactic tournaments, was getting on Sean's last nerve nitpicking our rules. It hissed, "You're being noncompliant."

"Yo!" Sean yelled into the megaphone. "Whose manz is this?"

A persistent lizard, Ludwig. "The Rules of Altercation were agreed on by the Council of Xerxes in the year 1,000,501 B.A. Everyone knows this."

Sean yelled so loud the megaphone squeaked. "I need a smoke! LARP's closed!"

An objecting chorus rose from the fighters, whom Sean dismissed as he stomped off. Nothing for me to do but follow. Out on the street I watched him mangle open a Newport carton. Much as I wanted to comfort him, I hated this tantrum. "Bruh, don't take it personal—"

"A dragon-ass nigga!"

"I don't think he—it—is a dragon." Ludwig von Bloodfang had bragged of its genetic superiority as a sexless creature. "It spawned from a mutated dragon egg."

Flushed, Sean took one drag on the Newport and fell into a coughing fit. Doubled over, bracing his palm on the nearest window, he tossed the smoke away.

"A dragon-ass nigga," he rasped, "gon' tell a nigga how to run his tournament. I'm ready to fight that fool my damn self."

"Come on, bruh." I massaged him between his shoulder blades. "We gotta make new rules. The game is changed."

"I know something of this." After the shock from Wę's sudden appearance, I laughed at their wondrous stealth. Then I noticed the weather, Sean's irascibility being like his own private electron field momentarily heating the two of us; the chill through my jacket made me wish I had a quilted torso like Wę, who in their stillness looked, for once, like a museum piece.

"Perhaps I could be of help. If you find me worthy," Wę humbly amended. "Though this is my first tournament, I participated in many drills during the wars."

"My nigga!" I cried, thrilled at the prospect. "Help us write badass rules for badasses. Obviously you been in a fight befo—"

"And I haven't?" If Sean had been holding something breakable that moment, there'd have been shards around our feet. Grunting, he turned away, muttered to himself. This concerned me, at the same time Wę was switching their knees back and forth, gloved arms crossed in unconscious mimicry of my shivering. By the time Sean turned back to us, heavy-lidded pragmatism veiled his emotions. He told Wę, "We can't let them see you helping. They'll think we rigging the game. Who's gonna watch our equipment while we gone?"

This called for someone we could trust. Someone who would hate to disappoint me. Quickly I checked the schedule. Then, absent any better option, I made a show of teacherly hesitation so Sean wouldn't think less of me, otherwise I ran fast as my knees could manage to the *Promised Neverland* fan panel fortunately—or was it destiny?—scheduled that hour. I asked Aaliyah if she'd watch the LARP. She hesitated but agreed, the darling child.

Fifteen minutes later we pulled into Sean's driveway. It was four thirteen. Met with screaming from the feline horde on the porch, we were reluctant to get out the truck, and when we did the horde surged forth to hungrily headbutt our shins on our way to the door. Wę, intrigued at what appeared to them as miniature lions, picked up a tabby in their arms. Bastet's daughter jumped back to the lawn after leaving a three-inch scratch on Wę's helm.

Later, I was opening tuna cans while Sean sat at the table with a pen and pad. He had yet to write, even though he'd puffed from the teensy contraption that beefed up his neurons, or so he claimed. He said, "Let's rig the game."

"Excuse me?" Wę replied from the living room. They'd been exploring Sean's life: old-school hip-hop and show tunes on vinyl; video game systems; the flat-screen TV; framed Mardi Gras posters; color-coded liquor bottles on a stand; a tuffet with a double-sided lid flipped to the wooden part covered in leaves, pipes, lighters, grinders, papers, and tobacco. My mess. It occurred to me, if I was to act a slob, I should do it at my own home, but lately I'd felt estranged among the OSU students I called roommates. Two Bengalis and a Ghanaian, they saw me as merely their landlord, and much as I liked their scholarly preoccupations and cleanliness, around them I couldn't help but feel the generation gap. To distract Wę from the devastation my retirement had wrought upon the bungalow, I showed them photos from Sean's Japanese vacation four years ago, of he and his mom posed in fanny-packed exuberance before temples and kitsch.

At Sean's proposal, Wę eased to the doorway, where they stared on him, their gaze no less impactful for having no eyes.

"I said rig the game," Sean repeated. "Call fouls on niggas. Give you easy points. Cheat."

"That's dishonorable like shit," I told him.

"Are we following the Code of Bushido now? 'Bullshitto.' The samurai were barbarians. You're a good person," he told Wę, and punctuated his point with a toothsome, dour grin.

"As a warrior," said Wę, "I oppose such a proposal entirely."

"Did your lord ever rape anybody when he was wearing you?" Sean asked.

I popped off. "Wę ain't shown us nothing but respect, you corny lightskin—"

"No," Wę said. "Let him speak."

"That's how Africans roll these days," Sean said matter-of-factly.

"Go in a village. Kill the men. Rape the women. Make the children slave soldiers. I say we tell a different story. See, I'm black. On the Black Team. I want these motherfuckers to see our people triumphant and if that means cheating, so be it. My LARP," he concluded.

And Wę considered this! "*Gently draw the string of wealth,*" they proverbed. "My victory would inspire others."

"If y'all do this," I let them know, "I don't want no part in it."

"White folks ain't fought fair in four hundred years," Sean sighed.

Before I could argue, Wę said, "*No pocket is better than one with holes.*"

"That means losing is better'n a tainted victory!" I translated, bellowing to drown out the small, treacherous part of me saying Sean had a point. Pissed off as I was, I reminded myself he'd almost died. I took his hand. "I'm here, bruh. What's going on? You know ain't nothing but love with us."

Again he sighed. He started writing.

We put on Black Star, smoked, and brainstormed. Our goal: create rules that would prevent the combatants, given their drastically increased skill levels, from killing everyone in the convention center, if only by accident. Luckily for us, Wę had fought supernaturals during the wars, when it wasn't uncommon for a vampire or hyena-man to attack armies on the march. Their expertise helped us write new rules in half an hour. I could already picture Wę's epic clash with the Marquis.

After a time the armor grew silent. They waited for a pause in our verbal barrage before they spoke. "If it would make you feel better to give me some hel—"

"Ignore me!" Sean said, drawing hair on the Sailor Moon he was sketching, restless as the cats were before feeding. "You should know by now I talk some shit!"

Upon our return a crowd of hundreds scrambled for positions around the fighting square. Aaliyah, understandably annoyed at our lateness, informed us the fighters had treated her well; good to hear, else I'd have raised hell. Or at least given the offenders a stern talking-to, as I felt truly incapable of getting mad about anything. Maybe I was still a little stoned. Thrilled at Aaliyah's offer to stay and help, famished as well, I put in an order for two liters of Mr. Pibb, a bucket of chicken, and those hot Cheetos she liked.

Standing on his chair, speaking into the megaphone, Sean held the notepad close to his flamingo-pink eyes. "Hark, niggas! The new and improved rules are: you get pushed out of bounds, you lose. You are only allowed to use the weapons provided. There will be no powering up mid-fight. Period. Everyone must stay in their first form. These will be physical fights. Period. No magic or chi or chakra allowed—"

"What about nanobots?" asked someone in a digital accent.

"I will not dignify that with an answer. We want a fun, fair contest. Warriors!" he hollered. "Through dangers untold and hardships unnumbered, you have fought your way here to the LARP. We shall battle! They shall remember our names!"

Cheers clashed in the air. Sean roared like a moose before he crumpled into his seat, drenched in sweat. "King Kong ain't got shit on me," he concluded.

Notably, no regular people had signed up, for obvious reasons. I was reminded of the game room at every con—how anyone who wanted to play for fun barely got to touch the controllers thanks to those guys who did nothing in life but perfect their *Smash Bros.* skills bogarting the equipment.

"We need a second tourney for beginners," I told Sean.

"Why?"

"So they don't feel left out. We gotta pause and—"

"Look."

I followed the arc of his pointed finger around the sidelines, where those regular folk I was concerned for had their cell phones out. Ready for spectacle. Then I looked over the fighters and held my breath long enough to let the scene fill my lungs like zephyrs.

"You're good," Sean said, hugging my shoulders. Again, "You're good."

Every match began and ended with a show of respect between combatants. Before the thunderous crowd, under glamoured stars, foam weapons sang through the air, their boom on armor like a ceremonial drum, the Greater Columbus Convention Center less a terrestrial place than a coliseum promised at the end of time.

Midway through the opening match, Wę versus Cormac, words failed me. I cheered like Dad and I used to do watching boxing matches. I wept.

"Aww. Don't cry, Mister," said Aaliyah.

"These is thug tears."

"But you're not a thug."

True! I'd led a decent life, happy for it, never seeking danger for danger's sake, and for this I'd been rewarded many times over.

There were clever feints, powerful attacks, shows of speed and strength, none so efficient as the Marquis d'Oblivion who, armed with a foam rapier, performed a single strike to the heart that felled his opponent within seconds. His longest match came in semifinals against a djinn named Solomon, master of the scimitar, who struck five blows nearly too fast for the eye; standing in place, the Marquis wove a defensive pentagon before he moved, his blade a thread of moonlight. Solomon crumbled, screaming, at d'Oblivion's iron feet.

And I thought: *Cheap-ass fighter, spamming one move.*

My dopamine molecules swelling like sea monkeys in tap water, I couldn't focus on commentating duties. All the clever sports references and professional wrestling callbacks I'd planned on using escaped me. Aaliyah took over, megaphone in one hand, filming with the other. "He just did the Thing with the Thing!" was my favorite line. "Everybody make some noise!"

As referee, Sean enforced every rule, including a disqualification for which he shamed the combatant from the square, while paying attention to time limits and scorecards, to the point I wondered where he found the energy. I could see him doing this, if not across the galaxy, then running martial arts tournaments on Earth. Sweaty and exhilarated, he confessed to me between bouts, should this happen again, we should do it round robin instead of elimination. That word spread warmly through my chest. *We.*

And Wę! Watching them do their thing swept me in worship, the other spectators my congregation. We exploded with cheers when Wę's strength bested Cormac; nodded in enlightenment when their cunning defeated Ludwig von Bloodfang; and wept when Xentax the Great, who through foul play cut Wę's spear in two, yet was, in the end, unable to best their opponent, knelt before the Edo in forfeiture. Victory through virtue.

Casting aside the broken spear—would I have to pay for that?—Wę climbed on my table, to stand like a colossus over the crowd raising phones and hands, noisome until the armor hushed them with a gesture. They roared, "A spear! In the name of all that is good! It has been my mission to serve, yet the wailing of d'Oblivion's demon women has woken a flame in me." Their voice was like fire in the sky, with a touch of vanity that, as happened when someone loosed their ego for the first time, sounded a little silly. "Dark times and ancient evils wrought. I see the bodies of Malnerean children on the plains. I smell the dust from Arcturus, where flowers will never bloom. And though this is no battle to the death, sunshine is lighting the ruins of forgotten graves. In Olokun's name, a spear!"

D'Oblivion, whispering with his banshees on the other side of the square, paused to regard the challenger. His eye-teeth clacked voluptuously. Directly in the path of that gaze, I was confused at first from the cold, hard knot in my guts. It seemed I could fear again—not for myself, but for Wę, based on the many young people I'd seen grow overconfident before someone bigger and badder taught them a lesson.

Aaliyah was saying something. I snapped at her, "What?"

The sudden disdain in her eyes informed me in no uncertain terms that I was the oldest, uncoolest man alive. "It's Con Ops. They want to talk now. You welcome," and she dropped the walkie-talkie on the table.

In our excitement we certainly hadn't been keeping up with local news. Since morning the major story was that a suit of armor from the museum, part of a traveling exhibit, had been burglarized overnight. Radio wedged between my shoulder and ear, I tried to keep calm as the Con Ops director, sounding frantic enough for both of us, told me there were cops in her office asking about my tournament. Did I know this person was wearing stolen property?

"Did somebody snitch on us?" I asked in anger, both at the rat and the woman on the line. The "property" she spoke of had been stolen from Africa. But even as I snarled the words, I felt foolish, and worse, impotent. There was nothing I could do to a snitch.

"Have you been online?" she barked right back. "There's videos all over TikTok of this person fighting in your tournament. There's police here. They're coming," and she was gone.

I felt like the air around me was turned to water. All the world blurred and, barely able to walk through the crowd, everyone buzzing like hornets in anticipation, it was only through grabbing hold of them, each person a crutch, that I made my way to ringside, where Sean was smiling at how it all turned out. Urgently squeezing his arm, I told him the news. He didn't care, however; the annoyance on his face echoed that elfin boy who loved anime, who, if you bored him, let you know that pretty people had better things to do. "Let them bitches come," Sean said. "I got the greatest warriors in the galaxy around me. You okay, fam?" he asked, because at that moment I remembered cop murders were never clean. A bullet always missed, or hit a nonlethal area, two, three, four bullets, blood loss, sepsis. I ran.

Fear was an open palm slapping me through hall, stair, and escalator until I met a high brown wall. Doors would lead me deeper into flight, not save me from the men after my blood. Sprawled on a bench, I struggled to breathe, searching for happy endings in a fog of gunpowder and iron, when a familiar heady smell returned me to the present.

"You should go," I managed to say. Fresh cuts looked like lipstick kisses against Wę's scarlet surcoat, and, shamefully, my first thought was whether a judge would find me culpable for the damage. My second thought: How many people saw that very armor, right before a yoke went around their neck?

"I have my strategy from fighting Igala," Wę said in their heroic new voice, ignoring my plea. "Draw your enemy to your territory, pretend to give ground, make him deplete his strength and"—they laughed a bit too long—"you'll have to see. Now tell me why you fled before my match even started," they demanded with a combination of intrigue and betrayal.

I hated my eyes, and I hated the floor, for the fellowship they found in each other. "The police are here," I said to the warrior's boots. "To take you back to the museum. They think . . . I don't know . . . maybe they think I had something to do with it."

"You speak of these 'police' like an enemy army."

"You could say that," I stammered.

"Then we must kill them," the armor said pointedly.

"It ain't that simple."

They knelt before me. A shudder stole over me. "I wish to understand," urged the sexless voice behind the mask, not unkindly, but with humanlike urgency.

Stammering, I told them that, over time, slavery was abolished in the West, but America passed laws to make sure black people were never free. I told Wę the men who once hunted runaways became an army called the police, charged with terrorizing our communities and returning us to bondage. Often they got overzealous and killed us.

"There's a part of me saying go face them like a man," I confessed. "But there's a part telling me even if they don't shoot, they'll imprison me, and I need to get in my car and drive straight for Canada right now. It's . . . Nothing changes . . . Death . . . So many . . . Am I a man?" I wailed, a hopeless, violent cry that surged up my throat like vomit. Meanwhile, Wę listened in silence. At last I said, "You should go. Don't worry about me. I'll think of something."

At my further insistence they departed with a heavy gait unlike their strut from before. Time melted to a puddle. I thought of Aaliyah, glad she couldn't see me cower. Perhaps it was shame that brought me to my feet and carried me to the LARP, where, God willing, I'd find my dignity in front of the assassins. I held to that image of Aaliyah watching me with respect, whatever should happen, making my way through the goblin slayers, priestesses, and wizards, alert for black uniforms.

Near the LARP, I walked straight into a crowd gathered on the mezzanine, overlooking the entranceway, under the vaulted atrium ceiling. A hunch told me Wę was involved in this, and, awash in a cold feeling, I bullied through to the plexiglass rail. Below, a larger crowd circled a group of people and, before anything else, I spotted Aaliyah in the front, breathing heavily, but she had her phone out and aimed straight ahead, whatever might happen.

Four cops had their guns drawn on Wę. They shouted at the armor to put their hands up. I determined, in retrospect, that Wę must have intercepted the cops on their way to the tournament, to keep Sean and I from harm. From the sidelines, spectators put their hands behind their heads to show Wę how it was done. Gut clenched, I heard their desperation—we couldn't afford another tragedy. And still I wanted to see their rage. Why did they always stand there and film? Those cameras never stopped the cops. Throw something!

Slowly, confused by the unfamiliar action, Wę put up their hands as shown. After a quick deliberation, the bravest cop stepped forward to cuff this tall, armored person. Then, with guns aimed at their proud back, Wę strode to the door as if through Ubinu's gates, their awestruck spectators still like the sculptures in Oba Esigie's palace.

One step from the door, the proud bulwark of their shoulders became an apologetic hunch. Wę stumbled to the side, collapsed hard on their shoulder. I heard their helm ring across the floor. I couldn't see the cop pull down their mask, but, from the crowd, astonished noises flew up to sting my eyes. And so Wę lay where they fell, lifeless, a relic from a conquered nation.

Sean kicked over our table when he heard the news. His bronze eyes, filmed with tiredness from a long day, still beautiful, burned at me. "I should've been there."

"The fuck would you have done?" Him or any of us? My anger would have me walk outside, punch the first white man

I saw, drag his bloody carcass to Aaliyah, and say, "You either a warrior or a victim." That was the lesson I wanted her to learn.

Instead I watched her, fresh tears on her cheeks, hand a flower wreath to a banshee in accordance with Japanese tradition. They bowed to one another.

"The winner via forfeit," Sean intoned, dour as pig slop, "the Marquis d'Oblivion."

Such a disappointing end to several hours' diversion made the crowd applaud like they'd just witnessed a listless cover band. Not one of them knew what Sean and I had lost, our heritage caged. And for all I cared, the fighters gathered reverently around the square may as well have been daydreamers in costumes.

From behind d'Oblivion I watched the Marquis inspect, pinched between his middle and ring fingers, the Red Lobster gift card. Softly he said, "'Tis my prize? A piece of paper?"

Already on his way out the square, Sean wheeled at the arrogant voice. "You trade it for food, dog. Go get your women some cheddar biscuits."

I saw the card burn to cinders, and a chill blew over my bones. Sean sighed. "Runner-up gets the prize, then. Now get the hell on. Fake-ass wannabe Ringwraith."

One of the banshees ate the flowers. I heard Aaliyah call her a bitch right when something changed in d'Oblivion; whatever the transformation, I couldn't see, but it cast a cloud on Aaliyah's face, like in that instant her dreams had been swallowed in dark matter. A moment later she was behind me, digging her nails in my arms. I shielded her. Like cracking glass, the air around us shimmered. Whatever swelled against that membrane was indifferent and elemental, perhaps a demonic vanity, perhaps one of the rote annihilations we structure our lives around never acknowledging. The banshees sang something low and lonesome.

Part of me thought, should d'Oblivion wipe us out, maybe

that would be a blessing. No more jails. No more museums. But Sean stood and faced the Marquis across three yards of carpet, and I, against all logic, readied to attack while his back was turned.

Sean looked unimpressed. He said, "Nah."

It was then a small, hooded figure strode past me.

"Kid, are you stupid?" I cried. "Get back."

"You're good." The boy in the beige hoodie had a familiar whiny voice, like wasps complaining. Smooth as sand down a hill, he gave d'Oblivion the lightest touch on the back. At his unspoken command, the Marquis shambled behind the boy like a pet chimp, as did his banshees, their harsh song changed to a Sunday-morning hymnal. What a strange boy: he carried in his skinny elbow a massive leather tome and, as he moved between combatants, he would turn the page with a papery crash, from one decadent illustration to the next. Individually he touched mech, bounty hunter, and mercenary. Soon all twenty formed a circle around him, equidistant like signs of a new zodiac, obedient to a boy who'd spent his entire paycheck on that hoodie, as to accurately match the character.

At last he pulled down his hood to regard Sean, and I gasped because he looked exactly as he had on the harbor: the ninja who stole my heart. Wisdom doubled his beauty, in contrast to Sean, descended from the boy, rendered gormless as a newborn from his transcendent past. Then the boy escorted his host to whatever history, futurity, or postmortem awaited them.

What I would have told Aaliyah, had I time or eloquence, was that as a child I never saw myself in the stories I loved. The epics. Those tales that felt like they mattered. Boys like me, girls like her played the token, the help, the wisecracker who died first. Certainly not the hero.

More than a foreign art, anime was *not white,* precisely what I needed at the moment I discovered it. Not because I wished to be Japanese, but to find my best self. From vampire princesses, telekinetic bikers, lovelorn cyborgs, and space bounty hunters I learned dignity, courage, and fellowship until such time I knew my history. Until I saw the heroism in my friends. Until I learned the people I admired—my parents, their friends, people who provided for their kids and lived joyfully—*that* was an honorable life.

With the fighters departed, the crowd wandered off, save a few stragglers recalling what was, to them, a stunt show. They spoke of a Nazgul cosplayer who did a scary illusion, unsure whether that came before or after the guy who stole the African outfit did the "no head" trick.

Sean stared out the window. Chicken grease smell, stains like swamps under his armpits, tragic lungs, his heart an egg buried in topsoil. I came up next to him.

"No," he said. "Not a single answer. Just as lost as you. Not a clue. Don't even ask."

Below, cars with high beams on moved incautiously through the sludge. Nervously I asked, "You saw me, right? You saw me ready to stand with you?"

"Of course," said Sean. "I'm glad it didn't come to that."

An avalanche of pent-up aggression. "How many times? How many times did we watch *Dragon Ball Z,* screaming, 'Don't just stand there. Hit the nigga while he transforming!'"

"*I* didn't watch that garbage at all."

"I was about to—"

"And what if he got you? Why's everything gotta be a fight?" He stared at his own bleared reflection. When he spoke again, he sounded elsewhere. "No black folks were harmed in the making of this LARP."

Aaliyah and I brought the spoils from Wę's fallen opponents: Cormac the Man-borg's Radiant Sword; from Ludwig von Bloodfang, a pink rose that grew once a millennia on the tallest dune in the K'k'khan Desert, powerfully fragrant with the aromas of lost civilizations; from Xentax a paper ticket, densely packed with typewritten text and authorized with the stamp of one Lord Orion, to next week's launching of the Galactic Cruise Line. Underneath the ticket was a list of instructions as long as my arm detailing how to locate the hidden platform at New York's Penn Station. From there, a round-trip voyage to the quasars and all stops in between.

I claimed the sword. It only seemed right Sean take the ticket. After all, part of him already existed out there. He could be Lavender Star, Lord of the Tournament. Jupiter alone had ninety-five moons. Surely one could make him a home.

"You can have it," Sean told Aaliyah without a moment's thought.

She tried handing him the ticket, saying, "I'm still in school!"

"How old are you?" Sean questioned, holding the rose under his nose. She said she was fourteen. "Kids these days be following rules. You gon' age prematurely if you don't wild out every now and then. I wasn't going on no intergalactic trip at your age, but I was going to a five-dollar matinee at that theater in Over-the-Rhine with the holes in the seats to watch *Princess Mononoke* while trippin' on some old-ass Dexamyl. Wut'choo know 'bout that, youngblood? Hold up!" he said when she tried to speak. "Uncle Sean ain't done. Them seats was like watching a movie sitting on the john. Then I had a wino buy me Henn. I got home, my mama whup my ass. My uncle Leon took the Henn. Then at night I go downstairs to make a sammich and there's Uncle Leon playing that crying-ass old Marvin Sease record that skips during 'Ghetto Man' and he gon' let it skip 'cause he ain't getting off that couch for nothing and he drinking the Henn hisself. He goes, 'Look at'cha, wit'cha swishy lil ass. Looking like Prince on guv'mint cheese. Boy, get in here and finish this bottle with me.' I can do that, you can hitchhike to New York and catch a intergalactic cruise ship. 'Can't take off school,' she says. *Got*damn."

"It's scary," she moaned.

"You kids ain't known nothing your whole life but famine and despair!"

"Take both," she offered. I was proud of her. "I don't need anything."

"A nigga gotta be a broken rec—" Sean hollered before a coughing fit had him hacking into his fist. It went on for so long, I suspected he was exaggerating to shut her up. Between drafts of water, he rasped, "Take the ticket . . . and have fun."

Though she remained reticent, she forgot us when her friends arrived, a group of *Promised Neverland* cosplayers. She ran to them screaming, "Omigod! Look what I got!"

I heard that moment waltz through Sean's breath. For my part, I placed it in the warm, secret, many-windowed library where I kept my dad's Saturday game of Spades.

"Damn glad I ain't never had no kids," Sean said after a long sniff from the rose. "Bruh. I got cognac. Let's go pour one out for Wę."

And we did.

WEIRD BLACK GIRLS

Bostonians like to say their town, when no more than a straw-and-timber fishing colony along the verdant opal of the bay, was so pretty the moon wanted to give it a kiss. That had always been my favorite explanation for why, in 1702, the settlement and miles of land leading toward it rose like a finger pointing skyward to fix at a 45-degree angle above the earth, a monumental divorce of the planet from itself that left the surrounding lands rocky and uninhabitable for decades afterward. This phenomenon proved pivotal for the American Revolution when inaccessible Boston became a key base for colonial operations, as well as a rallying symbol for the Redcoats, who, notably proud of their sun-drenched empire, refused to let this ragtag army of tobacco farmers deny them the added tan of a city in the sky.

At first I mistook Boston for a patch of stubborn leaves shining greenly among the autumn maples as our Amtrak twisted through wooded acres, the rails screeching underfoot. I was twenty-five. You had been twenty for a month. Reclined in the seat across from you, I'd spent Friday morning in a mixed state of introspection, anxiety, and admiration for the cedar-shingled cabins, the deer cantering within russet leaves beyond our window. At half past eleven I was reading a captivatingly masturbatory *Rolling Stone* article written by some Brooklyn white woman about her heroin addiction and other self-made problems, when you said, "There it is!"

Excitedly I gazed out the window. That first glimpse of Boston did violence to the imagination; for several beats my brain denied the existence of what I clearly saw from a distance, stretching the length of my arm: a leaning pillar of metamorphic rock. Neighborhoods crept along the surface of America's highest city like gray-and-red fungi. I saw downtown skyscrapers shining like crystals, and, squinting, thought I could make out Fenway Park upholstered somewhere along the center of the incline. The Charles River extended for a mile or so off the ledge before turning to blue mist. With every passing moment, I grew to accept the wondrous calamity as a part of my universe, denial replaced by a gluttonous desire to stuff as much of it as I could down my insufficient eyeballs. My gaze rappelled down Boston's earthen flank to several hundred feet of dangling vegetation and mud. Then, gazing up to where the city disappeared in the clouds, I pictured ruinous, deoxygenated Cambridge, where eighteenth-century poets claimed angels soared through the bone-cracking cold. Where they said the city's ungravitied trash clustered until it gained sentience and went man-hunting. I imagined the hidden harbor with blazing lampposts to dispel the eternal shadow on the water, the vacuum-powered tubes that carried goods to the city.

You rose on your knees to take pictures with your Polaroid disposable. God, you looked cute. We shared awe and excitement, our hearts shredding a guitar solo as our minds, unmoored from thoughts of past or future, sang anticipation for the unknown.

You threw both hands over your heart. "It really *does* look like a penis!"

"I hear it's a fine upstanding city," I replied. "California had the Gold Rush. Massachusetts had the blood rush."

The best joke I could manage on short notice. When you

refused to reward me, not even with annoyance, I pressed on. "I heard the witch Annalee used sex magic to make the earth orgasm. Then it just stuck that way."

"Everything's sex with you," you replied, pissing me off at your blatant falsehood. Had I not been a gentleman? Had I not asked *May I* every step of the way?

But you had taught me that girls, afraid to be thought unequal partners, liked to play games with their lovers. I forgave you since I understood your reasons, however disappointing. Empathy looked better on you than insecure bullying.

"I'm talking sex magic," I retorted. "A black tradition. Look up Obeah."

"I had an aunt my family thought was a witch," you mused, tilting at your waist to snap an angled picture. "It turned out she had a mental illness."

I laughed out loud, a touch theatrical. "When was this? The fifties?"

"Nuh-uh! This was recent!" you said in fake indignation that made your soft, high voice nearly squeak. I adored that voice. To me it was—more than shower water off a woman's shoulders, or the liquid black eyes of a doe, or a pair of feet squeezed into pumps and elevated off the earth—the most feminine thing I'd ever encountered. On the other hand, your words concerned me. Here we were, interesting, educated people on an adventure. The reminder that you descended from sexist, superstitious, sweet-mother-Mary-I-*do*-believe-in-spirits bog standard black folks was a bad portent. It made me want to talk more on the subject, to hear you renounce your family's beliefs, but since I didn't want to upset you, I said nothing.

I hadn't always been passive. Back in third grade, my parents sent me to a suburban Catholic school where I grew sick of the racist, unexceptional white kids and fanatical teachers. To get expelled, I concocted and executed a plan wherein, during the Christmas pageant, in which I donned a shiny metallic poncho as one of the stars standing against the curtain—not even the Star of Bethlehem, that had been a first grader named Evanee who'd grow up to serve time in Muncy for impersonating a tax collector—I stuck my hand down my crotch and yawned loudly for the entire hour. For some reason the nuns didn't hook me offstage, let alone expel me, so I suppose you could call my mission a failure, but I found it hard to reconcile that confidently sinister child with the man I'd become. Just the other day I'd called out a barista for giving me incorrect change, the rush of accomplishment I felt when he slipped that dollar bill into my palm either encouraging or humiliating—I hadn't decided yet. Someday, I hoped, when bravery came easier, such moments would feel less special; after all, I'd had the courage to woo you.

You were weird. Gloriously weird. Not *quirky*, as some called you; that's a nice word for dumb. You were a soft-spoken, lighthearted black girl into *giallo* horror and mysticism, who texted me at one in the morning to let me know you were tripping Robitussin with your white-girl roommates, prone to awkward rambling and sardonic asides that sounded innocent from your lips. That morning you'd gone on about the Devil. How fascinating, you had said, that he collects souls through backdoor deals and yet can possess people, as well. You thought it was kind of sexy he rebelled against God—*Blasphemy!*—before quietly admitting you didn't believe in Heaven or Hell—*Sweet Baby Jesus! That girl must think she white!* Though I'd have loved to discuss Baphomet's various incarnations all the way to Boston, you had such trouble maintaining conversation that you went quiet, in the way that a desert was sometimes quiet. I supposed this made sense—a two-day ride in the pinnacle of transcontinental luxury travel would exhaust anyone's verbosity.

And yet the longer you dwelled in silence, unease twisted my guts: your coming on this trip, which I'd proposed midsummer at the height of our courtship, made no sense. You'd slipped me the note at the last staff meeting, as our supervisor gushed over another successful summer of beautifying Braddock. *I'd still like to go to Boston.* Not a month since you'd dumped me outside the Cathedral of Learning, neither sadness nor anger on your golden-brown face; the aura of romance hung over this weekend in a way that felt potentially disastrous.

But anything was possible with positive thinking. The most logical explanation had to have been, perhaps subliminally, to the point you yourself were unaware, that you still wanted me. And I still wanted to take you somewhere special, somewhere neither of us had been before, and make it *our* place. We would get back together. I could feel it.

After a few more pictures you settled back in your seat, and immediately resumed work on the *New York Times* crossword. Pretending to read the awful magazine article, I studied you across the table littered in empty Rold Gold bags. Watched your intelligent fingers go back and forth over each precise, ruler-straight letter to carve your ink in the newsprint. You wore shapeless gray sweatpants, pink woolen socks, and a royal-blue Pitt sweatshirt I'd intentionally left on your bedroom floor weeks before; it had given me pleasure to think of you slipping it on when no one was watching. Presently the sweatshirt, which should have flattered your curves like most clothing did, puddled around you in bulky folds that made you look fat and ordinary. You sat curled at the corner of the seat, your afro smashed against the window. I remembered the textures—wooly up top, coarse in the middle, the base of your skull sown with calligraphic spirals soft like a rabbit's fur—and could feel those textures in my fingertips, a phantom reflex.

I pictured us in the Boston Library stacks: saw myself lifting your short skirt to take you from behind as you bit down on your lip, trying not to scream, your fingers splayed over the leather-bound Chaucer. Imagined you pregnant, your breasts hanging huge and trapezoidal on either side of your belly. Pictured your linea nigra like the shadow of a fir tree and your nipples the size of tea saucers. Surrendering to illusion, I flashed forward to bulkier, ball-capped, bearded, manlier me pushing our giggling daughter on a swing, in the park where you'd first proposed we make love. In my fantasy you were watching me from a bench, smiling with tired fondness, pregnant with our second child.

This fertile shade superimposed on the reality of you filled me with painful longing, so, to distract myself, I recalled a chinless streetwalker I'd picked up on Penn Avenue, whom I told frankly I only had a twenty, the look on her face appealingly dolorous as, bracing her black-sneakered feet on either side of the driver seat, she lowered herself onto me.

An unexpected flick of your eyes and you caught me watching you. Reflexively I smiled. Funny thing about eyes—no pair moves any faster than another. Yours were long and angled down at the tails. Almost diamond-shaped. Though I knew your ethnicity (black mother, Mohawk father) those eyes lent your features a wonderful glow of diasporic possibility.

"What's on your mind?" I asked.

"The crossword. I'm doing really well."

"Did they teach you about the Rupture in school?"

"Mm-hmm. Yeah. We had a Rupture pageant. It was kind of like a second Thanksgiving play in April because we had to dress up like Puritans. Yeah. And everybody had to go up and say who they were. And the music teacher made up this song to the tune of 'Stayin' Alive.'"

"How'd it go?"

Momentarily remembrance made your brow crease like a well-read book. Then you sang: "*Well, you can tell by the way I do my hair / I'm a Puritan, up in the air.* Um. *It's all right, it's okay / Boston was flat yesterday.*" Amusement tugged the corners of your lips. I was reminded, though you smiled often enough, you rarely laughed. Laughter was a surprised reflex, and it seemed little caught you flat-footed. "Mm-hmm. Yeah. I was excited because I got cast as Annalee—"

"The black witch? Are you kidding?"

"Ahem. The *accused* witch," you stated, calmly peevish. "My mom got mad about that. She, um, said I was being typecast. She complained to the principal, and I got recast as a rock."

"Better a rock than a slave who got set on fire."

"They didn't teach us that part."

"We didn't do a pageant. In art they gave us clay and little Monopoly houses and we had to design our own Bostons. And I went to Catholic school, so we were taught it was a miracle from God. Like, he raised the earth and killed a thousand people in order to make Boston better."

"We really didn't learn much about the Rupture," you said without emotion.

Since the moment seemingly called for laughter, I chuckled. "You weren't told it happened on the day of a mass genocide?"

"They told us the Puritans gathered the Native Americans for a party!"

I threw a hand over my face. "Fuck this country."

"I heard Annalee caused the Rupture with voodoo magic," you remarked, "*not* sex magic. And I like to think she got away." You chose that spot to end the conversation. A minute later you asked, "Do you want to do the crossword?"

I saw you'd completed half of it already. Anxious you might judge me for a pedant, I flipped to the front page for a glance at the headline. Obama was drone-bombing Middle Easterners. How very black of him. Since college I'd been proudly far left with plenty protest cred—Food Not Bombs, Iraq, Abu Ghraib, School of the Americas, Oscar Grant—and still hoped to play my part in creating a better world, after I'd recharged my batteries in a nice, long break from tear gas.

You rolled a pen across the table to me. "Here's the Bic. Ha," you droned. "Wasn't there a girl in your group named Bic?"

"Her name was Biqaela. Bic was her *nickname*. You thought somebody named their kid Bic? I know black people give our kids funny names"—aware I sounded patronizing, I softened my tone—"so I see how you might think Bic was her name."

"I never said I thought that was her real name," you argued, peevish again.

"Bic hated me at the end."

"What did you do to her?"

"I docked her pay. Girl was a shit worker. Girl kept saying she had anemia as an excuse to sit on the curb and not work. We're planting and she's just talking with that other girl."

"It sounds like she made you angry," you teased.

"I tried to be a nice guy, and I let her shit slide too much. It's crazy, too, 'cause she was the one with a kid. But when I messed with her money, she threw a hissy fit like a teenager."

"I think she *is* a teenager."

So were you when we started dating, as good a reason as any for this tedious and strangely touching show of respect for your peer. I remembered Biqaela—cinnamon complexion, dimples, and gorgeous tits. She wore tight T-shirts, gym shorts, leggings, and expensive-looking sneakers. The endearingly ditzy eighteen-year-old had slept through her interview for a counselor position and thus had to spend a fourth straight summer working one of the gardening teams. Every day she'd come into the flower patch with a carefree saunter. Flirtatious with staff and coworkers, always joking that she worked outside in order to tan and not be so light, wearing her cheerful vacuity like a panther wears fur. Until she forced my hand, I'd forgiven her laziness because I found her charming. The type of girl my dad warned me to keep at a distance when I took the job: cute hood-rats who saw men as sperm banks and babies as welfare checks. She already had a toddler with some nigga called Murda, which I'm sure worked out great for her.

"Those girls are fast," Dad had said. "They'll see somebody like you with a college degree and think they can get some money."

"Nobody would ever call a boy *fast*," I told him archly. We'd been sitting at the kitchen table in his apartment, drinking McDonald's coffee.

"They *are* fast." He stared at me over his reading glasses, signaling he wanted this information plugged into my brain. "And they choose to be that way. That's how we get babies having babies."

"*Babies having babies* is an outdated term. Black people live shorter lives, so we have kids earlier. That's basic evolution."

He grumbled in reply. During my childhood he'd shown nothing but contempt for women, having never forgiven my mother for divorcing him. However, like most passions in life, his misogyny had cooled over the years into scorn and helpless fear.

Thinking back to that conversation, how I'd submissively changed the subject to avoid hearing him spout the same old backwoods shit, I grew combative. I told you, "I'm not Malik. Didn't you say that's who I reminded you of? Malik would have let Bic's shit slide."

"You don't remind me of him anymore," you agreed after a hesitation. "You did. Physically. You ended up not really like him at all!"

We meant Malik from *The Real World* season 10. Oh, that season! My favorite because it had a trio of black cast members instead of the token individual. This being Hollywood, all were biracial and, hate to say it, cramming lightskins into one space started an unofficial competition over who could act blackest. They took on identities: your boy Malik, the smoked-out Bay Area boho; Coral the self-righteous Afrocentrist; hoodrat Nicole. Instead of one black person getting butchered by the editors into a belligerent, oversexed stereotype while their soul got cannibalized by their sociopathic white roommates—the virginal midwestern airhead, the boy-crazy bimbo, the condescending Republican, and the guy who became a WWE wrestler—*three* blacks got to have what amounted to a group meltdown on camera. I liked the season because it felt realistic. I think that's why you liked it, too.

"So you dated me because you thought I looked like Malik?" I prodded. "I know I have an afro, but I'm not some hippie."

"Yeah. It was surprising to learn you kind of hate white people," you muttered.

"You can't deny systemic racism. Can you really say—"

"No," you interrupted before I could escalate from Martin to Malcolm. "I don't want to talk about race." After dismissal, digression. "What are we doing in Boston?"

"We'll meet up with Matt and put our stuff in his apartment."

"After that?"

"Play it by ear."

"Sounds *goo-oo-ood*," you replied in a birdlike singsong. You probably considered my anger at white supremacy reverse racism. No doubt at Chatham you learned all kinds of intersectionality bullshit from white women who secretly hated you. Something about your sarcasm at that moment came off genuinely hostile, your antagonism stained in fear and confusion, like rust on an ax left in the rain.

Or perhaps you were just being a girl. Whatever your reason, the ignorance behind your brattiness made me feel tender toward you. To allow you space, I left for the café car. I asked if you wanted anything. You said no thanks. On my way down the aisle I saw humans of every stripe reading, typing, sleeping, or snacking. Fortunately their preoccupations kept them from noticing me paused at the steel door, watching your afro roll back and forth like a balloon losing helium, my love for you a beetle army scuttling up from my guts and out through my chest.

The only other traveler in the café was a small, ferocious woman alone at her table, shoulders hunched, blurry eyes and dogmatic nose aimed dead center at her laptop screen. She wore glasses, a fleece vest, long-sleeved shirt, jeans, and hiking shoes all colored the same dark brown. Woodsy Joyce Carol Oates massaged her cheek with her middle finger. Her other hand squeezed the cordless mouse she would, every minute or so, give a thunderous click. The copious hair pinned back from her sallow, efficient forehead was the color of campfire ash. Even as I ordered peanuts at the bar, I watched her, certain she'd been working all night, one foot in dream yet devoted to her task, which struck me as a beautiful thing.

"Thank you, brother," said the aproned server behind the bar, a tall, blue-eyed mulatto too handsome by half for the job, as he handed me the ten-dollar bag of Planters. I felt annoyed, because we both knew full well he wasn't so casual with the white folks. I should have made the punk call me *sir*. At a table I swallowed peanuts greedily.

I wondered if you'd come to Boston on impulse, unable to control the affection you still bore me, but hoping that in Massachusetts you might grab your blue heart barehanded like a trout from the stream, to have it in your power at last. Did you seek adventure? Or, on a darker note, did you travel six hundred miles to keep me in your thrall, pandering to your whim, even though you were sick of me? Faced with the possibility of a very unpleasant weekend, I wanted to march back and ask your true reason. But I was afraid.

I remembered, at the start of summer—before we met, you a watchful presence at training, dressed in an ingratiating pink skirt suit—I let a friend visiting from Maryland crash on Dad's couch. There'd been awkwardness that night, my proposal that we finally start dating met with a curt reaction confirming my suspicions, that all this time she'd thought of me, at best, as her gay black confidant like Meshach Taylor in *Mannequin*, at worst, an honorary white woman no different from her other girlfriends. Anyway. Next morning Dad stepped out of his room to find us at the kitchen table in our pre-coffee doldrums. He made chivalrous noises and then retreated to his room, where he stayed till she was gone. Later, he told me, in a voice full of Georgia and death, that I should be careful around their kind.

His cornpone terror made me want to bring one over every night. Not just any daughters of Aryas, I'm talking the most brain-dead snow bunnies I could find fogging up the dive bars with their booze sweat. Fun to think about, but I would never do such a cruel thing. I loved my dad. Besides, I'd sworn off white women after the Bay, burned out on bohemians: insecure, racist, self-destructive narcissists, each worse than the last. What I needed, I told myself, was a woman from the tribe.

Do you understand? I manifested you in my life.

On a notepad I wrote everything I wished to tell you. I wrote the rhymes you put inside me, the sadnesses you engineered. Hopefully in Boston we'd reconcile organically, even if part of me wanted to read you my words, so there'd be no doubt I admired you.

As I started on the eighth page, an irregular shadow fell

over me. She was a hawk-faced woman somewhere between her forties and sixties, fair-complexioned in a teal blouse and capri jeans. Her barely perceptible lips crooked in a smile that I returned twofold.

Before I could say hello, I was shocked into silence by the hippo-cat in her arms. The photos in books didn't do his ugliness justice. Moaning and snuffling, the size of a pig, he—as he let me know with an assertive twitch of his jet-black sausage—laid his white-furred belly in the crook of her elbow, four stubby hoofed legs dangling. Tufts of matted yellow fur emerged from the holes of the pink jacket she'd dressed him in. Other than pointed ears, his long face looked more hippo than cat, his muzzle shaped like a sack of manure, amygdaloid eyes black as charcoal. His maw cracked open to moo at me, his teeth like four dull hatchet blades, a show of prehistoric threat that made my spine go stiff and my bladder loosen somewhat.

"Shush," the woman told it fondly. Supposedly the creatures infested Cambridge, the offspring of a strange genetic pairing some years after the Rupture. The woman looked ready to adopt me, as well.

"Were you writing for yourself, or working on homework?" she asked.

Blood rushed to my cheeks. She thought I was a student! Mistaken for someone with a plan, I answered, "Myself. I'm a teacher," I elaborated; true, though I felt like a liar.

The concept of a black male teacher seemed to switch her brain off, since she neither spoke nor blinked for five seconds. Her patronizing should have angered me. But it didn't.

A petulant moo from her hippo-cat startled her back to reality. "How sweet," she said. "Well, keep working hard," and shuffled off in her tangerine Crocs to assail the mulatto with her pet's dietary specifications. Time passed before I realized, not only had I been smiling like an idiot from her attention, I'd been, under the table, pressing the heel of my palm against my crotch. Instinct combined with sexual frustration. You know I didn't want to fuck that lady. Come on. She was old enough to be my mom.

The world was browning, sleeping. I fantasized stepping off the platform into one of those bucolic New England hamlets and into another life. We could raise bees. Tap trees for syrup. Open a wooden knickknack shop.

At half past twelve I returned to my seat, but had trouble getting comfortable. I'd been putting on weight in my lower body. It had been a shocking revelation to see myself in the mirror with a sagging ass and thighs taking on a cylindrical shape. However I turned my knees, the dough on my inner thighs went in the opposite direction. For once grateful that the crossword had your attention, I crossed my khaki legs to sit on top of the seat, my ass a tuffet.

Before long the train ascended through stark blue-collar suburbs. Gravity pulled me down and my guts seized up. We traveled the top knuckle of the finger like a caterpillar up a leaf. For a minute I got to gawk out the window at the woods we had left, a pagan dream dispelled when warehouses and strip malls obstructed my view.

Unfolding a map across my knees, I followed our passage through towns forced into a linear pattern by the Rupture. Brookline, Quincy, Charlestown, Dorchester, South End. Then came a point when the earth to either side of us vanished, and the train slowed to climb a sharply angled suspension bridge. Outside and below, clouds frothed in what was, as far as I could tell, an abyss. To check my terror, I watched your pensive beauty until we made it across.

The conductor announced South Station. In a frenzy, we grabbed our luggage from the overhead rack.

The train hissed to a stop. We exited the platform into the mud-thick throng in the neoclassical relic, where white light through windows set high around the walls illuminated all the fast food, coffee, and pastries late capitalism had to offer, yet at the same time old-fashioned clocks above certain entryways set my heart to a winsome, Victorian pace. Hearing so many different languages had me feeling worldly.

At the ticket machine we decided on weekend passes for the T. As we studied the instructions, your hand slipped down your thigh and our knuckles grazed. I pulled away like I'd been stung.

"It's not awkward for you?" I asked. "Us breaking up and going on a trip?"

"Huh?" you exclaimed, as if startled. "Is it awkward? It doesn't have to be. We were on a thirteen-hour train ride. I would have said something if it was."

I didn't know how to answer that. All I knew was, were you to show me affection, I wanted it to be irrefutable, without a chance for accidents or misconstruction. We bought passes and retrieved our change. The dainty plinks as you dropped Sacajawea coins, one by one, into your pocketbook sounded nervous and sweet. It was one p.m. and our host, my old college chum Matt, didn't get off work till three.

We exited the station to the busy intersection of Atlantic and Three Sisters. Since the build of the city made an underground subway impossible, Boston had a light rail made of silver cars that roared above like rockets across a Golden Age science fiction book cover. Nearby a hustler sold Red Sox gear: he waved a shirt that said FUCK THE YANKEES, in place of the letter U a photo of Boston itself, a titanic middle finger. I chuckled at this. Also amusing was how you shuffled like a duck or church lady, with your high butt and wide feet, both hands around your suitcase handle, an awkward gait I was convinced you exaggerated for comedy.

I would have liked to shower, worried the high-altitude chill would freeze the dead skin in my scalp and crevices, clammy as rice pudding and undoubtedly putrid-smelling. The raw air shriveled my lips, clutched my throat, turned the skin on my knuckles to white scales. And yet the red-brick buildings packed in narrow streets filled my glass with fugitive delight: the need to explore until we chanced upon a place, anyplace, we might find comfort or distraction. These heritage homes, meetinghouses, and Tory estates had been part of Charlestown before the Rupture tossed them like flapjacks. Gray brick at the foundations of the florid Puritan elders marked where they'd been repaired.

Your silence forced me to try to ease the tension with observations. "Oh! A living statue!" Or, "They actually speak with the accent!" Or, "There's so many Dunkin' Donuts!"

"I wonder why that is," you replied. And, "I'm hungry."

"Hi, Hungry."

I suggested an artisanal burrito shop. Inside, I decided on the sushi burrito, you the bibimbap burrito. I offered to pay for our food and you let me. The cashier was a bronze-skinned girl in a pink hijab. If a marshmallow could become a person, it would have been her. Finding her blandness attractive, I smiled for her to no reaction. Ours was a red plastic table shaped like a nail driven into a board with one blow. The restaurant was a spacious, soulless gentrification abyss whose pastels and smooth edges made us agitated, gorging down our postcolonial burritos like a pair of troughing pigs.

We wandered to Haymarket. What they displayed in white-roofed stalls reflected that salvaged quality of a city that remade itself after being torn asunder. We saw trout that over the centuries evolved to breathe oxygen and travel on spindly legs, who tried like crickets to leap free from their tethers. We sampled a spicy chowder made from the edible Dorchester soil. We saw model sailing ships that glowed from within with bostonium. We tried on a local company's sneakers, crafted with lead in the soles to resist gravitational shifts. We explored a greenhouse filled with potted anemones. We swooned from an explosively sweet orange melon called deathdrake, which, the legends said, first grew from the corpses that littered Ruptured Boston, and it was for that reason that it resembled a small human in shape.

Like all New Englanders, Bostonians took pride in their ancestors' perversities. We saw cruel pillories where the condemned suffered under the sun, the gallows where the unfortunate took that trapdoor to oblivion. Though I hated such things, I appreciated them as evidence of the past. Before long we entered King's Chapel Burying Ground. Knowing Hester Prynne lay interred neither there nor anywhere, I nevertheless looked for her among tombstones furred in green-and-yellow moss. Of people who had lived, I found John Davenport, John Winthrop, and Elizabeth Pain. Certain names I recognized from the Rupture: the Arch-Inquisitor of Cambridge William Buttle; the famed executioner and madman Solomon Whitstone; Abe Cleveland, the slave notoriously denied his freedom after helping survivors from the rubble; the tomb of Mary, Sarah, and Emily Pureheart, the first victims of the calamity, crushed by a stone that fell from the church towers; at the western perimeter of the cemetery stood a chillingly long tomb dedicated to the anonymous dead, victims of both the Rupture and the lawless days that followed.

Submerged in the grass near the wrought-iron gates stood a bronze plaque that depicted "angeling," a unique form of stoning from the post-Rupture period. Using my suitcase for a seat, I silently read the inscription detailing the barbaric practice:

marched to Cambridge, that town of rogue physics, the condemned was booted off a ledge to float in the sky. From there the dour Protestants would toss rocks at the victim, who could see every projectile wobble in slow motion before implacable gravity brought stone to skin. Organs pulped, bones snapped, the victim was left floating in a death suit.

This fascinated me and should have fascinated you, given your tastes. But you made a point to act bored. I wanted you to tell me you were disgusted. I wanted you to say you hated this and ask to leave. So, feeling vengeful, I read the description aloud.

"That's pretty terrible," you woodenly replied.

"You're into Italian sleaze. *Cannibal Holocaust* and *Salo* and all that."

"I like those movies. Not in real life," and you patted sweat from your forehead with a napkin. "I am *soooo* tired. When I see a bed, I'm just gonna sleep for a million years."

"Want me to give you a piggyback ride?" I asked, half joking.

"I think I'm too heavy."

"I mean"—I paused to consider your feelings—"I know you're not supposed to ask a woman's weight."

"That's right. You're not."

"What're you? One forty?"

"You're not supposed to *guess*, either!"

I told you about the three days I spent in jail for protesting the Iraq War. After singing a verse from Prince's "Glam Slam," I switched to horny '90s R&B songs, at which you reminded me one of the guys from Jodeci raped a woman. Seeing annoyance could get a rise from you, I sang R. Kelly, "Bump n' Grind," the dumbest and raunchiest tune I knew.

"Stop it," you said.

It dawned on me I should have asked Matt to leave us a key by the door. Here I was dragging you around downtown like a fool. I asked a polo-shirted guide if she knew a place to kill time. She said St. Mary's had nice shops. "C'mon!" I told you. "We'll go see some rich people!"

My words came out sounding eager, idiotically so, though I secretly *did* enjoy pretty things. We walked seven blocks. St. Mary's did, indeed, look chic. While we checked out crystals in a Wicca shop window, you said, "This feels like the Great Depression. Like we're urchins staring at sausages."

"Poverty! It's hard being a black-ass man."

"It's hard being a black-ass woman. Everybody looks at you like a sex object," you elaborated after a reluctant pause.

"I don't think of you as an object."

"Thanks."

"You're a *person* to me. A sex person."

What an absolute idiot I was. But my annoyance at your mood had me feeling cruel, and I had to wonder, since you didn't seem overly upset at my bad joke, if somehow I was getting through to you. Hard to tell from the silence between us.

I got a text. "It's Matt. He's home."

"Thank god," you said.

On the bus ride to Jamaica Plain, you slept in the seat across from me, arms folded over your suitcase with your head down. You didn't look out of place among Ethiopian women who flittered on and off the bus like angels in pastel dresses and headscarves, but you came from the Rust Belt like me. A late-in-life miracle baby, daughter of a postal worker and a cop, a slit in your mother's belly your entrance to this strange world.

When you'd told me this, I remember saying, "Giving birth is crazy. I'm glad I don't have to do that."

"I'm glad I also don't have to do that" was your reply.

Your father existed as a hasty signature on a child-support check, occasionally glimpsed driving his squad car down weedy alleys between weather-beaten bungalows. One part absentee dad, one part oppressor, you had mentioned him twice to me, both times without emotion, like you wanted to keep your rage to yourself. On the other hand, I knew the black side of your family were good people, because I'd met your church-lady aunt in Wilkinsburg and adorably irritating little cousin. From what you told me about your mom, she'd sacrificed for her little miracle to have the go-out-and-play-back-by-seven-shooting-tin-cans-off-the-neighbor-boy's-fence West Virginia upbringing that had always sounded mythical to me.

Matt lived in a narrow, coffin-shaped apartment building. His voice sounded hollow and androgynous through the intercom: "I'm at the end of the hall." He buzzed us in. We walked a passage pasted in moldy floral paper that reminded me of cheap gift wrapping. His was the last door on the right, cracked open for us. I greeted him with a tight hug. He was tall, thin, and amiably handsome, his small-featured face crowned with brown curls starting to thin at the top. It had been four years. You introduced yourself with a hug that, for all this being your first meeting, showed plenty affection.

The apartment consisted of a combined bedroom and kitchenette, a hiccup of a bathroom, and a single window that opened to an alley. The clock radio in the nightstand said 3:16 p.m. Immediately you went into the bathroom to shower. I opened my backpack on the folded-out futon and unpacked toothpaste, toothbrush, soap and baggy of hotel shampoos, my shirts and cotton briefs. Matt grabbed two PBRs from the fridge and we caught up.

He worked reception at a law firm in Beacon Hill, a job he neither loved nor hated. Gave him plenty of time to check Facebook, he said. But it was his stepping stone to a career in human-rights law. Seeing as we were competing over which of us had found the worse layover in our flight from College to Life, I told him I'd been working three weeks at the Hudson News in Pittsburgh Airport. Straitjacketed in a blue cotton polo, I would ring up trail mix and Smartwater for travelers who stared right through me. Mostly I read tabloid stories about the tawdry divorce of a reality-TV couple with eight kids and the progress of Jennifer Aniston's eternal pregnancy. But I had a phone interview scheduled for tomorrow. Residential advisor at Pittsburgh Job Corps. Matt said good luck.

I could tell he enjoyed my company as much as I did his. Considering the boozing poltroon I'd been in college, that came as a relief. Matt suggested we meet at Whitman's later for beers with his girlfriend, Magali, a Brazilian woman who studied geology at Tufts.

Showered and dressed, you came out of the bathroom, your illustrious afro smelling of lavender. You wore a periwinkle tank top and pink cotton skirt hemmed several inches above your thick, insouciant knees. Your feet, besides being long and wide, were dense, thicker than your leather sandals with cowry shells on the uppers. The same outfit from our first date. With a nagging sense of loss, I admired your rounded brown limbs, your slightly protruding abdomen and full breasts.

In the middle of unpacking, you flung clothes and toiletries on the bed. You looked concerned. "I left my phone charger at home! Whatever shall I do?" You paced in a circle, making it a joke. "What oh, what oh, what shall I do?"

My charger wasn't compatible with your phone. This would be a problem because you got internet on yours. Mine was a basic flip phone.

"Can I give my mom your number?" you asked. "She, um, wants to be in touch."

I said yes. Matt gave us his number on the back of a receipt before handing over the spare keys, one to the apartment and the other the front door. "I'll sleep at Magali's," he said before he left. It occurred to me I hadn't told him we were no longer a couple.

For a time, you set about putting your things away, and it soothed me to hear your tuneless humming, your pointless comments to and about the furniture. A search of Matt's kitchen revealed his diet consisted of instant coffee, TV dinners, and canned beans. I smiled at that, and the squat IKEA particleboard bookshelf stuffed with law books, all so wonderfully bachelor-like. Inspecting the discarded carbohydrates burned into blackened, spiral-shaped corn dogs on his two oven skillets, I wanted to cook for you. Vegetable stir fry, white rice, mashed potatoes, a leafy salad with cashews, pinto beans, and fruit salad in a Valentine's Day–colored lump. The Pittsburgh Food Not Bombs Special, nothing groundbreaking, but served with love on a white tablecloth over Matt's plastic computer desk.

Lounged in an office chair, I asked, "Could you look up directions to the bar?"

"We should write it down," you replied. I produced a pen and pad from my pants pocket. You were condescending. "Oh, look at you."

"Get directions to the Singing Sands." We'd talked about going during the train ride. It sounded like the most magical place in the world: a beach where the crystalline sand whistled.

To my delight and surprise, you sat in my lap. Tapped away at your phone while sitting upright like an antenna. Prudently I touched your waist, kneading that endearing little fat roll. You gave me a peck on the lips.

"That wasn't weird?" I asked.

"A kiss is just a kiss." The way you said it sounded like a question. Or maybe I'd imagined that. Lying in bed we talked about nothing in particular until we fell asleep. In my dream, we went shopping for secondhand clothes in a nameless mountain town. It wasn't long before two white women talked trash to you. Thus instigated, you beat up them and their friends. At the point my guilt peaked, because I had watched without helping, a massive man with a black trench coat and a golf-ball-sized head snuck up behind you with a shotgun. But I kicked him over a railing and down a mountainside. Saved your life.

Your phone alarm went off at eight. "I only got in a fight one time," you told me after I told you my dream. "I was playing in the sandbox with my friend and he got mad at me for beating him in a game, so he punched me in the face. My mom took one look at me and said, 'Never let anyone hit you.' So she made me go back there and fight him."

"How'd that go?" I asked.

"I felt bad! We were both crying the whole time. I think I won. I bit him a few times."

"Sounds excessive."

"Nuh-uh! When you grow up in poor communities, you have to do violent things to survive. Because if people think they can mess with you, they'll keep messing with you, and your life will be ten times harder than if you just do unpleasant things. Like bite a boy on the playground. Yeah!" you affirmed with a prim little nod.

We locked up the apartment and made our way downhill to Whitman's. Say what you will about gentrification, I still saw plenty taquerias and Arab restaurants. The most obvious sign of change was an anarchist infoshop named the Lucy Parsons Center, which I made a mental note to visit while in town.

Halfway to the bar, I grew nervous from the pressure in my

bladder. There'd be a restroom once we got there, of course, but did I want to be doing a pee dance at the moment we met Magali? I suggested we find a restaurant, but you assured me that, maybe excluding my injured pride, you saw no negative repercussions should I urinate in the park across the street. With that we scoped out an oak in a secluded corner, where we took turns pissing on the roots.

Founded in 1953, Whitman's was constructed around the roof of a cabin that got buried during the Rupture. Instead of bulldozing it, the original owners, enterprising sons of Irish immigrants, rightly saw the potential capital in kitsch. The roof, eight feet in length and three feet in height, scalene triangular, made of shorn logs with a brick chimney, had over the years acquired a coat of signatures. I spied a tiny spot of unmarked chimney brick on which I wrote my initials and the year with Sharpie. You wrote on a log, THIS BAR EN-RUPTURES ME!!!

We joined Matt and Magali at a red oak corner booth, both hardwood walls decorated in portraits of Nantucket whalers. Magali, a freckled, diminutive woman in peasant blouse and skirt, had round and perceptive eyes. When I asked if her parents named her for the *Turma da Monica* character she said no, though my knowledge of Brazilian pop culture had the desired charm.

And her smile. The baroque curve of her upper lip around her long teeth. Attractive—no, *special*—because, as I would learn, she never grinned unless supremely amused at something, her default expression being a scowl that would have one thinking her humorless. I'd made six jokes before she beamed those pretty teeth at us one by one, turning her individual euphoria collective, and for several beats afterward her face stayed that way, as if waiting for some new amusement to give her an excuse to keep smiling. Observing her carefree rapport with Matt, I pitied him because no doubt men flirted with her, probably in his presence.

When the mannish bartender with her absurd platinum dye job asked, "Gotcha IDs on ya?" you whipped out a fake with the quickness. Impressed, I patted your knee under the table. Whitman's was quiet at that hour, mostly empty. I watched Magali rest her hand on the laminate table and Matt rested his over hers, an appealingly proprietary gesture from a gentle guy.

At her offer to buy a round, I hesitated. Lately I'd been caught between dueling modes when it came to drink, both fueled by a visceral sense that humanity was facing imminent extinction: in the first, dulling the pain with booze made sense; in the other, I should have my faculties about me when Armageddon fell. Typically I would abstain from drink for a day or two then binge until I blacked out. I decided to make that night a binge night. Three gulps and I finished my coconut gin, while you sipped yours with the quietude of a cat lapping water.

Over the hour Magali spoke about the legal nightmare she'd endured getting a student visa to fulfill her dream of studying the Boston soil. Startlingly lucid after three glasses of rum, she explained how early-twentieth-century geologists incorrectly surmised the minerals in the area—such as the bostonium that powered lightbulbs—had lain dormant in the earth until the Rupture revealed them. Modern science proposed that such minerals developed as a result of the Rupture itself. Imagine a force a hundred times greater than the pressure that turned coal to diamonds, a singular tectonic event in history, still unexplained three centuries later.

During her monologue I watched Matt, his mouth open while he pondered what—if anything—he had to contribute. Then he blurted, "Did I mention she's only twenty-two?"

"Stop that!" she yelled. "I am not fishing for compliments.

Besides, I hate how this country privileges youth. Experience is just as important, if not more. I love you even if you are an old man," she teased, pinching his chin.

"Você vai cuidar de mim na minha velhice?" he cooed. "Você não vai?"

She chuckled. "Só se você cuidar de mim, meu amor."

Learning Portuguese so he and his girlfriend could sweet-talk in public like Augie Doggie and Doggie Daddy? A little obnoxious. I could forgive him, though.

Magali asked us, "Another round?"

I was a traditional drunk: a corroded bloodstream led me to supreme gregariousness, my every opinion correct, my every anecdote hilarious. And there came a point during this especially loud round when Magali asked you about United Students Against Sweatshops.

"Mm-hmm. Yeah." You sounded flattered to know I'd told Matt about it. "Right now we're trying to get Chatham to join the Worker Rights Consortium. I think we'll win."

Worker Rights Consortium—the name transported me to the William Pitt Union in a nondescript classroom, pizza and soda and paper plates, the eight of us brainstorming how to convince Pitt they should join an anti-sweatshop organization when we couldn't even get people to attend our meetings. To passersby we probably looked like an AA group. The campaign, along with our club, died the minute we got our diplomas.

Matt looked contemplative. "Did Pitt ever join the Worker Rights Consortium?"

"They did!" I yelled. "And they never gave credit to student activists. Motherfuckers explained it as a fucking economic thing."

He scowled. "I remember that was a really conservative school—"

"When I talk with people about college, all anybody does is

complain about what we didn't do. First of all, it was just preparation for real activism. Second of all, we had real victories. Same-sex benefits? We won. Getting Boise Cascade to stop destroying forests? We won. How many people went to our anti-sweatshop fashion show?"

"Three hundred," he answered instantly.

"*And* we got Pitt in the WRC. It just happened later. We're fucking heroes."

You squeezed my hand, which startled me. Whether your gesture meant I should keep going or cease immediately, I couldn't tell.

Magali raised her glass. "To fucking heroes!"

We toasted. The bar was filling up, the ambient noise as comforting as the intoxicated bodies were claustrophobic. Drunk, you became a fount of communistic opinions. I enjoyed seeing Matt and Magali take to you so quickly.

You told us you might be inheriting a farm soon, but not from relatives. The way you explained it, many of your friends were black Pittsburghers decades older than you, two of whom you had met at Landslide Community Farm in the Hill, which I'd no idea you were involved in though I had friends in the collective. With an embarrassed air, you said these elders you knew were offering to cede you their twenty-acre land trust in Erie. Flippantly, you mused it would be cool to milk cows and shear sheep, but it really sounded like a *lot* of work. Meanwhile, I sat in awe. It was no surprise that other people loved you as much as I did. I pictured you at Landslide Farm, on a hillside overlooking Fifth Avenue and the Allegheny, on your knees before a planter made from a used tire. In an oversized dress shirt, trousers, and straw hat, you lovingly plucked radishes to place them in your basket.

Your words threw a Dr. Jekyll potion on my shouty alter ego. What did I have to say that was nearly as interesting?

"I'll get the next round," Matt offered.

"I'll get it!" I declared, guilty at letting Magali pay for everything. "I'm not broke."

"I appreciate that," he rejoined, "but I have a tab open."

"Seriously. I can pay for it."

"What is this pissing contest?" Magali groaned. "While you all figure that out, I'm going to the bathroom."

"Me too," you said quickly, and butted your hip against mine to shoo me from the booth. Left with a hard dick, I watched you two leave down the oak-paneled hall for your womanish trash talk. Then I told Matt, "You win."

"Four more gins," he chuckled wearily to the bartender.

"Magali's a jewel," I said to him. "I'm so happy for you."

Forever minutes later, you had yet to return. I can get paranoid, I know, but I think anyone would have suspected at least a tiny conspiracy. So I excused myself and left down the hall, out the back door into a trash-strewn alley where I found you two smoking a joint. Involuntarily I shuddered. Remembered an AmeriCorps party where you smelled smoke on my shirt and said, "That's gross." Watching you in all your hypocrisy got me shy. Middle school dance shy. I retreated to the bathroom to collect myself. Took a piss.

At the urinal next to mine was a dead ringer for Santa Claus in a denim jacket. Earlier I'd heard him and his friends complain about standing in line while the bouncer checked IDs. "We're obviously not under twenty-one!" one of them growled before they buffaloed inside and seized their corner of the bar to do shots and flirt creepily with the bartender like the obnoxious Irishmen they were. And Santa asked me in a rumbling voice, "You need help with that?" And I asked, "My dick?" And he said, "Yep. I'll pay."

"I'm good." I flushed the urinal with my elbow and left without washing my hands. Somehow, this yuletide interaction gave me confidence to return to the alley. First thing I did was challenge your hypocrisy. It made no sense to act righteous over cigarettes then hit the reefer.

After a leonine hit, you sheepishly replied, "That was tobacco."

"It's still smoke. You're still inhaling carcinogens."

You pretended to think it over a moment, shrugged. "Oh, I guess I don't think it's that gross after all!"

Jesus god, you. To fit in, I took a drag. My thoughts unhinged.

Lulled senseless, I found myself in the booth, in the corner with my arms around your waist. "Edge of Seventeen" was playing. Spend enough time in bars and you'll hear every song ever released as a single. Fortunately we'd chanced upon this bar and this song, the sixth-best track on *Bella Donna*, a bath in which I gratefully submerged, and when Stevie sang "I'm a few years older than you," I felt it in my soul and rode that euphoria until she made that noise and everything kicked into second gear at the point when a lesser song would have ended. I felt amazing. Perfectly happy being smashed and loving you.

The conversation had turned to Magali's youth in Rio, something she talked about straightforwardly, with neither self-pity nor rancor. Her late father had also been a geologist. The day of her seventh birthday he didn't return home, and her mom lied to her for weeks that he was on assignment in the Amazon, when in reality he'd been murdered. With his death their middle-class life crashed to a halt. No running water till high school. Gangs with AK-47s in the streets. Forced to live in shelters and the homes of abusive relatives. Solemnly she related her mother's excitement to learn she was dating an American.

"I'll get you the white picket fence and blond children," Matt snarked, his tone dry and sharp as a wicker chair. "House in the suburbs."

"Shush," Magali countered. "She seriously likes you. She

thinks you can get me a better life, but can you blame her? After all she's been through?"

"You're right," he demurred, but bitterness stained his brown eyes, like a piece of mud in chocolate. At Magali? Her mom? The American Dream? Any or all of the above, that acrimony felt precious to me. I appreciated having a grown-up in the room, a woman grateful and forthright, not a brat, her occasional overbearingness appropriate given her background and station in life. She'd found herself a milquetoast white man partly, I supposed, because she'd had her fill of thuggish masculinity. In return, Matt adored her. Theirs was a perfectly imperfect relationship that could work, if they wanted it to.

"We should wake up early to print my résumé," I reminded you.

"I'll set my alarm for eight," you said gamely.

My trusty wingman did the bragging for me. "He's got a job interview tomorrow," Matt told Magali. And to me, "There's a Kinko's near the apartment."

Magali was incredulous. "Don't *pay* for it. We can do it at Tufts."

"I wouldn't want to impose," I begged off. "Your print quota—"

"We're going." She'd tolerate no argument. "I am not from America. Here nobody helps each other. I am Brazilian. Don't worry about my quota. We have a very large endowment."

The neighborhood was named Braintree after the three colleges built into a colossal prehistoric tree uprooted during the Rupture and lodged like a splinter in the western end of town. On the T the four of us stood squeezed in a lump of humans, safe among one another. It felt great to be part of a cohort, like Matt and myself in college. I gazed out the window and down at apartments built on top of the roots. Yellow lights. Red-and-blue lights.

We disembarked into a hyperactive mass of college kids swarming the three-level station. From every direction, girls dressed provocatively declared their intentions to dance and drink. Like an impatient battering ram, Magali extended a palm to push through the rubbernecks while you and I, holding hands, did our best to keep up. Down twisting tunnels that echoed with pop tunes from the buskers, my overstimulated brain conjured valiant fantasies. Some frat boy would snatch you around the waist. I would ram the punk with my shoulder and send him flying. Or the flow of kids pushing onto the train would carry you away, but I, intrepid, would leap atop a wooden bench to grab your hand before the flood washed you out to sea.

We rested on the escalator that carried us upward with no end in sight, like ascending the throat of God.

"This is pretty epic," you noted.

Eight minutes later the escalator deposited us in a wide glass-walled corridor. Outside, gargantuan branches reached into the pulsing night like Cthulhu's brown-skinned brother doing aerobics. It occurred to me the room we stood in was constructed against the tree trunk, a grand and terrifying thought. Out the left window I viewed Boston University, composed of a dozen redbrick buildings attached to the tree like cuckoo clocks, with more lecture halls built in cavities within the trunk. On Magali's insistence we moved to the right window, where she cheerfully pointed above us. There, hanging from the underside of a branch, the steel spires of MIT resembled a dozen titanium stalactites glowing with light from a hundred tiny windows.

On our exit from the station the bat-wing doors made that shy, dipping motion into their slots. At the top of a translucent stairwell I paused in fright because, under the steps and through the glass, there loomed several hundred feet between us and the Braintree lights below. Vertiginous, I backed toward a wall smeared in advertisements and threw my shoulders between Robert Pattinson's and Kristen Stewart's smolderingly empty profiles. I stared out the windows at three branches upon which the Universalist Church built its utopia of nonsectarian learning, each connected to the others by translucent walkways bridging the sky like arteries pumping blood to the gabled Georgians lined in a row like a regiment of royal dragoons.

I spoke to you through nervous laughter. "Fear of heights still there."

"Maybe you could wait here for us," you suggested. Rather than soothe, your words made me want to dash my brains on the wall. There seemed no way around this challenge, so I stripped off my shirt to the tank top beneath, tied it around my eyes, and extended my hand to you.

"Just lead me," I demanded with forced boldness.

You did so, down, up, through the corridors. Comforted in the dark, I regained enough spirit to make unfunny jokes. And yet there came a point, suspended in the void between Heaven and Earth, that it hurt to realize this was the closest intimacy we had shared in weeks, even going back to before our breakup. You had set your boundaries shortly after we started having sex. "I don't think we should do it every night. I don't want to be a, um, loose woman, as my mom would say." And I asked you to repeat that, hoping I might hear something different the second time. Instead, you repeated the lines word for word, and when you said "as my mom would say," you gave my hand a zesty squeeze.

Things only worsened from there. You grew colder. Thinking back to this, I was sullen when you told me, "You can take it off."

"And put it back on," I heard Matt drolly amend.

Sight returned, I found us in a brutally ordinary hallway with three elevators on either side. Nearby a couple dozen palm-sized geodes floated in the air, glowing from within with violet light, and, giving one a curious push, I watched it drift until it bounced gently off the chrome wall. Magali buzzed us through a plexiglass door.

Our reflections shimmered over stones that called to mind garnet, topaz, and quartz but were in truth nothing I'd seen before. Cracked open, the crystals seemed like living things on the walls, mischievous with ancient power. Farther in, the cave became office space, ready-to-assemble and beige. In the print room Magali logged me onto her account. The desktop background showed a picture of her and her cohort in a mine, dressed in orange coveralls, posing with pickaxes around a boulder as tall as herself, black as pitch and marbled in veins red as aneurisms, cracked at the top and emitting toad-colored smoke.

On Yahoo I downloaded my résumé from an email I'd sent myself and printed it. Plucked the warm document from the tray to find the indentations jumbled.

"It's fine," I told Magali when she offered a second printing. "So long as I can read it."

"*I* can't read that," she retorted. "Like I said, billion-dollar endowment."

Afterward Magali visited her cubicle to attend to a matter that occurred to her at the last minute, but I had no doubt was in some way relevant to mankind's survival, and Matt, the dutiful boyfriend, helped her carry a box of files from the meeting room. It was as if I'd turned twelve again, left alone for hours in an after-hours jazz club while my mother, accompanied by her saxophonist boyfriend, saw to adult business in the back, while men played Spades and, feeling as if spiders were building webs over me, I passed the time reading.

Unlike me, however, you had no patience for waiting; you hurried us down a hall where the stones glowed extra bright, the smell from their emittance like burnt toast buttered in limestone. At the first opportunity you ducked inside a men's room furbished in toilets and sinks cleaner than antique china, courtesy of what had to be Earth's most efficient custodial staff.

You, sitting on the floor beside a toilet with the deadpan, guarded air of a woman in a Caravaggio, fished a tinfoil ball from your bra, opened it on the toilet seat to reveal your sizable weed stash. Rolling the joint, you told me that if we exhaled into the bowl and flushed at the same time, it would air out the smell. I doubted this, but made no objection, despite my terror. During my brief career as a smoker there had been more freak-outs than sing-alongs, more doomsday visions than philosophical tangents. I could recall a night in Baltimore when, my car locked in a parking garage, I had a panic attack for seven straight hours, the sensation like my head was on fire, all because I smoked with some dudes; on top of that, for someone like me, who once walked three hours through Manhattan to avoid the bus fare, drugs seemed an expensive habit. Tonight, however, I did them for free, and I did them for you.

Finished with your joint, you crumpled the tinfoil into a ball you then noted looked like a one-eyed, demonic bulldog. You named your creation Berneticott and, setting him on top of the flushometer, said he would protect us. A little while later we determined, after I told you about my last encounter in a restroom, that had I taken up Santa's proposal, it would have been an awkward situation at best, since even on his knees he was probably taller than me. For this particular scenario, you decided, I would have to either sit on the paper towel dispenser, or, if we stayed in the stall, insist on the giant hairy Bostonian doing a handstand in order to service me. But forget about me. What about you? What about these older people who loved you so much they would gift you forty acres and a mule? To which you mused a mule would be a pretty useless animal nowadays, unless you taught it a skill, like embroidery, or trained it to be a spelling bee champ. And for a while you spun the tale of how you should move to Hollywood and find another old person, like Snoop Dogg, and convince him to give you a dinosaur, but a kind and sensitive one, like a velociraptor.

From there we raced around the reception desk in office chairs. Illuminated in geode light, you beamed a melty smile to the ceiling, as if it were telling you knock-knock jokes. I listened to you muse about how, if black folks failed to trim their edges, those edges would keep growing until everybody's face became a mask made of curls.

For the first time, it felt like I was sharing my unique happiness with another person: since childhood I'd been keen to climb, crawl, stride, and creep into places where I'm not welcome. Places where I'm too early, too late, unknown, uninvited, unregistered, banned, barred, mistrusted, or despised. On occasions when I'd find myself stirring dust in an abandoned building, or scoffing hors d'oeuvres at someone's thesis presentation, or absorbing eulogies at a stranger's funeral, artificial notions of stability curtsied before Chance and Risk.

This I was pondering when a shadow stretched toward us from the adjacent hallway. A guard, I thought, followed by the image of our black bodies bullet-riddled. No time to waste, I grabbed your wrist and hauled you up from the chair. I hurried you through a cubicle labyrinth that ended at the top of a titanium stair. Scooped you in my arms and bore you two flights down to a waiting area furnished with pastel vinyl sofas and what looked like the Dark Crystal, a lavender stone twice as tall as a man. Squatting behind a second reception desk, cautious as turtles, we listened for danger, fighting to appear calm for each other, even as our staggered breaths told the story.

"That was security," I whispered. "They catch us, they'll kill us."

You nodded understanding. Inwardly, I rejoiced to find us on the same page, even if it took imminent death and marijuana to put us there. You reminded me of the crystals, cracked open at last to reveal the luminescence beneath your beauty. There was no one on earth I would rather die with. "Find us weapons," I ordered.

Off the desk you passed me a Rolodex, then armed yourself with a letter opener. Feeling I might burst from affection, I said, "Tell me your dreams."

"My dreams?" You sounded confused.

"When they come, I'll shield you. But if you die and I live, I want to honor your dream."

With lucidity that bordered on robotic, you told me, "I'm thinking of becoming a food healer. I'd like to create kitchens where black people can cook healthy meals together. And they don't have to be family. Just people in the community. We have generational hunger that affects us physically. Sharing a kitchen with strangers and working together to make something good can create a healing space. And then everybody can eat together. And it'll be great."

Generational trauma I'd heard of, but hunger? Weird. Like, California weird. Nor did I understand what made you an expert in "food healing" studying poli. sci. at Chatham. In any event, knowing your dream bound me to you. I promised, "I will absolutely start the project if you die."

"Shush! I hear them coming."

Rather than wait for the attack, I jumped to my feet, Rolodex held high to bludgeon our fascist assailant with the fervor of a Zulu warrior. At the foot of the steps Matt stood holding a stack of prints, in no way surprised at the state he'd found me in;

befuddled Magali; and, between them, a paunchy Indian man in thick spectacles.

"I am sorry if I scared you," he said. "Please forgive me."

"This is my colleague Rajit," said Magali, and introduced us with our names.

Matt looked bemused. "Maybe you shouldn't smoke pot."

Awareness of how stupid I looked weighed on my chest like one of those X-ray aprons at the dentist. Nevertheless, you laid your head on my shoulder.

Matt and Magali parted from us at Arch-Minister Station. I caught the sarcasm on their faces right before the train door closed. Not much later, on our way out of the Jamaica Plain station, you said, "Let's get more drinks!"

A stop at the convenience store for two tall boys. Brown bag in hand, you jumped on my back so forcefully I nearly dropped the manila envelope containing my résumé.

"Go that way!" you beerily commanded, pointing in the wrong direction.

"Do you even know where we are?" I shot back. "You're like a mahout."

"What?"

"Someone who rides an elephant."

"Stop body-shaming. I'll bite you."

"That means *I'm* the elephant. Chill."

Seeing a storefront door recessed between two bay windows displaying bisque dolls in Victorian garb, I carried you into the alcove. Breast to breast and lip to lip, we returned to the love I knew had never truly died. Even your boozy breath stank deliciously to me. Over your shoulder I saw teenaged boys stroll past, and I cringed.

"Aw yeah! Get it!" they cheered and moved on, thankfully, after a good long look.

At last we continued walking, half our steps stayed with kisses. We had a wonderfully incompetent conversation, about what I can't recall. A disorienting mix of memory and anticipation carried me like a charge in an electric current. We had agreed, when we started dating, that our coworkers shouldn't know about us. None of their business. At work we flirted through deadpan whispers that no one would have guessed crackled with erotic energy. Typing student reports in the computer lab, you might dryly solicit, "Let's show up late to the next meeting with our clothes inside out and backwards." Once, you slipped me a note that read, "You're like a fresh pair of jeans. Fits nice and it's fun to get you off."

Back in the apartment, I poured us tap water from a groaning faucet, my back to you, my heart yours. I asked if you liked Magali.

"I did!" I heard you tumble into bed. "Things got really serious when she started talking about her childhood. I didn't know what to say."

"She's interesting."

"*Too* interesting, don't you think?" I asked what you meant. "I just don't know about people who tell you how interesting they are when you first meet them." But every dude does that. "And most *men* are intolerable. She just seemed a little, um, not full of herself, just, um, not humble? I think everybody's interesting if you really talk to them."

"Some people in this world are boring. And humility is an overrated quality," I stated, disappointed to hear you act catty toward a more successful woman. I cut the light. In bed we bonked lips. Your hair smelled like autumn wind. I remembered you collected Indian dream catchers and there you were—a wind catcher.

Nearly suffocating each other pulling shirts and bras over

our heads, we managed to get naked with many apologies. Matt's futon coughed up a musty odor as I rolled on top of you. Eyes screwed shut, you gathered the green plaid sheets in your fists and clenched my hips between the moons of your knees. Wan streetlight guided my hand to your lower back, and I told you I loved you. At those words you relaxed in my arms.

I froze, unsure of my next move. Like a silent film projected over your dim outline, I saw nights between our breakup and the present when I'd drive from the airport in Dad's wagon, take the Fort Pitt Tunnel then the Oakland exit to Garfield, Highland Park, Lawrenceville. My whole life women had portrayed themselves as inaccessible, but in the hour when artifice dissolved along the planet's axis they showed their true selves—friendly, sincere, and available like oxygen. They wore heels, latex, booty shorts, long tees, and sweatpants. The more pitiful they seemed, the more I wanted their hollow eyes in my passenger seat. Mostly I bought lap dances and blow jobs, to avoid STDs. Some performed their job with porn-star aplomb, others behaved stupidly, some were barely conscious, others were bored. One skeletal girl I found weeping on the curb in front of GetGo, terrified of a person she called Daddy, and in my car delivered a dreary monologue about how she wished *Pretty Woman* would happen to her. Annoyed at her unsexy behavior, yet sympathetic, I paid her fifty bucks for a handy.

I always departed these women with a blissful, nurtured feeling. But they weren't you, just your replacement. And now, in the moment I should have focused on you, I found myself recalling the night I chased a pale blonde down an alley, as she complained to her voluptuous, noirette friend what a cheapskate I was. When I caught up to them I asked, politely, if she could return the shirt she threw on before storming out of the backseat: my Hudson News polo, complete with my name tag.

Fortunately another minute of making out got me back in the mood. You. My black beauty, elemental, pastoral and pasture, ready for my seed. I went down on you because I remembered you liked that. On your left rib cage, below the breast, a bear paw tattoo rose and fell, like the bear was petting a cub.

Not a minute later you grabbed me under my armpits and pulled me on top. Your navel disappeared within your stomach folds. Sweat glistened on your cheeks. I entered you. My feet pressed in an upside-down triangle between your larger feet, I rejoiced in how our bodies fit. You ground against me, eyes closed, your lips a cousin to a smile.

Caught up in your skin and your mercy and the gin in my blood, minutes passed before I realized you weren't fucking me back. Lust became humiliation, at which point I shriveled. Rolling over, I dropped my toes to the cold linoleum and sat there, my shoulders curved, gazing shell-shocked at the lifeless dick between my chubby thighs.

Without a word, you turned your coldhearted back to me, feet curled under you, hands pressed under your cheek to simulate sleep. I went in the bathroom, and, to let known my displeasure, punted the wicker clothes hamper. It bounced off three of the four walls before landing in the tub.

Dawn slipped like an envelope through Matt's window. Already dressed in jeans, sneakers, T-shirt, and a hoodie, I struggled against the tiredness grinding my eyeballs like a shoe stamping out cigarette butts. I drank cheap coffee in the office chair and watched you, small beneath a heap of linens, open and close your eyes for long minutes, until you finally sat up. Your deflated "Good morning" began a pageant of avoidance disguised as pleasantries we lobbed at each other with cold formality. *What do you want for breakfast? Can I borrow some soap?*

Matt's shower, it turned out, had the kind of pipes that made you dance under scalding water. Turn the dial a centimeter to the right, freezing water. A strange mercy, then, that the pain helped me forget you until I turned it off, and as geriatric plumbing belched in the walls, everything came back to me. Twenty minutes later I watched you emerge from the bathroom in a red tank top, a preposterous robin's-egg-blue cotton short skirt tied at the waist with drawstrings, and white tennis shoes. Your outfit reminded me of something an eighth grader who wished to appear womanly might wear as she stepped into an older boy's car.

Our destinations: Harvard, then the library. Phone interview at four. On our way down Centre we stopped for breakfast at Annalee's Voodoo Biscuits. Above the door hung the image of the slave woman as some island Rosie the Riveter who, instead of a hammer, raised in her fist a chicken biscuit. Your eyes flashed my own displeasure at her red madras wrap, her grinning honey-colored face like that of a supermodel, the short-sleeved ahistorical plaid dress they put her in, belted with a red sash to accentuate the athletic *V* of her torso. Having chanced upon the second-most-offensive East Coast mascot—the future of the Annalee character had been as vehemently debated as the Washington Redskin—I took you inside for "Caribbean" pastries, certain you would hate the place. I reminded you the real Annalee was a woman in her forties with black teeth, while the Mexican cooks fried up four chicken biscuits, two for each of us.

"So racist," I said on our way down the street, gobbling sandwiches to fight my hangover. Later, on the platform, I could no longer hold back. "I can't believe I went soft on you."

You swallowed audibly. "I'm sorry you feel that way. Um, nobody should feel that way."

On the train you sat across from me, one arm wrapped around the crochet purse in your lap. Dark sunglasses on, you looked mean as a swan, and I wondered, *What the hell did I do?*

For a time I watched the world go by. Everything in Boston was a potential collapse. Fenway's aquamarine dazzle distracted the eye so one didn't notice that the bricks warred with one another, laid at odd angles to keep the five sides upright on unstable earth. To sail the Charles showed courage because one never knew when gravity might return and flush the river, including the people on it, off the edge of Boston. Eavesdropping on obnoxious weekenders wearing Red Sox gear, I heard, soldered into their blustery declarations, vestigial fear of another Rupture. It invested Bostonians with manic fatality, friendliness that seemed genuine, hostility equally genuine, pride in their matchstick existence.

Every stop yielded interest: a trio of men chatting loudly in Amharic; a majestic onyx woman with a baby strapped to her chest; a tired-looking Asian girl in a green hoodie and jeans ripped at the knees, raccoon-eyed with mascara, probably a methadone patient, a pungent half-smoked cigarette between chewed fingernails black from equal parts polish and bruising. I drank in the multicultural beauty of this place, disappointed at your acting above it all, as if hurting me justified blinding yourself to delight.

"You heard that version of 'You Got Me' with Jill Scott?" I asked. "It's like the perfect R'n'B song. There's a part where she starts scatting at the end that's, like, the blackest thing ever."

"You know I . . ." Your voice trailed off. You slipped into a sincerity-retardant slouch. "We've already talked about Jill Scott. You know I listen to her."

I was sick of your bullshit. "You shouldn't have called me a reverse racist."

Even in sunglasses you looked away, out the window. "I don't remember that."

"Yeah, you do."

"The Chris Rock joke? That was weeks ago."

"When I said black women aren't attracted to white men and date them for status, you agreed with me. You said your old boyfriend was an average white man."

Your eyebrows proclaimed such a shocking display of insincere innocence, I had to wonder if you were a true sociopath. "I don't recall."

"You could have disagreed. You could have said you loved him. You said he was an average white guy who sat around playing computer games all day. You said when he tried calling you a few months ago you didn't want to talk 'cause you thought he was just lonely."

"I don't like talking about that," you said in a voice high and hollow, like an out-of-tune guitar string. Hardly decisive in your meanness.

"Don't ever settle," I told you. "You're a beautiful woman. You're smart. You're cool."

"Thanks, buddy. Thanks, pal."

"I'm being sincere." It was then that the conductor announced Harvard as the next stop. "We're checking out Massachusetts Hall," I said. "This isn't up for discussion. I'm not asking consent."

You finished the miserable joke. "Just take what you want?"

In Harvard Square the flower-bordered sidewalks thronged with undergrads, future despoilers of the world. The international students provided an appreciable brown element among pink-and-pale New Englanders in straw sailing hats and khaki shorts. Warm winds shook the well-pruned trees so their shadows contorted on the cobbles. You whipped a sun visor from your purse and jammed it on your forehead, though the weather was temperate.

Historical records said the Rupture, for all its magnitude, lasted less than three minutes, during which Harvard's Massachusetts Hall flew from its moorings in Cambridge to crash in what would later become Chinatown. After many decades the university fathers, having given up on reclaiming their real estate in the clouds, rebuilt the university around the crash site. We followed one of the cracks from the impact, as thick around as my waist and filled in with bronzed gravel. Massachusetts Hall was a brick-faced Gothic structure that looked normal three fourths of the way across before it split with a diagonal crack from foundation to peak; it had been paved with brick, an architectural scar. Gantries covered the longer side of the roof, reconstruction threatened over the decades but never begun because, like much of Boston, the appeal lay in its shabbiness. The white bell tower curled in on itself like a claw, kept upright by an ironwork balustrade. The stained-glass windows mounted high in the walls depicted events such as the Fire of 1831 or the Cambridge Revolt of 1790. They said the hall always had a breeze, often mild, sometimes strong enough to blow books out of students' hands.

"Take my picture." I stood on the Harvard seal embedded in the pavement. Feet on the VE and RI. Eyes on the clouds, I declared, "I can feel the knowledge in the air."

You took the photo with your disposable camera. Then I told you how, a few days before our trip, I'd visited the Club Fair at Pitt. You said that was weird.

"Why?" I asked.

"There's nothing you could really learn there."

"I have to see what the youth are up to!"

"You really want to go back to school," you flatly replied.

For passive-aggressive sniping, Harvard Square proved the

perfect theater, and the longer we carried on in this painfully artificial manner, the more perverse pleasure I found in it, to see how deep we could dig ourselves into the hole. For all that, I wanted to at least snatch the bitchy visor off your head. It seemed too fake—the punch line to a joke with no setup.

I tried to keep the anger from my voice. "Is there anywhere *you* want to go?"

"I'm okay."

Before long I was wandering the campus bookstore, alone. It seemed a good time to split up. Around me employees were making barricades out of boxes from which they unpacked shrink-wrapped textbooks. The worst part, it occurred to me, was you were right: I *did* miss grad school. After dropping out I'd moved to the West Coast, where the cost of living left me trying to stretch my last five hundred bucks while sleeping on a mattress in an Oakland house where I lived with three anarchists, two migrant workers, and a racist pit bull who bit my shin every time I came home. My biggest win of late had been tricking a dozen teenagers into thinking I knew anything about life or horticulture. I was tired of fighting. I was twenty-five, broke, drunk, living at home with my dad, and, worst of all, in love with a brat.

Girlish tittering—two coeds who darted behind a shelf the moment I locked eyes with them—made me aware I'd been muttering at an invisible you. I took deep breaths, went to my comfort zone. In bookstores, I would always read biographies to discover when famous people got their big break. I left Film Studies knowing Scorsese directed *Taxi Driver* at thirty-three.

Around one o'clock we met up again at the station. "What did you do?" I asked.

Your answer: "I just kind of walked around."

But you looked upset. "Are you okay?"

"These guys came around."

Alarmed, I took your hand. "Did they do anything to you?"

Your tone had a bitter edge. "It was nothing. They were just being men. With penises."

Seeing as you would have refused any comfort I offered, it seemed kinder to say nothing. Neither of us spoke on the platform. Then I sang Jadakiss: *"Niggas be hatin'!"*

"I really don't like that word," you moaned.

Ten feet from us stood a jittery woman at the platform edge. Pale and plump, she wore black jeans and a black button-down blouse. In her forties, a slim face beneath hair coarse, brown, and lusterless. Like a fat Isabelle Huppert, a dour turn to her mouth and passionless eyes that suggested, had mental illness not brought her vulnerabilities to the surface like sewage from a blown-out manhole, she would be a real bitch. Her arms were flabby and freckled. Heavy breaths rocked her enormous bosom as she backed up, walked forward, wrung her blue-veined hands together. One of the buttons across her belly was undone and I wondered if she'd forgotten to fasten it, or if her clothes simply couldn't contain her. I imagined offering her consoling words on the subway. At her Quincy apartment she would fill me in on her diagnoses. I would fuck her while she lay on the bed and I kept standing, pants around my ankles, a wild man.

The Orange Line train braked in front of us. The doors hissed open and I watched her step back, eyes startled and wet. I wagered she would enter. Sometimes I did that—made bets with myself over mundane things. If I bet correctly, I had a victory for the day, and a wrong bet cost nothing. With a quick and intrepid stride she propelled herself into the car, and my toes curled in victory.

You were exhausting work. Childish. Nothing about your huffy reaction to every little thing reflected a grown woman's spite. An hour Downtown had me noticing you weren't even that weird. Just a collection of cutesy habits.

Someday I might handle such acrimony as yours in a mature way, but for the moment I hadn't the slightest idea how. The middle schoolers I used to teach treated me horribly, and I'd met their disrespect with petty tyranny that finally, at my wit's end, had me shouting in their miserable brown faces. In a similar vein, I pummeled you with more singing, more observations. You made me, in short, an intolerable windbag.

Before the statue commemorating the Tuber Strike of 1939, I let you know the Tubers' Guild used to make slaves carry goods up the shafts, no elevators then, only ladders and their aching backs. One of those slaves, a woman named Clara, discovered bostonium. Over the next decade, hundreds of blacks acquired radiation poisoning from digging up the mineral. Though the histories said otherwise, the Lunar Creole Revolt of 1861, during which Cambridge natives burned down the harbor, had been a direct response to this atrocity. An indigenous woman hearing indigenous history, you said, "I don't like talking about those things."

You showed no interest in the gold-gated Boston Opera House, built to replace the original burned down in 1852 by the Fireside Poets, named for the many eulogies penned in their arsonist wake. Abolitionist insurgents, they joined the resurgent Puritan Empire in guerrilla rebellion against Boston, though they held no political union with Oliver Cromwell II. Their names were "Black" Henry Longfellow, John "Redhand" Whittier, James Russell Lowell, Oliver Wendell Holmes Sr., and the greatest zealot, Ralph Waldo Emerson. Having escaped the gallows that awaited his fellows, Emerson continued setting fires around Boston well into the 1860s, before he disappeared into the fog of history.

It seemed you wouldn't allow me the slightest grace. As wanderlust carried me like a tide from one landmark to another, I wondered if I dragged you around as punishment for your behavior, or from some doomed attempt to impress you.

Outside the Boston Library, you made us halt. "Um, your interview's in two hours. We should make sure we have time to get back."

From icy to empathic. The whiplash made me confused and grateful all at once. In the marbled foyer, the slight tilt under my soles told me this place had been built on an angle. I imagined the whole sandstone cube sliding down the incline, crushing the surrounding buildings on the way. Under the arched portico connecting modern wing to antique, we agreed to rendezvous in the courtyard.

Our second separation that day. It saddened me how relieved I felt getting away from you. Free of destination, I walked the center of an oblong chamber lined with Palladian windows where hundreds read quietly at tables arranged in neat rows, under high buttresses that called to mind a whale's rib cage. From Jonah to Revelation, in the adjoining chamber I ascended a grand stair to the mezzanine, where there rose from floor to ceiling a triptych: the first painting showed angels reaching down from Heaven for hundreds of pleading unfortunates; the second depicted Puritans making the pilgrimage to Cambridge in belief the New Jerusalem stood upon its crest; last came their descent, their already dour faces darkened in cosmic disappointment.

On the second floor I found the Rupture Room, the walls hung with antique maps that looked made from prehistoric hides. Eight leather-bound volumes were opened in glass cases against the walls. In the center lay three black stones from the Church of the Arch-Minister, each half as tall as myself. My attentions turned to a middle-aged guide who, like an intelligent housefly in thick eyeglasses, recited sanitized history to the tourists cattling behind him.

"Is Cambridge safe to visit?" asked some potbellied Midwestern harridan.

The guide faked laughter and pointed to a map, repeating its words. "There be dragons."

Fascinated by it all, I stopped to read a heavy tome opened to a journal dated May 1782.

"The stream ran his course northwest and westerly, and so keepeth his course without any tarrying some twenty miles, where at this nearness to the clouds took on a peculiar aspect. The fresh water which had run downhill now flowed uphill in what seemeth a gross resistance to science. With a Shippe of some fifty cubits, we proceded north on the mountaine into the hinterlands of Boston. The country we navigated some three or fourscore miles until we saw people upon the sandy shore. The delegation was of white men, though their dress was similar to that of the savage, demented so after years without civilized contact. They welcomed me into their home, as they claimed was their custom.

"Their religion and Ceremonie I observed was thus: three or foure dayes after my taking in the house where I lay, seven of them, each with a rattle began at ten a clocke in the morning to mourn the leaving of the moon. The peculiar gravity inspired them to create a number of floating idols in its Honore and it became clear to me that they worshipped the moon like pagans of olde. They begat with extreame howling, showting, singing, and such violent gestures, and Anticke actions as would startle a civilized man. At the end of each ablution, they would Laye down two or three grains of wheat. I beheld a Ceremonie in which the warriors, as their initiation into manhood, floated off the promontory and into the skye. They would curve back, though one unfortunate youth missed his turn and descended slow as a pebble in water to the clouds . . ."

His cursive came to a frilly halt at the edge of the page. A curator's annotation next to the book called this particular captain a self-aggrandizing propagandist, his claims worth scrutiny. Nevertheless, it mesmerized and horrified me to imagine that young man in his slow, fatal fall.

Cambridge, CB, the Bridge, Angel City. On the news they spoke of it like the third world. Then again, they said the same of Detroit. Maps displayed what people once believed lived there: something with an ostrich body, human head in its chest, and three snakes for a tail; a corkscrew-tailed dragon roosting atop the Old College building. Creatures like those so lovingly inked on the time-soiled paper seemed to me no more impossible than hippo-cats.

Monsters on the brain, I departed the room while tourists jammed the buttons on their cameras like psychotic presidents nuking the world. Halfway to our rendezvous, anxiety shrank my stomach to an olive pit. First chance, I ducked inside an ornately macho men's room heavy on the marble and brass, decorated in framed poems wherein Whitman beardily declared his mastery over time and space, a bathroom where you wiped your hands on a single DNA-clotted cloth hanging almost to the floor, like they believed the towel dispenser a superhero who required a cape. Behind an oaken stall door, I jerked off to the woman at the train stop.

Feeling slightly better, I found the central courtyard, built around a colonial cabin that had famously landed upright and unharmed on that spot. Guarding the saggy house was a negro in a black suit, most likely a footballer in high school, now a living barrier to the photo-happy Chinese sticking their heads through the windows, in spite of his repeated instructions not to. I had to laugh at his ridiculous job. Venetian columns boxed the low hedges that boxed the cabin, and there you sat next to one of them, a straw in your teeth, gnawing it like an old salt on his pipe as he regards his mistress the sea.

I thought ahead to the moment when, disembarking in Pittsburgh, we would go our separate ways. For my own selfish, cowardly reasons I wanted to marry you. I could endure your contempt for years, decades even, let you degrade me into dirt. A fate preferable to loneliness.

After we reconvened, you suddenly took an interest in the history, so, frustrated and eager, I accompanied you to a long chamber resplendent with artifacts, beneath ziggurat lamps spaced so far from one another they seemed as gold buttons fastened on a gray coat. On either wall stood glass cases displaying curios, antique books, and photos of long-dead personages on parade or in ceremony. You took particular interest in pictures of the Senya: three Boston slaves who in the 1830s fled to Cambridge, where through science or miracle they were transformed into a moose-human-eagle hybrid. Captured in blurry daguerreotypes, clearly shot from a distance by timid photographers, the Senya looked like winged black idols above the snarled grass, marshland shepherds to whom Pan himself would have ceded his staff.

A plaque told us the Senya were eventually hunted down, their remains now stored in the Kennedys' private collection. Adding insult to injury, there lay, behind the glass, the original handwritten draft of Whitman's famous ode, which he published and got paid for, while his subjects rotted. *"Swift like water, the Senya flies / And though I yearn to touch his wing / The beauty of his symmetries / Make sight itself an awesome thing."*

You were calmly expressing your anger when someone said, "This room is off-limits."

The employee had on oxfords, black slacks, and a gray sweater-vest over an aquamarine dress shirt. He had a hubristic schnoz and wave of dead-looking auburn hair.

You looked nonplused. "We just walked in."

"Security shouldn't have let you do that."

"What security?" You shrugged.

Later, in Jamaica Plain, we stopped for ice cream at J.P. Licks, a converted firehouse, its most interesting aesthetic being the plaster mold of a hippo-cat head next to the black awning. How hippo-cats related to ice cream, I'll never know. Inside, they had the air-conditioning on a frigid level. Standing in the line, which wound all the way to the door, we were undecided when we reached the register.

"Caramel apple!" I blurted as soon as the manager laid his hard blue eyes on me.

"I'm thinking pumpkin custard," you vacillated. "Oh, no, I'll have pumpkin praline—caramel apple! I'll have that."

"Are you sure?" asked the manager.

"Um . . . I think so."

He turned away, then wheeled back around. "You *sure*?"

"I don't know!"

The man barked a laugh. "I'm just givin' ya a ha'd time. Caramel apple!" he roared to the teenaged employee.

On the curb we ate our cones in tranquility. For the first time that day, I noticed your perfume. It smelled like pencil shavings in stale sweat, like ingenuity and chaos, like Boston.

A call from a West Virginia area code. The woman said she was your mother. Her breathless voice conjured a plump lady pacing her apartment, worried sick for her baby in New England.

"It's nice to meet you, ma'am," I greeted.

"It's nice to meet you, too. I'm just checking on her."

I observed your terse, polite conversation. "We just went to Harvard and Tufts," you lied to the mom who, you once told me, would dance around the apartment to *Purple Rain*. She'd put on the movie but fast-forward through the sexy parts, as protective of your innocence as a coral reef protects the shore from storm.

After she hung up, I asked if everything was okay.

"Mm-hmm," you nothing'd. Moments later you remembered to pass me my phone. "She's just doing the mom thing. She's . . . I don't know."

"An alcoholic or something?"

"No. She's just, I don't know, a little silly. She doesn't take good care of herself. She expects us to take care of her if she gets sick. I'm not sure I will."

Horrifying, to hear you degrade your paisley mom who was certainly proud of you, who taught you to defend yourself, who took a knife to the gut to birth you. I bet she was a real Prince fan, too; ask her favorite *Purple Rain* track and she'd say "Take Me with U."

It was then I winced at hate puked from my subconscious. *You are mentally ill. You are a sad person. You smell. The world will eat you alive! You're an arrogant kid! How dare you look at me like that! I hear that tone! Grow up!* That was the war my mother waged on her children. As a short-legged, snot-nosed, tear-eyed human I dreamed of running from her. To Narnia. To Redwall. To some seam in this world that sheltered black boys. To my father in Pittsburgh, who watched, and watched, and watched, his eyes as cruel as her tongue.

Now that I was grown I simply ran, even when standing still. You mother-hater. You ingrate. Don't you know my love for your black ass grew from the compost?

I said, "You have a sister, right? Can she look after your mom?"

"Mm-hmm. Yeah. She's older. Ha. You're closer to her age than mine. That's funny."

Now I was Humbert Humbert. All day I'd given you time to yourself, yet you goaded me.

"I *am* twenty-five," I continued on your horrible trajectory. "In two years I can join the Twenty-seven Club."

"What's that?"

"It's a secret."

"I'll bite you."

"I'm the one who does the biting. Remember you spent a week wearing a scarf to work?"

"Those hickeys were hardcore!"

"You can't do that."

"Yuh-huh. One time in high school there was this guy who talked all this trash. So I bit him so hard I broke the skin."

"He sounds like a wuss."

"Nuh-uh! He was *aaaall* man."

Before you finished I'd pulled down the neck on my hoodie, exposing my shoulder. It seemed right to flash a pervy grin, dirtier than a kitchen floor. Pathetic, really, that you were trying to make me jealous of some phantom dude. You opened your mouth, eyes leveled at mine in plea, apology, or a pitiful attempt at seduction. Dismally you closed your jaw until your teeth clicked like a pair of pliers, then you returned to your sitting position, staring into space.

On my shoulder, a blood crescent.

I had 10 percent battery left on my phone, so, soon as we got to Matt's, I plugged it in the socket next to the bathroom door. Sitting on the floor, I tried to clear my mind, switch from an itinerant headspace to a professional one. Meantime, you arranged the pages of my résumé in a row in front of me, as well as a typewritten sheet of answers to the "tell me a challenge you had" type of question. At quarter past four we sat waiting for the ring.

"I think you should call them," you proposed.

An excellent idea. The phone picked up. First I spoke with a receptionist; then a security guard; then five minutes of Steelers talk radio funneled from WDVE; then the head of the men's residence at Pittsburgh Job Corps picked up. I could hear, in the background, about a dozen indistinguishable male voices. Intermittently she'd yell at them to stop cussing.

Asked about my experience, I answered in my shiniest voice, "I have recently worked with high-school-aged youth."

I pictured her short and stout, with the nervous energy of a chinchilla. Exactly the way I pictured your mom. She asked, "What did you do there?"

Glancing at you, I repeated, "What did I *do* there?"

You pushed forward that page.

"I taught urban gardening," I slowly read, "but there were elements of mentorship and job training. I did education on sustainable living as part of Braddock's urban renewal. Really, my job was about building character. Teaching kids the strength of personality to succeed in life."

The woman on the other end explained to me the "kids" in the dorms were rough. For many of them, their options were either Job Corps or jail.

"Well, I grew up in Garfield," I explained to her. "My dad lives in Swissvale. I've earned privileges in life, but none of that means anything if you don't give back."

She asked if I could interview tomorrow. I said, "Unfortunately, I'm out of town."

"What about Monday?"

"I'll be traveling Monday. But I can do Tuesday."

She agreed on one p.m. Tuesday and hung up. Instinct told

me I had the job on lock. Another gig trying to help negroes who'd given up on themselves long before anybody else did. Zora said the black woman was the mule of the world. Not even close—social workers are. All the same, when you embraced me I felt victorious.

I looked up directions to the Singing Sands. What gave us pause, other than the two hours it'd take to get there, was the cost for the ferry. How about we just enjoy the city?

Dusk found us wandering the Kennedy Greenway. The park occupied a stretch of land that had been dynamited to make the earth even. During the Rupture the area stayed underwater for longer than other parts of Boston, and as a result naturally bloomed with aquatic flora in terrestrial variants. On either side of the walkways grew red algae, green Posidonia, and white pond-weed. Black water caltrops grew on stems as long as a man's leg. Pedestrians gave a wide berth to the roving bladders of sargassum floating through the air.

To experience level earth after so many altitude changes may have made me delirious. When I finally realized we'd walked clean across the Greenway, we were at the foot of the Charlestown Bridge. We turned around.

For a second time I observed the whimsical carousels and abstract sculptures, the parents, friends, lovers, children, business-people, pregnant women, joggers, and dogs embroiled in predictable rituals I felt privileged to witness. Mutely following along, even your obedience felt hostile, and I loathed the part of me that liked your pain. Obviously you found this wandering torturous, to the extent I realized the swollen feet and sleepless nights had been torture for me, much of the time. But that's the price for adventure.

At length we crossed what some would call a park, smooth stone cubes for seating and a grim Dadaist playground built atop concrete pavement. Hazy night had fallen. From down the block a red trolley came ambling until it drove parallel to us. On the side in carnival lettering it read BOSTON GHOST TOURS. Spotting us, the hollow-cheeked driver grinned like a jack-o'-lantern and clanged a bell. Tourists screamed as one, *"Eeeeeeeeeh!"*

We kept walking. Halfway across we heard them scream again at other pedestrians. By the time we reached the opposite side of the block, the trolley had come back around to us and a row of pink faces gaped over the sideboard. *"Eeeeeeh!"*

"That's really annoying," you said.

An artificial lake. Standing at the iron rail, we stared at yachts moored to the dock, listening to them groan like sleeping albino elephants. It felt like a moment of truce. Every so often the earth rumbled under our feet, commerce through the transport tubes.

I thought now, perhaps, the moment to ask why you'd been acting this way. But I was interrupted by the approach of five men: black, younger and more stylish than myself. The gold chains glittering against their dark clothes sent contempt through me. Their tall leader, smiling benevolently on us, had a cute babyface. His Celtics jacket hung from his shoulders to his knees like a comfy iron maiden. By his leer I knew his intentions for you.

"Y'all from around here?" he asked.

"Naw," I replied, and inwardly reproached myself for telling him. "You?"

"CAMBRIDGE!" The boys shouted their hometown the way people from Brooklyn did, with their whole bodies. Their spokesman continued, "It's just, I ain't never seen no one like y'all before. Y'all both got afros. Did y'all plan it that way?"

"Naw," I answered flatly. "We just have hair."

He aimed to keep us talking until you succumbed to his

charms. Young men had irritating faith in their ability to pull off such sorcery.

"Is y'all brother and sister?" he asked. "Dating?"

"Dating," you answered quickly.

Where are you from? What brought you to Boston? His questions I answered truthfully if crankily, still wary of his motives.

"Pittsburgh, huh?" said the boy. "Why'd you come all the way out here?"

"It's not that far," I retorted.

"It's far to me. Don't tell me y'all came all the way just to come. I ain't never heard of nobody doing that. Yo, if y'all ain't got nothing going on, we was just—"

"We were having a private conversation when you interrupted," I interrupted, *basso voce*. "Can you let us alone? Please?"

From that point I expected him to drop the pretense and talk to you directly. Anyone else having thoughts like mine would be a racist, but I'd escaped enough boys wanting to kick my ass for breathing the same air as them. I knew the violence my people were capable of when the night wedded with self-hate.

Make your move, I thought in the boy's direction.

But, like choreography, all five threw up their hands in theatrical innocence. Because they were so fucking cool, right, and I was some Urkel losing his shit like a white boy. This came as no relief. The breath stayed hard as stone in my lungs.

"Just being friendly," said the leader. "Being friendly don't cost nothing. Y'all heard the man. They having a private conversation."

Above all else I had to keep from making fists, order my hands to stay relaxed.

"But check out Cambridge," the kid said as he backed away. "It ain't like people say." He turned to leave, thought a moment, and wheeled around. "Just so y'all know, make sure you don't go that way," and pointed down the wharf.

"We'll get jumped?" I asked.

"White boys," he answered soberly. "Mark Wahlberg–type bitches."

Commerce roared as I sat on the concrete, for however long, with my arms over my face. Wondering if the adrenaline would pass, or would I have a heart attack right there?

By streetlight we returned to the park, where we sat on a cube, hip to hip, barely room enough for the two of us. I slouched forward. You laced your hands contritely between your knees. We guttered like candles as some paces away, languorously aglow, like souls taking the long way to Heaven, half a dozen sargassum floated through the playground.

"Why?" I asked you.

"Why what?"

"Why are you acting like this?"

"I can't help—"

"This trip has been really hard on me," I said, hating the balefulness in my voice, desperate to make you understand. "I've been trying to make it work and you've just been so standoffish and bratty. Why did you come if you just wanted to treat me like shit?"

A hesitation. "I guess I've always been like that. A bit of a brat."

"You were never a brat. You were charming and smart. I loved you because you didn't act your age."

"You know—"

"I love you."

"I'm really glad you feel that way about me," you said morosely.

You fought hard to keep your soul from me. Too late. How could I forget your love for family; your compassion for those younger and weaker, like the middle schoolers on your gardening team; your pride in being black; these jewels you tried to tarnish in your bizarre plan to make me hate you.

"You're a girl," I laughed, nearly manic. "Just a girl. When you dumped me, I didn't do anything. I just let it happen. *This* is our real breakup. All this negativity—"

You yelled my name to make me stop. Bent over with your belly curling into your lap, you looked pudgy and defeated.

We took the T back to Matt's. There we plummeted into bed like a pair of used Christmas trees to the curb.

I woke in the morning to find you gone. Confusion turned to panic before I remembered you stating your intent to visit the Native American House up the street. Glad you'd found something to occupy yourself, and maybe make you happy, I decided to visit the Lucy Parsons Center. I gathered my strength and rocking-horsed on my spine, before sleep could drag me under again, out of bed for a triumphant dismount in my mismatched socks, black cotton and navy wool.

I walked to the center. Everywhere Bostonians went about their rituals at a relaxed pace. After a weekend in Jamaica Plain I could find my way around, identifying streets by sight and comfortably walking parks shaded in red oak, their leaves crackling at autumn's gentle breath. I wished we didn't have to leave the next day.

I arrived at Lucy Parsons, a storefront on Centre. Protest flyers crowded the windows and, from the awning, a photo of the fabled anarchist organizer stared on our modern world with judgment and wry amusement on her attractive face. The scene revived for me memories of cooking Food Not Bombs in punk kitchens around Pittsburgh. It had been like Sunday church for me, chopping onions while dissing the government, some local band screaming from the CD player. Nothing beat the satisfaction of unloading our car at Market Square and serving the homeless a hot meal.

Upon entering the shop, blue-eyed suspicion fell upon me from a volunteer who should have been less concerned about niggas shoplifting and more with keeping her balance on the stepladder as she hung CrimethInc. screen prints with twine. A plump little yellow-haired Marxist in a plaid shirt, she was cute enough to forgive her racism. During my time in the store I noticed her brusqueness with most customers, dedicated to clerical tasks with an attractive air of simpleminded misery that reminded me of a piglet caged in the slaughterhouse.

The Cure crooned from a stereo. Everywhere I saw posters about Cambridge, which, since the colonial era, had been the site of seventy-nine uprisings. "1792–1795—Remember the Free Cambrian Nation," read a screen print. A giant poster showed cop cars burning during the 1974 Busing Riots; much artwork fetishized the guillotine, which had seen its only official use on American soil during the Anti-Clergy Riots in 1790; illustrated on zine covers were Lunar Creoles, black freedmen who joined the Wampanoag in the marshland between Cambridge and the rest of Boston, in what would become a thousand-strong maroon colony.

Pillowed in familiarity, I searched the zine rack, smug, because I knew most of this stuff already. Nonhierarchical organizing, harm reduction, dumpster diving, old hat, got it covered, thank you very much. Finding books on polyamory, I was reading a chapter about the different types of polycules when I noticed an average-looking white man had sidled within kissing distance of me. He wore khakis and a Dropkick Murphys shirt with a big shamrock in the middle. Something about his arrogant, boring demeanor reminded me of every person I'd hated in high school. He asked if I was poly. I said yes and he attacked with a kindred smile. "Don't you think the primary/secondary distinction is hierarchical?"

His voice, like that of a charmless parrot, injured me like a red-hot pepper smeared over my brain meat. However, I told him no, I didn't buy those distinctions at all. Polyamory meant following our animal selves. "Whoever heard of a *primate* having *primaries*?" I asked, liking how cute I sounded.

"Nobody owns anybody," he fervently agreed. "It's all outdated bullshit."

"Fuck hierarchies," I compounded.

"We're just not meant to live like that!"

His flirting reeked of entitlement, but I flirted back. Who knew? Maybe I was gay. It wasn't like I'd ever been particularly good at being straight. Anyhow, he continued proving my assumptions about him correct when he summarized Emma Goldman's theories with Wiki-like shallowness, and, when I told him I disagreed with much of her commentary, he continued to babble as if I'd said nothing. His name was Zack Epstein. Recently he'd bought property in Cambridge but totally wasn't a gentrifier, no, *he* was in danger of getting gentrified from property taxes. After all, he was no millionaire, just a sound engineer at WGBN. He invited artists to live in his condo, a scenic workspace for them to weave truth and beauty over this misbegotten world. "I do it like Europe," he bragged.

"So they don't pay?" I'd been intrigued by the European trend wherein squatters functioned more like long-term house sitters than trespassers.

"They pay," he contradicted himself. "But they might as well not. I'm charging way below market value."

In the span of five minutes he'd

—invaded my personal space

—ignored that I am educated

—misused radical rhetoric

—admitted to being a landlord

—and was one "I don't see color" away from winning Yuppie Scum Bingo. But he invited me to a party that night at his house, and I hesitated not from any ethical dilemma, but my fear of visiting Cambridge at night. "It is safe?" I asked like some bourgeois asshole.

"It's not as bad as it used to be." He placed a compassionate hand on my shoulder. "I can pick you up. How about the Marina at seven?"

We exchanged numbers. Then he said, "I don't place your accent. Where are you from?"

"Pittsburgh," I replied, unaware I had an accent.

"Pittsburgh." His gaze quivered with dreamy sincerity. "Bro"—he embraced me—"I'm from Cincinnati."

What a poser. But I wanted to glimpse his world. I'd been staring at mine long enough.

At the apartment I found you in bed, one leg stretched and the other bent, holding Matt's well-thumbed *Autobiography of Malcolm X* close to your eyes. You wore a navy-blue T-shirt and brown cotton shorts. "How was the Native American House?" I asked.

"It was pretty cool," you opined from behind the book. "I liked the, um, artifacts. There's a strong indigenous history here."

"Lunar Creoles," I mentioned, pouring myself some cloudy water from the faucet.

"I was aware," you bluffly replied.

Then I told you a gay yuppie had come on to me at the infoshop. "It was gross," I chuckled. "I'll never know what it's like to be a woman, but it felt like what you talk about when guys catcall. Like he thought he *possessed* me."

"White men are the worst with that," you commiserated.

"I've never felt as endangered with other men as I feel with them."

"He invited us to a party," I went on, reclining in the office chair. "I told him to pick us up from the Cambridge Marina at seven. I can just picture him waiting there."

"That's really mean."

"That's the point."

"But you're not a mean person. Why would you do that?"

"I can text him and cancel," I conceded in shame.

"Do you want to go?"

The answer was yes.

"Maybe," I replied pettishly. "Do *you* want to go?"

"It just sounds more interesting than hanging around here listening to the people down the hall get drunk."

I clapped my hands with excess enthusiasm. "Let's do it! To Cambridge!"

Since our train left in the morning, we decided we'd head straight from the party to the station. Nap on the benches, vagabond style, then sleep on Amtrak. So, sacrificing the remaining juice on your phone, we looked up directions from Cambridge to downtown; the buses ran every two hours, their regularity legendarily suspect. Taxis didn't come at all. Our best bet was to catch the T to South Station before the trains stopped running at one.

After lunch at a sandwich shop, we slept awhile. Then we made the bed, packed, checked that we had everything. You wrote Matt a thank-you note in swooping cursive. We signed it, locked up, and slid our keys under the door. Dressed in sweaters and jeans, on the assumption temperatures would rise in Cambridge, we embarked for a wild and insomniac night.

Early evening found the car sparsely populated, ourselves and five others adrift in their private worlds. You laid down your suitcase on a scoop-backed seat, sat cross-legged on top of it, and leaned your elbows on your knees like some mountain guru. I sat across from you, grateful. The train lurched up the long, gradual slope in the direction of Cambridge.

On our way I gazed out the window at rust-colored marsh glistening like bronze in the twilight, a land pandemoniac with stunted trees that looked less like flora than nesting aquatic cephalopods, thick of trunk, limbed with translucent tentacular branches flowering bulbs at the ends like red tassels. Under wintry winds they bowed their pale arms. I squinted at the marsh and could swear I saw wild hippo-cats snuffling the foliage, lean and toothsome, as long as full-grown alligators.

You and I talked about activism, music, and Italian exploitation flicks. You said *Goodbye, Uncle Tom* had been formative for you. The scene where the little white girl ran through the field with a naked black boy on a leash was burned in your brain.

We talked about how Paula Abdul songs were so effective precisely because she couldn't sing. We talked about white fragility. We discussed whether or not this world was a simulation.

Our train approached, encased in miles of barbed wire, the quintuple colossal cylindrical warehouses where goods hydraulically sent from the harbor were received. Ceaselessly their mammoth doors ingurgitated and expurgated trucks carrying goods to buyers. Next the train took us directly over a crater, property of the Boston Company, the latest tyrants to control the local geology in a history of bloody conflict. I searched for Magali in the red-lit gantries among miners in hazmat suits, who looked to me like astronauts on Mars. The world took on a dreamy haze that centered in you.

"We are now approaching Cambridge." The conductor sounded weary through the speaker. "This is the end of the line. Please check your seat to make sure you have all your belongings."

I expected the capital of the Puritan Empire to look like a colonial reenactment. Either that or a treacherous, rundown hood patrolled by gangs. With the bullet-shaped T car at our backs, we descended a wide, piss-smelling staircase from the platform into a large, low room. Caution in your brown eyes, you crossed your arms against the clammy chill, and first impressions told me Cambridge would lean more toward the "hood" side of things: the station was occupied by two dozen or so homeless people reclined in fitful rest along fives rows of pew-like benches, or sleeping on the square-tiled floor outside shuttered fast food kiosks, or muttering in conversation with themselves while a single police officer strolled the parameter in droopy-lidded boredom. In every way it reminded me of San Jose Diridon Station where I'd spent a miserable night after missing the last train to San Francisco. I grew nervous of the time. A quarter to six, we needed to hurry.

For a long moment we studied a glass-encased map nearly hidden behind cracks and graffiti. Next we sat on a bench and collaboratively drew a route in my notepad, after which we headed down a long and dimly lit commuter tunnel slimed around the edges with congealed black water. Out in the parking lot, I gasped for breath, the air too thin for comfort. *Idiot!* I told myself. How had I not taken altitude into account?

Our gasping brought over a little man in a suit too large for his frame, double-fisting liters of oxygen. "You need these," he exhorted. "You won't last without them."

"How much?" I rasped.

"How 'bout forty dollars?"

Five minutes in Cambridge and I was getting conned. Before handing him the money, I requested to test it, and, surprisingly, he agreed. I fumbled the plastic off the suction cup and took a hit. An icy sensation spread through my face and chest, rendering me adrenalized, like I'd just finished watching *Die Hard*. Tell me to jump off an exploding skyscraper and I'd have done it. Quickly I handed him two twenties.

Alone I might have saved the money. But I wouldn't watch you suffer.

Sipping air, hauling our luggage, we crossed a shoddily paved square dominated by a dry fountain, at the center of it a plinth upon which a graffitied bronze goodwife radiated piety, one hand held up in oath, the other on the Bible that grew from her chest along finely soldered lines. The neighborhood we entered reminded me of Detroit in its abandonment, though not so sprawling, the streets and interlocking blocks built to cram as much real estate as possible, pathways branched between apartment complexes like the repurposed horse roads in Europe.

Some would call the neighborhood "dead," their lame definition of "life" defined by white faces and usefulness to capital. But I saw life in the smell of barbecue from behind a chain-link fence, in the friendly clink of beer bottles, in the rap thundering from a Monte Carlo. From the crowds outside the bars, barbershops, and salons. Even commerce showed its unwelcome face in warehouses and fish-smelling produce wholesalers. I began to think this place was, in fact, the utopia Black Radicals envisioned, where our people could live unmolested.

Street names changed every three blocks to accommodate a history rife with regime change, and it came as no surprise to discover ourselves lost among vacant rowhouses. First opportunity, I led us inside the sole heartbeat on the block, a convenience store.

Smoking a cigarette behind the counter, the clerk, a Lunar Creole in a panda hat, listened with a tough-guy leer as I asked which way to the Marina. At first it perplexed me why his counter didn't have bulletproof glass before I noticed, in a window above the liquor rack, a teenaged boy, or, if you choose, a sniper in his nest. There followed a conversation that made me feel like an asshole because I tried, but the clerk's accent shrank every three syllables to one, and we both grew frustrated.

Five minutes into this awkwardness, the bell chimed. Enter a perfumed black man in a wig and stockings, cravat and shiny-buckled shoes, a gold-threaded crimson jacket with tail-coats and matching short pants. He purchased a snuff box, and, as the clerk searched under the counter for the good stuff, I asked the colonial-looking fellow for help. Kind and plainspoken, with a more manageable accent, he looked over our map, promised us a short walk to the Marina, and redrew our route. Then he wished us luck. So the clerk wouldn't think less of me, I bought tuna sandwiches, one for each of us. Now I had no money.

Outside, we watched the wigged driver mount a black Berlin carriage driven by two robust colts. In the shadowed cab sat an old dark woman in a mulberry gown. She neither moved nor spoke, but watched us from under frowning brows, a luxuriously portly hippo-cat sprawled in sleep on her silk-swaddled shoulder, the pet clothed in a onesie sewn with pearls. From the part of my brain marked SECRET FILES came a conspiracy theory that the Nantucket black bourgeoisie—those who cloistered themselves from whites and poor blacks alike to hoard generational wealth in peace—actually lived in Cambridge. Secretive as vampires, they had spread the rumor to hide their true enclave on top of the world.

"Weird," you said, watching the carriage amble away with hearse-like slowness.

Adhering to the map, we encountered our most chilling roadblock within sight of the square: a police station with an armada of squad cars, vans, and K-9 units out front. We hurried across the street.

Soon what had been cemented in my mind as a ghetto became a colonial marketplace. Before us stretched a cobble-paved area that had been left miraculously unharmed during the Rupture, save for a half dozen craters where stones had fallen; in a ring around the square stood the governor's mansion, jail, church, mill house, dry house, post office, and town hall in their original condition, puritanically compact, built from decaying gray brick. Notably absent was the Church of the Arch-Minister, which over the years had been set afire, dynamited, bullet-riddled, and finally whittled to nothing by tourists making off with the stones.

At the center of the square stood a wooden gallows that creaked in the wind. There a quintet, boys and girls, the Cambrian future, drank beer under stars chanting billion-year-old space madrigals in voices made of fire. Lopsided, a half-moon loomed so large over the square I felt I could pull it from the sky and use it to chop bread. Though I looked for Annalee's stake, it made sense it would have been dismantled long ago, if not destroyed in the Rupture itself.

Through a glass of half-truths and legend, in a world teeming with hate, I saw Puritans gray, miserable, and murderous. The British Crown had been right to exile the Protestants, who, upon settling Massachusetts, established a fundamentalist tyranny with imperial ambitions, Cambridge the base from which they terrorized native and settler, French and English, Huguenot and Hessian, servant and slave. From New France to the future Georgia, their inquisitors arrested accused witches, indigenous, Catholics, Anglicans, and Antinomians by the thousands.

The day of the Rupture had been one for feasts and fiery speeches, until, full to bursting on lamb and Scripture, come from town and farm for the holiday, Puritans, their crucifix hearts craving scarlet, turned to the beadle's hollering bell. At six in the evening a steel-plated phalanx marched to the square bearing muskets on their shoulders, for half the army had been summoned for the spectacle. Behind their parade, the condemned came shackled. Clothed in tattered hemp, they had marched for miles from the dungeons outside the city, during which some died from the strain, and rather than unshackle the dead, for such a thing would be too dignified, the army forced the living to carry their fellows' corpses into Cambridge. Children gawked from behind their parents' legs at people such as they had never seen before, wretches of all skin tones whose pleas were met with, beyond mere indifference, anticipation through the assembly, a silent scream to call down the night as nonbelievers were halted before twenty stakes, lined down the square like teeth sharpened to points.

"A flame to cleanse the wicked," thundered the Arch-Minister from the gallows. "The greatest fire the New World has seen!"

In the illuminations he looked average. Another white man in a wig. But he promised, from God's chosen land in Massachusetts, they would tear down the Vatican, overthrow the demon gods of the Orient, and purge the Mohammedans. Starting with the witch Annalee.

"I curse you!" she yelled as flames consumed her legs. "You shall die this day!"

The moment she finished her curse, they said, smoking fissures cracked the Arch-Minister's monumental vanity of a church, and volcanic rock imported from Spain took to the air like ash flakes from a furnace. Where Goodman Pureheart's virgin daughters stood a steeple fell, and those who were once living, breathing girls became three marble angels in the tympanum above Boston City Hall's Congress Street entrance. Those patriarchs and robust women of whom Hawthorne wrote so critically plummeted like black-winged birds to the earth below, their carcasses a bloody autograph across the Fenwick meadows. With the destruction of Cambridge, so fell the Puritan Empire, stretched thinly across Massachusetts and too racked with infighting to sustain itself in the aftermath.

Or so I'd imagined it. Back in high school that history was like catnip to a Korn-loving goth. Somewhere in my mom's garage lay folders of violent colonial westerns I'd set in the Rupture Era, about Puritan pirates and faery archaeologists.

We came to a beach. Nearby, winos picked through the ground, which, I soon learned, was not made from sand but garbage. Extending fifty feet from where we stood, and stretching for an apparent mile in either direction, trash twined in a dense, lumpish black shore that looked both solid and unstable at once, treacherous to walk. Stank like trash, too.

Beyond that shore, nothing.

We stood in the shadow of a gloomy ship-mast jutting at an angle from the earth. Attached to the pavement with hooks, the rigging that stretched from ground to square topsail looked recently installed; inversely, the wood was blackly rotted, slimy with ancient seaweed like a fragment from a ghost ship. It wailed low in a wind that made the two of us shiver.

You stretched your tennis-shoed toe to the beach, to test the firmness, and it made a crunching sound like sand. That brought a disapproving cough from nearby.

"Careful now," warned a husky-voiced man atop a red lifeguard chair. Somewhere in his sixties, he wore a Patriots jacket, blue jeans, and yellow Crocs. His face, silver in the autumn moon, was long and handsome, serenely wrinkled. He wore his white hair in a Jheri curl. At his left elbow a radio played Sam Cooke and the Soul Stirrers on low. Tipping down his spectacles, he asked us, "How y'all doing?"

To reach his chair, which stood a ways down the broken sidewalk, we crossed the trash. Plastic bags, wrapping paper, snot-crusted tissues, and takeout containers crunched underfoot. Granulated debris blew in swirls over the beach. A pain in my big toe—my sneaker ripped open by a CD case.

"We're fine," I answered the man once we reached him. "You're a lifeguard?"

"You could say that," I think he said, his Cambrian accent even thicker than the clerk's. "I guard lives. You're not thinking of ending yours? Jesus loves you. Young couple like you got a lot to live for."

Nailed to one leg of the chair was a sign that read THE CONSEQUENCES OF JUMPING FROM THIS LEDGE ARE TERRIBLE AND FATAL. Like the Golden Gate in San Francisco. And, like that suicide spot, they would rather risk the deaths than ugly the view with a fence.

At that moment a harsh wind blew, causing us to shudder, causing empty bottles to whistle in a show of elemental poetry that made my breath catch. Garbage shards blew off the ledge like snow from a mountaintop. Our knees turned to wind chimes.

"Have you ever had to rescue anyone?" you asked the man, after the wind died down.

I believe he said, "More than I can count. Ain't lost a one yet, neither. Got my trusty lasso here to pull 'em right down. Some succeed in jumping," he admitted frankly, "but they never do it on my watch. I started after my friend jumped," he reminisced. "He was a daredevil type. Wicked brave, wicked stupid. He didn't fall. He just floated away, and we never saw him again."

I felt ready to cry. I felt your shoulder against mine; you had inched closer.

"That's a mast from a brigantine got stuck up here," and he

pointed to the ancient wood. "Them was spy ships they used in the wars. Beautiful boats, they was."

Oliver Cromwell II probably didn't consider them so beautiful, I thought. Descended from the despot, or so he claimed, he'd made it his mission to revive the Puritan Empire over a century after it fell, mainly by means of piracy around Boston Harbor, to disrupt commerce and starve the city. Municipal leaders hated Cromwell such that, following his arrest at a Cape Cod orgy, they left his fate to the naval captains he'd vexed. In a massive operation for the time, they set up masts and pulleys in Cambridge Square, the narrowest point of the city, to keelhaul Oliver Cromwell II under the length of Boston. His last word was, "Please."

You asked the lifeguard, "Is this the Marina?"

"Over on the other side, baby girl."

Before leaving you told him, "Take care."

"All right now," he farewelled.

The air grew chiller on our way back across the square. The teens had flown to wherever delinquent kids went after drinks. Through a whining iron gate we descended stone steps through tiers of well-pruned roses interspersed with scarlet currant bushes. We reached a tiny lamplit park containing a pond, within whose waters I glimpsed copper wishes. At the edge of the pond a brick column supported a plaque that read: "A Project of the Cambridge Heritage Society. Each rose is planted in honor of Black Americans killed in the Rupture."

A waist-high black hemlock wall ran the length of the promontory. We looked out at the world. Below, clouds raced like gray-sailed shallops sundering the empyrean on their path to the cosmos, and, below their condensational flotilla, the world looked as it did from a nighttime plane, a miasma that appeared as antimatter at the beginning of time. Cities like scattered diamonds. To our left, two handfuls of smoldering campfire embers.

"New York," I discerned. I asked you, "Where do you think Philly is?"

You pointed past New York at a patch of gold dust. At the same time, I glimpsed red lights blinking on a jet drifting west to Ohio. My mind's eye followed my organic eye to where clouds thickened over dead coal towns and Mennonite farms. I thought, if I squinted, I could see the three rivers. The wooded hollows. The secret stairways. Did you see them, too?

"Could you imagine throwing a penny off here?" You chuckled. "It would make a crater."

"This is probably a date spot," I mused.

"A good one," you declared. "People tend to lie on first dates. So you take them here, and they have an existential crisis, and then they tell the truth. Mm-hmm. Yeah. How else are you going to know if your date is half gremlin, or if they have eight kids, or if they're actually dead, and you're on a date with a ghost?"

I could see you pushing me off the ledge. Except in my fantasies, I managed to contort just right so that I belly flopped safely into Boston Harbor. Then I walked all the way up Boston, dripping wet like Daffy Duck, to inform you *shit like that* was why I didn't date black girls.

My next vision showed me jumping. To traumatize you. Your disembodied shriek sounded so real in my head that I, scared of myself, backed away from the ledge. On a bench I listened to you comment on what you saw.

Come half past seven I had yet to hear from Epstein, though I'd shot the punk five texts, my phone at 40 percent. Feeling panic coming on, I asked you for an oxygen can, only to find it empty.

"Shouldn't have trusted someone I don't know," I said through deep breaths. My composure fell to mania. Damn near broke myself in half laughing at my own foolishness. I screamed, "How the hell do we get down?"

You didn't answer.

"We're fucked!" I said. "I can't believe this."

You swallowed. "We can go back."

Shame had its teeth in me. Visions of our American-style deaths circled like buzzards.

"What if the train is delayed? What if we miss our Amtrak? This always happens. I always do stupid shit like this. Did . . . did I plan this?" I asked you. "Subconsciously. Did I plan on trapping you on top of the world?"

"You're kind of scaring me right now."

"I can't breathe. Fuck. If it was just me it'd be one thing. I'm sorry. I'm freaking out."

"Yeah. That can't be good for your health, either."

"You are not helping!"

Without another word, you sat next to a currant bush while I breathed to still my heart. You looked chagrined. Suddenly I pictured my dad in his beige corduroy armchair, where he always relaxed that time of night, zoned out to cop shows. Desperately I wanted to call him. Hear him tell me it would be okay. That was the secret I'd held from you: I hadn't a clue about independence. I kept breathing. In. Out. In. Out. Out. Out. In.

"Let's head to the station." This wisdom came from my mouth, somehow.

Immediately after you agreed, a gilded coach driven by four black stallions reined to a stop at the top of the garden. Smiling on us from the front seat was a driver in colonial livery similar to the earlier driver. Sinuously pudgy fingers drew back the red velvet curtain. Out peered a round, cheerful, youthful face gleaming with cosmetics perfectly matched to her purple-black skin tone.

How she gazed on us caused her chins to puddle around her jaw in concentric circles, her demeanor like that of an Arabian mare who could eat, if you had oats, but if you left her to dream in the straw, she wouldn't mind.

"Praise Oshun!" exclaimed the woman in the window. "Are you going to Zack's? Get in!"

No sooner did we step inside than she flung her voluminous arms around us. Smooched me right on the Adam's apple, then planted a kiss on your eyebrow. Her embrace was like being wrapped in a mattress.

Four lanterns lit the well-upholstered cab. In their light the woman glistened like the sun off clashing swords. Across from us, she took up almost her entire seat, as wide as she was tall at five feet, in a violet silk flapper dress, the same color as her lips and eye shadow, girdled about her billowing waist with a red silken sash. Her hair was shorn almost to the scalp.

"Where are we going?" you asked, seated next to me with your hands in your lap. Your question made her grin, her teeth like piano keys. Her lips stretched back into pointed tips beneath deep-set eyes small and merry; her sleeveless dress revealed every quiver of her arms as she clenched her fists in delight.

"You should ask my name first," she insisted, her voice bright and booming. "I'm Annalee, and I'm so glad I found you. The last thing our people need are two fresh young things out there in the cold. You two are just the cutest little cinnamon buns. I just want to eat you up!"

Had I not been on edge, I would have liked her sensual presence. Outside, mansions dotted the craggy landscape. The stores looked like Norman Rockwell had designed a neighborhood based on a Washington Irving story. Iconic New England.

"I just knew you were going to dear Zack's," Annalee continued. "And I didn't even have to use divination."

"The real Annalee could have," you pointed out. "I mean, the original Annalee. Is it a popular name in Boston?"

Of course black Cambrians would make that a baby name. However, at your observation, Annalee rocked with laughter made all the more disconcerting because it sounded neither condescending nor hysterical, but entirely good-natured.

"You are *succulent*," she whooped. "I hope I'm not being too forward, but if you were a fruit, you would be a blackberry. I *am* the real Annalee. You couldn't have known," she forgave an apology no one had made. "Do they still speak of me in Boston? Those patriarchal, anti-black, colonizing hypocrites? Perhaps. Perhaps not. I don't want them to know what I do up here."

So, not just a rich woman, a *crazy* rich woman.

"You two are smart enough to know I speak true," she determined, handing me a golden bowl of dark cherries that I held in my lap and never touched once. "You remind me of myself when I was your age. Even if it was three hundred years ago. Oh!" she exclaimed. "You seem unconvinced. It's all right, babies. I got you."

She pulled down the collar on her dress. Against the cleft in her massive breasts hung a necklace made of three hempen strings. They called to mind sketches of Annalee, an emaciated slave being led by rope to her death. The present Annalee, noticing my eyes on her bosom, shot me a coy look that bristled my neck hairs. Like a burlesque dancer, she peeled up her skirt hem and there, on her shins, were burn scars all the way to her knees.

"I'm sure I look more svelte in the books," she laughed, and let her skirt fall like a curtain. "But it's normal to gain a couple of pounds over the centuries."

By the time her driver reined in the horses, the stars had

triplicated. We stepped out onto a sprawling, pebbled field dotted with sickly grass. It looked like somewhere people got murdered. Why then, I wondered, was I so calm?

We had reached the end of the road where the cobblestones lost their symmetry. In the center of the street bricks lay disarranged in the mud like teeth on a broken zipper. Behind us the road snaked back a mile or so through the antique homes, to the Marina. In front of us, like a titan's funnel, loomed the bottom story of a tower turned upside down and jammed in the earth. Stretching my legs, which ached after what amounted to three days of hiking, I wondered how we'd get back, but more than that I wanted to make Zack's party.

"You're nervous," Annalee noted, and I realized she was speaking to you. "That's understandable. There's so many people in this world who can't be trusted. And so many black people go missing. It's horrible how racism forces us to have these fears. I'm the spiritual leader of Cambridge. I would never hurt visitors, especially friends of Zack's. He lives in the condos, and I really want to guide you so you don't get lost. What can I do to make you feel safe?"

"I feel safe," you volunteered. And that was that.

Annalee led us up a shoddily made brick stoop, through the tower door, then immediately down a moss-furred stairwell attached to the inner wall. Brazier-bound electric lamps lit the way. At the rear of our trio, my sense of vertigo made me aware the steps had been built at an angle, the sensation like descending and ascending at the same time. Bracing myself on the pockmarked stone wall, I watched you switch your suitcase to the other hand. I readied to catch you if you fell.

A staggering odor of sunless places usurped the homogenous, electric smells the wind grudgingly carried from the cities. The cone shrank until we reached a dirt floor and a rough-hewn doorway buttressed by decayed brick. Annalee, who never stopped speaking, to the point I can't recall half of what she said, led us into a chapel-like room that reminded me of colonial meetinghouses in Philadelphia. Several black men sat around the tables. Dressed in a mix of modern and eighteenth-century clothing, they bowed to Annalee, who complimented each man on some small thing about his appearance, before letting them resume activities such as boiling tea or debating philosophy, each visibly happy to earn her approval.

Kindled memories married the dimly lit figures and relaxed social mores, such that the men seemed to change before my eyes into Pittsburgh punks. Our first date felt like a hundred years ago. I'd asked you out at the First Presbyterian on Braddock and Parker, where the gardening groups convened before we started our day. That had been the third time we'd ever spoken to each other. That weekend I took you to a fundraiser dance at the Free Ride bike co-op in Wilkinsburg, staffed by punks and paid for with city money after the spin-the-wheel of municipal branding landed on BIKE FRIENDLY CITY! Like Annalee's sanctum, that stretch of postindustrial neighborhood had a capital-R Romantic quality. Stunted trees grew alongside the warehouse, and, if you looked down, you'd see wildflowers between the palimpsest of railroad tracks. Several staffers also volunteered with Grow Pittsburgh, a gardening program adjacent to ours. Watching those tight-shirt-wearing scenester fucks buy cheap houses in my hometown made me hateful. Still, the wolf in me had planned the role white devils would play in my seduction; if you recognized them from Braddock, I schemed, their greaser hairdos might create a visual synchronicity between work and the co-op. They would make you comfortable.

That night we drank screwdrivers and danced chastely to songs from middle school, three feet of space between us, allowing me to appreciate the innocent—yet alluring—movement of your body. After a while the DJ, my boy Sean, spun the throwback slow jam, "Freak Me" by Silk, and you claimed me with an arm around my waist.

All of a sudden my nostalgia collided with the reality that I was, at present, among a cult in a dungeon. I swooned and would have fallen had Annalee not caught me by one arm and, expending zero effort, hauled me to the wall, where she stood me upright. On the ceiling, I noticed flies' sticky remains purply pulsing phosphorescent, as if their very essence had leaked from their broken exoskeletons, airborne romance and daring escapes from hippo-cats written in mortal braille from cornice to cornice of the dank, ancient chapel.

Annalee's face filled every corner of my world. She smelled amazing, like coconuts and printer ink.

"Are you okay?" she asked with great gentleness.

"I just had a weird flashback." I was moved to honesty by her tone.

"L*oooo*ve," she smiled. "You're a sensitive little danish."

Whereupon she swept us away into the next room, describing the various and multitudinous libertinisms she'd committed in this subterranean realm. She paused every so often to point out barbed, spiked, and incendiary devices she'd used. Sometime during her monologue about pegging Benjamin Franklin, I began to tear crumbs from the tuna sandwiches I'd purchased earlier. Your eyes met mine, and I put a finger to my lips.

So it went, room by room, each connected to the last by tunnels lit with ensconced torches. Kitchens, dining rooms, parlors, libraries, bedrooms cobwebbed and mildewed. With a cold feeling I realized we walked the dismembered cadavers of several colonial manses. Some of the dusty, drafty rooms tilted at a slant, some upside down, some cut in half with portions of their walls made from packed dirt, but all had been left unmolested, not a spoon missing from the china sets, not a diamond purloined from the chandeliers we stepped around. To no surprise the French paintings on the walls depicted orgies, every one of them.

Wherever we went, loiterers bowed to Annalee. For all I told myself we followed a madwoman, facts about the historical witch challenged my skepticism. Latter-day scholars theorized she'd been a maroon, born in Africa, taken to Barbados, a freedom fighter captured and sold into slavery a second time. Like Tituba, Annalee snitched on her owners, naming them goat-worshipping, broomstick-flying, baby-eating pagans. But unlike Tituba, a victim of circumstance, Annalee had been described as a charismatic woman versed in several languages, with a penchant for poetry and a voice like cinnamon. Small wonder the Arch-Minister wanted her to die first—he feared her, even when he had her shackled. Presently I listened to her diamond-studded slippers shuffle on the cobblestone, listened to the fabric shift along her capacious back.

"I'm a gardener," the fat woman metaphored. "I plant my little Cambridge flowers and watch them bloom. Sometimes I have to prune them so others may grow. Gardener. Priestess. Mother. Fairy godmother. Mamadjo. Dominatrix. Mistress. Coven leader. I am Annalee," she declared, "Destroyer of the Puritan Empire and Lady of Cambridge. I assure you I'm a big softie," she promised, giving us a wink over her shoulder. "With a big heart. But I do have bite."

I wondered if, instead of "Hansel and Gretel," we had found ourselves in "The Juniper Tree." You know—the one where the kid actually gets eaten.

To you I whispered, "She makes a move . . ."

"Shush," you whispered in turn.

"Don't whisper, dear." Annalee sighed on our way through a

kitchen crowded with men playing card games on barrels, as in ye olde tavern. "If you have something to say, say it."

"I was asking her the time," I answered meekly.

"It is a quarter to nine, though you could check your phone seeing as hers is dead."

Spooky.

You asked her, "Can you tell us about the Rupture?"

Silent for a time, she seemed as one in the grip of a black and traumatic dream. When she spoke at last, amusement tinkled her voice. "I've come a long way to become this luscious plum that I am. What kind of human being wishes to own another, *hmm*?" she inquired sharply. "To subject them to the Middle Passage and put them in chains not once, but twice. I'll tell you: the kind of people who wish for the world to be enslaved. Who would shackle feminine desire and beat childhood innocence under Scripture. Such was the world the ministers envisioned. A world where even the thought of freedom was impossible.

"But they were men. Powerless men. There is real magic in this world beyond the promises of their silly patriarchal god. Magic in my hips. Magic between my luscious thighs. *You* know," she teased, batting her kohl-slathered eyes at you. "They try and steal it from us, package and sell it. They love to throw their bellies around. But our bellies are bigger, eh? What do decrepit old men with flat cocks know about black mother goddess pleasure?

"While I sat in their cells, I communed with Gaia. I sent my lust deep down and stole the heart of this world. And when my lover heard what might have been my last gasps, she grew excited. Oh, let me tell you how excited she was!" she boomed with fire in her eyes.

You stated the obvious. "Um . . . You made the planet orgasm."

"Told you so," I whispered.

Annalee threw both hands to her belly and chortled. "You say that like it's a bad thing! The planet seemed to like it. And my lover kept me alive. She still does. It is my mission that no man ever controls Cambridge. Over the years I have set sides against each other in mutually assured destruction. Sometimes that meant fermenting revolt to keep the numbers in check. Sometimes I had to let those little boys in Boston know who runs things here. You *know* those little boys wanted to mine Cambridge for minerals. They kept it up for *decades*. Do they have nothing better to do? They forced me to go down there once."

In a study filled with moldering books, she spent some time rummaging the drawers. At last she found in an armoire an aged photograph she blew the dust from. In the picture a woman, thinner, yet with eyes like the woman before us, scowled evilly from a Fenway Park skybox.

"I cursed them," she crowed, taking the time to light a kerosene lamp. "The Red Sox have never, nor will they ever win a World Series."

Then we entered a chamber so vast we couldn't see its parameters beyond the shadows. You made no objection when I took your hand. Time had swept all from the room save a soft, sweet scent of decay and a throne in the center made entirely of pearl. Annalee's lamp caused the facets to wink upon its smooth contours, like a single jewel gifted from the ocean.

There'd been an era of mad kings. They massacred the armies Thomas Jefferson sent to subdue them. They ate human flesh and nearly drove Cambridge to ruin, until, as the last great act of his career, Benjamin Franklin convinced the beleaguered Cambrians to rejoin the union in 1795. Part of the agreement had been to rig the Electoral College for a Massachusetts native, the pencil pusher John Adams, to hold the highest seat in the land.

Suffocating on the centuries, I shivered to think how much bloody history had been Annalee's fault. What of the 1865 Boston

Riot, when racists invaded Cambridge and lynched twenty-nine black people? What about the Black Radicals of the 1890s, who wished to make Cambridge the Palestine for our people, but disappeared without a trace? Had they disrupted her plan somehow?

"Ask her about the Black Radicals," I whispered to you. "Why'd she let that happen?"

"You ask her," you said out the side of your mouth.

"She's obviously on some Girl Power kick. If I ask her, and she's really a witch, she might eat us."

"She's just a crazy person."

"If she is, then why's it matter?" I snapped.

"A crazy person could eat us, too!"

"Are you asking about the maroons?" Annalee asked, even as she kept walking.

You drew yourself up to your full height. "Yeah. Why'd you let the white people invade and slaughter the Lunar Creoles? They could have made Cambridge a free state."

At that Annalee wheeled around. Damn. Either I'd forgotten the Creole Massacre, or, more likely, there was only so much pain the mind could handle. But you were indigenous as well as black, and in that moment, when your eyes met hers, your blood cried for knowledge. Your demeanor threw the woman off her game, and long moments passed before she spoke.

"The Lunar Creoles pissed me off," she said at last. "They were quite patriarchal."

You didn't let up. "What about now? The gentrifiers?"

"What is wrong with new people?" Annalee replied without pause. "I know what you're going to say, but nobody is getting priced out of Cambridge. Just like the white people can't get a place without me. Some of the spots here are condos, some are going to be luxury glamping. And if anybody gets too powerful—" She drew a finger along her throat, then burst with laughter. "Gentrification is inevitable. It's like when crack appeared. I disapproved, but everyone wanted to smoke it so badly. So I controlled the rise and fall of the kingpins. The same goes for whites. Every Cambrian is one of my babies. Tonight I check on my white babies, then off to see my other babies.

"I plan on leaving here soon. Do you know I'm on Instagram? I'll add you. There's such a big world out there, with so many people lacking spiritual fulfillment. I want to create my own nonprofit: Black Girl Sorcery!" she declared. "Why am I telling you this, you wonder. After three hundred years I deserve to gloat a little. What are you going to do? Go to the surface and tell them you met the *real* Annalee? Believe me," she sighed, "I would have made a utopia. This patriarchal, racist, ableist, sick system of ours literally drains years from the life of black people. It exhausts us."

"I know," you said quietly.

"Alas!" said Annalee. "That evil was too great to fight, even for an African fairy mermaid tigress witch. So I made *myself* the utopia. Everywhere I go there is love, and sex, and food, and sensuous touch. People see me and wish to throw off their shackles and roll in the furs like animals. I can't wait to inspire more luscious youths such as yourself."

"Luscious?" I laughed, to break the tension. "I have a neckbeard."

"A luscious neckbeard!" her voice echoed like strawberry seeds cast to the wind, and I felt like my face might melt, I blushed so hard.

An indeterminate time later I heard New Wave from the end of the hall we trod. Annalee led us through iron doors into a frigid, sprawling room with no outer wall. Human language cannot describe my awe, confusion, and disgust when met by several dozen hipsters drinking and dancing in front of open sky. The DJ announced, "Annalee's in the house!"

People cheered for her. They were white as knuckles.

Hugging them on her way through the crowd, she asked where Zack was. We found him on a horsehair couch doing bong rips with some girls in indie band shirts. Excited to see Annalee, he then saw us, and he looked confused, followed by realization that made him fling a hand to his forehead.

"Awwww!" he cried. "I'm sorry, dude. I forgot. I'm sorry. Let me make it up to you." He poured two drinks from the punch bowl and shoved them in our hands. With the trembling smile of someone unsure whether or not this negro he'd screwed over intended to stab him, he exclaimed, "Glad you made it!"

"Yeah," I returned.

"I picked these two up on the roadside," said Annalee, embracing him. "They have been absolutely delightful. Maybe when we get the chance let's talk about how you can *actually* make it up to them," and with a surreptitious movement of her hand pinched my ass. You grabbed my hand. I felt like, if I tugged hard, I could pull that hand right off.

Annalee seated herself at a long table in a corner of the room, where Epstein gloatingly presented her a steaming wine-battered catfish on a platter. Everyone stood around and applauded as she consumed it. Mouth full of fish meat, eating with her hands, she seemed a barbarian, someone who predated civilization to the point she saw no value in it, who had caught fish barehanded, hunted in winter, seen enough empires fall to smirk knowingly at late capitalism. A hungry woman who smacked her lips and sucked grease off her fingers, in between hitting a joint the length of her face.

After devouring all but the bones, she joined the crowd watching Epstein get rigged to a harness. He seemed in high spirits, joking with women, flirting with men. Everyone gathered near the open ledge, but I kept back, though close enough to stare out and realize, to my terrified wonder, we stood in the hull of a warship embedded in the underside of the landmass. More than traveling to Boston, we had traveled *through* Boston to stand on the most precipitous real estate on earth. Above and below, eighteenth-century boats jutted from the soil, an empty gulf yawning between them; slopes, pirogues, brigantines, schooners, pinnaces, barques, Dutch cargo fluyts and Spanish galleons that had chosen the wrong day to dock in an English port, merchant galleons dealt karmic comeuppance for trading with a genocidal dictatorship. All had battered hulls and broken masts; however, in a number of them I saw lights in the captain's quarters, and people on deck. I noticed warships outfitted with stained-glass windows on cabins for nepotistic lords, bulwarks, quarterdecks, and gunports. The cold breath of death blew over my shoulders to realize those behemoths once belonged to the Protestant Vengeance, the armada for which the Puritans had destroyed the Massachusetts woodland in their quest to create Hell on Earth. I could hear the wood groan around us, feel the hull roll beneath my feet.

"Release me!" roared Epstein, so his friends shoved him off the ledge. I saw him drop for a heart-stopping moment, then he floated like a feather skyward, his hairy arms in Jesus pose.

"Angel me!" he called, spinning before the moon.

A large-eyed, skinny girl tossed up a piece of rusted machinery that wobbled through the air until it socked him in the gut. He grimaced in pain and screamed for more. Tires, boxes, and empty wine bottles followed. The word *angeling* seemed wholly inappropriate because every object had him looking more and more like a floating trash heap. At last, spherical with garbage, he brought his palms together in namaste.

With effort, his friends hauled him back down to the landing. Trash fell off him and he collapsed to a knee. Coming from behind us, Annalee swept his limp body in her arms.

"A drink for this man!" she called. Applause all around.

From that point, it was like every other hipster party.

I sucked at parties. The longer I stayed at one, the more my introversion felt like a handicap. Why can't I make friends? What's wrong with me? You seemed uninterested in socializing, a far cry from your gregarious self at AmeriCorps parties. If anything, our mutual discomfort made me comfortable. I enjoyed your company.

After several drinks we climbed a ladder through a berthing area divided with bulkheads into a dozen or so artist lofts, and continued to the open air and a spacious deck under the last of three sail-less masts. We tried to go up on the foredeck, our way blocked by a girl in a denim jacket who insisted on making conversation. Cheek to palm, eyes halfway closed, blond hair oozing between her fingers.

"You're just so cool," she complimented you. "I just met you and you're, like, the coolest person I know. Your hair and, just, your everything."

"Thanks," you said.

"I need your number! I need it right now. We have to be friends."

Afterward we made for the gunwale. It felt good to have privacy, relatively speaking. I counted fifteen people on deck, more on the poop and foredecks. "She's going to look at her phone tomorrow," you mused, sipping a White Russian, "and be like, 'Whose number is this?'"

Around the mast, musicians sang a sea shanty. Two men on electric guitar, an appealingly frumpy girl with sleepy eyes on tenor sax, a mandolin, a synth, and drum kit. A pale girl in a black blouse and tulle skirt put on tap shoes, placed down a piece of burnished wood, and danced.

I smiled at you. "The white people are singing and dancing for *us*. What could be better?"

More women made their way on deck to dance. Young, old, and in between. Before long a wail rang out from the quarterdeck, where Annalee stood at the rail with her arms out. She rotated her hands and with that stirring the women's dancing grew more fervent. More than ever, I believed her a charlatan, this "coven" of hippies and yuppies her pathetic marks.

I don't know why I had the idea. Maybe to amuse myself. Almost like a child daring another, I dared myself. *Do it.*

So, when the women lay exhausted on the deck, humming in their spiritual afterglow, I asked if they knew what a food healer was. Everything you told me in the Geology Department, I told them, and with my words they rose like chemically enhanced cash crops to cluster around you. Shy at first, you struggled to answer their questions until a woman who looked like a rich lesbian said you should be getting paid for your ideas. That got you going.

Girl, you could charm the planets from their orbit. Little Pluto would charge to the front of the line on your word. What seemed to me pan-African nonsense took on weight in the wondering, awestruck reactions from the women become your *ad hoc* coven. Equally interested was Annalee, who descended to the deck but, rather than try to sabotage you, as I would expect of a black woman scared another might steal her marks, she offered encouragement.

When music played again, you struck up a dorky-yet-on-beat dance to get the others dancing. You made pop culture references that only black people would get. You spoke vaguely and dismissively of the social justice topics you majored in, yet rambled for minutes about stuff you clearly knew nothing about. You said things that made no sense, like Brandy should play Whitney Houston in the biopic, even though they looked nothing alike and Brandy was old now. You made sweeping statements like "Marriage is for silly people." When you weren't talking, you moved between your newfound confidants with a cloyingly cute bobble-headed shuffle.

This I watched in growing discomfort. Like the horrible parties that summer, when you would abandon me for those brainless kids, you offered them your best, even as you denied me. Punished me. Three days in the company of a charmless, abusive, monosyllabic Neanderthal.

Below deck, in the kitchenette, I met a girl. She was the sax player from the jam session. We started talking. Except for you, this was my first one-on-one conversation with a female since coming to Boston. A small, shivering, horselike thing, she drunkenly rambled about jazz complexities. She told me it was hard, as a progressive, to navigate her sister's conservative Judaism. As if I cared.

"I can't even really see you right now." She sounded frightened. "I don't know where I am."

"I'll take you home," I told her. "Don't worry. I got you."

I asked myself, *What if she says you raped her?*

And I answered, *You'll spend the rest of your life in prison*, aware of the risk. Though nowhere near as drunk, I struggled to remember how I'd gotten below deck in the first place. Then I remembered fleeing you and your indifference.

I fled again. From myself. On the quarterdeck I stood beside the wheel. Ships stretched into the distance like hulks in crime-dark water, like nameless gravestones in scorched earth. To my surprise, I had phone reception, though only 15 percent left on my battery. I called my dad, anyway.

"Hello?" he greeted.

Tears spilled from my eyes. "Black bitches ain't shit."

"Black bitches ain't shit?" he repeated to ground himself

in the conversation. "Most women ain't shit, son. Most people ain't shit."

Truly, I thought, there was nothing in this world lonelier than a lonely black person. Small wonder, then, that we bought into God, devils, and portents. Otherwise, there was nothing to believe in but yourself . . . and the several billion loaded guns pointed your way.

"What the fuck do they think is gonna happen?" I said. "That we're so fucking disposable. They fucking trash us, and suck up to the white man, and sleep with him, and take his money. Every bad thing they blame on us, when they outnumber us three to one. There are no good black men? I've seen the niggas these bitches let impregnate them. No fucking standards. What do they think is gonna happen?" I demanded he tell me. "When the men are all dead? They think the white man will take them to wife? Fucking morons."

"Where *are* you?" he asked after a pause.

"Cambridge."

"Cambridge!" He sounded shocked. "Why in God's name are you up there?"

I'd told him I was visiting Boston, but had left out most details, including that you were coming. To learn this, his voice went cold. "You took that little girl to Cambridge?"

"It's not that bad. It's fucking gentrified, like everywhere else."

"I'll have to take your word on that. Does her mama know you did this?"

"Nah. She just knows we're in Boston."

"Good! Whatever you do, never tell her mama you took her to Cambridge."

I moved to the rail and stared into darkness. "I'm on the underside of Boston at a hipster party in a Puritan warship for her. She's been bitching the whole time. Now she's ignoring me."

"I don't know what to tell you. Women make no sense."

"I feel like I'm gonna die. I was ready to go home with this drunk white bitch."

"No you weren't."

"What do you think about that?"

"I don't think anything. You didn't say anything." I heard him sigh. "It's not that serious."

"It feels like it is."

"You want advice, I'll give you advice. Have a sense of humor."

"I thought you might say something more useful."

"What do you want? You're grown. That's what I say when people ask me about my children. I say I don't have any children. I have a son and a daughter. Do you have anywhere to stay in Cambridge?" he changed subjects.

I checked the time. "It's eleven. We should get to the station."

"There's something to take your mind off things! Get your ass off a Puritan warship and get to the station. How are you on money?"

"Good."

"When do you get back?"

"Tuesday morning."

"Need me to pick you up?"

"I appreciate it, but I think we can catch the sixty-one. I should go."

"Okay, Bub! And can you do me a favor?"

"Yeah."

"Get that little girl home safe."

"Of course. I love you, Dad."

"Love you, too. M'bye."

Sometime later I found myself on the poop deck with a pretty Puerto Rican with a huge ass in yoga pants, and a fuzzy pink sweater. She told me about her research into the poisonous effects of bostonium mining on drinking water in black communities. In her green eyes, I saw Annalee approach. You and Epstein flanked her, the witch all smiles.

"A food healer!" shouted Epstein, and hugged me tight. "What a concept! I'm sold, bro. A kitchen for blacks and Mexicans—"

"Blacks and indigenous," you corrected.

"Blacks and Indians to come and cook! You two have a dream and I believe in it. Stay here as long as you need to set up your practice. I *will* ask you for rent down the line, so you better be ready to pay up. But for now . . . you know . . ." He lost his thought. "Fuck Orlando! Boston is the place of magic! I'll give you the guest room. Settle in."

Annalee clapped her hands. "I'm so happy I could facilitate this. Now, if you'll excuse me, the Mastingtons are holding a ball for little Johnny's sixteenth birthday, and may the gods strike me for a triflin' negro if I arrive a moment late."

As it happened, you had specifics to debate with Epstein. Parameters around the length of your stay, which sounded reasonable enough to me, but he argued nonetheless. You two went on for a while, point for counterpoint. Respectfully I let you handle your business. I was simply no good at conflict, whereas you seemed suited to it, your demeanor amazingly calm. Come to think, you had a natural affinity for altercation, maybe even a desire.

What a prospect—a new life in Cambridge. I wondered what you wanted. What would you envision when free to dream?

Just like that, we had a small room in the crew quarters, the walls partitioned with bulkheads. We had a chest of drawers and a king-size bed with a bronze frame. Mere moments after we placed our suitcases in the corner, our next-door neighbor, a skinny blonde in a magenta '80s aerobics outfit, came and welcomed us. It seemed polite we should sample biscuits from her startup, Emily's Authentic Hardtack, authentically baked on a New England warship. Which did we like best? I preferred Rage Against the Gluten, whereas you liked the Barack O'Biscuit, both of us bullshitters, because her biscuits were all equally tasteless.

When she was gone we reclined side by side in the light of a single bulb, still fully clothed on top of a patchwork quilt. We stared at the ceiling. There was still time to catch the T, and I figured we would do so; first, we had to make sure Annalee was gone before sneaking out on her gift.

"What did you talk about?" I asked. "You and Annalee?"

"Spells. Psychedelics. Mostly psychedelics. She really likes shrooms." You giggled. "And my food healer idea." After a quiet, "I guess Zack's our landlord now."

"I have a feeling we'll hate him," I said.

"There will be conflict," you said matter-of-factly.

"Are you on shrooms right now?"

"Don't judge me."

"Congratulations on achieving your dream."

"This is different from how I saw it happening."

"Boston's a special place."

"I have a Women's Studies presentation Tuesday."

"I have a job interview."

"Amy probably forgot to feed the fish. If they're dead, I'll kill her."

"So . . . how long are we gonna wait till we leave? Because we don't have much time."

"Leave?" you piped. "I don't want to leave. This is more interesting than doing a presentation or feeding fish. Um, do *you* want to leave?"

Not anymore.

From there you took me back up on deck. It was empty, the

smell of pot the only evidence human beings had been there at any point in the last hundred years, the night quiet except for ships grunting and groaning. The clouds looked bland, I thought, fat and dark, like sponges that soaked up the abyssal color around them. In Toltec tradition, you told me, everyone had two faces. The day face was the one you wore most of the time, the night face what you wore before the gods, because to come as a mortal was an insult to them. Thus, in ceremony you masked yourself as a bird or beast, some grand ferocious thing. What you wanted to do, you told me, was to wear a mask during the day, so when you went to sleep, sublimity would carry over into your dreams.

We tried to return below, only to find the hatch locked. First we knocked with our fists, but no one answered, so we stomped the wood until at last a voice from below cursed at us. When tired-looking Emily opened up, she said we'd woken everybody. And when we descended through the quarters, the artists we met along the way, universally angry, told us they had work in the morning. Such things were beyond our infantile understanding, they implied.

At the entrance to our room, Epstein stood in a cream inner robe and red satin outer robe. He looked like a count. He pointed to us. "What are you doing here?"

Before you could explain, he ran down the hall to put distance between us, wildly gesticulating and, when you tried arguing, screamed something something this wasn't a playground, something he believed in diversity, something we were crazy.

Gringos. Cavemen. Sisterfuckers. Brotherfuckers. Colonists. Red-faced apes who want to bang their own daughters. Grave robbers. Book banners. Unwashed stringy-haired honkies. Crackers. Devils. Demons. Orcs. Beckys. Karens. Amys. Pattys. Brads. Kevins. Barbarians. Villains. Murderers.

Cultureless despoilers. Columbuses. The Euro-plague. Fascists. Thieves. Killers. Jailers. Torturers.

Like the shampoo-hating, sun-allergic cunt he was, Epstein cast us from his place. I would have been angry, were it not for the fact that, in hindsight, he'd done exactly as I had expected him to. Really, I was concerned about you. There, in front of the iron doors, never to be welcomed again, you wept into your hands.

"How do we get back through that maze?" you cried.

"Remember the sandwiches?" I said.

You flew into my arms.

My phone was dead. Five blocks from the upside-down tower, we stopped, sweaty from hauling our luggage, before an Ichabod Crane dance hall converted into a home. We asked directions from the men guzzling forties on the porch. Gruntingly clueless, supremely stoned, they summoned from around back two women in Celtics jerseys. The more conventional woman looked young, possibly younger than yourself. The other woman, her elder by many years, was human from the waist up, an old gray moose from the waist down. Instead of arms she had wings, her feathers black like well water. Atop her square head was a pink satin hair bonnet with holes for her long, furry ears. Inviting us onto the lawn, the umber-eyed woman knelt on one cervine leg to hear our story.

"You tryin'a get to the station?" cried the Senya. "Ah you crazy? Station close in fifteen minutes."

"We can run," I reasoned.

Her *hmph* sounded like that of a frustrated horse. "Run to the station? Tha's wicked fa'. You got the ca', Nu-nu?"

"Day-day coming with the ca'," answered the other woman.

"How fa' she?"

"'Bout a minute. Nana, I don't mind driving," Nu-nu offered.

"Y'all need tea?" asked the Senya. "War-ter?"

You smiled. "I'll have tea, please."

"Thank you so much," I told Nu-nu outside the station.

"Don't stand there!" she yelled from the Honda Civic. "Run!"

Suitcases under our arms, we raced to the stall. Fucking card wouldn't go. Catching the station attendant asleep behind the glass, we hopped the stile. Holding hands, we raced up the steps to hurl ourselves into the last car. I heard the doors hiss closed behind us.

We arrived at South Station. Through the skyscrapers, a clock tower read two fifteen. The sign on the door said they opened at five.

Nothing to do but wait. We dropped our luggage on the pavement, relaxed our sore bodies on a stone bench. Shaped like a scythe, it faced a pedestrian area paved in black-and-gray brick. You laid your head in my lap.

I knew with dreary acceptance that I would love you forever. I imagined ten years in the future, a coffee shop, the two of us youthful in appearance at the dawn of middle age, our black uncracked, gracious and content with each other, happy for a familiar face.

What I want to tell you is: I still don't know why you came to Boston.

"How are you?" I asked.

"I'm wonderful." Arms folded under your check, you nuzzled my thigh. I stroked your hair. Smiling, you drifted to sleep.

I watched you. I watched the streets. I heard someone approach. The thin woman wore thigh-high red stiletto boots, a red leather bikini bottom, and a white fur coat. Under her bustier, a loose fold of stretch-marked skin hinted she'd had at least one kid. Her gold wig brought to mind Tina Turner and I felt connected to her, like I would anyone who honored the old school. Seeing us, a smirk creeped in at the corner of her lips, like we made her long night worthwhile.

"Beautiful black couple," she said on her way to the curb, where she waited.

ACKNOWLEDGMENTS

Zora said, "There are years that ask questions and years that answer." The years since my last collection had a lot of questions. Here are the people who answered some of them.

Liz Hand, Melinda Noack, Dan Parme, Jess Simms, Nathan Kukulski, Liz Abeling, Shawn Maddey, Ben Passmore, Tasha Casini, Wendy Trevino, Endria Richardson, Hannah Levy, Alex Smith, Danielle Truppi, Spenser Tierney, Dr. Maria Seger, Alissa Nutting, Jessica Martinez, Courtney Morgan and the Lighthouse Writers Workshops, Steven Dunn, Adrienne Oliver, Ben Taylor, Dawn Rivers, Matt Gereghty, Joshua Leonard, Toni B, Kim Vodicka, Christine Stoddard, Sean Smith, Zoë Levitt, Yona Harvey, Heidi Asundi, Alex Mattraw, Rebecca Gomez Farrell, Lourdes Figueroa, Emily Nagin, Christopher Cotman, Pamela Bradby, Kate Horvath, Daniel McCloskey and the McCloskey family. Antifascists the world over, the city of Oakland, CA, and the Republic of France.

My editors at Scribner, Kathryn and Rebekah. Mark, my agent. Kelly and Gavin at Small Beer Press. The writing of this book owes a debt to various and sundry authors who've inspired me, but especially Mary Gaitskill, the world's greatest living writer, who has long been my lighthouse in the storm. Last but not least, my father Dr. Elwin Cotman, who held me in his arms, and read to me about the day a mole left his home to go explore the riverbank.

And my people. I love being black.

ABOUT THE AUTHOR

Elwin Cotman was born in Pittsburgh, Pennsylvania, where the postindustrial landscape greatly influenced his love for myth and adventure. He is the author of three prior collections of speculative short stories: *The Jack Daniels Sessions EP, Hard Times Blues*, and *Dance on Saturday*, which was a finalist of the Philip K. Dick Award. Cotman holds a BA from the University of Pittsburgh and an MFA from Mills College.